GIRL

IN

THE

ASHES

Willow River Press is an imprint of Between the Lines Publishing. The Willow River Press name and logo are trademarks of Between the Lines Publishing.

Between the Lines Publishing
1769 Lexington Ave N, Ste 286
Roseville MN 55108
btwnthelines.com

First Published: April 2024

ISBN: (Paperback) 978-1-958901-76-2

ISBN: (Ebook) 978-1-958901-77-9

Library of Congress Cataloging-in-Publication Data

Names: Weissman, Douglas, 1986- author.
Title: Girl in the ashes / Douglas Weissman.
Description: Roseville, MN: Willow River Press, an imprint of Between the Lines Publishing, 2024.
Identifiers: LCCN 2023055212 (print) | LCCN 2023055213 (ebook) | ISBN 9781958901762 (trade paperback) | ISBN 9781958901779 (ebook)
Subjects: LCSH: World War, 1939-1945--France--Fiction. | LCGFT: Historical fiction. | Novels.
Classification: LCC PS3623.E4594 G57 2024 (print) | LCC PS3623.E4594 (ebook) | DDC 813/.6--dc23/eng/20231211
LC record available at https://lccn.loc.gov/2023055212
LC ebook record available at https://lccn.loc.gov/2023055213

GIRL

IN

THE

ASHES

Douglas Weissman

Thank you Lisa for the idea, the inspiration, and random moments when I would interrupt you to read a line I needed to share.

One

Mr. Maraud was naked and strapped to the table. A cloth muffled his voice. Odette put on gloves with precision, taking care that each finger slid effortlessly into place. She wished she could burn her fingerprint into his cheek, remind him of the burns he gave his daughter, how he let the cinders brand her shoulder, her legs, or how he ashed his cheroot in her hair. She had followed him for a week, watched as the cigar glowed in his home's midnight darkness, listened to screams as the embers cooled on his daughter's skin each night after dinner, as his wife dipped the dishes in soapy water and hid behind the sounds of the radio. Odette was eager to shove a cigarette into Mr. Maraud's eye. But she didn't smoke. She flicked his ear instead.

She stood in the apartment cellar and brought a peach to her mouth. The flesh was soft. The juice rolled down her lips, slipped onto her chin, and splattered on the floor. She took a cloth to wipe away the juice. A collection of clay plates, pots, and cups rose out of the dust on the table behind her. They had a rudimentary design— homemade. She placed her dripping peach in a bowl. Another peach in the bowl had rotted, its fuzz black with mold. A maggot wiggled in the flesh. The table surrounded a neat stack of wood, framing the pieces like a cabinet. The fire in the kiln flared and the heat prickled her skin.

Mr. Maraud thrashed about the table and whimpered.

"Calm down Mr. Maraud," Odette said. She ran her finger down his cheek and wiped away a bead of sweat dripping from his bald head. He looked like a mole, with dark eyes—marbles sunken into his face—Odette thought. *He should have stayed with the other moles underground, the vermin.* His cheek felt sticky against her glove. He didn't try to scream. Outside, the street had an eerie quiet. She normally watched random feet shuffle past through the cloudy basement window, but the absence of life made her shiver. A rhythmic thump disrupted the silence. It had sounded like a storm in the distance, rolling slowly across the fields until it landed in the city. But the rain never came, only the thunder.

Mr. Maraud thrashed again, with a series of low thumps that imitated the storm brewing in the distance. He had exhausted his voice from the hours he had screamed without success. It was the same every time; they all started with threats, promising the different ways they would take their revenge on her. When that proved fruitless, they screamed hoping someone would hear their stifled cries, would notice they had been missing for a day or two. Then they begged for their lives. They apologized; they offered riches; they vowed to change—as if her mother had been given the same mercy from the grocer—as if he would have given someone else the mercy for which all the men now asked—no, thought Odette, *for which they begged.*

Mr. Maraud flinched and moaned.

"You have something to say Mr. Maraud?" She took the cloth from his mouth. He stretched his jaw.

His voice was hoarse like he had swallowed sand.

"Please," he said. "Forgive me. I know better now."

Odette stifled a yawn. "Of course, you do, Mr. Maraud." Odette shoved the rotten peach in his mouth. He gagged. She took her knife and severed his ear. He couldn't scream. She waited. He spat spittle and chunks of mold. He gurgled. Saliva wept down his cheeks. She stuffed the rag in his mouth pushing the remaining peach farther down his throat. The thunder outside grew louder.

"You all know better once you are on the table. Death has a funny way of revealing first the worst in people, then the best. Was it not just last night you promised to—what was it—rip out my womb and have your wife roast it for dinner?" She leaned over and whispered into the severed ear. She nearly touched her lips to the blood leaking to his neck, a false intimacy she craved. He let out another muffled cry. "The truth is, Mr. Maraud, you might be sorry. You may even be forgiven."

Mr. Maraud closed his eyes, a sign of relief, the reaction Odette had hoped for.

"But not by me."

Odette traced her finger from down his neck, brushing the glove against the wispy hairs on his shoulder and arm. She craved this moment, the realization of death, of finality, of regret. She savored their eyes when they glimmered, the look, how they went from hope to despair until the last second right before they passed out. Odette wondered about the glimmer. She wondered if it came from seeing G-d, not Death, because to them—to herself—she was Death. She would eternally wear that mask to them, for them, but in that last second of their waking life, the glimmer would show in their eyes, and they would even smile. But then—she would miss it if she blinked—a look of terror would set in; that was when Odette believed they had been received, they had been measured, and then, they had been denied—and she witnessed all of it.

She took Mr. Maraud's wrist, ready to slit her knife down the vein. The thunder pounded against the building and shook the room. Jackboots marched down the street, the jagged stream of successive boots visible through the frosted window. Mr. Maraud's wrist slipped from Odette's hand. Her fingers shook. She tried to blink the cellar into focus but couldn't concentrate. The fire in the kiln heated the basement.

She reached down for his wrist once more, but he flailed and hit her in the nose.

"Damn it!"

She caught hold of his arm, dug her nails into his skin, and sliced at the veins. She dropped his arm and took a deep breath as the blood dribbled out and tapped into the waiting bucket. She turned back to the table where her butcher's knife sat near the collection of clay cups, bowls, and plates. Mr. Maraud screamed and flailed once again. Blood squirted from his arm as he pulled away his straps, reached for the gag in his mouth, and fell to the floor, his face pressed to the concrete. Blood draped over the floor like dark velvet. Odette bent over Mr. Maraud's body, sat on his back, her composure gone.

"Look at the mess you made!" she said. "It could have been so much easier if you just stopped squirming." She took her knife and dug deeper into his skin, twisting the blade into the artery until blood flooded out of his wrist like a wave crashing against the cliffs. She dropped his arm in the carpet of dark velvet enveloping the stone. It splattered across her apron, across her shoes, across her face once more, baptizing her in the blood.

No one escapes their mess, she thought.

She breathed and breathed again, each inhalation slower than the last. She wiped her hands on her apron and patted her hair. Perhaps this baptism would be the last, the final body exsanguinated, burned, evaporated; her final purification into a world she never asked to be part of.

The fire in the kiln roared. Normally she loved the sound of the fire. It made her think of an animal, a beast, hungry for whatever she would feed it. It listened to her commands but could also bite, the scars on her hands a testament to its hunger. The kiln was her reflection, the fire that roared inside of her, one that faded after she fed it but never died. She stood from the body knowing the blood would dry and wash away, leaving only traces of her cleansing until the stains, like the memories of Mr. Maraud, disappeared. She ignored how her shoes splashed in the puddle that had formed around Mr. Maraud. She threw his shirt, his pants, his socks, and his shoes into the fire box with the wood. She grabbed the butcher's knife from the table. Mr. Maraud lay limp on the floor, far from the man he pretended to be at his home, at the bank, when he beat his wife, when he put out cigarettes on his daughter's back. The thunder on the street grew louder. Dust shook free from the ceiling and rained over the cellar. The boots on the cobblestone stomped and scraped and stomped in unison. Odette squeezed the knife's handle tighter until her knuckles turned white. The fire in the kiln raged.

"You're ruining everything," she whispered to the window. And the boots kept stomping past, trampling the words Odette let slip onto the street unaware, uncaring, unashamed of how the thunder shook the city.

Two

The thunder over the city had faded, replaced in the streets by a sterile quiet, absent of birds, absent of footsteps, absent of the children drumming their sticks against the buildings. The heat from the kiln had disappeared in the night, and with it, Odette felt the fire inside her calm. She cleared the ash from the pit. She wore a mask and apron to keep the powder from creeping inside her nose and mouth. The first time she had cleared the kiln, she hadn't known to wear protection and she choked on the ash. It had been nearly ten years but she still felt the raw grainy remnants of the powder scratch against her throat whenever she opened the grate. She raked the bottom of the kiln and collected the ash. Mr. Maraud's clothes joined the former wood, exploded cups, and his disintegrated bones. Draining the blood from the body released between nine to fourteen pounds. Clothes provided another two to five pounds. Fat and bone and sinew made up the other percentage of weight. Fat and skin burned away in the kiln's intense heat. But scattered pieces of Mr. Maraud remained, bone shards and teeth mostly.

Odette sifted through the ash and placed the remaining bits of Mr. Maraud in a mortar. She ground the fragile pieces with a pestle to make a finer ash than what remained in the fire.

"Odette," Aloysius said. He lowered his voice and tapped against the door. She could normally hear his lame leg thumping against the steps. She had told him time and again not to bother her in the basement. His mother had given him the same speech. He never entered Odette's studio without permission, but he often waited by the door.

The first time Aloysius had knocked on her door after a night with the kiln, Odette nearly choked on her heart, worried he would quickly look past the door and see the beast hidden inside the cellar, hidden beneath her skin. In that brief moment when her heart jumped into her throat and stopped beating, she vowed to keep the beast stowed in the cellar, trapped inside to never let Aloysius see.

She was twelve years old. Her legs had just sprouted. She had not yet begun strapping down her chest. Ali's mother made Odette spend the night in the basement feeding the flame, stoking the blaze, and watching as the bits of body melted away.

"You didn't ask for this mess," Ali's mother had said. "But now you're stuck cleaning it up." The skin melted. The bones cracked. "Clean it all up and clear it all away."

Aloysius had knocked in the morning and brought a croissant for Odette thinking she would be hungry. Odette never thanked him and instead slapped him for interrupting her. He never mentioned the smell. He never looked at the fire. He never entered the room uninvited again.

Odette pounded the teeth and bone faster making sure all traces of their structure disappeared before she opened the door.

"What is it, Ali?" she said.

"The city feels empty," he said. "It's like what we always dreamed about." He didn't blink at her mask or her apron covered in gray powder. He took his finger and rubbed it over her arm, taking a layer of ash with it.

"And what do we have here?" he said. "A poor cup, a plate we will never know?"

Odette's smile hid behind her mask, and she tried not to laugh.

"A bowl, actually," she said. "I'll have to make another."

"You have hundreds of bowls.'

"And now I have one less."

"Come see the city with me. You won't recognize it."

At first, Aloysius hadn't known Odette in person, but from afar, and he thought he knew her better through distance than he could have known her close up. She was quiet and rarely spoke to anyone but her mother. She kept her eyes to the floor when people spoke around her. Not when she walked or was lost in thought, though. Then she kept her eyes to the sky, along the rooftops of Paris, or peering down the hidden lanes and alleys, as if she knew someone lurked in the shadows. Aloysius kept to himself too, drawn to Odette for their similarities and not their differences, her idiosyncrasies, not her oddities. She pummeled boys who tried to light ants on fire with a magnifying glass. She made Louis San Michelle's nose bleed when she caught him terrorizing a cat. The boy had placed the cat in a box with handmade large slits—the cat wailed as the boys threw stones at the box trying to hit the cat. Odette used her elbow, and Louis's nose crunched. Blood gushed down his face, stained his shirt, his knickers, and flooded the cobblestones dark. He held his nose as water filled his eyes. Odette picked up the box. The cat scrambled away. Odette walked back to Louis and kicked him in the ass. He fell to his hands and knees, blood running from his nose like a broken faucet.

"You think it's fun?" Odette demanded. "Are you defenseless? Is this fun?"

She took the same rocks Louis had used on the cat and threw them against his ribs. He dropped to the streets. Each rock hit his skin, his ribs, his back, with a dull thud. Odette ran out of rocks. Louis tried to stand but fell back to the ground. He coughed and dust burst from between the cobblestones. Blood seeped through his shirt.

"You didn't answer me," Odette said. She picked up more rocks. Louis curled into a ball. Odette dropped the rocks one by one on the stone. Louis flinched at the sound. He sobbed and his tears fed the stream of blood around his cheek. Aloysius had wondered what his father would have done in that moment, if he would have helped Louis or Odette, if he would have helped the cat? But Aloysius hadn't chosen a side. Even if he had wanted to save the cat—to help Odette—he was not his father. He was not confident and courageous. Aloysius was a coward who hid in the shadows while Odette had strength. She had the spirit Aloysius wished for. The air had smelled of dust and heat that day. The cat had taken to its hiding place around the boxes and trash of the nearest butcher, where many of the feral felines called home in the summer, drawn by the smell of the meat ready to rot, the bones untouched, the sinew held tight to the tossed away skin. Odette and Aloysius had been eight at the time. Aloysius knew they belonged together, like a torn loaf of bread, each a piece missing, each broken in the wrong places but when brought together made a whole. Their fathers had died from the Great War. They had been brave men who gave way to brave children. Odette was brave. She made Aloysius want to be brave too.

Two days later, Louis's older brother Francois dragged Louis down the street by his elbow. Louis had two black eyes and a bandage over his nose. He ached when his brother pulled at him. His body was sore with bruises around his back, around the shoulders, and his ribs had cracked in two places from the rocks. Francois threw his brother towards Odette and told her to apologize.

"I only did to him what he did to the cat," she said.

"It was a cat," Francois said. Louis cowered at Odette's voice and again at Francois's, not sure who would hurt him worse.

"And?" Odette said.

"He is not a cat. He is a person."

"Not much of one if you ask me. If a person treats an animal like that, how will he treat someone else?"

"You're just a filthy bitch," Francois said. "And I'll give you what all bitches deserve."

Even at eight, Aloysius knew it was Francois's father talking. Typical adults, typical men: when all else failed, punch down.

Francois flexed his fist. Odette grinned. Ali could spend days studying her grin—it appeared rarely, like a rainbow, but instead of colors and sunshine, her grin promised blood.

"Apologize or—"

"Or what?" Odette's voice dropped. Her eyes broke into a hateful stare framed by her bangs. She clenched her fists and let her nails dig into her skin. Aloysius imagined that the slight pain was supposed to ease her mind, calm her down; instead, it stirred her rage, reminding her of the pain to come—pain she was eager to feel.

Francois pushed his brother aside. Aloysius stepped in front of Odette.

"You can't hurt her," he said.

Francois punched Aloysius in the mouth. He flew to the ground. Odette cracked her knuckles and waited until Francois moved within two steps. He reached back his fist. Odette kicked him in the groin. He bent over in pain. She grabbed his hair and drove her knee into his face. His nose opened the same way his brother's had. Francois fell to the ground.

"What kind of person are you that you want to defend someone like that?" Odette said. She spit on Francois as he writhed in pain. His moans sounded like the wails the cat had made when in the box. Odette moved to Aloysius. He put his hand out to Odette, sure she would help him up. She slapped it away.

"If I need help, I'll ask for it," she said. Aloysius met her eyes. They had a deep brown color, like dark chocolate, bitter and sweet. She reached her hand out and gripped Aloysius's wrist to help him up.

"Thank you," he said.

"No more helping," she said.

"Unless you ask," he said. She nodded.

"My name is Odette," she said. "You are Mrs. Moreau's son."

"Aloysius," he said. They stood in silence. Francois's moans faded to whimpers.

"I'm sorry," Louis said to Odette.

"You should apologize to the cat," Odette said.

Louis tilted his head. "I don't know how."

Odette thought for a second. "Well, the next time you see a stray you should give it a good home."

Louis nodded with innocent excitement—without the vindictive smile he had when torturing the cat in the box.

"But if I ever hear about—"

"You won't," Louis said. He helped Francois up from the ground, and they hobbled away together; this time Louis set the pace.

"You're very brave," Aloysius said in the absence of the other boys.

"No, I am not," she said. "I don't like when people think they can do whatever they want because they're bigger."

"Then you help those that aren't as big," Aloysius said.

"Sometimes."

"Are you scared when you do it?"

"Sometimes," Odette said.

"That's being brave."

"I shouldn't be scared," Odette said.

"I get scared sometimes too," he said.

"But you do it anyway?"

Aloysius looked away and hung his head.

"But you did today," she said. She touched his shoulder. He looked into her face, strong and calm once more, and found a tender smile. Different than the ones his mother gave him, with the corners of her lips turned down, and distant eyes filled with remnants of sadness. "Were you scared?"

"I didn't think very much," he said. "I wanted to help."

"Like me," she said.

"You make me want to help."

She leaned in and kissed him on the cheek. "We can walk home together."

They stayed a few paces apart, the way they would continue to walk for the rest of their lives together, far enough for people to not get suspicious but close enough to touch one another if they needed to reach out.

Through her mask, through the stale musk of ash in the air, what Odette smelled was the lingering scent of iron from Mr. Maraud and the bleach she used to scrub the floor, the scent of accomplishment and a job well done. Then she recognized the pleasing aroma of Aloysius's cologne, a mixture of jasmine, sandalwood, and sweet orange. She nodded.

The air was still around the cobblestone streets. All the window shades were drawn. Children didn't linger on the stoops or kick soccer balls. The distant rumble of tanks and footsteps left their mark on the parade route, but the sky was clear, blue, and sunny—absent of the storm. A sugary scent from the tank exhaust hung low through the city. It hid the lingering smell of copper that clung to Odette. She had drained the blood and spilled what was left into the drain before leaving the basement.

Once, when the kiln had broken, Odette tried to drop the flayed flesh outside of a butcher shop. The shops no longer threw their rotted meat out for collection. The day Odette realized this she had almost thrown open the bag into an empty street where piles of pig intestines and hooves often tumbled over. The butcher waved. Odette went inside to buy a sausage. The butcher told her about regulations he had to follow. He could still drain blood into the sewers but now had to "properly" remove all meat from the shop, rather than feeding it to the dogs, cats, and vagabonds. Odette bought her sausage and thanked the butcher that day, taking the bags to the Seine and hoping they wouldn't float. She removed loose stones from the path and stuffed them into the bags. She stood and watched the bubbles disappear, waiting for the bags to rise to the top, waiting for a young couple to stroll by in search of a hideaway, finding instead a bag of amputated prune-like fingers and decaying molars. But the bags never returned to the surface, nor did any of the flesh.

"Isn't it eerie?" Aloysius said. The dull thud and drag of his leg echoed after him as they walked. They kept a steady pace; the same pace they had set years ago. A pace from which they rarely ever strayed.

"What is?" Odette said.

"The city. It's more like a picture of itself, all quiet and empty."

"I suppose."

"Yes, I'm sure you would," Aloysius said with a smile.

It did not feel like her city, the Paris she had grown up in, or the one she explored during the day, where children played in the parks, women sipped coffee at the cafes, and bakeries puffed with fragrant brioche in the morning. This felt like the Paris after midnight, where serenity acted like a blanket that hid law-abiding citizens from corners of detritus, as if the darkness could cover the grime of bar fights and beaten prostitutes and the blood leftover on the streets come morning. But now that same quiet laid the truth bare for Odette: it was never the darkness in which the shit thrived. The fire inside her prickled a little at the thought as she and Aloysius walked beside the river and listened to the absence.

Three

The wind coursed over the streets, fluttering the café umbrellas. The dirt sprung from the crevices of the city as if they were leaves but the leaves had browned, died, and fallen weeks before, leaving the city barren and lifeless. If Odette arrived early enough to work, she could sneak in and avoid Ms. Gerhardt. How often had Odette arrived on time only to be berated about the fact that only Philistines arrived late? How many times in the past two months had Ms. Gerhardt found a new reason to reprimand Odette? Her pointed nose reminded Odette of an arrow, sharp, narrow, and great for piercing another person if she got too close. Odette had fantasized once or twice about chopping it off and feeding it to the fish in the Seine. Her round face, broad shoulders, and the folds of her neck only sharpened her nose.

Odette clenched her coat tight against the endless push of the wind, tipping her head to protect her eyes from dust and stones as she walked to the hospital. Summer and spring breezes carried the aromas of flaky pastries and the gentle nutty scent of macarons. At night, the stars flickered above a city flooded with the fragrance of melted butter, poaching pears, simmering berries. In the winter, Odette yearned for the rich, decadent perfume of melted chocolate as it drifted out of the confectionaries, settling over the thin layers of snow spread across the cobblestones. Autumn always felt stuck between the fragrances Odette adored and the reminder of looming darkness. Autumn was the season her mother died. Autumn was the season she discovered the unavoidable demon that ate at her insides. Winter was when she descended into the depths of the beast, like Dante into the pits of Hell, wondering how many layers she would have to travel before reaching its core. Unlike Dante, she hadn't witnessed anything holy and instead, came face to face with herself—unholy—the true beast.

"The story of Beauty and the Beast is charming," Aloysius had said. "It's a fairytale."

"Fairytales are for children," Odette had said.

"They're for all types of people," Aloysius said.

"Other people, maybe," Odette said.

They had sat at the edge of a pond, eating ice cream while watching the ducks swim across the water. Aloysius's mom had reminded him of the story. "She probably thinks I'm the beast."

"Never. You are the beauty."

"Beauty is a girl."

"She doesn't have to be—"

Aloysius dropped his ice cream, scaring the ducks away, and Odette found herself descending the pits of herself, layer by layer, following Dante more than a fairytale. Finding first, the unavoidable pain of the monster, desecrating her memories with a veil of blood painting the walls of her past. The blood coated her every thought, turning the images of her mother red, smelling of vomit and dried piss. The photo of her father, still resting on the table beside Odette's bed, with a face she could trace from memory—a trimmed mustache, hair parted down the center with the impeccable pride of a soldier, memorialized in his uniform—painted crimson where his skin once was. The second layer fought with her, ripping at the skin between her legs with its fingernails. Come morning, when she woke outside of the layers of the underworld, her skin had healed without a trace around her thighs, but blood and torn flesh were stuck beneath her fingernails. Until the morning she awoke with fresh scars on her wrists and tiny indentations on her thighs, bandages soaked with the brown that blood turned once oxidized. Then she fell deeper into the third layer; a comatose state of paralysis, with the monster whispering in her ear—laughing at her body, mind, spirit, past, present, future—screaming that she had nowhere to go. On the fourth layer, she met the beast, shook its hands of wrinkled skin and found that the monster's skinny fingers and yellow nails resembled her own. Black horns had turned to black hair; the demon's yellow eyes had turned brown; the ominous laugh, the nefarious hushed whispers, had softened, gelled, and formed the familiar tone of Odette's voice. She emerged from the inferno, like Dante enlightened by her journey, but unlike Dante, without a familiar light found at the top of Purgatory, eager to scold and yet, redeem her. Odette emerged from the subterranean, sub-spiritual, and subconscious into the park—which looked as though no time had passed—half-expecting to find her mother and the grocer face down in the water surrounded by broken glass. She half-expected to see her own feet bloody from having stepped on the glass, with her knees broken open from having kneeled on the glass, with her hands weeping from the wrists, having been cut by the glass as she shattered it over the Grocer's head. A head which didn't prove hard enough as it split open and leaked. Dented-in and gushing, it hit the floor with a squish instead of a thump. Aloysius touched Odette, and she recoiled, the ice cream melting over her fingers and dripping into the edge of the pond causing the water to ripple.

The wind, as if angered by the absence of leaves, took out its aggression on Odette's body. It didn't bite; it chewed on Odette's cheeks and pushed through the thin slits in her coat, needling her skin. It seemed eager to punch and whip the neoclassical pillars lining the streets, rattle the windows of the boutiques, and flip the café tables; leaving puddles of whatever coffee and wine and grease remained in the city.

Odette entered the safety of the hospital and quickly lit a cigarette away from the wind. It had once been a place to help people, a place where Odette could offset the nights she spent stalking the unsuspecting men of the city. Men who thrived on chaos, on fear, on provoking others, and on exhibiting their power, when really, the more they postured, the more it showed the cracks in their armor. It represented their fears, their worry of not being more masculine, of not having enough force over their world, of not having enough money to pay for food, of not having good enough looks to attract admirers, of not having enough power to hold sway over their families, the government, the bank, the city, the world. The more they had to posture, the weaker they looked. The more they argued, the smaller they became. Until Odette could pick them up by their collar, hide them in her pocket, and take them back to her table in the cellar. Until they all but disappeared. Men, she thought, were easy to manipulate; they were just too stupid to know the world had been doing it their entire lives, and instead, blamed women for their troubles, their pain, and their ignorance.

The hospital was a refuge, a place that couldn't break when Odette touched it. It was a place that always stood for safety and the help of others until the day the head of the hospital turned his office into a suicide den— a place of intentional death, instead of healing and life.

When Odette first started, she shied away from the other nurses and the patients, attempting to use the hidden bandages wrapped around her breasts as shields. The longer she worked, the more the other nurses included her in their conversations, the looser the bandages became. The nurses welcomed her the way their superiors had welcomed them into the folds of nursing in the fast-paced city. Back in a time when people entered the hospital with bones protruding from their forearms after a bicycle accident and head-wounds gushing with blood from bar fights or lover's quarrels. Eventually, her wraps slipped away completely, and Odette emerged as a nurse.

Once, Odette met a man in the emergency room who needed stitches after his wife slammed a frying pan into his head. He had brought his mistress into their home for an afternoon when the children were in the country, and the wife found a pearl in their bed. The man claimed he had slipped on a loose bar of soap in the tub. The wife hadn't been as coy about the incident. She told all the nurses she hit her husband with the frying pan; not because he had a mistress, but because he bought his mistress pearls when his wife still had to wear the shoddy copper earrings he purchased for a wedding anniversary that turned her skin green. She kept his house and bore his children; she at least deserved the pearls. Then again, she had said, she recalled how her husband made love and thought maybe the mistress deserved the pearls more than she after all.

The moment Odette touched the suicided head of the hospital, the day the Germans entered the city, she felt the change in the halls, in the office, in the air.

The nurses wouldn't enter the office. They crossed themselves and whispered about curses. They spoke about demons in hushed tones. The doctors refused to enter the room as if staying in the hall kept it from being real. They kept ordering nurses to enter, but the women looked away and spat on the floor.

Odette entered the room. The doctor hung from the ceiling; his legs dangled like a child held by their father ready to kick any second. But he couldn't kick anymore. The note on the desk referenced the occupation, his refusal to work with the Germans, his anguish at the France he didn't recognize, the Paris of his youth gone in an instant. Odette took the doctor down in silence but left the note on his desk for others, for the next hospital head perhaps. She placed the doctor on a cart and rolled him to the morgue. She passed the nurses, the doctors, first witness of sickness but now purveyors of death in the city, they embodied despair with heavy shoulders and rancid eyes creating an army of sadness. Because of them, Odette knew, not all life was created equal. To Odette, not all deaths were equal either.

After Odette handled the body, the nurses looked at her differently, as if she had put the wraps around her chest back on, as if she had tainted the hospital, as if she had an incurable infectious disease on her hands, one they would all catch if they associated with her.

A nurse pushed a cart filled with instruments down the hall as a woman in a doctor's coat turned the corner. She wore black heels and strutted with her shoulders back. Even the male doctors walked with a sense of urgency, their shoulders hunched, always looking over their notes or hurrying as if one missed step would mean a patient's life. But the woman walked as if a patient's life would wait for her, as if she chose when the patient would live—or die. Blood dripped from the doctor's coat. Odette knocked over the cart, shattering the instruments on the ground as she grabbed a pair of towels and ran to the doctor, opening the coat in search of a wound, ready to apply pressure. The doctor stood like a child amused by a squirrel running at her feet.

"What is it you are looking for?" the doctor said.

"You're bleeding," Odette said. The doctor stared with a bemused smirk; the first time Odette noticed it. "You're bleeding?" Odette repeated.

"I assure you—what is your name?"

"Odette. Odette Lefebvre."

"I assure you, Odette, had I been bleeding you would not be the first to have noticed." As the doctor spoke, the blood on her coat dried. "You are very observant."

"I think most people notice when blood is on someone," Odette said.

"But most people choose to ignore it. Most people do not know to apply pressure. Most people would not call for a doctor—especially for a German, no?"

Odette blushed, realizing, if the doctor *had* been bleeding, most of Paris would have been quick to let her hemorrhage, with a sort of beauty Odette could quantify in the image of a blood-red pond fed by the woman. Odette hadn't considered the doctor was German. Would it have mattered? Should it have mattered if she had known?

"What is it you do here?" Ilse asked.

"I am uh—"

"Odette, I don't have time for nonsense. Are you a head nurse?"

Odette shook her head.

"And why not?"

"I was not allowed," Odette said.

"Says whom?"

"Ms. Gerhardt." Odette pointed to the bear of a nurse who stood above the scattered utensils with a look of disapproval. Her glasses clung to her pointed nose as if guiding her eyes as they caught the overhead lights and glared.

"What else did Ms. Gerhardt say?" Ilse asked.

"I shouldn't," Odette said.

"Believe me, *hase*; you should."

Odette paused, wondered why the doctor would call her a rabbit, and cleared her throat, filling the hall with the sound of churned gravel. She looked from the doctor to Ms. Gerhardt. The woman's mouth twitched. Odette tried not to smile, but the edges of her thin lip flicked in eagerness.

"She said the French folded under pressure. That was why we lost to the German forces. That is why we should only take instructions and not give them. We cannot handle the pressure of the hospital."

"Are you dumb—Odette?"

"I can do the work," Odette said.

"That is not what I asked," the doctor said.

"I assure you, doctor that I—" Ms. Gerhardt said.

"If I wanted you to answer, Ms. Gerhardt, I would have asked you the question. Are you trained, Odette?"

"No, doctor."

"Do you have training?"

"Yes, doctor."

A silence hovered over the hall thick like wet clay.

"Must I ask what you have training in or is it implicit?"

"I am sorry, doctor. I am a trained nurse."

"With experience?"

Odette nodded.

"Pulling information from you is like pulling a rotted tooth," the doctor said.

"I have trained in emergency situations but have mostly been changing sheets and sterilizing equipment."

"I can see that." The doctor looked to the hall where the fallen instruments remained scattered across the floor, lifeless, motionless.

"Dr. Kohler," Ms. Gerhardt said. "She was the one who found Dr. Le Angles."

Dr. Kohler eyed Odette, the same way men would look at Odette when they thought she was an easy target, a doe ready for the slaughter. It was the same way Odette would look at the men she hunted, with the same interest, the same intensity, and the same understanding that they were nothing more than deer. The hairs on the back of Odette's neck stood. She fought the urge to cover herself. On cold nights, she would leave the windows open to feel the same chill, let the breeze roll up her neck. She would sit with Martine in her arms as he purred, enjoying the scent of the frosty air as it rolled through the flat. It excited her.

"That explains it," Dr. Kohler said.

"Doctor?" Odette said.

"I am sure we'll speak later."

"Yes, doctor."

"And Ms. Gerhardt," the doctor said. "Make sure the new schedule is on my desk by the end of the day. I will be looking them over from now on."

"But, doctor—"

"That is all." Before Dr. Kohler turned the corner, she took one more look at Odette. The chill returned to Odette's skin, this time running down her back. She looked at the floor expecting to find a pool of blood but met the light glinting against the polished tile.

Four

The scent of fresh peaches permeated the air; it turned Odette's cheeks flush. She ran her fingers over their skin and enjoyed the touch of the soft fuzz. She wanted to roll her hands over the rounded angles of the fruit until the skin faded away, revealing the juicy flesh. How long would it take? Hours? Days? Weeks? She could already imagine the way the juice would wrap around her finger, the same as when she submerged her fingers in a pool of blood. Her nail would sink into the crimson, absorb her skin, leaving a reflection of her hand shimmering in the blood, her face serene from the fresh kill, the same face she made—she imagined—when she rubbed her fingers against the peach. When her skin emerged from the blood, from within the flesh of the peach, the juice would slowly drip down the length of her finger to the tip, with the final drop dangling, waiting, and with one final breath, drop back to where it came—from the peach—from the bloody pool.

"Fresh," the bagboy said.

"Excuse me?" Odette said. She avoided eye contact.

He motioned to the peaches. His voice cracked and reeked of pubescence.

"Would you like a sample?" the boy said. "We're not supposed to but—"

She shook her head but continued rubbing her fingers over the peaches. The boy looked at her fingers, the way they traced the fuzz across the surface. It reminded her of being a girl—the hair on her arms and legs wispy and fine. It reminded her of being twelve, on the cusp of womanhood but so far from being a woman. She hadn't blossomed but she had grown. Her legs had grown long, her torso had grown long, her hair had grown long. Boys hadn't noticed—men noticed; she still played football, tag, skipped rocks along the Seine, but when she walked home from the riverbanks, men watched, their eyes lingering, following—their gazes pursuing her home. She hadn't become a woman, but the men all wanted to *make* her one.

"I like the way the beans feel," the bagboy said.

Odette pulled her fingers from the peach. The memory of the men and their lingering eyes, their burning eyes—their corrupting eyes—faded away.

"I've changed my mind," Odette said. "I would like a few." Her mind drifted as she yearned to touch a peach—to taste one.

Odette only visited the grocer at the busiest times. If by some coincidence a crowd hadn't formed that day, Odette would wait for another day, another time, to not have to face the grocer, the assistant, or the bagboy, alone. In the anonymity of the crowd, she felt safe to choose the produce without being noticed. She shopped at the market more than three blocks away from her home so as not to pass a face she recognized when not in need of groceries. She shopped little, rarely bought the same thing twice, not wanting the grocer to predict her order. But she needed a peach, always a peach or two when in season. She had changed grocers three times in the past three years after the grocer recognized her, asking if she wanted a peach with her order. She would shake her head no, then buy the peach from a different grocer near her, thinking her sporadic purchase wouldn't draw attention. The second time she had to change grocers, the shop owner was flush with pride. A gap-toothed smile made him look younger than he was. He had just had a son. He gave a single free item of his choice to each customer. Odette didn't know if he recognized her or not, but he gave her a peach for free. Citing his happiness as a new father, he encouraged others to feel happy as well even if it came through a single carrot, or an apple, or a pear, or in Odette's case, a peach. Odette tried not to accept the peach. The grocer insisted, his smile only growing wider, making the gap look bigger, making his face look younger, making the familiar scent of peach turn rancid in Odette's nose. She took the peach in the end, turned the corner, and threw the peach down the drain in the hopes the rancid smell would go with it. It didn't; the stench of rotten peaches stayed with her the entire day, the following day as well, fading only when she bought a new peach from the grocer on the corner.

Since she was a teenager, she always kept peaches in a bowl beside her sink. The perfume filled the kitchen and spread to the entire flat. It seeped into the curtains. It swept over the rug to the point Odette could find the aroma before she entered through the door. She kept the peaches and waited for them to turn, waited until they were soft enough to peel with a flick of her pinky. The smell rose until it became too sweet, too rich, and she drowned in it, as if she had dived into a deep pond of peach perfume.

The last time Odette had tried to eat one of the peaches, the juice ran down her chin and clung to the tiny, imperceptible hairs on her skin. The soft texture became squishy on her tongue and fell apart beneath the strength of her teeth. She remembered the flavor—the sweetness, the subtle hint of the country in the dirt that hadn't washed away. The chewed flesh turned to maggots in her mouth that wriggled and crunched and tickled the inside of her cheek. She spat the meat into the sink and vomited. Stomach acid burned her throat, the back of her tongue, and her nostrils. She felt as though chunks of the peach were stuck in her cheeks. She clutched the edge of the sink and wretched more, and wretched more, and gagged—her entire body heaving—gagged, and wretched more, until she put her back to the sink and sunk down to the floor, legs to her chin, arms cradling herself against the memory of the grocer who broke through the door. The man had licked Odette's cheek, pulled his belt off and lifted her mother's skirt, gripped his hairy and sweaty and fat fingers around her mother's neck, yelled and grunted, as he choked her mother, the sound muzzled, her throat constricting as the grocer grunted. Her mother's eyes had bulged, turned red—almost popped—until her eyes turned the same color white as his knuckles, her cheeks the same color as his cheeks, and her feet stopped kicking. Odette grabbed a vase from the countertop, and knocked a peach onto the floor, and the peach rolled to the grocer's feet. She slammed the vase onto his head, and the glass shattered around them.

"Your peaches," the bagboy said.

"Excuse me?" Odette said. She finally looked at the boy. His eyes were green, light like the lettuce rather than the cucumbers. This time, the boy looked away.

"Oh, right. Thank you."

"You're welcome." His voice cracked.

The scent of peaches drifted upwards from the bag. Odette inhaled. She tried not to gag.

Five

Odette knocked on Agnes's door ready to ask for the mail. Aloysius opened with an excited smile.

"I am glad you are here," he said. "Come in for a coffee."

"Coffee?" Odette said.

"It's an occasion," Aloysius said. "An occasion calls for coffee."

Agnes glared at Odette from across the room.

"Good afternoon, Mrs. Moreau," Odette said. "I just came for my mail."

"It is on the table there," Agnes said and gestured with a slight nod. She had pulled back her silver hair, but the frayed bangs framed her face with a distinct disheveled look, unlike her usual poised appearance.

"Thank you," Odette said reaching for the envelopes.

"Don't be silly," Aloysius said. "I have so much to share." He grabbed Odette's wrist and gently pulled her into the apartment. Unlike Agnes's composed personal appearance, her apartment was always covered in papers and scattered mail, half-read books and decomposing catalogues sent from New York, London, and Milan. Aloysius hobbled when excited as if his body tried to keep up with the speed at which his mind raced. "Sit,

sit." He pulled a chair from the table in the kitchen and motioned Odette to sit. Agnes joined her with a stern look but refused to meet Odette's eyes.

"You must have had an exciting day," Odette said to Aloysius.

"You should know about excitement," Agnes said.

"Mother," Aloysius said. "She is our guest." He placed an espresso in front of Odette and another in front of Agnes. He had mixed one teaspoon of sugar into both cups.

"Ali," Agnes said. "You shouldn't be so liberal. We don't know how long our supplies can last."

"Mother," Aloysius said, his eyes cast down at the sugar bowl. "Sharing with our neighbor is important."

"Says who?" Agnes said.

"You," Aloysius said.

"And the Bible," Odette said.

Agnes made a noise, shook her head, and waved away the comments as if that would erase the past, the words, or Odette's biblical reference. "Of all things you should quote," Agnes said. But Odette wasn't sure to which of them Agnes spoke.

Odette took a sip of her coffee trying to savor the flavor she assumed would soon dissolve. She wondered what else would disappear. Agnes savored the coffee as well; perhaps she indulged in the slight sweetness the sugar added or the way the bitterness became muddled. Odette had never noticed she and Agnes took their coffee the same way. Aloysius remained in his gendarme uniform. He must have just gotten off work.

"Did something happen at work?" Odette asked.

"More like is happening," Aloysius said.

"They have called him back after a lunch break," Agnes said with a sneer. "There has been a—what did you call it *ma souris*? A development?"

"Yes," Aloysius said. He sat down with a large cup filled with a double espresso. He poured cream into the cup as if it were a waterfall, splashing down into a pool of coffee. Aloysius stared at the cascade as he spoke.

"We have autonomy." Agnes cleared her throat, her eyes scowling at the milk, and he stopped pouring.

"We?" Odette said.

"The gendarmes."

"Okay," Odette said. "What does this mean?"

"We will not be under the thumb of the Germans."

"Nothing will change," Odette said. She tried to understand Ali's excitement, but the more he stood smiling the less she grasped.

"There is talk of disappearances," Agnes said.

Odette took a sip of her coffee. She let the bitter and sweet flavors coat her tongue before she acknowledged Agnes.

"We have reason to believe they've been murdered," Aloysius said.

"I don't understand," Odette said.

"We will be able to investigate. Not the Germans."

"There are murders every day," Agnes said. "We just finished a war."

"Sadly, I'm sure there will be more disappearances, too." Odette said. "How can we know who has disappeared, who has simply left town, and who might have been taken at the front?"

Aloysius waved his hands through the air as if wiping away their concerns. "No, no. I am not explaining this right." He leaned in close. "This is not some mother looking for her son who did not come back from the front or a wife eager to find her husband after a drunken night of debauchery. This is murder. It has to be. These men do not just leave their families. They are—"

"Respectable?" Agnes said.

"They must be," Odette said hiding a sigh. "If the gendarmes are serious about pursuing their disappearances."

"Do you remember the English story of Jack the Ripper?" Aloysius said.

"Someone killed a prostitute?" Odette said.

"It is a very dangerous profession," Agnes said. She sighed and took a sip of her coffee. She glared at Odette but said nothing else.

"No, mother. It wasn't a prostitute."

"But it is very dangerous," Agnes said. Odette nodded.

"Yes," Aloysius said. "I meant, that is not what I mean. It was a man."

"A male prostitute?" Odette said.

"Do male prostitutes exist?" Agnes asked.

"I said it was not a prostitute!" Aloysius snapped. He took a breath, sipped his coffee, wiped his hands down his shirt, and continued. "I already told you what we found, mother. Why do you ask questions like these?"

Agnes finally looked at Odette. "I must have forgotten. It sounds so vile. I can't believe it has happened at a time like this. It is hard to imagine such a person out there in the world."

Odette took a sip of her espresso as Agnes gave a slight nod, her frown looking like melted candlewax.

"A woman came to the station with a few teeth she swore were her husband's," Aloysius said.

"His teeth?" Odette said.

"One was gold," Agnes added.

"If you remember, mother, you can continue the story."

"I could never," Agnes said.

"There were four teeth in all," Aloysius said.

"Her husband had been missing for days but suddenly, she found his teeth near the front door," Agnes said with an air of surprise and wonder.

"His teeth?" Odette said. "She could tell they were *his* teeth?"

"Of course not," Agnes said. "But she knew the gold tooth well enough. Even the worst of the police figured that quandary out."

"Thank you, mother."

"I was not talking about you," Agnes said. "But you must admit that your department has done nothing about our current situation."

"France signed an armistice, mother. It is not a situation. We lost. Paris is an open city."

"And your department will let these *people* do whatever they want while here."

Odette kept silent about the war, about the influx of Germans. She had been so cautious about the bodies, about grinding their teeth, about not letting her victims struggle. But sometimes the men didn't want to follow Odette home. Sometimes they knew they had power at home and not on the street. And sometimes Odette had to convince them with a punch to the head instead of the ego. Agnes must have known where the teeth came from with the way she kept looking at Odette. Why was Aloysius so excited for the emergence of random teeth?

"The point is," Aloysius interrupted. "The administration does not want to look bad in front of the Germans. They put someone fully in charge of the case to figure out what has happened and to track down the person who did this."

"What about the teeth you found?" Odette asked.

"Of course, we will try to identify the man too." Odette and Agnes stared at him blankly.

"I mean," he said, "I will try to find where he is first, but if we can't, we will try to identify where the man went." Aloysius sat up proud, his chest puffed out.

"They put you in charge of this?" Odette asked, dreading the response.

He slumped a little, folding inside of himself at the question. "Well, no" he said. "But this could be the case of a lifetime."

A lump filled Odette's throat, making it hard to breathe and harder to swallow.

"Yes," Odette said. "It *could* be."

"It could also be nothing," Agnes said. "And that's why no one else cares. You are chasing a phantom's teeth, *running after the moon*."

"I have the support of my superiors," Aloysius said. His voice quivered.

"It sounds like you have their load and not their support," Agnes said.

Aloysius stood from the table, said farewell, and shuffled out the door to return to the police station. Odette sipped her coffee and avoided the stare she knew Agnes pointed in her direction.

"You need to stop," Agnes said.

"Stop what?" Odette said.

"If the German's don't catch you in the act, the police will."

"Since when have you worried about the police getting involved?" Odette asked.

"Since now," Agnes said. She stood from the table, grabbed her coffee, and took the remainder of Odette's without asking if she had finished. She placed the cups in the sink with a heavy clink. Odette had never worried about the police. She had taken so many precautions to hide any trace of her activity. Agnes was right. Odette hadn't worried either…until now.

When Odette was fifteen, she heard a group of women twittering on the street. They spoke in hushed tones, like the water of the Seine brushing against the bordering walls, but not as soft, not as gentle. Their twittering took on a harshness, an edge, as if the water carried a bicycle that clanged and smacked the wall with the water's movement. They hid their voices as Odette walked past. The quiet made their voices louder. She didn't need to hear what they said. She already knew.

The girl's as flat as a boy.

Her mother disappeared.

Where are her breasts? They should have come in by now.

Her mother ran away with the grocer and left her behind.

Her mother was un-Christian.

Perhaps that's why the girl has no figure.

I don't think her mother was a Christian at all.

Her mother…Her mother…Her mother.

And as their voices bounced around the street and echoed in her head, she felt a heat burn in her stomach, heard the subtle crackle as a fire started. Until eventually the voices rang out.

"She's broken."

For the first time since the Grocer pounded on her door, Odette felt the surge of violence stir. It felt a bit like nausea and excitement. Her hands shook. Her heart turned to powder. Her knuckles ached, awakened by the memory of the blood that once soaked her skin. But she had promised Agnes she would try to keep her knuckles clean from now on, and Agnes, in return, promised to teach Odette what she had learned during the Great War. The lessons first started with pottery.

"You always need a vessel to carry the important merchandise," Agnes said.

"What would important merchandise be?"

"In the army, it was anything from morphine to canned goods, or even socks."

"Will I need to carry around socks in this vase?" Odette asked.

"Don't get any ideas," Agnes said. "Or I will make you do the wash."

Then the stories of the horrors at the front turned to lessons, with Agnes stuck in the medical tent—men bleeding from their eyes, their ears, open wounds; spritzing from their stomach, a gunshot wound to their anus. Odette relished the stories, the gorier the better, each time imagining someone she despised as the soldier dying from blood loss or screaming in agony. Most often, the grocer took the place of any and every soldier tortured from mustard gas or on the verge of an amputation. After months of learning how to make vases and listening to the stories of the Great War, Agnes told Odette she was ready, and just this one time, they would go on a hunt together. Agnes gave Odette two rules—and in a world of rules, only two felt freeing and debilitating all at once. The first rule was to do everything in Odette's power to never get caught. The second rule was no women, no children.

"But why no women?" Odette had asked thinking of the clan of women chirping on the street.

"Cunning," Agnes said. "It's a world run by men. It's a world made by men. Are you going to fault the women who play by men's rules?"

They made a date for their search party; then Odette found a man at the park—his hands cupping the breasts of a young girl, the girl slapping the man's hands away, and the man cupping her ass instead, and the man turning to Odette, *When you're ready for a man*, he laughed—and Odette had to make an excuse to march away from Aloysius so she could follow the man home. She ran back to Agnes in the night and told her the story of a man attempting to take advantage of a girl. Agnes wanted more proof saying: "When you cut, you cut once, and you cut deep. There's no turning back from it." It was her way of saying, *you better be sure*.

"You have so little rules in life," Agnes said. "You need to follow the ones you do have, and everything will be ok."

They waited another week and took turns following the man to make sure he was the right choice. Then, one day in the park with a different girl, he tried again. This time Agnes interrupted him pretending to be a woman selling flowers to lovers. She returned to Odette and said, "He'll do nicely." That evening they found the man at a tavern sipping wine and fibbing to another man about his latest exploit in the park, conveniently leaving out the woman who interrupted before he could start, allowing the girl to run home unmolested. Odette lured the man out from the tavern and back to the apartment. Agnes waited in the cellar with a thick sheet and metal pipe. She wacked the man in the head—he hit the table with a clang on the way to the floor. Agnes placed him on the sheet and restrained him. They would wait until he woke up before speaking to him.

Then a knock boomed from the door. A gendarme stood waiting.

"Are you ladies alright?" he said.

"Of course," Agnes said. "Why do you ask?"

"I heard a noise," he said. "At this time of night, it is usually something unsavory."

Agnes leaned closer to the officer as if to tell him a secret. "She's all thumbs," she said pointing to Odette. "She's studying nursing at home. If she doesn't read through the night, she'll never make it."

The gendarme gave Odette a partial look. "She reminds me of my sister," he said. "She always wanted to be a nurse."

"What did she become instead?" Agnes asked.

"She died of influenza when she was thirteen," the gendarme said.

"It struck my husband too," she said.

The gendarme nodded and wished Odette good luck.

"I thought your husband died in the war?" Odette said.

"The gendarme doesn't have to know more than we need him to," Agnes said.

"Is that one of my rules?" Odette asked.

"It is now."

Six

Hunger in the city came fast and with little warning for those who had not previously seen the signs. But Agnes had noticed the writing in the sky if not on the street long before the Germans arrived in the city.

By fall, Agnes took to using a cane when walking the streets. She shuffled, much like the men who had returned from the front after the Great War. Men who had shrapnel stuck in their knees, or thick splinters of wood buried deep in their feet that they never could tweeze out no matter how far they dug in the knife—or how much more they bled—until they finally gave up on life and had no more taste for blood, theirs or others. Agnes's shoes scuffed cobblestones with a familiar drag. Her step, not like her son's, who slightly scraped his foot on the stone, hoping no one would notice if one leg didn't lift as high as the other. He hoped no one would see it took him a half-second longer than the rest of Paris to take the next step, that his rhythm didn't fall in line with those climbing the steps from the metro or crossing the Rue de la Paix. While her son attempted to fit in desperately with the city, Agnes slowed down using the cane like a third leg as if the weight of the occupation had finally broken her back. Outside her apartment, the gravity of the city felt much heavier, pulling her down to the floor. *One day I'll end up sprawled out like the rest of those poor idiots,* she thought and spat. She carried her bag to the grocer's using the cane to propel her forward, slowing with each clack. Those behind her walked around, while those in front of her sped past until she eventually faded into her surroundings, not as a Parisian marching to the indifferent beat of daily life, but as part of the backdrop of the city. She could have been another streetlight, another park bench, or perhaps, another rubbish bin in the park where people would stuff her full of garbage, as if the city hadn't already stunk of waste. Perhaps no one else smelled it, but to Agnes, it radiated off the very ground, the buildings, the people, especially the people who kept pushing through the city as if they had somewhere more important to be. *We're occupied,* she thought, *there is nowhere else to go and nowhere else to be.*

People would flock to the food, she knew, so Agnes took to shoes first. The store was empty of people and Agnes practically had to pound on the counter to get an attendant's attention. He puffed his cheeks and looked around Agnes until he finally faced her.

"Four pairs," she said.

"Perhaps you should take your money to the grocers," he said. His thin lip reminded her of a lizard. She waited for his tongue to slip in and out of his mouth.

"Four pairs," she said again. The Great War lasted four years, she thought. This one shouldn't last longer; *it couldn't last longer.*

When she arrived at the grocer's, a small crowd had already amassed. She elbowed her way to the front of the line. The women apologized to one another over Agnes's head, as if they had bumped each others' hips, instead of Agnes. The few men in the shop towered over her and scowled, both at the indignity of doing the shopping and the shame of waiting in line. They shrugged and grunted and grumbled when Agnes pushed through, but she ignored their hollow reprimands. They all held their ration cards tight in their fingers, hoping today the grocer would have enough produce or dairy for a full meal: fully-grown onions they could sauté in oil, refills of butter having disappeared from the shelves days before the Germans arrived, or crisp butterhead lettuce with enough crunch to withstand a healthy pour of vinegar, or succulent grapes, juicy figs, or ripe blackberries whose juice pooled in their mouths, rather than the last batch that nearly disintegrated between Agnes's teeth as if the earth itself rebelled against the invasion. The grocer passed over Agnes, taking the cards and francs from members of the queue, from those around her dressed as if headed to church, or the men stinking as if having stumbled out of the brothels of Montmartre. She waved her hands but the grocer, like the rest of the city, ignored her as if she had turned invisible. She tapped her cane, stomped on the floor, yelled with the rest of the crowd, "Monsieur! Monsieur!" in an attempt to get the grocer's attention. He never once looked over the counter at her. She felt alone, helpless, and starving. Her legs shook violently with hunger hidden behind her long black skirt. For a moment, she understood how the women and men must have felt during the Siege of Paris in 1870 when a popular chef cooked an extravagant Christmas meal for the Parisian aristocracy using animals from the zoo. If Agnes could, she would break into the zoo and steal an elephant. She could hide the meat in her apartment, make a stew to simmer on her stove, and let the rest cure and dry. Then, by the time winter came, she could enjoy the jerky alongside some beets, brussels sprouts, and sweet potato, although she knew by the time the snow fell the whole city would be relegated to Jerusalem artichokes and turnips—just like the last time. Agnes tried once more to get the attention of the grocer, but he passed right over her for a man with an unlit pipe in his mouth. Agnes let out a contemptuous breath and, for a moment, wanted to whack the man in the shin with her cane.

Instead, she scuffled through the crowd and back onto the streets of Paris. She turned into a dark alley, shook out her feet, then stood up, pulling her back straight, letting the bones crack, creak, and pop back into place. She gripped the cane tight but no longer used it like a leg, holding it more like a baton to ward off hooligans if any of them would take notice of her.

Her stomach rumbled; she should have eaten breakfast. The mad wave of conversations stemming from the grocer grew louder, more acute with anger, with words of disappointment and broken promises. She made her way to the butcher instead, knowing he would have some meat for her, knowing her stomach wouldn't have to wait much longer for a decent meal. She entered the shop, and the butcher gave her a familiar nod.

"Madame Moreau," the butcher said. He watched her from over the counter. The wrinkles on his forehead made his eyes look droopy and sad, creating thick layers up to his bald head. Unlike the grocer's, the butcher shop stood empty. The familiar thick scent of warm meat in the summer never materialized; instead, Agnes found the recognizable stench of bleach.

"Smells like you'll never have meat again," Agnes said.

"Some mornings are much more prominent than others," the butcher said. "I didn't know your 'ailment' had worsened."

"In fact," Agnes said, "it has grown considerably bad. Not only am I lame but invisible."

The butcher shook his head. "Tragic."

"Yes," Agnes said. "Very tragic. I spent an hour leaning on this cane at the grocer's and he didn't even acknowledge my existence. Can you imagine? An old, feeble woman like me. Didn't look at me once. Not once."

"I see," the butcher said. "If you need some help—"

"A woman like me could always use a hand." Agnes smiled. The butcher reached out a hand and Agnes offered the bag she had brought from home. He turned around and popped open a hidden closet before placing a collection of groceries, meat, coffee, and even butter inside.

"This is—"

"Our secret," Agnes said. She knocked on her cane with her fist. "So is this." The butcher smiled back. Agnes took the groceries and walked to the door.

"Like you're invisible, you say?" the butcher repeated.

"I could have been on fire, and they still wouldn't have noticed me."

"Unbelievable," he said.

"No one wants to look this far into the future," Agnes said and winked. She opened the door but before stepping out, hunched over the cane and once more shuffled her feet over the cobblestones. Parisians avoided her, moving around her as if she propelled them by an invisible wall. And she did propel them, she knew, simply by being her, by being old, by wearing out her welcome in the city, on the earth, until she could have been just another body buried in the Cimetière de Montparnasse or a broken lamp post dark in the night. But unlike a dead body or a lamp post, Agnes had ears, Agnes had eyes, and while standing in line at the grocer's, heard people speak, heard their secrets, learned their names, memorized their faces. She could, would, wait for another day the grocer ran out of food, had more time before her stomach truly rumbled and her legs had weakened from starvation. Until then, she could keep hiding wood in the cellar or pigeons on the roof. She carried the groceries home, tapping the cane to the street as the city passed her by, as if she had become another forgotten stone they walked over. She smiled knowing she, unlike many of them, would survive.

Seven

The flowers in Paris never bloomed after the winter frost, choosing instead to stay dead, embodying the degradation Paris had felt upon its occupation. A city once vibrant and known to the world as a beacon of multitudes, resigned to decrepit leaves—crinkly, cracked, stepped on, and forgotten with barely a memory of what once was. The seasons changed but couldn't bring the color back to the city.

The sun scorched the cobblestones and the stucco facades until the entire city held a hint of the summer mountains with the aroma of baked stone in the morning. The smell dissipated early when the char of chicory coffee spilled out of the cafes and open windows from the surrounding homes. The entire city could have fled south after the invasion, Odette thought, and the damn bitter, burnt stink would still hit her like a punch to the face.

By mid-afternoon, Odette expected the pungent sting of rotten and rotting flesh to pour out of the butchers. With no way to keep the meat cool—the heat quickly melting the ice meant to refrigerate the perishables—what little pork, beef, or even horse the markets had either cooked slowly or birthed maggots, which erupted into flies. Flies plagued the streets, making people cover their noses and mouths with scarves beneath the broiling sun to keep the black clouds from their nostrils and mouths. But a stray fly always managed to get through unnoticed, until caught in the spittle at the back of Odette's throat.

Odette had promised to keep a low profile since the arrival of the Nazis. She had promised Agnes, she had promised Aloysius, and she had promised herself, holding dear to the promise that the most important thing was to not get caught. The city died around her. People disappeared around her. The old couple in the park that walked every day no longer sat on the park bench sneaking touches as if they were still love-struck teenagers unable to stray from their chaperones. The pigeons no longer loomed around the outdoor cafes and along the windowsills. Some of the apartments had been plastered with so much shit, it looked like the paint had chipped. What was left looked exactly like what it was: shit— splattered, stuck, and never washing away.

Odette tried to spend less time at the apartment. Time away from the whispered arguments between Aloysius and Agnes, away from children's voices she imagined drifting through the walls, and away from the silence screaming from the empty apartments that people fled after the Germans approached the city. Even at night, the heat pressed down over the streets like a freshly extinguished furnace, with the air sticky from humidity. Martine stood at the foot of the open window, splayed out as if run over by the milk cart, in need of refreshment. Odette rolled atop the sheets and ended in the same position hoping for a breeze that never came. The next morning, she left as early as possible in the morning hoping to avoid the heat before reaching the hospital.

"You don't need to be here today," Ilse said.

"But it's Thursday," Odette said without any conviction, without any reasoning behind the comment other than she had made the effort to get to work. Ilse didn't respond. She looked down at her papers as little droplets of perspiration lingered on her forehead. She kept writing. Odette lifted onto her toes to see if she could see what Ilse wrote, but it was upside down and in German.

"You are still here?" Ilse said.

"What should I do?" Odette asked.

"Get away from this awful heat. Climb a mountain. Jump in the pond. You are not needed here today."

Odette stuck to a strict schedule most days. She rarely strayed from the schedule unless it was important and often gave herself enough time to account for travel, traffic, or a shift in the schedule but not an overall, complete change. She turned on her heels and walked at a slow pace through the door waiting to hear Ilse call her back. Ilse didn't call.

A German bureaucrat carrying a bouquet of flowers bumped Odette as she walked down the corridor nearing the door. The bouquet erupted with flying color. It reminded Odette of the gardens Paris had before the war, the rainbows that had turned crusty and brown. She felt like she hadn't seen a flower since before the occupation. It could have been days or weeks or months but maybe even longer; had it already been a year?

"I beg your pardon, mademoiselle," he said.

He spoke eloquent French, like a poet or a professor of ancient languages who understood the value of a sound, let alone an entire word. He was short and stocky, like a chimpanzee Odette had seen at the zoo, down to the brown hair poking out of his hat.

"You must be looking for one of the nurses," Odette said pointing to the flowers. "No one has brought flowers like that when visiting a patient for a long time."

Before the war, lilies meant purity. Men would bring flowers to the nurses, to their sweethearts, to the women they courted, and the women swooned at the waterfall of petals or gasped at the creamy clove aroma. After the war, a lily practically meant marriage if a man could get his hands on one, afford one, and parted with it to the hands of a woman. Odette would never, but she knew plenty of women who would open up their legs like a blossomed lily if they received one, let alone an entire bouquet.

"A doctor actually," he said.

"A doctor?" Odette asked. She tried to hide her puzzlement, but it draped her face. Was it so outrageous that he should bring flowers to a doctor or simply that he would do so in the daylight?

"Dr. Kohler," he said. "I am her husband."

"Her husband?" Odette asked. "I didn't realize..."

"She doesn't like to mention me at work," he said. "I know this." He lowered his voice conspiratorially. "She thinks it undermines her authority." His smile formed slow with lips like molasses revealing rows of porcelain.

"You can find her in her office, past the administration desk and down the hall."

He tipped his hat, handed Odette a single lily, and left her alone with her flower intact.

The wrath of the sunlight had yet to corrode the day and the people. As Odette walked back into the heart of the city's remaining life, she wondered how a woman like Ilse could have a husband: a strong woman, a capable woman, a woman who chose career over family? Yet, in the end, she had both while Odette spent so long choosing one, fed the idea that a woman could not have both, should not have both, and would be lucky enough to find a husband. What sort of life would that have been for her, where every night she would lay beneath her husband on his whim, in his stink, and wait for him to convulse on top of her and fall asleep so she could have a moment to herself? But she also thought of Aloysius, of midnight coffee, of Martine sleeping at their feet. Perhaps a life as a wife wouldn't be completely deplorable, she thought, especially if she could keep her job, her life, and her Death.

Women and men walked along the narrow cobblestones; those that could afford it sat at the cafes and sipped fake coffee. German soldiers on leave drank real coffee, with real cream, and snacked on real bacon. She hadn't eaten real bacon since before the occupation. Her mouth watered at the smell of the grease. The newspaper recently had an article about the police arresting a man who had broken into a restaurant to try and steal their rations of meat and coffee. An accomplice who noticed the lock on the refrigerator chose instead to try and take the bacon grease. On his way out, he tripped and spilled the coagulated fat on the street. Late night passersby didn't call the police and instead tried to collect as much grease as they could with their hands; grit, soot, and cigarettes be damned. Odette couldn't say she wouldn't have done the same if she had been there. The smell of sunflower leaves had already replaced tobacco, with most Parisians preserving whatever cigarettes they had left while German tourists— and those who associate with German tourists—could afford real tobacco.

Stranded motor vehicles lined the edges of the streets like boulders after a rockslide. The sweat pooled underneath her uniform as she imagined the wetness turning her coat transparent. Thankfully, it hadn't— yet. She longed for a moment to sit at one of the tables at a café, ignore the soldiers and visiting Germans, and play her favorite game. As the city passed her by, she would pick out a man in the crowd and imagine their faults, their failures, and more importantly, their sins. She would create a life for them absent of the measures of morality, figuring out the ways they made themselves seem normal in the public eye. The man with polished brown shoes couldn't get an erection without beating his wife. On some nights he would hit her too hard, breaking open the skin on her cheek or busting her nose so the blood splattered onto his shoes, making them endlessly in need of polishing. The man with the oversized blue coat liked to walk around Montmartre at night and flash his flaccid penis to the working girls. One night, one laughed at the pathetic sight of his shriveled skin in the cold. The man took his shame out on the prostitute with his fists, his feet, his elbows, and when she lay on the ground bruised and beaten, he threw down a few francs before spitting on her. Odette would then think of following the men down the street, always at least ten paces behind. She imaged she would visit stores across the street from where the men would shop, wait in cafes near where the men would work, busy herself near the corner where the men lived until an opportunity presented itself. She would picture a way to lure the men into her trap—an empty space she found safe enough to cut them, gut them, and make them repent for their awful sins. During droughts the game kept Odette calm, collected, sane, kept her from acting out and getting caught. But she didn't have the money for a coffee or cream or bacon. She couldn't sit and play, ease the fire inside her with imagined justice. Her palms grew sweaty. The stench of rot hit the air. People pulled their scarves to their mouths and left the streets behind, eager for the safety of their apartments where they could hide behind lemon zest or perfume. A German soldier stood in front of her. He pinched his nose in the air and left a half-eaten steak on the plate. A splotch of red stood out on his pristine uniform. It resembled blood, but Odette wasn't sure if it was from an animal or a person. His wastefulness alone was enough to make Odette want to bleed him dry.

"Excuse me, soldier?" she asked. The sun reflected off beads running down his forehead. Thin strands of hair made him look older than his mischievous eyes did. Odette wondered how much mischief this soldier had gotten up to, how much he had seen and done before he arrived in Paris, or after he had wandered the streets of Montmartre. "Do you have the time?"

He licked the remnants of juice from his lips and looked Odette up and down, the way a lion gazes out over a herd of gazelle. Odette had entered a zoo, but instead of staring at the animals, she stood in the cage leering out at passersby. She had often felt like the lion in the zoo, where people on her street—where women around her apartment—would stare as she walked past, whisper with toxic breath, point at the wild beast. But now, she felt crammed inside the cage with the rest of Paris. Part of her wanted to defend her space but part of her wanted to turn around and laugh at the other animals forced inside the enclosure. The soldier was lanky like Aloysius but thinner. She tried to shake the thoughts of her friend away. She didn't need him ruining her fun; he wouldn't approve.

"You are a nurse?" he asked with a German accent.

"Did the uniform give me away?"

"The hat," the man said.

"Does that mean you have the time for me?"

The soldier smiled. Bits of masticated steak stuck in the spaces between his teeth. Odette didn't know if the odor of decay came from the butcher's shop or the soldier's breath. He took a golden watch from his pocket and checked the time. He placed the watch back by digging two fingers into the pocket first to help the watch slide back in easily. He reached for Odette's arm.

"I do have the time for you," he said. "I have always appreciated the attention of a good nurse."

Aloysius's voice filled Odette's head. He whispered, "stop," and, "don't." When that didn't work, his voice grew louder. "You don't know what you're doing! This will only make it worse!" She ignored him both in life and in her head.

"I can give you better attention somewhere private," she said. The soldier smiled again, with the bits of meat in his teeth growing bigger. Odette looked from his teeth to the steak left on the plate. She wanted to wrap the remainder of the plate in her coat and carry it home. She would probably attract the stray cats and dogs with the smell of steak, but she didn't care. It took all her strength not to jump on the table and tear at the leftovers. The glory of the kill would be better than the price of the meat, she thought.

She walked away from the table. The soldier followed two steps behind, close enough for her to feel his lanky body shade her but far enough to not be conspicuous. The voice yelled louder. They turned down a blind alley, narrow and dark, with just as much heat as the remainder of the city. The kids that often kicked soccer balls in the streets had run down to the Seine to jump in the river. They looked like the only people having fun in the miserable heat. Odette knew the alley. She had run through it as a kid after winning at marbles, after the boy Michael accused her of cheating. The soldier followed her. No one had seen. The soldier wanted the attention, with sweat dribbling down his cheeks and scraps of steak saved for later in his teeth. He wore a wedding band. He wore a bloodstain on his uniform. He wanted to tell his friends about the French women's hospitality, about his time in Paris, where he "experienced" the culture. He had earned this as much as the men in her game had earned their just rewards.

"Are all French nurses this attentive?"

"I am a special exception," she said. She reached for the bun in her hair and pulled out a sharp file she used to keep the bun in place during her shift. She flicked her hair from side to side. The soldier's sweat fell to the ground. Odette gripped the file tighter.

"What would your wife think?" she said and pouted.

"She passed away," the soldier said, not falling into Odette's trap, the sin of adultery, the eroticism of the forbidden.

This is wrong, Agnes's voice said. She stood up straight. The hair on her shoulders made the heat of the day worse. Sweat fell from behind her ears. Odette pointed to the bloodstain on his shirt.

"And this," she asked. "Did you cut yourself shaving?" She pouted again. "Or did I overhear you telling your friends it was a—what was it— a Frenchman who left that there?"

The soldier blushed. "You heard that?"

Odette nodded and made a sad face. The soldier leaned in close. His words hushed. "I was showing off for them. That's all. It's tomato sauce."

The soldier licked his finger and scrubbed away part of the stain.

"See?" he said as if it helped. Odette looked at the red color of the stain and how blood—real blood—turned brown when it dried. The voice in Odette's head returned.

He is a German tourist—a soldier on leave told to wear a uniform and be on his best behavior. The city is riddled with them. This could get very bad. He doesn't deserve this.

The man leaned in for a kiss. Odette held tight to the file. She imagined sticking it into the side of his neck, covering his mouth so he couldn't scream, cutting the jugular to let him bleed out quickly. His body loomed over hers like a question mark. He came close enough to jab. His breath smelled of meat and vinegar. But she had spent so long protecting herself by hiding in the shadows, by following a routine. She couldn't step into the light now. Instead, Odette stepped away with the file tight in her fist.

"I never did get the time," she said. "I believe I must be going."

"But—"

"I hope you enjoy the remainder of your stay," she said.

She heard the children laughing as they jumped into the Seine. The voices in her head kept silent. She didn't look back at the soldier. She stuck the file in her pocket and then heard the thunder before the rain.

Eight

Aloysius's leg thudded against the stairs, each step audible from Odette's apartment. She sat in her chair and stroked Martine as she waited for Aloysius to reach the door. She had left the door ajar in wait. Aloysius tapped at the door with his foot.

"You know the door is open," Odette said.

"I don't want to be impolite."

"Ouch!" Odette winced at Martine's sudden swat. She had petted him too much for one sitting, she knew. She often felt like a cat, eager for love but eager to not seem too needy. Too many pets, too many people, too many noises could cause her to turn just as quickly as Martine had.

"I heard you cry out," Aloysius said through the door. "Was it Martine?"

"Just come inside, you."

He pushed open the door and carried a tray in his hands full of fake coffee and two depressing madeleine cookies. The slight bitter aroma of the roasted and brewed chicory filled the room before emptying out of the open window. The day's hot wind had given way to a cool, still evening.

Aloysius handed her the chicory and sat in the chair near the window. He dropped a wisp of sugar into his cup and mixed it around with his pinky. He raised his finger to his mouth, first sucking away the coffee, then to hush Odette—reminding Odette that his little idiosyncrasy was their secret.

"It is ungentlemanly to stick my fingers in things," Aloysius said.

"It is unladylike to have a man in her room without a chaperone," she said. "But this is Paris."

"Not anymore," he said and took a sip of his coffee.

"It will always be Paris," she said. It was a city of light, and light gave way to shadows, where she thrived. In any other city she would get caught or someone would have noticed the missing people sooner.

"I heard, when the Germans arrived, they tried to put a flag on the Eiffel Tower," Aloysius said.

"The elevators were broken," Odette said.

"It wasn't a coincidence. A group of men broke them to keep the Germans out. But they just took the stairs anyway."

"I never saw a flag up there."

"They wanted it on display in time for Hitler's arrival. They didn't account for the wind. The flag lasted less than a full day before it was torn to shreds."

"You can fight man, beast, and darkness—"

"I know," Aloysius said, "but you can't fight Paris."

They sipped their chicory and Martine returned to Odette's lap. He purred against her thighs, but she refused to touch him, letting him rest in peace against the warmth of her body. She eased back in the chair, her muscles relaxing.

The city had turned black for the night, and in the darkness Odette and Aloysius listened to the music from the old man's apartment upstairs. It was always the same music each night, with the crescendo of Paganini's "Caprice No. 5," peaking at exactly 9:06. The cats ceased their yowling in the alley. The pots and pans that usually echoed from Agnes's kitchen mellowed. The streetlights had faded earlier until they resembled starlight and eventually went dark. Aloysius opened the window wider. It didn't matter to Odette how cold the night air was, whether it bit her nose or froze her fingertips to the point she would have to wrap her hands around a hot cup of coffee and lower her face into the steam. The voices rose with the instruments; the drums pounding, the choir echoing, the jubilation falling and rising, falling and rising. There was always an added layer of violin that trailed away from the phonograph, twisting and curving with higher pitches, lower octaves, and a tapping of strings unattached to the choir. Then the music would stop, the clang and clatter of dirty pans resumed. The cats screeched below. Martine leapt to the floor, settled down, and purred amidst the comforting noise of the outside world, making him feel like a wild cat in the wilds of the Parisian night. Although he would never step outside the door for fear of having to actually defend himself.

Aloysius had started this ritual years ago without knowing it. He had offered Odette coffee one evening after her mom died. He thought she needed company. He continued to bring the coffee at the same time every week. Odette found comfort in the routine: the coffee, the music from Mr. Tureshko, and the soft eyes Aloysius offered her. She killed her first man on the same day and made it home by the time Aloysius came to her door. She had been sweating so bad she worried Aloysius would comment on the sweat soaking through her coat. She worried he would notice the musk of her body odor overtaking the delicate spritz of perfume she had used in the morning—she was almost out of her mother's perfume and couldn't afford more but couldn't bear to be without the scent in her apartment. But Aloysius knocked on the door, gave Odette her chicory, and sat on the chair near the window making polite conversation and waiting for the music to start. Her body relaxed, the perplexing and paranoid thoughts racing through her mind eased, and she felt comfortable in his company. Her heart rate pounded during that day and relaxed that evening, giving her the only restful, dreamless sleep, she would have until the next time.

"We are almost out of coffee," Aloysius said.

"I can make the *coffee* for next time," Odette said. She looked to the kitchen, her can full of resin that still smelled of roasted beans but was now filled with chicory. It wasn't the coffee that Odette cared about.

"We have to get more ration coupons tomorrow," he said.

"I can go with you," she said.

"I know." He finished his drink, put it on the tray, and pet Martine. The cat continued to purr and nuzzled his head deeper into Aloysius's thin fingers.

"Next time I will supply the coffee," Odette said.

"Okay," Aloysius said with a thin smile. He took the tray and went to the door but stopped before opening it. "Where do you go?"

"What do you mean?"

"In the music," he said. "It takes you somewhere but I—"

"It isn't anywhere great," she said. "It is somewhere familiar is all."

"But where you do go?"

"Why so curious after all this time? Jealousy?"

"The streets might be…" Aloysius blushed as he lingered in the doorway. "Those teeth—things might be unsafe from now on. I wouldn't want you getting hurt. You have to be careful—"

"Just remember which one of us needed taking care of," she said. Aloysius looked down at the tray resting in his hands. Odette felt sorry for her joke and tried to laugh it away. "I just mean—"

"I know," he said. "We use your coffee next time."

She sighed and looked once again to the diminishing beans on the counter. "Of course."

Aloysius carried the cups with him, leaving only the echo of his bad leg behind.

Nine

The Arc de Triomphe pulsed with bodies, an endless mass of breath, heaving in and out together. Men and women singing the Marseilles while holding the Cross of Lorraine. The cold surprised Aloysius. The damp air made his bones ache, especially around the knee. It was always worse in the cold. It made him feel brittle and want to hide in the shadows of the city, rather than limp down the cobblestones. The wave of students hummed together, sounding more like mosquitos than a choir. Aloysius stood with his precinct. They had already been standing in the cold of the late fall day for an hour without any direction. Batons in hand, they were ready to beat back the crowds once the order came. It made him itchy; it made his knee ache; it made his mustache twitch.

Aloysius hadn't been self-conscious of his limp at first. He hadn't realized he even had a limp. His mother never told him how the polio had scattered his motor functions, how, from what she could see, the virus attacked the nervous system, how it tore apart his motor neurons until whatever was left inside him most likely resembled the scarred earth after the battles of the Great War Aloysius always revered. But it wasn't until he went out to play with the neighborhood boys that he learned he walked differently. He didn't step one foot in front of the other; he needed to sweep his left leg out to the side; he couldn't bend his knee; his hip often ached if he walked on cobblestones for too long; the inner sole of his left shoe faded much faster than the heel of his right foot.

It had taken him two months to learn how to walk again. But his mother never mentioned he walked differently than he had before he got sick. He hadn't noticed; he had gotten out of bed, happy the dream of swimming in a sea of warm water while wrapped in a blanket had ended. He was happy he could walk at all. In stories, characters who reached death and had sprung back to life would talk about how the grass looked greener, the water tasted sweeter, the touch of another person felt purer. But for Aloysius, his revelation was the beauty and the ease of breathing. He didn't remember the way his muscles ached. His mother never told him about how he would scream in his sleep because of the pain. That she would spend all night with a sponge in one hand dabbing his forehead and her other hand wrapped within the fingers of Odette's mother. His mother never told him how that was the moment she fell in love.

The mothers had exchanged fleeting glances and quick brushes across the skin, enough to make his mother forsake the butcher, but not enough for them to consummate their mutual affection, their mutual love, until Aloysius's screams brought them together—as if his physical anguish embodied their inner turmoil. The mental pain of not voicing how much they cared for one another turned physical and ached in their hearts. It made them want to scream out like Aloysius, with their want to caress each other for comfort. But all the words went unspoken between Agnes and Odette's mother and they hid in their silence. Aloysius forgotten along the way.

"How much longer?" Aloysius asked Dufour, who stood a bit hunched and stepping side to side. His body already answered before his voice spoke. "No word yet?"

As far as Aloysius knew, none of the officers wanted to be there, but as the crowd grew, as their song echoed out from the Arc de Triomphe as if projected by a radio, the more anxiety shook the line of gendarmes. How many of them wanted to join the students? Aloysius just wanted to go home and rest his knee. It was Armistice Day, and he should have been at church lighting a candle with his mother or watching the parade. He should spend at least a minute honoring his father, a hero of the Great War, rather than listening to a group of whining students. The song pinched at his nerves, plucking the pain in his bones with every note rather than bringing a sense of honor or nostalgia.

Dufour swayed, nearly dancing to the music; the autumn chill turning his eyes glassy.

"Are those tears?" Aloysius said. Dufour pushed Aloysius away. Aloysius nudged Dufour. The officer didn't push back, their quick and often mismatched game ended before it began. Aloysius always envied Dufour's mustache, how it filled his face, full and black, while Aloysius felt his hair grow in whisps. Dufour looked like a proper Frenchman, a gendarme people could look up to, could fear—a wolf overlooking the sheep. Aloysius felt like a boy in man's clothing, the shepherd's child left to watch the flock.

After the virus faded and Aloysius could once again stand, walk, jump, and run, he stole an hour from the house and ventured into the alley where he knew the neighborhood boys would be kicking around a ball. The muffled sound of shoes tapping the stones echoed against the buildings as the kids shouted instructions to one another. Aloysius watched as the boys kicked the ball between them, elbowed one another, edged one another into the walls, and kept kicking the ball wide of their makeshift goals.

"I want to play," Aloysius said. "Whose team am I on?"

At first, they ignored him. They didn't even look up from their game. Then the ball came to Aloysius. He trapped it with his good foot and picked it up.

"I said, I want to play."

"You can't play," a boy said. "Look, you can't even use your feet!" All the boys laughed. The heckler took the ball from Aloysius and kicked it back into play.

"Hey!" Odette shouted from the end of the alley. The boys stopped and stared. They knew better than to ignore Odette. Her reputation had spread across three *arrondissements*. "He said he wanted to play. Every day you complain about needing another player to make the teams even."

"No we don't," the boy said.

"The deaf dog three buildings away hears you and howls each morning because you all won't shut up."

"We don't want him," the boy said. "He can barely walk. And he thinks he can play with us?"

"Oh yes," Odette said. "And you're the next Boyer."

The group pointed and laughed at the boy. Aloysius marched through the crowd of boys, pushed aside the pouting boy, took the ball, and reached Odette.

"I don't always need your help!" he shouted. He kicked the ball down the street. The boys screamed and ran after the ball.

"But I thought you wanted to play."

"I wanted—no, it wasn't about—damn it, Odette." Aloysius started to stomp away.

"Well, what was it then?" she yelled after him.

"I wanted to be normal!" he ran home trying to fight the tears.

Agnes was in the kitchen; *like always*, he thought. She always had something to clean, a letter she needed to write at the table, or she snooped through another tenant's mail. But no matter the time of day, if Agnes was at home, he would always find her in the kitchen.

He tried to run past her, but she grabbed hold of him. She shook him gently and wiped the tears away from his eyes. He hadn't managed to make it the entire way home without crying. He had tried to push the feeling down into his stomach until it turned into a knot, but instead, it just rolled out like the Seine during the rain, unstoppable. If he hadn't let it out, the tears would have consumed him and everyone else around him.

"Leave it alone," Dufour said. He continued to bounce back and forth. Between the swaying crowd and Dufour's dance, Aloysius started feeling seasick. He needed to get back on land, give his focus to the ground, the sky, the sound of an order. Then Dufour stepped from the line.

"We haven't gotten the order yet," Aloysius said. He gripped his baton tighter, about to follow Dufour into the crowd, stick held high, head held tall, knee aching, and ready to break up the unlawful demonstration. But Dufour dropped his baton. He unlatched his cape and let it fall to the ground. He tossed his hat. His voice rang above the sea of students who absorbed him like a drop of rain.

"Dufour, what the hell are you doing?" The ache in Aloysius's bones turned to a roiling in his stomach as he worried for a second that the crowd swallowed Dufour whole. In a way, it had, as the wave opened and closed around him with students cheering, slapping him on the back, passing his possessions between them like souvenirs. But instead of drawing Aloysius in, the louder the crowd grew, the more it repulsed him. The sound pushed him back as other gendarmes joined Dufour in the sea walking directly into the wave and drowning in the crowd. Aloysius refused to drown.

"What is it boy?" Agnes said.

Her tone always cut through him. Aloysius rarely listened to her words anymore. Too often they contrasted with her tone. She'd ask what happened, but she really meant, "what did you do?" Or she would tell him everything will be alright, but her tone said, "you will get nothing in this world if you don't toughen up." And now was one of those moments when her words could have conveyed concern but instead, they only revealed her exasperation.

"The other boys," Aloysius said.

"Did they hurt you?" she asked. "You can't let the other boys step all over you like that."

"No, it wasn't just—-"

"If you don't stand up for yourself, no one ever will." The tears rolled faster down his face. "You think you're the only one who's suffered?"

Aloysius tried to speak, but the words came out as sobs. She grabbed him tight around the shoulders, her fingers pressing into his clothes, into his skin, into his muscles. His body convulsed in his mother's hands. He couldn't make the right sounds. She shook him harder.

"Damn it, boy," she said. "Stop it. Stop it now."

"The boys—it wasn't—it was—"

Then Agnes slapped him. He could never remember what it felt like, if it stung or if her fingers bounced off his skin like rubber. He could only remember the surprise; not on his face but on hers. The shock that seeped out of her skin and crept into the wrinkles at the edges of her eyes, her lips. She put her hands to her mouth. Silence filled the kitchen except for the steam rising from the espresso machine; until it sang. Agnes reached for her son.

It was too late.

Aloysius had already run out of the apartment, with the thump of his leg sounding like a betrayed heartbeat as he disappeared.

Behind Aloysius, a German battalion fixed their bayonets. The remaining officers stood fast ready for their orders. But the orders never came. The Germans charged. And Aloysius followed. He crashed into the wave and the students fell apart. He tore down his baton with the crack of a bone, the subtle resistance of a shoulder, the slight crunch of a skull blinding him to the panorama of the Place de l' Étoile. The ache in his bones disappeared. The anxiety from the police line had faded. Aloysius swung his baton like a tennis racket and tasted blood. The Germans waded through the wave as it shattered like glass. And Aloysius still followed. Dufour emerged from the crowd. Students scattered around him. Officers embraced the terror, casting a net over the scrambling, terrified fish. And the Germans pushed through with their bayonets inching closer to Dufour. And Aloysius led the way rushing forward as if his leg had never bothered him.

Ten

Paris had become a city lost in time—dark, empty, and confined to a memory. Odette struggled through the cobblestone streets of Montmartre, winding beneath the shadow of the Sacre-Coeur. The pristine façade bleached the hilltop and even made its silhouette look white. She would have hated to see what the basilica would look like if Paris hadn't become an open city, if they had chosen to fight instead. But with the decision to open itself to the Germans, it also punctured the lungs of Paris and let the air slip through until every street deflated.

She needed to breathe. More importantly, she needed to burn. She set out in search of normal when normal, like the city, felt too much like a fleeting memory. But unlike the city, she could hold onto her normal. She avoided the corners and cafes where the Germans would drink their wine and stuff their mouths with rich beef and real butter. She couldn't stand the scent of the butter, of the men, of the fat she wanted to sink her teeth into— of the butter, of the men. The Germans filled the doorway and hall of the Moulin Rouge with the windmills acting like a beacon. Like an ancient light that screamed to men from across the country, a bonfire of legs, tits, and sex, reaching out its scorching hands and pulling them through the door. Sex, the ultimate offering, the easiest offering.

The Germans yelled with drunken slurs, not that Odette could tell the difference much as their voices carried through the arrondissement. Drunks were the easiest prey. They thought little, questioned less, and drooled at the slightest hint of what Odette hid under her dress. They'd follow her across the entire city. As she wandered down Rue Androuet, she hoped to find the drunk she had followed for the past two weeks; desperate for him to have continued his routine, to stumble out of the bar and fall into the stench of beer and piss. Wine was alcohol in France, but President Petain had put an end to that. He had pointed his finger at the bottle as the source of making France soft and for "undermining the will of the army." Trying to find a decent bottle was akin to having a fairy grant Odette the gift of a precious jewel every time she spoke. But with the influx of Germans came an influx of beer, a taste of home rather than a taste of France. And a good man always knows how to adapt, Odette thought.

Like clockwork, the man stumbled out of the bar with the vapors of past beers flooding behind him. He stumbled up the cobblestones and toward his home where he would find his wife sleeping, most likely, where he'd wake her with the demand of a steak, most likely, and when she didn't comply because no one had any steak, most likely, he'd beat her until her face turned red, then rusted, then black, then blue, very likely.

On the first night, Odette had lingered outside of their apartment and listened to the soundtrack of the night turn from quiet, to yells, to screams, and back to quiet. The woman poked her head out onto the street with a rag soaked in blood and took in the air. Odette had wishes for a cigarette in that moment, for her and for the wife, almost post coital in the knowledge that she would feed the beast soon.

She bumped the man and giggled.

"I'm terribly sorry, monsieur," she said. She glanced away, shy, playful, engaged. And he took the bait quickly, ferociously.

"Where are you off to at a time like this?" he slurred. His breath stank more than his body, soaked in the rot of stomach acid. "You know there's a curfew in effect. My place is very close by. I'll keep you—" he hiccupped. "Safe."

"I could never impose on you like that," she said. "But perhaps you could escort me home."

He wavered. She misjudged his fear of curfew more than his lust for vice.

"It's just so dark and my mother is in the country for a few days." She found the glint return in his eye, the safety of the assumption. They would be alone. He could have her until morning when it would be safe to return home. But more importantly, he could have her at all.

"I couldn't in good conscious—" he hiccupped again, "let you make your way home alone. Not when the country is in such a state."

It was easy to hook a drunk. They always succumbed to vice. He walked her home trying to sneak a peek at her cleavage, trying to slip his hand up her skirt, grab her ass, or slip his tongue into her ear like a snake. And then, when they reached the apartment, she would linger in the alley for a moment to make sure anyone—Aloysius—wasn't nearby. She'd take out the flask clung to her thigh, pretend to sip, toast to his health, and let him chug the rest until the man, and the last drop, fell into the cellar. Odette had trouble luring back the men with fewer vices, those she couldn't tempt with cheap brandy or a low-cut blouse. Those men enjoyed sadism for the sheer love of terror. And it was in those men that she found fearsome kindred spirits, the men whose eyes glinted and whose hearts pounded at the thought of pain, of blood, rather than just succumbing to the moment's passion. She lured them with the same sense of terror that led them home, the promise of producing pain. Now and again, she would wake up on the wrong side of bruised after showing her commitment to the man, to the cause, to the beast. But with time, the bruises on her collarbone, the cracks in her ribs, faded like the memories of those men.

"Maybe I should get home," the man slurred.

"But we are so close," she said. "Just there." She pointed. She tapped at the flask. But when the man wavered again, she lifted her skirt and he drooled. She pulled out the flask and he smiled. He pulled her close and reached for it. He took a swig. She pulled it back. He tried to kiss her, but she turned. She wiggled free laughing, happy to be away from the skunk of alcohol and rotting teeth. Then she turned, glanced back with a smile, and ran to the cellar door taunting the man who stayed behind. He succumbed, like they all did, took the flask again, and as she had planned, fell through the door and onto the table where Odette undressed him, tied him up, and waited until he woke up with a hangover and a gag in his mouth, with the fire roaring inside the kiln and inside her, with his clothes already turned to ash waiting for the rest of him to join them.

As the kiln roared to life and the heat filled the cellar, Odette felt normal—for a shallow breath—leaving nostalgia behind for the comfort of the familiar present. But something didn't feel right. And the echo of German songs rang through the street taking the second of comfort with it. And she realized the peaches hadn't rotted. And noticed she hadn't bought the peaches. And the German voices left with the stench of the man rotting behind.

Eleven

The hospital had an eerie quiet since the Germans arrived in Paris, as if the functions of the hospital had shifted from helping the sick and dying to serving as a holding pen for those needing arrest. The hospital had become more of a jail, the entire complex one large cell holding undesirables who had sought a refuge from their pain and instead found deliverance into the very hell they had sought to escape. Even the scent of the hospital changed, from disinfectant to the acrid stench of fear, an aroma Odette knew well, one that stank of sweat and piss, the same acrid pheromones that filled the cellar when she worked.

Odette took her lunch outside on a bench, choosing to stay away from the other nurses and their judgmental eyes. She judged herself enough already and didn't need the weight of their stares. She took off the mask she had taken to wearing, a Death mask, in its own way. It created a wall between her and the hospital as if the people could infect her with their presence, their pasts, the non-existent futures. All she wanted was to keep their germs away, not inhale their scent any more than their breath. She ate a small baguette stuffed with brie. She sipped some water. The doors to the hospital looked old and decrepit. The entrance took on the silhouette of a face lined with angry eyes and sharp teeth that swallowed all who entered. Odette felt lucky enough to get out each night after her shift.

"Mind if I sit?" Ilse said. She wrapped herself in an impeccable white coat, always a white coat, while others in the city couldn't patch their torn, ratty coats, or afford new garments, Ilse always exited her office with a pristine white coat, even if at the end of the previous day she had left with a layer of blood soaked into the arms, lapels, and chest. "It gets so stuffy in there. I hate being in there all day. It is so—" she stopped as if waiting for Odette to try and finish her sentence. Odette didn't try. Instead, she sat quietly, thinking herself patient and respectful, waiting for Ilse to finish and noticing for the first time the scent of lilies drifting from Ilse's skin.

Ilse had never imagined she'd be in a place of power, in a position of power. She had felt so powerless as a child: daughter to a veteran of the Great War, a man who sought peace in pain, feeling balanced only when his fists bled or his back ached, or he caused another the pain on the outside that he felt on the inside. Ilse spent most of her time at home hiding from her father, pained by his pain, both outside and in. His Catholicism made the pain worse, both outside and in. She had once overheard him question his god; "How could a god of peace, a merciful god, ordain such death?" he whispered to a friend in the parlor days after Ilse's mother had died. Her father had continued in his raspy whisper, a half-voice leftover from an encounter with the mustard gas on the field, which often turned into Ilse's savior when her father turned to the belt or the fist as he got winded easily. Her father's voice carried in the high ceilings of their Prussian apartment in Austria. "It isn't even the death. It is the torture. I hear them every night, those screams. Do you remember them?" The friend nodded, an affirmation Ilse couldn't see and at the time took as the silence of confusion, the same confusion she felt. His voice fell beneath the aroma of croissants, the scent of strudel, the whip of the wind that rattled the window. Ilse could never appreciate what her father had seen on the battlefield, not until she recreated the screams herself.

"Drab," Ilse said. "Is that the correct word? It is so dark and there is this feeling in there like no one wants to be there. Like Death has thrown a blanket over the entire building and waits. Yes? Like death is just waiting for us all." Ilse took a bite of her baguette and smiled. She spoke with food in her mouth, but no crumbs fell out. "I apologize if I sound so dark. It must be the German side of me. I did love Nietzsche at university. I think he offered me a different perspective on my studies. Have you read Nietzsche?"

Odette shook her head.

"How about Machiavelli?" Ilse asked. "Italian, but still good. Don't get me wrong. I am not one of those people who think the only thinkers come from Germany. I'm Austrian, you know. We have our own thinkers. And don't get me started on those wonderful minds from France. I just mean to say, Italians are many things, but fastidious isn't one of them, yes? I like to think of them as romantics, poets...lovers?" She raised her eyebrows and nudged Odette with her elbow. Odette blushed.

"There is life in there," Ilse said. "For a moment, I worried I spoke to a statue. I know you are aware of the things the other nurses say about you."

Ilse had grown up wanting to defend humanity from the pain of death, the pain that haunted her. Her mother had grown weak in such a short amount of time. Her cough became bronchial, filled with rocks. Her arms grew thinner. She spit blood into handkerchiefs until the white cloth dyed red. Morning, noon, or night, her mother would smile fierce and strong, with white teeth as bleached as the handkerchiefs she carried in her purse, unused but available. Without notice she would double-over, the rocks clanging together in her lungs once more and the blood oozing into her mouth, staining her teeth as much as the cloths she carried. It took more than a year of her mother's cough tearing at the fabric of her insides, the blood filling up her mother's lungs until no cough could drain them, and she drowned in a pool of her own blood the doctors found after they declared her dead. Drops of red rolled down her cheek, like tears from her mouth to her hair. Ilse's father couldn't watch. He had walked out the door and to the closest beer hall to drown in a liter. It was the first time Ilse saw him weak, not the storm wind but the flower, not the force strike but the stricken. It nauseated her.

Odette had heard the whispers, felt the unsubtle stares. She didn't spend her day hiding around corners waiting to catch the tail-end of a conversation about her, but it wasn't hard to stumble into a wall of nurses avoiding eye contact or shuffling off like the women from her youth, the birds, Agnes had called them because of their incessant twittering. She worked hard; she worked well; and she worked the jobs no one else had the balls, no, the ovaries, to do. Those jobs enticed her, especially the ones others had no stomach for, the ones they thought a *normal* person wouldn't have the moral conscience to do. And perhaps they were right because Odette didn't have a normal moral conscience. But it certainly didn't mean they knew what type of person she was.

"You must have known," Ilse said as if reading Odette's mind. "The way they avoid you, the way they whisper when you walk past. These are the types of people I stay away from personally. I have enough voices in my head without worrying about those of other people. Would you agree?"

"Yes, doctor," Odette said.

"No, no, no," Ilse said. "We are at lunch. Please, call me Ilse."

"Yes, madam," Odette said.

"You must understand me," Ilse said. "If I wanted to be called madam, I would throw dinner parties and lunch with the wives of the German defense department. I am a doctor. Did you work hard to become a nurse?" Odette nodded. "Tell me how hard you worked."

"I worked hard, mad—" Odette paused. Ilse looked hard into Odette and nodded. "I studied every night for five hours after working ten-hour days, six-days a week. They let me have a free day on Sundays to attend church."

"Did you go?" Ilse asked. "To church, I mean?"

Odette started to lie, but the look Ilse gave told Odette she'd see through the lie anyway. "No, mad—"

"You worked hard it sounds like. I worked hard too. Especially being a woman in a world run by, well, not women. I learned how to cut an artery and not get any blood on my coat if you know what I mean. If I wanted people to know my status, you would call me doctor, not madam, not commandant, doctor. But you will call me Ilse."

Odette nodded.

Ilse watched through clear eyes, clearer than they had ever been before, glassy and reflective, wide open with a slight shimmer. Death had taken her mother; it didn't have to take anyone else. She didn't want to cheat Death; she wanted to stare Death in the eyes and know she had defeated him. Her mother's cheeks had turned blue. The doctor told Ilse to leave but she refused, unable to leave the side of her mother even during an autopsy. Ilse could wait outside the door and return when they had studied her mother a bit, the doctor had said. Ilse still refused, wanting to see what the doctor would do in Ilse's absence more than caring about leaving her mother's side. The doctor carved through the chest with a saw. Stale blood oozed from the wound and flooded into the cloth they had laid beneath the body, a more gruesome vision than when her mother had spit nonstop into the handkerchiefs. The doctor explained that if they studied what had happened to Ilse's mother, then they could possibly fight the disease so others wouldn't suffer. It was fate, Ilse thought, that she refused to leave, feeling the same as the doctor in a way. The doctor reached his gloved hands into Ilse's mother, opening the skin. More blood poured out. The stench of iron and acid stung Ilse's nose. She twitched her nostrils and tried not to turn away.

"What did you do instead?" Ilse asked.

"Pardon me, mad—Ilse?" Odette had finished her sandwich but wished she could take another bite of something to keep her mouth full so she wouldn't have to talk. She couldn't understand the nuances of the conversation, the way Ilse stared at her, the way Ilse's voice took on a complex array of tones unfamiliar to Odette, whether due to the woman's accent or Odette's inability to share consistent social norms. It thrilled and scared Odette at the same time.

"Instead of going to church," Ilse said. "What did you do to make your day of rest—hmmm—*perfect*?"

"I spent the time at a café reading or walking in the park looking at the birds."

"Fabulous!" Ilse said. She slapped Odette on the knee and pointed to the rooftop of the building across the street from the hospital. A Eurasian blue tit perched in the rare quiet of the afternoon. "I love to watch the birds. I have noticed the different species around the parks since arriving. My father would take me into the Dolomites on weekends. We would search for purple heron, Eurasian griffon, and golden eagles. At first, I wanted to spend time with my father. But then, over time, I became obsessed with the birds. I think it was his enthusiasm, yes? It was contagious. Sometimes we would even take rifles to hunt for quail. Have you ever hunted, Odette? It is quite thrilling."

Odette nodded.

"I must admit, I must know more about your expression. Are you nodding your head because you agree hunting is exhilarating or are you nodding to reassure me you are listening?"

The question caught Odette off-guard. She was unaccustomed to Ilse's direct form of conversation after spending years learning the nuances of French subtext, the importance of using metaphor and analogy to make a point. Ilse used both but Odette wasn't sure which type of language she was supposed to read into and which Ilse meant as fact.

"Both, I presume."

"You presume?" Ilse asked. "That will not do. I have asked you a question and expect an answer. Come with me." She stood and expected Odette to follow. Odette took her trash from the bench and went to take Ilse's as well. "Oh, child, just follow. You do not have to clean up after me."

"I wanted to leave a clean—"

"Clean is important but following orders is also important. I told you to follow, not to clean. You must stop."

"Stop?" Odette asked.

"Giving more than what I demand of you," Ilse said. "It will get you in trouble."

They re-entered the hospital, breaking through the mouth of the angry face and venturing deep into its throat. Ilse kept talking as if giving Odette a tour of the hospital Ilse had run for months, but Odette had silently run for years. Ilse pointed to the rooms they had changed as if Odette hadn't been part of the overhaul. Ilse crafted elaborate stories about the reasons the hospital needed the change. "This place was so old and decrepit; it needed new life and new technology…the lights went out…the space was too small…different heads have different visions…etc." At the end of the twists and turns of the hospital, they entered Ilse's private office located opposite of a locked room offering access to German staff and a select French nursing crew, which Odette had noticed none of the gossiping women were on.

"I never thought I would die in a hospital," Ilse said. "I figured I would be in the mountains, hiking, looking for birds. Have you ever thought about it?"

Odette nodded again.

"Please, Odette—may I call you Odette? You must stop with this nodding and head-shaking business. I ask you a question because I want you to respond with an answer. I want words, more than one. When I ask for a doubloon, I expect buried treasure in return, yes?"

Odette nodded but caught Ilse's stare once more and said, "I understand, Ilse."

"Great," Ilse said. "Tell me, do you expect to die in a hospital? I had a colleague in Munich who hated hospitals. He had a deep fear of them since his mother died in one run by nuns after a carriage accident. He became a doctor to overcome his fear. He thought facing his fear would help him. I don't know if it did help, but he never missed a shift in the hospital ward. Do you fear hospitals?"

"No, Ilse, I do not fear hospitals." She had given Ilse more words than one. She thought it would be enough, but the way Ilse kept staring, waiting for more words to spill form Odette's mouth like an open bank vault made her nervous, a feeling that both thrilled and scared her, for the only other times she shared this feeling was before a hunt. She kept talking, without knowing why. "I thought I would die in the Seine," Odette said.

"That sounds romantic," Ilse said. "Very French of you. Throwing yourself over one of the beautiful Parisian bridges after being scorned by a lover, yes?"

"Yes," Odette said at first, hoping the lie would hold. But the more Ilse stared, the harder it was for Odette to keep the lie intact, as if Ilse's eyes pulled the letters desperately apart. "I mean, no."

"Which is it?" Ilse asked. A spry smirk turned her stare into a look of encouragement instead of disdain or demand, taking pleasure from the power she held over Odette knowingly or not, but Odette had a feeling that Ilse knew.

"Yes, I had dreams of throwing myself into the Seine but not because of a lover." Not really, she thought. "Because of something I did, a rule I broke."

"It must have been a very important rule if it causes you to jump into the Seine."

Odette nodded, snapped to attention, and said, "The most important rule I have."

"Your rule, not even a rule of the city, a law of Paris or of the occupying force? What is this rule?"

Odette froze and kept the words at bay. Her fingers trembled, but she kept them hidden in her lap. A scream pushed through the quiet halls. Odette looked to the door expecting the noise to burst into the open, but no one came.

"You must forgive me," Ilse said. "Sometimes I get carried away with my games."

"This was a game?"

"No, no, not a game. An interest. You must admit, you are a very interesting person."

"Am I, mad—Ilse? I don't know how interesting I am." Another scream tore through the quiet. A knock filled the room and overtook the silence between Ilse and Odette.

"Dr. Kohler," a German dressed in the SS uniform saluted. "You asked to—"

"Is all that noise from you?" She didn't solute the soldier back. "You are supposed to take prisoners quietly. People will be too scared to come to the hospital if they think every person who enters these doors gets arrested." The calm and collected tone had turned stern, demanding once again.

"But doctor, we—"

"People need their care. We don't want the streets filling with blood and disease running rampant because *you* thought better of it. Who are you to *think*? What is your name?"

"Doctor, I thought—"

"Again, you thought. It is not your job to think. It is your job to listen to orders. Listen and do. Have you listened?"

"Yes, doctor."

"Then why aren't you doing?"

Odette took a silent delight in the way the doctor scolded the soldier. She thought back to a German private at a café who took pleasure in the way he fondled the French girl, the way she couldn't fight back, the way she watched and turned a blind eye to his gnarled fingers, his slimy tongue. What had become of the girl? Odette hadn't thought about her since that night, when she decided then and there to keep her life together by avoiding the Germans; so far it had worked, but how much longer could she bear their haunting touches, their laughter, the way they toured the city above those who lived here, who were born here? The way they thought themselves better, yet wanted their fingers knuckle-deep inside French women and stole French art and watched French cinema. Hypocrisy took more time to swallow than the actual moral divergences.

"Yes, doctor." The soldier turned on his heels and the screams stopped. A moment later two soldiers walked past the door dragging a man across the tiled floor.

"Whoops," the doctor said. He had squeezed the lungs too hard, puncturing a small hole that spouted blood like a fountain. It arched out of Ilse's mom's chest and painted the doctor's chest, his gray beard, his glasses, and made the stench worse. "Just like the others."

"Others?" Ilse said.

"You have managed this far," the doctor said. "You can obviously take a big shock. Your mother had tuberculosis."

Ilse nodded.

"In the end the victim's lungs fill with blood and they drown."

"It can be prevented?" Ilse asked.

"That is what we hope. That is why we are studying the victims, like I said."

"How close are you?" Ilse asked.

"It is not only me," the doctor stumbled. "It is the global community of physicians."

"Are you any closer than you were ten years ago?" Ilse asked.

"We have made great advances," the doctor said with Ilse's mother's lung still in his hands. "Fifty years ago, most people didn't live to be ten years old. Your mother reached thirty-six."

Beneath the dull glow of the hospital lights, Ilse counted the years from that moment, as if her life had begun then and not at birth, as if the blood from her mother's lungs had baptized her anew, differently than the holy water of the church and the pain of her father's belt. Ilse was thirty-five, the head of the program on the way to curing tuberculosis, cancer, ulcers, on her way to striking disease from the earth. What was it they said about making a strudel? It didn't matter how many eggs she used because of all the people she would feed in the end. She never thought she would live past her mother's age, as if her mother's life defined the end of Ilse's, but she edged closer and closer to thirty-six with a loving husband and a career as a god. Nothing could stop her, not even the barrier of her mother's past life.

"I apologize about those, monsters?" Ilse said. "You know better, yes? I am not a hard woman to please. I ask for simple things and expect them. I do not require the world on a platter. I ask that the job is done the way I want it done. This is why I'm asking you these silly questions."

"They are not silly," Odette said.

"No?" Ilse asked.

"I find them, interesting."

"Yes," Ilse said. "That is what I thought of them too, which is why I like to ask them to people I hope will help me."

"Help you?" Odette asked. "I already work at the hospital."

"Yes, but you can do so much more, better than those *soldiers*. Can you keep a secret?"

Odette nodded.

"So can I," Ilse said.

She motioned for Odette to follow her and brought her to a room from where the soldiers had dragged the unconscious man.

"You will work in here until I think you have proved how close you can hold a secret."

Odette wanted to laugh at all the secrets she had kept over the years. If she took a second to laugh at every secret, she might be laughing for a year. How wonderful it would be to laugh for an entire year, to carry enough happiness to laugh for a year. She had watched women at the cinema laugh at the clowns on screen until tears rolled down their faces. The last time Odette smiled that large, she had thrown the final finger of a fat man into the kiln and cherished the pun she made to herself. She couldn't remember the exact wording, but it had something to do with time, fat, and fate, perhaps.

"What would you have me do in this room?" Odette asked.

"Be interesting," Ilse said.

Twelve

"You shouldn't crave it," Agnes said. Crave was the wrong word, Odette thought. They stood in Agnes's kitchen. The room smelled of musty letters and soap. Odette searched for the soft aroma of orange blossoms that meant Aloysius was home, but the steam from the hot water soured the damp scent of paper.

Odette didn't crave it. Not like she craved a good slice of camembert melted over toast. It didn't make her salivate when she thought of it. Perhaps compelled was a better word. But what would Agnes have said about that? About a compulsion? The French were so good at giving into their compulsions, of enjoying the pleasures of life, but it wasn't life Odette wanted to take pleasure in.

It wasn't pleasure, exactly, but whenever she finished, it was a weight lifted off her shoulders. No, not her shoulders, more like a boulder taken off of her chest. It allowed her to feel again, the way she felt when her mother was still alive or the way she felt when the grocer was still alive before she shattered the vase over his head and cracked his skull. At the time, all she could remember was how more blood than water splashed down onto the floor.

"You need to help," Odette said. "It's—I don't know. Maybe it isn't."

"Whether it is or isn't," Agnes said," I don't have to do a damn thing." Agnes scrubbed a pot hard. She poured boiling water over the inside and scratched at burnt crumbles stuck to the bottom.

"I never burned a single thing in this kitchen until you and Ali became friends. Now, all I seem to do is burn things." She used the crux of her elbow to brush the hair away from her face.

"You said I needed to learn—"

"I never said I'd be the one to teach you, especially after all this time." Agnes's words felt sharp like nails. She had become more and more annoyed over the months, and Odette felt Agnes retreating whenever Odette knocked on the door, said good morning, or asked about Aloysius.

"But who else—"

"Damn it, girl. Ask the butcher for all I care. He knows best how to chop—"

Odette's mother had candlestick holders hidden under the floorboards. It was a relic, a family heirloom her mother had once said. Odette rarely thought of it. But on the night her mother died—on the night her mother was murdered—her mother's blood spilled and seeped beneath the floorboards. At the time, Odette felt removed from her body, from her mind, from the smell of bleach and the stench of blood. She stood over her own body watching the blood disappear, watching the grocer's limbs disappear, watching her mother's body disappear. But the trail of blood led downward, away from where the bleach had reached. Odette picked at the corner of the floorboard where the blood hid and dripped down onto the candlestick holders made of brass and silver. Then she forgot about them until a warm July night years later. Rare fireflies flittered around the edges of the open window. Odette should have been sleeping but she had stayed up reading *The Secret of the Tomb*. Aloysius always said it wasn't really a Lupin story but Odette preferred Dorothée to Lupin; she was strong, she was bright, and she was the only one intelligent enough in all of the stories to solve Lupin's puzzles. There were plenty of Lupins in the world, Odette had thought, but there weren't many Dorothées.

The clamor from the floorboards shook Odette from the story. At first, she had thought someone banged on the door. She put on her slippers and walked to the edge of her room, peered into living area where Agnes had pulled back the carpet and peeled the wood away. She took the two candleholders, left the floor broken, and put the candleholders on the table. She filled them. The Friday evening had been unusually quiet but as Agnes stood in front of the table with an unlit match, Odette felt transported to another place entirely, a meadow or a wood or deep under the sea where sound ceased to exist altogether.

Agnes held her breath, looked to Odette's room, and saw the girl awake, poking her head where it didn't belong. Agnes waved Odette over, gently—her hand a soft, welcoming breeze carrying Odette into a place she didn't understand.

Agnes reached her hand to Odette's, her skin warm, wet with sweat, a familiar tender touch she hadn't felt in years.

Odette said nothing. Agnes let go, lit the match, and the smell of sulfur filled the room. She put the flame to the wick and for the first time, Odette truly heard the gentle crackle of a wick catching fire.

"Your mother showed me these," Agnes whispered, her voice as soft as the crackling flame. "She always said her birth year was a cursed year. Did she ever tell you that?" Agnes stared directly into the candles. She closed her eyes, covered her face with her hands, and mumbled words Odette couldn't understand, a language familiar but distant.

"How did you know where—" Odette said.

"1894," Agnes said. "Did you know that? Born in the shadow of *l'affaire Dreyfus*. Like she already knew then she needed to hide." Agnes turned to Odette and cupped her hands around the girl's cheeks. The tenderness remained in her fingers and the way they caressed Odette's chin. It had been so long since she had felt such kind hands, a gentle touch, she had forgotten what it felt like, forgotten how warm it felt, forgotten how much her body craved the quiet and intimate touch of someone she cared for. She nearly melted into Agnes's hands.

"Then 1906," Agnes said. "Your grandmother dies, Dreyfus is exonerated, your mother inherits these candlesticks, and she knows she needs to bury their meaning deep down where no one can find them."

"You found them," Odette said.

Agnes shook her head. "No," she said. "Your mother showed them to me." Agnes put her hand to her chest and Odette wanted to reach for the woman's arm, to put the woman's hand back to Odette's chin, to let them stay close for just a whisper longer.

"Friday, July 12, 1935," Agnes said. "Alfred Dreyfus died tonight. He was 75 years old."

"Did my mother know him?"

"Only in the way so much of France knew him—the betrayal, some say a hero, but a silent one, a reluctant one. How many of us would have preferred banality to being falsely branded a traitor? So many forgot. No— so many chose to forget. But unlike so many, your mother saw the warning signs. They were all over the place then, they're all over the place now." Agnes turned back to the flickering candlelight.

"What did you say?" Odette said.

"The warning signs—"

"No," Odette said. "When you lit the candles."

"They were a prayer your mother taught me."

"I thought you went to church for that," Odette said. She took a breath for what felt like the first time since Agnes had entered the apartment.

"I do," Agnes said. "Your mother didn't. Your mother's people don't. Your people…"

Odette took a step away from the table, from the candles, from Agnes.

"Blessed are You," Agnes said. "Lord our G-d, King of the universe, who has sanctified us with Your mitzvot, and commanded us to kindle the light of Shabbat."

The flicker of the candle faded into silence. The room once again sat empty of sound. Odette couldn't hear her own breath, but her lungs inflated rapidly then deflated until she felt dizzy.

"Why now?" Odette asked. "Why now!"

"I see the warning signs," Agnes said.

She stepped to Odette with her arms outstretched. Odette moved away.

"Your mother would have wanted you to have these." Agnes walked to the door. Odette stood in place watching the wax melt away from the flames, each droplet quickly running down the stick and pooling at the base. It reminded Odette of blood.

"Don't blow them out," Agnes said. "Let them burn."

And Odette wanted to let them burn; let them burn and disappear.

"Hi, Ali," Odette interrupted.

Aloysius stood in the doorway to the kitchen with a soccer ball under his arm.

"Chop up what?" Aloysius said.

"Meat, of course," Agnes said.

"Yes," Odette said. "I wish to learn to cook but your mother was telling me she doesn't have the time."

"But mother," Aloysius said, "It is for Odette. Could you not teach her how to cook a couple of meals while there is still at least a little food?"

Agnes stopped scrubbing the pot. She released an audible sigh that sounded like exasperation but what Odette knew to be aggravation, as if the sigh held every secret Agnes ever kept from her son but mostly this one. Ever since that night in Odette's apartment, Agnes had not looked at her the same. It was as if she avoided Odette completely, as if Agnes didn't want her around Aloysius, as if Agnes didn't want her around at all. Agnes had helped Odette out of a tight spot, a bloody spot, more than a spot of blood but instead of putting the feeling to rest, swept under the rug, or more accurately, incinerated in the kiln, Odette's desire for blood grew, especially after the Germans arrived. She noticed men in uniform browsing maps in the street, picking their heads up and glaring at her. She knew they wondered what she looked like naked. She watched as men beat their wives only to have the women resemble some misshapen thing, the way her mother would have looked if she had lived. She found newspaper clippings of women the police dug out of the Seine, of girls murdered in dark alleys, or children discovered in brothels. Each new story, each new vision made Odette's blood boil more until she couldn't stand it any longer. She hadn't just come to Agnes for help. She came to Agnes for permission.

"Agnes," Odette said. She looked hard at the woman who had visibly aged since that night. Strands of white shone through her gray hair and the creases at her eyes; the laugh-lines had disappeared completely as if she had never smiled a day in her life. It had been nearly a decade, but Agnes looked as though she had lived a completely different life in those ten years. Odette pleaded in silence hoping Agnes would see the need behind the girl's eyes.

"Mother," Aloysius said. "If she wants to learn to cook that badly, is it really that much of a hardship?"

"Boy," Agnes said, "do you always have to be so damn valiant?" she scrubbed the pan and sighed. "There's just too much damn German food in this city."

Aloysius broke into a gentle grin. He crossed the kitchen, kissed his mother on the cheek, and held the ball out to Odette.

"There's a game in ten minutes," he said.

"I have to miss this one," Odette said. "If your mother will help me cook, I would like to start my lessons right away."

Agnes's head snapped to the couple. She finally understood what Odette had asked of her, Odette knew.

"I'll let them know you aren't coming. For some of them, it might be a relief. Victor says he still pisses a little blood." Aloysius chuckled.

"They shouldn't get too comfortable. My elbows will be back next game. Especially for assholes like Victor who think I'm a dancer at the One Two Two." Odette forced a weak smile, but Aloysius didn't notice. He took the ball and left the flat.

"You want lessons to start right away?" Agnes said. She threw the pot in the sink. The harsh clang pounded in the kitchen like a single bell piercing an empty sky. "What have you done?"

"It wasn't my—"

"Damn it, Odette." It was the first time Odette could remember Agnes using her name since that night, so often choosing to omit her name altogether for something like girl or child. "You can tell me what happened, you can say nothing at all, you could make up a damn story, but don't you ever tell me that it was not your fault."

"But he—"

"There will always be a he, won't there?" Agnes loomed over Odette and forced her finger into the girl's face. But she wasn't really a girl, not any longer. "You may not like your choices, but you always have one. And you made this choice. Like it or not, it is your fault. Accept responsibility, accept who you are, and move on."

Agnes once more breathed a heavy sigh. She took her finger out of Odette's face, wiped her hands on her apron, and took Odette by the shoulders. Odette flinched waiting for a harsh grip, but Agnes pressed against Odette's shoulders gently.

"I won't always be around to help you fix it."

Thirteen

The day had started friendly enough, with the last of the pottery drying, the mugs she had made, the plates she had formed, the bowls she had fashioned, and even a few frogs she had crafted modeled after the tadpoles she imagined growing in the ponds formed by the rains along the Seine. When the clay dried, when the peaches started rotting, when the fire inside the kiln ached to burn once more, Odette knew it was time to hunt.

It started as a flicker, the way a match might fizzle before sparking. But even if the match failed to spark, she still needed to light the flame. It wasn't a craving as much as a compulsion. Once the flame came close to sparking, she wanted fire to rage, contained—in a way—but the powerful burn that spread from her toes to her eyes aching for release. She nearly felt her eyes turn red, her cheeks flush from the excitement, from the heat, at the thought of the fire catching.

And then it did, not as she expected, not as she planned, but one thing the arrival of the German's had told her was that perhaps following plans wasn't all what Agnes had said it was. Sure, careful planning had kept Odette from harm for this long, but that may not have been the planning as opposed to Odette's methodical approach to action, her awareness, how her adrenaline made time slow to a crawl until she felt superior to those around her, able to glide between rain drops, outrun bullets, or simply sense a man minutes before he ever arrived.

And then he did arrive, not as she expected, but she wanted to shake away expectations. The city lay in a puddle of putrescence, a foul smell covered by lavender or musk oil, as if the boulevards flooded with perfume to cover the stench of the back streets. But she found it, the way it drifted from the empty shops once filled with fabrics or the way it weaved in and out of the lines of people waiting for their weekly rations. Beyond the dry plates and rotten peaches, she had tried to keep her expectations as free flowing as the sea. For a moment, she had thought of a sailor, one dressed in the flash of blue and white before she remembered the war. Then she thought of a cobbler wondering what the man could have done to necessitate her appearance. How far she had come from the girl who hid her body underneath bandages. Now she used her body the way the men expected her to, and she would arrive like—in darkness—ready to take the man away from his shoes and the life he had chosen. But then, as she had lowered her eyes to her shoes and toed the frayed edge from the inside waiting for the fabric to break open any second, a soldier stumbled out of the nearby door. He stank of sex. He stank of wine. He stank of blood oxidizing on his fingers. It turned rusty and brown ready to harden and crust away.

His shirt was half torn and hanging from his shoulder. His blond hair was ruffled and dangling over his eyes. His boots were still polished. A woman drew back into the door, a loose robe hanging over her shoulders. Perhaps no one else would have noticed the frayed sleeves, the tiny holes that showed the aged elegant and graceful garment as pockmarked. Perhaps someone else would have only watched the soldier, watched his hair sway like a grandfather clock before his eyes counting the time he had left. Perhaps someone else would only have paid attention to the woman's battered cheek, her broken nose, her frayed hair, her chipped tooth.

Perhaps anyone else would have kept walking, stepped around the soldier and averted their eyes from the woman thinking *collaboration horizontale*.

And Odette may have noticed and thought all those things but only after she saw the soldier, knuckles bloody, the grin dripping down his chin like drool, and the wine nearly turning his skin red; only after she watched his hair tick back and forth across his eyes telling her to follow the rhythm like a metronome; only after first thinking, *easy*.

"Good evening, private," Odette said. She stopped rubbing her toe against the thin layer of fabric keeping her shoe intact. "Rough night?"

The girl hid in the frame half behind the door. She tried covering her face but shot Odette a glance of a warning, "don't trust him." Odette stared at the girl through the door, nearly able to see her torn undergarments, her tattered stomach covered in scratches like she had rolled around the bed with a boar leaving bits of blood and skin underneath the soldier's fingernails. He was young; he was drunk; and more importantly, he was unimportant. Odette nodded to the girl in the door and winked. The girl cracked into a smile showing more of her broken tooth. She covered her mouth and ducked inside the door.

The soldier spoke French words with a German accent and German words with a drunken slur. Odette struggled to understand. But she didn't need to understand him. She only needed him to understand her, her lingering stare, the finger she grazed across the chest, the way she swayed her hips as she walked away. Could she keep him upright for the walk back to the cellar? Could she keep him intrigued the entire way? She led him by the remains of his shirt like a dog on a leash. Part of her tingled at the sensation, the power she had over the soldier, not just for what she had planned to come but for how he followed her every move and command before she had even stuffed his mouth with cloth or had him choke on a rotten peach. If she wanted, she could have him bark and eat off the floor.

But then, as can happen with dogs, he turned, no longer content to follow her like a happy puppy with sporadic treats of lingering glances and the promise of a meal. He pulled on his leash, caught Odette off guard, and dragged her into an alley where the reek of trash nearly matched his breath, rotten from wine, butter, and fish. He grabbed at Odette as she tried to pull away. He clutched her ass, bit at her neck. She pushed at him with her elbow against his chest, her forearm to his neck, until he caught her arms to her side. He slobbered on her cheek leaving a trail of grease on her skin. Odette rolled her eyes with disgust and annoyance. She told him to stop and wait, but he didn't understand, and he spoke German that she didn't care to understand. He let go of her arms and pulled her skirt. Odette punched him, catching his chin, and she finally understood the term "glass jaw" because it shattered. And he crumbled to the cobblestones. And he slammed his head on the street. And he broke. And she looked around in the dark. And she tried pulling at his shirt. And she tried kicking him. And she tried pushing his chest as the blood spilled more and more from his skull. And she pulled him behind the trash. And she covered him. And she looked around in the dark once more. And she walked away counting the footsteps until she reached home and could hide in the comforts of Agnes's help.

Fourteen

Food and sex, Agnes thought. That's what the Germans want when they come to France. *All I want is food and to be left alone.* While others in Paris slept-walked through occupation, Agnes was too old, too stubborn, and too annoyed to change her eating habits for the sake of a war France had already lost and the Germans she didn't care to know. She went to meet the black marketer who would sell her the food she couldn't get from the country, the ingredients others around the city waited for in lines that lasted hours or tried to forget completely.

Her age had already worked to her advantage. Parisians avoided her and Germans ignored her. She swayed through the crowds like an infectious disease, her age keeping others at a distance.

Agnes, old, frail, silver-haired, with hands made of glass and veins resembling thin rivers of ice water ready to break through the wrists, had surprisingly leathery fingers. She had told Aloysius the texture stemmed from years of scrubbing pots and pans clean until her skin blistered. What she hadn't told him, what she never planned on telling him, was where she learned how to scrub pots and pans so clean she could use the tin as a mirror. In fact, she had used the tin as a mirror originally, on the day she met Aloysius's father at the front in Bastion during the Great War. The field had once held poppies, but no one could imagine what the poppies looked like during fighting when limbs sprouted from the soil like dead tree roots and the limp bodies rotted in the mud where delicate flowers once lay. The sky held the same color brown as the ground, the color of shit, smeared across the horizon, across the floor, over the air until it filled Agnes's lungs.

She had met Henry Dupoise after he had been shot in the ass. He arrived at the medical tent face down, teeth wrapped around a horse bit. His stringy, greasy hair framed the sweat dripping down his forehead. He lifted his eyes to meet Agnes's. The agony in the lines mapping his face faded into bravado. He laughed away the pain.

"Tried to show the German's what I was made of," he said.

"You nearly succeeded," she said. "A few centimeters higher and your insides would have been your outsides."

"I guess I'm stronger than they thought," he laughed again.

"Or shorter," she said. She took red hot tweezers from the fire and blew on them. They glowed against the cold of her breath.

"What do you plan on doing with those?"

"Seeing what you're made of," she said. She took her free hand and punched Henry in the nose. He screamed and put his head back down, like an ostrich scared of the coming lion. Agnes then took the red-hot pliers, dug them into the open wound, and pulled the bullet from Henry's plump flesh. She dropped the bullet into a bowl with a tiny clank. The bullet didn't look like it came from a German rifle. It looked too small, well rounded, and had hit him at an odd angle. Agnes then took another hot poker from the fire.

"Damn it, woman," he screamed. "I'm in enough pain without your help!"

"And when your ass turns gangrenous and you can't sit down, you'll certainly not need my help then, either."

"An ass can get gangrene?"

Agnes nodded. The poker pulsed with red and orange streaks in the flecks of cold air drifting through the tent.

"Can an ass…fall off?"

Agnes nodded again. "I've never seen it, but who wants to look at a man with half an ass?"

Henry took the chomp in his mouth and bit down hard again. Agnes placed the poker against the flesh of Henry's left cheek, soldering the wound shut. The scent of burnt flesh overtook flurries of snowy air along the winter western front. Henry continued to sweat.

"Does this mean I'll get a discharge?"

"If I had known you wanted a discharge," Agnes said, "I would have let you get gangrene. You should be back to the front in a week. Five days if you're lucky."

"Back to the front?" Henry yelled again.

"I'm becoming close friends with your screams, private."

"I would have been better off with half-an ass," he said.

"You say that now," she said. "That's because you haven't tried to sit down." She slapped the side of his ass covered with a blanket swollen with drying blood. Henry winced.

"You and your damn meddling," he said.

"I live for meddling into the lives of French men. My mother always said, if Frenchmen had their head on straight, they wouldn't need French women."

"My mother always said," Henry started, "if you can't do something right—"

"You should stay out of war," Agnes finished.

Over the course of the week, Henry attempted to charm Agnes with his looks, with his witticisms, with his card tricks, but nothing took until the seventh day, after his orders back to the front came. He had two days of leave before needing to return. He stayed for an extra day, continuing his jokes. Agnes saw the way he looked at her. But she also saw the way he looked at the other nurses, the way he joked with the other nurses. She knew from the moment he came into the tent, ass up and head down, he would have spat his charm like a serpent with a silver tongue at any of the women on the compound; she just happened to have had the red-hot poker that day.

On the morning Henry was set to leave, a convoy of men arrived at the compound from the front. Sunrise had been serene, empty of the brown sky, with a tempting promise of tranquility, returning birdsongs, Christmas carols broken by the cries of young men shattered into pieces resembling broken children. They cried for their mothers, daughters, wives, sons, and fathers. Bombs fell from the sky adding to the chorus of screams, the earth's quake. Medics brought the bodies into the tent by the tens. Agnes ran to each man, each boy, finding the beards they wore was nothing more than blood and dirt smeared across their chins. Henry appeared in the tent as Agnes applied a tourniquet to a soldier's leg. The blood had squirted from the artery. Agnes had seen blood, had watched it gush from cattle and sheep on her father's farm. Her brother never had the stomach for the slaughter. Agnes carried indifference to the animals' deaths. She ignored the confused or strained looks in their eyes. She plugged her ears to their deep, guttural gasps as their lungs filled with blood. She concentrated on the way her father wielded the knife, the way he cut through bone, the different ways he could kill an animal without it feeling any pain, so he said. Henry touched Agnes's hand, finishing the tourniquet for her. Then Agnes fell for Henry, for the laughter he had given her over the week, the fun they had stolen for one another during the ensuing madness. The tourniquet loosened and the blood from the artery spouted from the soldier's leg like a spring onto Agnes's dress, her chin, her lips. She shooed Henry to the next patient and tightened the bandages hoping it wasn't too late. She took a wet cloth and wiped away the smeared blood and dirt from his chin, returning the man to the boy he had been before arriving at the front. The screams carried on into the night. The medical tent had become a morgue. Agnes spent the night washing the faces of the dead men, trying to bring back each boy in the hope the water could turn back the clock. She scrubbed nearly one hundred soldiers that night. Her hands had numbed from the cold. She couldn't feel the tips of her fingers by morning. Henry took Agnes's hand at sunrise, tore away the blood-soaked cloth from her hands, and replaced it with a cup of coffee. They sat and watched the sun return an inky blue over the icy horizon. She married Henry the next month during a week-long leave. She continued to smack his ass with one, if not both hands, every chance she had. It wasn't until after the war, when the bodies had stopped flooding into the tent, when Agnes's fingers remained leathery, never recovering from her night gripping tight to the cloth like angels to their wings, Henry returned to his smile, his flirtations, his card tricks, and also added liquor. One night in a drunken stupor, he broke into the wrong house and demanded a meal. The neighbor beat Henry with an iron rod and threw him on the stoop of Agnes's building, the building she had bought from the money she made as a nurse, by selling a portion of the land her father had given her after he died because her brother couldn't tend to the flock. Henry had become Agnes's flock, a black sheep, a dumb sheep, a drunk sheep far from the man who had jumped into the fray to help her tie a tourniquet but just as clumsy. She had settled into the city, into their arrondissement. She knew the grocer, made friends with the tailor, and grew fond of the butcher, who always had an extra chop for her to take home. The butcher, who once said she glowed yellow like the sun after a rainy winter day when she hadn't seen Henry in nearly three weeks. She was pregnant. She hadn't told Henry yet. She hadn't seen him for so long. She didn't know if she ever would and didn't think he'd even notice if he ever came back.

She brought Henry into the apartment. He lay on the kitchen floor. He spat out a tooth. It clicked as it hit the tile.

"I did it," he mumbled.

"You sure did," she said. She dabbed at his face with a wet towel and almost laughed at the parallels. All she needed was a hot poker or a truckload of dying soldiers to complete the nightmare.

"I was never shot," he slurred.

"I believe you were," she said. "I pulled the bullet from you myself."

"Damn you and your meddling," he said.

"I believe that has become our birdsong, Henry."

He scraped the mucus from his throat with a loud cough and spat the mixture of blood and snot onto the floor with a sickening thwack.

"I did it," he said again. "I shot myself in the ass. Then you…I just wanted to…then you."

The thought of the bullet returned to Agnes, who remembered the small caliber, the angle she had to reach into his skin; then she thought of the scar on his butt, the nights she had traced her fingers over the tissue with a silent relish at its coarseness. She had known all these years, and she had chosen to ignore it until he said it out loud. Suddenly, neither of them could ignore it. She lowered her voice and pressed her hand to her stomach as if to protect the ears of her unborn child.

"You were a good soldier," she said. "You did your best. Everyone was scared." But she couldn't ignore it any longer. They had all been scared, true, but how many men—how many boys had she washed that night who hadn't had the foresight to shoot themselves in the butt, the leg, or even the head to escape the coming death? If the leather texture of her fingertips returned to a smooth surface, maybe she could forget the night of frostbite, of bloody beards, of a camp paved with bodies. Instead, she rubbed her rough skin against his cheeks. He sighed. She held his face in her hands and squeezed like a vice.

"You do not belong here anymore," she said. "I will not raise our child in the presence of a coward."

He opened his eyes. The blood dripped from his cheeks revealing his busted skin but quickly showing a newfound sobriety.

"A child? We—"

"No," she said. "I. You do not live here anymore. You have chosen to live a life as a hero, to have fought and died bravely in the Great War as a protector of fallen soldiers. You wanted to pull every last man from the field. You thought they all deserved a proper Christian burial."

"I did?" he asked, understanding spreading slowly across his beaten face.

She nodded. He returned the nod. She went to bed and sobbed silently against her pillow. In the morning, Henry had gone. She went to the butcher.

"You are blue today," he said. "Take an extra chop, please."

Agnes demurred. "You already give me an extra," she whispered. Her hands rested gently on her belly. She didn't look up.

"Then take another. If there is one thing I won't miss in this shop, it is another chop."

"Until there are no more left."

The last customer in the store left, leaving Agnes alone with the butcher. He leaned at the door and found the essence of Paris in those passing by the window but never seeing past the glass.

"Non, mon coeur. As long as I am alive, I will always have an extra chop for you."

Months later, Agnes discovered that Henry died in a bar fight after he was caught cheating at cards. She had spent all her tears on Henry already. Her stomach had grown. Any tenants who had known Henry had left. Those who remained had forgotten the drunkard who sometimes stumbled into Agnes's apartment late at night and slept until noon on most days. After the war, most people turned a blind eye to the drinking and late hours of former soldiers. Most people turned a blind eye to the irregular outbursts of former soldiers. After Agnes rid her apartment of Henry, she never wanted to turn the other cheek again, and every time she entered the butcher's, he had an extra chop waiting for her.

The Champs Elysee glowed in the afternoon, and she wanted to bask in it. The aromas of butter, fat, and cologne sweltered into a single cloud, aromas she couldn't find in other districts in the city that sweltered with sweat, despair, and hunger. But on the Champs Elysee, the Germans sat at cafes, and the young women on their arms drooled as they stared into the boutique windows where fur coats draped down mannequins and diamond bracelets caught the fading sun and sparkled.

Somehow, as the crowd parted for Agnes to pass, she carried the feeling of both obscurity and significance, worried that she would both fade into an apparition and yet be famous as the ghost of Paris. German officers lounged around her, enjoying rich fraisier and gooey crème caramel. Agnes's mouth watered remembering the sweet marzipan coating her tongue, the way vanilla lingered in her mouth, how the strawberries cut a tart note that helped balance the pastry. She remembered the first time she tried the *new* strawberry in 1933. The wild berries were small and could bleed too tart, but the new strawberries were news across the country, more popular than the cinema. And when Agnes bit into the strawberry, she practically melted into her seat at the table. Then melted further when she topped the berries with sweet cream and sipped her coffee, finding the euphoria absent from her husband, the ecstasy she had once found in the Butcher, the kind that made her toes curl and spine tingle.

An officer laughed and slapped the table with his hand. Around the soldiers, her toes curled for a different reason as she ducked into an alleyway that connected to Ledoyen restaurant's delivery door. Agnes pictured the officers waxing philosophical at the tables Flaubert wrote at, Monet scribbled at, and Dali drank at until the clocks melted. But the very artists they craved to absorb through osmosis would never sit in café and share their thoughts about art and beauty or what remained of the thought.

Agnes knocked on the door, waited, and knocked again. The alleyway behind the restaurant was quiet but carried hints of noise from the boulevard, sporadic bursts of laughter and the swirl of conversations. The door broke the quiet. Agnes fought the urge to shush the man on the other side. But it wasn't a man; it was a boy, barely old enough to grow a mustache.

"You're early," the boy said.

"I'm old," Agnes said. The boy shrugged, accepting her excuse.

"Do you have it?" the boy asked. He held the door open with his body but leaned into the open air allowing the cool breeze to carry his words away. The clatter of the kitchen spilled into the alley with clanging pots and pans mixed with the chef screaming at the cooks to rush the orders for the German officers. The boy looked back and blushed, ashamed by the service, the rush, or perhaps the fact that he would rush inside shortly after and spit in their soup?

"Of course, I do," Agnes said. "Why would I waste your time if I didn't?"

The boy shrugged again. Agnes wanted to slap him in the back of the head and tell him to speak up. But instead, she passed him a thin stack of papers. The boy shuffled through what looked like official documents until he found a collection of photographs showing nude women. They posed. They postured. In a number of the photos, they kissed or played with one another's nipples. The boy stared; his mouth hit the floor. Agnes stepped on his teeth and poked him between the eyes. *It shouldn't be this easy*, she thought. But she was glad it was.

"Don't make me wait," Agnes said. The boy shook her finger away. He headed into the kitchen, grabbed two bags, and placed them at Agnes's feet. Agnes nodded. The boy looked back at the papers.

"Get back to work," Agnes said. "You don't want the Germans waiting." She winked. The boy turned and the door closed with a loud thud.

Agnes looked into the bag. Butter, truffles, a jar of chicken fat, eggs, wine, coffee, fresh spinach, potatoes. She could avoid another month of Jerusalem artichokes and rutabagas while the entire street reeked of boiled cabbage. Too many in the city couldn't remember what the days during the Great War had felt like, and they sunk back into accepting the absence quickly. But not Agnes, if she could help it. Controlling food meant controlling the population, and when people eat well, it felt like power. The Germans have it, the French want it, and Agnes would be damn sure she would keep it. Who could survive on one egg a week, let alone ten ounces of bread? Was it ironic or fitting that the embodiment of French and Parisian exuberance was the heart of the black market? Was it even more telling that the restaurants on the boulevard didn't need to adhere to the same regulations, rations, and price orders as the rest of the city? Agnes knew before Paris opened, if she wanted to stay safe and stay alive, she needed to follow the Germans the way people follow rats on a sinking ship.

And then Agnes slammed into a brick-wall of a man. She stumbled backward and dropped a bag. She nearly lunged to the ground to check the eggs but noticed the polished boots of the officer first.

"Madam," he said. "I am terribly sorry. Are you hurt?"

Agnes waved the officer away. "Please," she said. "Do not make a fuss." She straightened her skirt noticing for the first time the creases around the waste bleeding down her leg.

"If not me," the officer said, "then who?" He smiled a perfect smile. His chest broad, his chin broad, his face broad, his waist thin, his coat shining like a black diamond. "People tend to pay too little attention to the important things."

"I am certainly not important," she said.

"You must be important to someone, I'm sure of it."

Agnes's surface cracked. She smiled and slightly glowed bringing her back from a ghost hidden in the crowd. The thought she may be, may once have been, could be again, of importance to someone—

"You are too kind, but I really should be getting home."

"Please, let me help you," the officer said.

"I couldn't," Agnes said. Her pulse pounded in her ears reminding her of life and death, the choices she has made and the choices she wishes to make again. She tried not to push the officer's hands away. No too eager, she thought. *Not too fast*. She caught the slight scent of strawberry on the man's breath.

"Did you have the fraisier?" she asked.

He stopped reaching for the bag. "How did you know?"

"Strawberries," she whispered.

"I beg your pardon?" he said.

"You have a bit of cream on your collar. It smells of strawberries."

The officer rubbed the cream off his collar, smiled, thanked Agnes, and picked up the fallen bag before she could grab it. He handed it to her. Her heart dropped. She only hoped he would stomp on it and make it quick.

"Madam," the officer said. "You remind me of my mother." He leaned in closer to her. "I would want her to have eggs and butter too." He nodded, tipped his cap, and walked away disappearing into the crowd. Agnes waited. She couldn't gather the strength to pick her heart up off the floor. She held the bags. Her reflection stared at her through the window, her face topping a mannequin draped in a silver ballgown, her cheeks draped in tears.

Fifteen

The birds of Paris have disappeared, Odette thought. Aloysius had pointed it out to her earlier that day when they walked through the park. They had kept a body-length between them so no one in the park would get suspicious. The only thing worse than having no one was having someone that might get taken away.

Aloysius was always kind to Odette, always looked out for her, and she kept an eye on him, whether he knew it or not. He liked to think he was her guardian angel, but in truth, she was his. She kept the boys from beating him up at school. She kept the girls from breaking his heart. She kept the pain from the outside world from breaking through his glass box of kindness and care. Odette always thought it was glass because of how easily it could be shattered. He had told her the night before that he loved her. They sat in her empty apartment with the window open. She stroked the spindly gray hair of her cat Martine as he stretched on the sill overlooking the city. Aloysius sat on the chair and stared at them both. He tipped his head down until his chin touched his chest. Odette thought he had fallen asleep the same way Martine was about to, the way the cat purred himself to sleep, like a hypnotist lulling its volunteer into unbeknownst relaxation, complacency. Odette caught wind of the words, the gentle whisper like a familiar breeze she had forgotten about.

"I love you," Aloysius said with his soft, timid voice. Martine purred harder. The silence of the city wedged between Odette and Aloysius, threatening to pull them apart. She knew she needed to say something, tell him what he wanted to hear, to keep him close, to keep him near. She had spent all those years of their youth protecting him, making sure the world couldn't hurt him after the world had tried to break her—in a way it had. She couldn't tell Aloysius she loved him—couldn't or wouldn't? She looked forward to his company. She remembered the way they had played in the street when little, how they helped the old woman on the fifth-floor apartment before she passed away and left the apartment to Mr. Tureshko who lived there now; Agnes thought the woman had fed the cats milk, but it was actually Aloysius and Odette. The woman could barely make it up and down the stairs once in a day, let alone enough times to bring enough milk down for the clowder of cats. But those words felt like a wall Odette couldn't climb over. Her throat turned dry. Her skin became uncomfortable. Martine reached farther out the open window as if his fur, too had become too unbearably hot. He stopped purring and lashed out at Odette. His claw dug deep into her hand. The cut stung but did not bleed at first. Aloysius lunged across the room, took Odette's hand in his, and covered it with a handkerchief.

"It isn't bleeding," she said.

"Yet," he said.

Martine started to purr again. Aloysius's breath was warm, sweet, and tainted with sourness from an empty stomach. He glanced down at the cloth. It had absorbed a drop of blood. "They always bleed eventually." He grinned. Odette gave a soft smile of agreement but wasn't sure if it was meant for the cat scratches or the men Odette had taken in her lifetime, thinking *they always bleed eventually.*

Aloysius leaned in closer to Odette. Martine jumped from the windowsill. Odette turned back to the window, to the city, and listened to the nothingness—the emptiness of Paris at night.

"There aren't even any pigeons sleeping on the ledge," she said.

"They're gone," Aloysius said.

"That's what I just said." She took her hand from beneath the handkerchief and rested it on her lap. The blood had thinned but the cut continued to sting.

"I meant, the city is empty of pigeons. People have eaten them."

"Have you?"

"I tried to catch one in the park the other day," Aloysius said. "I thought it would be a nice treat for mother, the taste of meat again. I thought she would have appreciated it. She is so sad lately."

"Everyone is sad," Odette said.

"Lately?" Aloysius asked.

"Always."

"Tell me you love me," Aloysius said. His voice was stronger now than when he had told her. She gathered the strength to look at him, into his brown eyes, the same brown as his coat, the one he thought his father had worn during the Great War. Odette knew the truth; Agnes had told her. Agnes had confided in Odette as a conspirator to keep the truth from Aloysius, and Odette had agreed. That's what caring for someone was, she had thought at the time, keeping them from harm by whatever means necessary, including lying, and she would never let anyone hurt someone she loved, not after her mother.

She had kept Agnes's secret ever since, but when Aloysius wore the coat, she couldn't help but want to tell him. She wasn't sure why. She didn't understand the urge to say what would hurt him, like the truth would, when the lie was so much sweeter, kinder to him. The coat didn't fit. It looked exactly like what it was, the coat of a larger man over a boy trying to stand in the man's place—the shoulders too broad, the length cut too short. Aloysius was built like his mother, tall and slender, while his father had been a brick wall in pants. That's what Odette's mother would say.

"Please," Aloysius said, his voice returning to a whisper.

"I can't," Odette said. She felt the words scratch against her throat. She had wanted to exchange them for the words he had wanted to hear. She had wanted him to find another reason to smile in the empty Parisian night, without knowing how many more nights Paris would feel empty, but she couldn't get herself to say it.

"Because you don't love me," he said.

"Because I can't love you,' she said. "I *can't*. Someone like me—"

Aloysius reached for Odette's hand once more. She winced as his fingers brushed the cut and smeared a thin streak of blood across her skin.

"You are no different than anyone else. You're trying to survive."

"No one else needs what I do." She spoke the words hoping he would understand, wishing he had always known, but he stood in the dark with the rest of the city.

"Yet they take it anyway," he said.

She rested her head against his chest. His heart beat with a gentle rhythm, like a lullaby. She closed her eyes. "Is this what love feels like?" she asked.

"I don't know," he said. "How do you feel?"

"Comfortable."

"Safe," he said.

"Calm," she said.

"Fulfilled," he said.

The next day they walked along the gravel path of the Tuileries Gardens worried everyone would know what they had told each other, the secret they shared in a time when secrets got you killed, secrets got you hurt, but everyone dealt in secrets. Odette looked for birds in the sky, in the trees, and found a lone pigeon cooing in the shade. She had kept secrets bigger than this one, longer than this one. Perhaps one more secret wasn't so bad. Odette reached across the gap between her and Aloysius and entwined her fingers tightly with his.

Sixteen

Heat clung to the city making the buildings sweat and mimic the perspiration dangling from Parisians and Germans alike. But the French tried to ignore the heat by embracing it as their own, as if they claimed to understand it, they would not feel it. As if by not feeling the heat, they would not sweat. If they did not sweat, it was another way they could set themselves apart from the Germans. The city felt like an abandoned village with little life outside of the breadlines, which uncharacteristically for Paris, filled with rowdy women and bashful men hoping for a taste of food before rations ran out for the day. The heat, the lines, the near promise of food with the more likely result of continued hunger turned the air ripe with tension, a smell Odette equated to the day before a body rots, when the acrid aroma settled beneath the surface of the skin but had not yet been released.

Odette followed Ilse along the cobbled lanes of Paris away from the hospital.

"I need your help," Ilse had said. Odette had only nodded her assent unsure of how to proceed with her new boss. Ilse kept pursuing a relationship beyond the half-lit galleries of the hospital, asking for drinks, to visit a café, for Odette to show Ilse the hidden life for which Paris was known and all but invisible to visitors or newcomers like her. But Odette never knew that side of the city, too often hiding in the comfortable seclusion of the cellar, or the familiar flavors of charcuterie accompanied by the soft-spoken tone of Aloysius and the musical whines of Martine. But Odette could no longer avoid Ilse's invitations, especially after she offered Odette time on the clock without needing to stay at work.

"Trust me," Ilse said. "This will be fun."

They made their way to Lévitan, the first department store in Paris. Odette remembered the first time her mother took her to the shining façade on Rue du Faubourg Saint-Martine, the way the blue and gold tile mosaic shimmered in the sunlight, the soaring arched windows capturing the high fashion of the day, compelling more and more women to enter in search of the perfect garment both accessible to them yet unique enough for no one else to be wearing. As of June, 1940, the shining façade no longer promised the opulent displays of furniture and fashion. Odette walked between the arching glass windows following Ilse into what was once a familiar maze embodying the grand aesthetic of the city with subtle hints of perfume and charred wood scattered around the different galleries, which had given way to the stuffy scent of mothballs with the former rows of loungers, chairs, and pianos transformed into stacked boxes of plates, glasses, pots, pans, and watches. The organized showcase felt more like a warehouse empty of life, empty of importance. Small, makeshift signs hung loose to tables with words written in German. Ilse wandered through the aisles glancing at the stacks of goods resembling a marketplace on the other side of the Seine rather than the elegant shop Lévitan once personified. Rows and rows of watches and clocks looked to have taken nearly half the ground floor, with dangling signs pointing to the upper stories where bedroom sets were positioned. Odette imagined hearing all the clocks at once ticking, with each hand slowing, the seconds stalling into minutes, the minutes pausing for hours while the gears still turned, synchronized to her heart rate.

Ilse reached for a golden pocket watch stuffed beneath a silver wristwatch. Odette examined the wristwatch wondering where it had come from. Roman numerals marked the four points of the clock with yellow and black colors against rounded silver strands making the glossy band. She held the piece up to her ear but couldn't hear the gears moving even though she swore the tick of each hand grew louder. She shook the watch. She looked at the hands. She listened again—nothing—before placing it back on the pile from which she found it.

"Do you like it?" Ilse said.

"I'm sorry?" Odette said, the question catching her off-guard.

"It's a gorgeous watch," Ilse said. "I may have to buy it for myself."

"Buy it?" Odette said. "I couldn't? I'm sure it's much too expensive for me."

"Nonsense," Ilse said. She picked up the watch and tapped the glass looking for the hands to move. "It doesn't work. Is that why you put it back?" Ilse waved away the question and motioned Odette forward. "Take it to him."

"To who?" Odette asked. She looked around the long empty rows in the cavernous space and saw only herself and Ilse.

"To him," Ilse said pointing to a small man with large glasses and a ribbon of hair wrapping from ear to ear accentuating the wrinkles crinkling his forehead. He stood hunched over a table eying an open pocket watch, tinkering with the small gears. Perhaps that was where the sound of the ticking originated, Odette thought. The walk to the man seemed a trudge, slow and begrudging, the sole other person in the room, at least that she saw, but others could be hiding behind the stacked plates or the elaborate displays of perfume creating a waiting geyser of aromas ready to erupt.

"Pardon me, sir," Odette said. The man didn't look up from the watch. Odette cleared her throat and tried again.

"Sir? Excuse me, sir?"

The thick glasses on the old man's face magnified his eyes when he looked up from the watch, showing the bright green irises contrasting the silver strands of hair.

"Forgive me miss," the man said. "It has been a while since anyone called me sir. How can I help you?"

"I was wondering if you could—That woman told me you could fix this?"

The man held out his withered hand covered in liver spots and shaking yet with delicate fingers somehow steady against the trembling palm.

"That is what they keep me here for."

"Keep you?" Odette said.

The man flexed his fingers with impatience. Odette brushed the man's fingers as she passed the man the watch releasing the cool, blemished silver to his hot, emaciated skin and noticing how the liver spots imitated the blotches on the watch, but silver was much easier to polish away than time.

The man looked at the watch and froze. He lifted his glasses up and down rubbing his thumb over the face. He checked the watch's back, tracing his fingers over an inscription Odette had not seen.

"This is a nice watch," the man said.

"Yes, I thought so too."

"I had one like it once. It had an inscription too."

"What did it say?" Odette said. The man continued turning over the watch in his hands. A veil of tears formed in his eyes but never fell.

"It—I'm sorry, what did you ask?"

"The inscription," Odette said. "What did it say?"

"Nothing important."

"It must have been important enough for someone to etch it into your watch."

"It was from my wife. Our anniversary after a silly quibble, the kind husbands and wives married for decades know. Are you married?"

Odette shook her head. Too often she felt like she should have had dreams of marriage, perhaps images of herself on an altar with a man or beaming as he carries her over the apartment threshold, or simply picturing herself in a wedding gown seen through a boutique window. She never bothered with these thoughts. They never crept into her mind even after Aloysius said he loved her. The watch no longer felt like a found treasure but a needle hidden in a mound of other needles, where she could have reached into the pile on the table and found another beautiful watch covered in gold, or jewels, or handmade from wood, each adding to the cacophonous ticking, yet, she found this one, gave this one to the old man, the one that reminded him of his own watch. Then Odette noticed the table of candelabras and candleholders. Silver and brass and gold filigree that reminded Odette of the decorations hiding under her floorboards—proof enough for those punishing history, even if it was a history she never understood, connected with, or knew. The candleholders—the candleholders in hiding—were enough to make sure she disappeared, leaving nothing behind but their filigree, if they were worth enough.

"Did he fix it?" Ilse asked from down the aisle having moved on to looking at a gathering of music boxes. A caped man and terrified girl circled one another with a tinseled musical number complimenting the inescapable tick of the room.

"Not yet," Odette said.

"Well tell him to hurry it up," Ilse said.

"I'm sorry," Odette said to the man. "I can put this back."

The man sniffled as he looked down, already replacing the face on the band. He slid the watch over the table to Odette with the hands looking up at her clicking the time away, as if returning movement to the entire room now that she could witness time's passage in the watch.

"Oh," Odette said. "Thank you."

"It said, 'To help catch the passing seconds.'"

"That sounds lovely. Did it work?"

"Work? I'm a horologist; of course, it worked."

"I meant—no." Odette said. "To catch the seconds, did it help?"

"It made me far more aware of all the seconds I let slip by," the man said.

"Good," Ilse said. "It's working. Let's get out of this place. I can only spend so much time here before I either want to buy everything or burn it all. Some Parisians have all the taste and leave nothing for the rest of them."

Ilse linked arms with Odette and guided them out of the store. Ilse's usual scent of lilies replaced with jasmine and bergamot. Odette inhaled. It reminded her of her mother. *Perhaps another way she hid herself*, Odette thought. *Easier than hiding under the floorboards.*

"Do you like it?" Ilse said. "I think it's too ethnic."

Ilse said as she grabbed the watch from Odette. "There's an inscription! *Pour aider à attraper les secondes qui passent.*"

"To help catch the passing seconds," Odette said. As they exited the store, she took one last look at the man as his body shook, clenching what was left of his hair in his fists, shaking his head. Odette had heard the dreaded screams of dying, desperate men, but rarely did she hear the silent cries of a broken man. Perhaps, at times, it could come in the way of ticking watches, the ghost of time passing, or time gone by, those moments in which Odette suddenly felt lost to the past without any chance of trying over.

Seventeen

The night was surprisingly cold, and Odette shivered as she sat against the stone floor, resting her back against the stone wall but melting to the heat of the music that pulsed through the door. Mr. Tureshko played with fire the way the kiln turned the cellar red-hot. The way the kiln emptied Odette when the fire faded, when the steam released, when the ceramics cooled, when the only detail left of the stolen was wrapped in a harmless cup or a painless plate or the image of a ceramic peach glossy with glaze. But Mr. Tureshko brought his fire from a different place, and after Odette had cleared the kiln of the dry and cool pieces of the past, she remembered the music and sank into the floor not ready to return to her empty apartment and listen to Martine's judgement.

As Mr. Tureshko played, a familiar fire percolated in her heart. It felt comfortable instead of empty, more like a room in which she wanted to spend time rather than a cold cell from which she wanted to escape. Mr. Tureshko's violin filled the city with music. And Odette often imagined herself gliding over Paris's rooftops on the musical notes lifting and lowering over the balconies. She could peer in the windows of the aristocrats in the seventh *arrodissement* and watch how the rich make love, gently as if made of porcelain, but then she'd glide to the Marais and watch couples make love with abandon, rough and animalistic inside seventeenth-century mansions that remind them how fleeting time can be. If Odette could fly through the city on the notes, she'd stop in the bakeries feeding German tourists and stuff pain au chocolat into her dress. She'd steal coffee beans or hide cream in her shoes. And for a fleeting moment each night, Mr. Tureshko made Odette think it was possible, not flying on the musical notes, but escaping. Then the music ended. She sank back into the cold stone, in the cold hall, in the cold city, where she could never get comfortable.

Odette stood and dusted off her dress. Mr. Tureshko opened the door, his face melting with sweat and satisfaction. His suspenders clung to his shirt accentuating the watermarks. He pushed the bridge of his glasses up his nose, saw Odette, and adjusted his tie.

"You might as well come in," he said and smiled.

Odette stepped past Mr. Tureshko and made herself at home at the table covered in open books, in an apartment made of books, that smelled of old leather and worn pages, and that crackled with the sound of old paper and the gramophone Mr. Tureshko had not yet turned off. He stepped back inside and pulled the needle from the record filling the room with the echo of a scratch. He poured tea. He handed Odette a cup; it steamed. He sipped his cup. It did not steam.

"I expected you sooner," he said catching his breath.

"I'm surprised to be expected at all," Odette said.

He looked down at the layer of books in front of him, glanced at a particular passage, smirked, and turned the page. He looked back up at Odette as if he had forgotten she was there.

"You aren't so unpredictable, I fear," he said.

"That means I'm reliable," she said.

"It means you're easy to understand."

"I don't think everyone would agree with you."

"Anyone with an open eye can see it," he said.

"Can they?" She tried to smile, to make the question sound playful but it came out as acidic as it felt, with a touch of anger, concern, and bitterness. She had lasted this long because of her organization and skill. She was not predictable; she was precise.

Mr. Tureshko turned another page. He dabbed a wet cloth over his forehead. As his sweat faded, the liver spots on his head pronounced themselves with more authority. He had aged since the Germans arrived. His music had grown more passionate, always structured, always pristine, but once touched with sadness now riddled with anger.

"Why do you do it?" Odette asked breaking the silence.

"I like reading."

"No," she said. "Play." She nodded her head to the violin by the window. In another life, perhaps he could have played in the Paris Orchestra, studied in the Paris Conservatoire, found the convergence between the audience and artists at the center of a sunken stage where music elevated the entire auditorium and not just the musicians.

"I've lived in this building for nearly eight years now," he said. "You always listen through the door after you've finished in the cellar."

"That is consistency."

"That is routine. And routine is predictability," he said.

"And what about you?" she said. "Playing the same song every night. You may as well play La Marseillaise at sundown."

"It is routine," he smiled. "And routine is predictability." He sipped his tea. "I play because I must."

"Must you?"

"Why do you listen?"

Odette sipped her tea. It smelled of ginger but tasted of mint. It warmed her up among the books and cozy ambiance of his apartment. Better than the antiseptic and flower nettles, if Agnes is to be believed. Mr. Tureshko will probably have to burn the books by the time winter comes just to keep warm. If Agnes was to be believed, Mr. Tureshko should have already run from Paris.

"It's beautiful," she said. "So, I shouldn't listen?"

"It moves," he said. "Music moves. It stirs. You know that feeling, that need for movement, to capture whatever that feeling is that causes you to stomp your foot. Why do you spend so much time in that cellar, otherwise?" He lifted his eyebrows as if he had made his point. But had he, Odette wondered. Had he known the entire time? "The ceramics you make, you must be driven to create such pieces."

"They are amateurish and rudimentary."

"So is music," he said. "And then one day it becomes necessary." He stood from the table and took a book from the shelf. "Read this. It's all about music and art." Odette pushed it back across the table.

"I don't need an assignment."

"It talks a lot about our need for beauty because of our fear of death."

"We've all heard that story, haven't we?" she said. "At least, the need for men to create because they fear they will be forgotten."

Mr. Tureshko turned the book over in his hand, opened it to a specific page, read a passage to himself, and closed it. A paper poked out of the binding. The paper looked like an official document with blue words faded with bleach. Mr. Tureshko pushed the paper back into the book.

"Everything fades with time. Some things just take longer. Other things need encouragement."

Odette wrapped her fingers around her teacup and let the heat singe her skin waiting for it blister, but it never did.

"Are those the papers you need?" She knew about the restrictions for Jews in the city, the papers they needed, the stars they had to wear, a star Odette realized she never saw Mr. Tureshko wear. "I notice you don't have a certain yellow tinge to your outfit."

"I don't believe I have ever owned anything yellow. After this long, I don't think I ever will."

"What about the Germans?"

"The Russians couldn't make me wear red. The Germans can't make me wear yellow." Mr. Tureshko pulled the book back away from Odette and examined the pages once more, taking the paper from the folds. "See, I'm an immigrant but not an undesirable one." He put the paper back and closed the book, replacing it on the shelf.

"You know, maybe you don't need to read this. But sometimes, just sometimes, you can find beauty in the most unexpected places." He grinned again.

"The same as Death," Odette said. Mr. Tureshko's smirk turned into a smile. He sat back across from Odette and wiped his face with a handkerchief once more.

"But really…why?" she said.

"Does art need a reason?"

"Maybe art doesn't but you do."

"No," he said. He looked to a book opened to a marked map of Europe. "I don't."

"Is it about life?" she asked. "Is it about living?" She wanted desperately to know how his violin made him feel, if it could give her the same resolve as the kiln, give her an alternative, the way athletes find their game, whether tennis or football, the way a chef finds their special dish. Perhaps Odette didn't need to continue into the fire. Maybe she could pull herself back and take the violin instead.

"Perhaps," Mr. Tureshko said. "Once. But not anymore." He gazed around his apartment trying to memorize every detail, from the books on the shelf to the tea still steaming in front of Odette, and his violin resting on a stand near the open window. "Now, maybe, it's about death."

"Whose?"

"It's all the same," Mr. Tureshko said.

"Until Death comes for you," she said. She smiled pretending it was a joke, but Mr. Tureshko took it as she meant it. He gave a half-hearted chuckle—the puffs of air the only indication of his laughter. The scent of ginger from the tea had faded from the room replaced by the crisp chill of the night. Odette's heart pounded, a drum to the music Mr. Tureshko had stopped playing.

"I think it's time to go," Odette said.

"I always appreciate the company," he said. "I don't get much these days."

He hadn't had much company even before the German's arrived, but Odette said nothing. She reached the door.

"And you?" he asked. "Why do you actually spend so much time in the cellar?"

Odette hesitated. She breathed. She found the lingering flavor of stale mint on her lips.

"Death," she said.

"Maybe you should write a book," he said.

Mr. Tureshko reached from the table and grabbed his violin.

"Could I ask one favor?" Mr. Tureshko said. Odette waited silently by the door. "I was meant to see a man, about some documents. Hi, my name is Dr. Eugéne. Could you—"

"Of course," she said.

The chords to *Pavane Pour Une Infante Défunte* drifted into the night. Odette never felt like a princess, but the longer the song played, the more she felt the familiar pull of the music, the violin, the slow buildup. And then, for a brief moment as she opened the door to her flat, the song filled her, burning a hole in her stomach.

Pavane Pour Une Infante Défunte: Pavane for a Dead Princess. Tonight, more likely, Pavane for the Princess of Death. And it felt right.

Eighteen

The more blood Ilse drained from the bodies of the critters who entered the hospital, the more despondent she became, as if they drained her of her essence every time. She couldn't help but twitch a little when she stuck the needle into their veins and sucked out whatever she could gather from their emaciated bodies. It wasn't that they didn't feed them, the hospital just gave them as much sustenance as needed in order to gather the information necessary. When one died, another took their place. It wasn't hard to find another body in a war, especially this war. She had listened to her father exclaim the honor of war, the honor of armies, how all *men* should take pride in their death.

Ilse had always had a love of cowboys growing up. Her father had called it an obsession. What had her father known of obsession, with his military medals polished every Wednesday night, his shoes polished every Sunday morning, his horse brushed every other afternoon. He called it a schedule; Ilse knew better. She knew his life couldn't or wouldn't carry on if he strayed from his *schedule,* the way a mental patient had to string the same words together over and over again to feel sane, the way some felt compulsive enough to wash their hands on the hour every hour, which sounded sanitary until the sanitation ruled your life. Cowboys brought Ilse joy rather than pain. She would sit in her room after hours of studying human anatomy and the way a virus could attack the central nervous system in an instant shutting down the electrical faculties as if blowing out a candle. She would move on to the movements of men, their mechanical arms, their provoked pride. They clung to honor as if it had claws. They clung to their own mythology as if it held truth.

Her father was the same as a cowboy wrapped in the antiquated guise of the Hapsburg military. He believed in honor, emperor, country, and the myth of his own making—that the empire was in fact the center of the world. But in the end, he screamed, squealed, and cried like a pig, or as he would have said, like a girl. Except Ilse had seen girls die with more honor than her father had. Ilse had killed girls, female animals who had died with less than a whimper.

When younger, Ilse replaced the lush mountains of the Dolomites with the red rocks of Zion, Utah. The rushing river through Salzburg became the mighty Colorado. Donkeys ferried miners up and down the canyon walls and mining towns filled with the tapping of the piano, *Camp Town Races*, far from the tinny melodies of Mozart and forlorn rhythms of Chopin that only reminded her of her mother. The dry air of the American West could have saved her mother, but they never had a chance to know.

Ilse would regale herself with stories of Wyatt Earp and the Okay Coral. He had called for calm, yet saw the cowboys pull their guns, and without hesitation drew his, squeezed the trigger, and came out on the other end. After her mother died, Ilse thought the story was named the "Okay Coral" because Wyatt Earp survived; he was "okay." She was learning English at the time and didn't realize the word had been stamped over the coral long before Earp arrived in Tombstone. She had always thought it odd, even when young, a town would carry the moniker tombstone, as if it could draw anyone in with a name like that. But the mining town had drawn plenty of people in and laid claim to enough of them as well. It served them right for trying to find fortune in a place called Tombstone.

Yet, her father, the man of pride, honor, a man of king and country, wept like a river when she had plunged the knife into his back. Growing up, Ilse had noticed no scars on her father's body. She had never seen as much as a hair out of place, a piece of skin discolored, let alone a representation of his past battles, a missing finger, papercut healed poorly, which made her wonder how much he had actually given to G-d, to king, to country, to his family. She lay awake at night throughout her life recalling the words of the cowboys as if they could give her direction, guidance, the way others recited scripture, believed in the word of the Lord, she thought of the last rights cowboys took before dying, when they would tell their partner in arms, "look after my horse," or something with real panache like, "the river don't care when you go, as long as you go." She wanted to call her colleagues *par'dner*, spit tobacco, and gamble in towns made out of dustbins. Instead, she went to the finest schools in the Austro-Hungarian empire, and her father told her chewing tobacco was uncivilized for a lady and a gentleman. She never saw the dustbin towns, never rode through the trundling rivers dividing the blood-red rocks, and never could get her hands on a cowboy hat. She settled for the vague memory of her mother reading her a bedtime story about a cowboy and Native American who became best friends riding through the desert.

Her mother would take her hands and make a triangle. Ilse followed along. They put their triangle hands on their heads like hats. Ilse's mother would tell the tale first from the cowboy's point of view, the way he galloped out beyond the civilized streets of town to fight the Indian no one could ever defeat. He found the Indian sitting on a boulder with a crow on its shoulder staring to the horizon with his back turned to the cowboy. Then Ilse's mother would switch to the Indian's point of view, retelling the story as to how he had arrived at the horizon with a crow, his back turned to the cowboy but knowing the man would show up, the white man who no

Native could defeat. They sized one another up, as did their animals—the horse and the crow. But instead of fighting, they held out their hands to the other and became the day and the night, caught in endless revolutions but never giving fully into the other's strength.

"But we have night and day here, mother."

"But that is far beyond our horizons, dear. Now go to bed."

Instead of glory and battle, her father had wrapped himself in a blanket of patriotism no one questioned because of his service, but when all the men in his unit died under him and he returned home from the carnage of the trenches or the torn-up bodies of the cavalry, no one as much as whispered.

Ilse had seen the carnage of war in the blood she drew from her father, in the DNA she took from the people she collected over time in the hospitals across Europe, in Vienna, in Munich, and now in Paris. Except these people never looked her in the eye, which she preferred. She felt they looked too much like dogs when they stared at her, either begging silently for forgiveness or challenging her authority. She preferred it when they looked away, or better yet, when they struggled. She preferred when they had a sense of decency to fight a little, but not beg. When a little girl entered the hospital earlier that week, Ilse wrapped her fingers around the girl's wrist to take her pulse and noticed Ilse could fit her entire hand around the girl's bones and touch her fingers together. The girl didn't look away. She didn't plead either. She had softness in her eyes. She had a lively stare but no life in her limbs. She could barely hold up her head. They had shaved her hair. Ilse would not have lice in her hospital. She would not subject her nurses and staff to lice. And she would refuse to shave her own head, one of the principals her father had drilled into her. He had made the nursemaid go through Ilse's hair with a fine-tooth comb and take out every louse she found. The maid, furious with the job, pulled and tugged at Ilse's hair as hard as she could.

That night, she and her mother made triangles with their fingers once more, and at the end of the story, took their imaginary cowboy hats from their heads, and placed them somewhere safe until the next bedtime story. But the next story never came, and Ilse's cowboy hat remained unused and forgotten in its safe place, left to gather sand in an imagined dustbin town far from Salzburg. Ilse no longer put on her cowboy hat when reading about America's West, but she continued to ask herself "what if," thinking of the ways it could have saved her mother if her father hadn't needed his ritual, hadn't clung to his obsession. No, Ilse's connection to the West had nothing to do with obsession but had everything to do with deficiency.

When Ilse saw the nursemaid again, she returned the favor by taking her lice-filled clothes before they were burned and placing them in the maid's bed. This girl didn't have lice. Ilse leaned in closer and asked how the girl felt, a ritual with all the patients. Despite the look of things, Ilse wanted all her patients to get better. No, she didn't care if they died, but she cared if they didn't. She wanted them, needed them to latch onto the cure. Not for the Reich—fuck the Reich—but for herself, to prove she could, to prove she was as smart as she knew, to show all the men who had made her lie, cheat, steal, and kill to get to where she was, that she was smarter than them all along. She had put the stories of Wyatt Earp aside long ago and looked back to her books on the central nervous system, quickly remembering the passage on inhibitors, theories for and possible remedies against. She had jotted down their information and decided then it was time for a test, a showdown, a duel, and she would see who drew fastest, her or her father. She had won.

The girl in bed took on the same signs as all the other patients but held onto a shred of light, a bit of decency, held onto a shred of strength. Perhaps she just didn't know any better.

The girl didn't respond with words. She nodded. Ilse opened her mouth and found the girl's tongue a healthy red. Her teeth hadn't yet rotted. She squeezed the girl's bicep, tapped her knee for reflexes, and found nothing had changed. This girl might hold the cure after all.

"I come from Austria," Ilse said. "Do you know where that is?"

"Doctor," the nurse said. "We have others we need to—" Ilse put her hand up to the nurse, who was obviously uncomfortable with the way Ilse was speaking to the girl, to the patient—to the animal. Ilse didn't respond to the nurse.

"Do you know what Austrians do very, very well?" The girl shook her head.

"They make chocolate." Ilse pulled a chocolate from her pristine white coat. The girl's eyes lit up, but she made no attempt to move. She held her head straight and tall. The nurse nearly fell over keeping herself from reaching for the piece of chocolate, a delicacy she hadn't had since the Germans arrived, Ilse thought. "If you keep getting better, I will give you all the chocolate you can eat. We can make you a fountain of chocolate. That sounds good, yes?"

The girl nodded again.

"Put your hand out, *Par'dner*," she said. The girl did. Ilse placed the chocolate in the girl's hand, careful not to touch her. The girl took the chocolate, shoved it in her mouth, closed her eyes, licked the small ring left on her palm, and silently delighted in the treat.

"Doctor," the nurse said. "May I—do you have—"

"Come along," Ilse said to the nurse. "You are right. We have others to attend to. You make sure this girl gets better. Keep her on the same regiment. We have lots of chocolates waiting for her."

Nineteen

The November rain fell hard on the city, flooding the Seine and causing miniature creeks to form between the cobblestones. Odette, Aloysius, and Agnes sat in the kitchen. Agnes blew the steam away from her espresso. Odette dipped a biscuit into her fresh cup and let the buttery, crumbly texture soak up the espresso until soggy. Odette couldn't remember the last time she had tasted real coffee not made from chicory or chestnuts, let alone a biscuit made with real butter; she wanted to linger in the moment, the aromas, the supple fat coating her tongue.

A piece broke away from the cookie and sunk to the bottom of the cup. Odette would sip the espresso until dry, relishing the last flavor of cookie and coffee in a single gulp with the leftover cookie rolling around at the bottom of the cup. Aloysius sipped at his espresso while holding the plate. He had told Odette, at the station other officers called him the Brit, because the way he drank his coffee reminded them of how the British drank tea. Although, none of them had ever witnessed the way someone from England drank tea; they gathered their intel from the movies they watched and the cousins they all had who had been to England, a country they all called cold, heartless, and drenched with rain and sadness. "They just

122

work," Aloysius overheard one of the officers say. "All the time. Just…work." He repeated the sentence as if stunned into horror, staring off into space with the rest of the men who had the epiphany that the English didn't take time to enjoy a sunny day. But according to the travelers among them, Britain never had a sunny day anyway.

Aloysius broke the silence. "We have made a breakthrough in the case of the teeth we found on the side of the Seine."

Agnes coughed and brought her hand to her mouth, trying to keep the espresso from spilling out.

"Are you okay, *maman*?" he asked. Odette continued to dip her cookie into the espresso.

Agnes rebounded, placed her espresso onto the table, and ignored the question.

"We?" Agnes said. "I thought you were alone on that theory."

"Well," Aloysius said. "I…I made a breakthrough."

Odette patted her hair down and tried to seem uninterested hoping, if she spoke, Ali wouldn't hear her heart beating in her throat.

"Do they still call you that horrible name at work?" Agnes asked.

Odette looked up from the swirls she made in her espresso and cocked her head. "Name?" she asked. "What name?"

"It would seem my little mouse does not tell you everything," Agnes said.

"He tells me enough to know he doesn't like when you call him little mouse."

Aloysius coughed this time, spilling his espresso over the lip of the cup and onto the saucer. Odette bit her lip and stemmed the urge to lap up the wasted coffee.

"You presume to know more than me about my son's likes and dislikes when you don't even know the names they call him at work? Did you know they tease him?"

"They're jealous of his success and dedication."

"You are so daft," Agnes said. "And blind. Daft and blind. I'm amazed he tells you anything at all."

Odette smirked. Outside of the kitchen, outside of the apartment, outside of Aloysius's ears, Agnes spilled her history, her thoughts, her fears to Odette, like a confidant, like a friend. But inside Agnes's kitchen, the tides turned, the history of their relationship slipped into a different arena, one where they vied for the attention of Aloysius, the only man they both had affection for, thinking he couldn't have enough affection for the both of them. It was a petty battle, both Odette and Agnes knew, thinking this man they shared, who was filled only with love, couldn't conjure enough attention for the two of them, and therefore had to choose between the mother who raised him and the friend with whom he grew. When they crowded around Agnes's kitchen table, the room shrank, the mail Agnes had kept over the years stacked like towers, compacting the trash they had received offering a sense of the past. While photographs of loved ones filled people's homes, remarking on the family they held dear, Agnes's apartment had a single photo of herself holding Aloysius when he was six. She always said, "The hardest part of the photo was getting him to sit for minutes on end. Look at his leg. He kept fidgeting. This was the best photograph, and his leg looks all blurry. The odd thing, he came down with a severe fever two days after this photograph was taken as if the photograph foretold his getting polio. Then he could have sat still for hours without any problems." Agnes smiled at the irony but covered her mouth, worried the smile could be taken the wrong way. She placed the photograph back on the mantle and traced her fingers over the glass, over her baby boy, before he became…*tainted*. She had used the word once when referring to the way he cowered at loud noises and could never stand up the way his father had.

"Stand up?" Odette had asked.

"Oh, you know what I mean," Agnes said. "Would you want him defending your honor?"

"I would never need him to," Odette said.

"You're right," Agnes said. "But it didn't answer the question."

Odette had never been able to rid her thoughts of the word Agnes had used, *tainted*, when referring to Aloysius, making Odette wonder how Agnes had referred to Odette. Could it have been worse? She wasn't just tainted, she was broken, and then everything she touched shattered into the same degree of ruin, spreading the pain of loss and the cracks of a fractured world until those cracks sucked free any remains of life.

"The teeth came from a man," Aloysius said, bringing the conversation back to the table, to the work he found important.

"Are you still on about the teeth?" Agnes said. "Who cares about stray teeth? They were probably punched out of someone's face after a tavern brawl."

"They were hidden in a vase," Aloysius said.

"Like an urn?" Agnes asked.

"What is the name they call you at work?" Odette asked. "Why do they call you a name?"

"Someone probably dropped their poor mama off the Ponte Nuif. I wish for the same beloved farewell from my family," Agnes said.

Odette took a sip of her espresso. The fresh heat had turned tepid. She spotted fragments of the soggy cookie crumbs clumping beneath the waterline. "You said you had friends at work."

"It wasn't an urn," Aloysius said. "It was, it was a pot. There shouldn't be teeth in a pot."

"You said you had friends at work," Odette said.

"Which is it little mouse, a pot or an urn? It sounds to me like someone found the leftover ash of someone's life. Ashes to ashes and all that." Agnes turned to Odette, sipped her espresso, and leaned over the table. "As for you, you are his only friend. Don't you get it. He has spent his entire life following you around like a lost puppy. You are a cat, a street cat. We could leave you in an alley in Marseilles and you'd find a cubbyhole to hide in and a sailor to eat." She turned back to Aloysius.

"Maybe I shouldn't have called you my little mouse, I should have called you my little pup, loyal to the end. She could beat you with her lead pipe, and you'd spend the rest of the night wondering what you did to upset her. Perhaps, little mouse, it isn't you." She sipped the rest of her espresso until the cup ran dry, sucking at the empty air for any excess drops lingering on the porcelain.

Aloysius slammed his fist onto the table. "That is enough, mother. You of all people have no right—"

"A right?" Agnes said. "My right is as your mother. As your protector. As your bringer of life. What life have you brought into this?"

"And what of the lives you've taken?" Aloysius said.

Odette knew better than to get between them when they fought. She wanted desperately to defend Aloysius, to speak up for Mr. Tureshko, but Agnes had already said her peace, and Odette knew nothing new would come of it.

"Have you heard a word?" Agnes asked, "one single word? What makes you think she needs your defending? What makes you think those poor bastards need your defending? They made their choices."

"And they thought they could trust you."

"With what?" Agnes said.

"With their lives!"

"A poor old woman like me? You're awfully strong when talking to your mother. Where was your voice at the Arc de Triomphe? Or at the station? Where was the lion then?"

"We only told each other the truth, you said," Odette said. Her voice trailed off, sinking like her cookie into espresso. "I thought you had a life outside of..." she wanted to say, "outside of me," a life he could live away from Odette, away from the pain she brought, from the destruction her affections assured them both. She had been proud of all the people he knew, the women he met, the friends he leaned on, drank coffee with, danced with, or talked to on those nights she hunted, on the days she worked, during the years after the police had caught her, after the guillotine.

"Truth is—" Aloysius said.

"Relative," Agnes said. "Like your damned urn in the Seine."

"Why would someone drop an urn in the Seine, mother?"

"Why would someone throw teeth into the Seine?"

Odette took her finger and scooped the soggy cookie out of the cup. She sucked on her finger tasting the sugar, the butter, and the soaked-up bitterness of the espresso. She pulled her finger from her mouth with a loud pop. The noise caused Aloysius and Agnes to stir, stop dead in their argument to stare at Odette who looked up from her cup with a gaze ready to burn through the stacks of mail. She turned to Agnes with a voice simmering with apprehension and shaking with anger. She let the words drip from her mouth like poison, the way she had first thought of killing people, with little drops of venom in their coffee at a café or trickled into their soup at home or in a restaurant filled with people, so everyone could watch but no one would know. Agnes had taught her that killing was a private affair, one she should savor in the security of a secluded location, where she would relish the screams and the pleading, the stench of blood, shit, and sweat that make fear, the calm after the heart-thumping adrenaline faded. Yet here, in the kitchen, Odette wanted to make her murders public.

"Your *little mouse* is no longer little. He stands on his own two feet, which you try to cut out from under him over and over again." She turned back to Aloysius. "And you said you have only told me the truth. But you lie to me almost every night when you tell me stories about work, about your life. I wanted you to have a life away from me!" She stood up to leave.

"I don't want—" but once again the words caught in Aloysius's throat. A stack of mail fell to the floor. Agnes cursed.

"Can't you see, you stupid girl, he doesn't want a life away from you. He only wants a life with you, and you've done nothing to discourage him! It's going to take me hours to organize that stack of mail!"

"I can speak for myself, mother."

"No, you cannot. I've been speaking for you for years because you haven't had a voice."

"Did it ever occur to you I've had a voice; it just wasn't louder than yours?"

"No," Agnes said. She bent over to pick up the stacks of mail and tried to brush through the dates, the names, and place them back on the counter.

"Just get rid of it!" Aloysius screamed. He took the pile from the floor and threw it out the door. Agnes gasped. Odette stormed away from the room. Aloysius opened the door to the apartments. The sound of paper fluttering in the rain and wind filled the air, the flooding streets.

"It's garbage, mother! It's all garbage." Aloysius took his coat and hobbled into the rain. Odette called after him from the hall, but it was too late. Aloysius disappeared into the splashing rain. If Odette listened hard enough, she could hear the sound of teeth dropping into the water one by one with the rain washing them away with Aloysius's footsteps.

Twenty

Agnes's apartment was cramped with walls plastered with letters. The wooden furniture hid beneath the stacks like the base of the French Alps, supportive but forgotten beneath mounds of snow and granite boulders. The letters clogged the windows. The room stayed stuffy with thick, moldy air as if the apartment hadn't been opened in the more than sixty years since it was built. The concierge said she kept the letters as rodent deterrents. She could hear them scurrying across the papers throughout the day. But rodents didn't bother the apartment or the complex because of the cats that hung out in the alleyway at the edge. A woman had taken to offering a stray milk one day, then a second cat appeared the following day to have the leftover milk. By the end of the month, the woman had taken to offering milk to more than six cats that decided not to leave the area. They lingered in the garbage thrown into the alley. They sifted through fish and chicken bones. They took the milk from the same woman on a semi daily basis. Then they took to the rats, keeping at least the building rat free. No, the landlady preferred the papers because they made her feel important, they gave her a sense of pride over her job and a sense of power over the people in her building, those who never spoke with her more than a good morning or

129

wondering if she had seen their mail, even when she asked about their family, their job, the weather. The only one in the building who was worth a damn, other than her charming Aloysius, was Odette. It was a shame what happened to that poor girl's mother. And who had been there to help poor Odette? Agnes, that's who. She had helped rear the girl through troubling times, through the moments after the crash, when Agnes heard the vase shatter and the body thump. While other women lost their hearing with age, Agnes's had improved, able to hone into the subtle shifts of sounds in the air around the building. She could hear the cats when they rifled through the garbage or when they fought one another for their territory. The man on the fourth floor masturbating in the bathroom while his wife was getting groceries, old Mr. Tureshko on the fifth floor who played his Russian music and thought of his days in Eastern Europe with fondness; why anyone would think fondly of Russia was beyond Agnes. On that dark night, the one when the lights on the streets had gone out, Agnes heard the vase break and body thump on the second floor. The shouting had started minutes before. Odette had shrieked. Her mother had yelled for the man to leave, for help, but no one ran to intervene, not Agnes either. The man grunted and screamed, his voice low—muffled to some but not to Agnes. He said Odette's mother led him on, that he had given her peaches, that he deserved payment, that Odette's mother needed to pay up, that he was kind to her, but that was when his kindness ended. The man on the fifth floor played his music louder. The couple on the fourth floor glanced back and forth at one another, their forks scraping against their plates as they ate a crunchy vegetable—carrots? No, celery—with their overcooked chicken. Agnes didn't want to go up the stairs. Odette always waved hello, always asked how Agnes was, always asked after Aloysius if he wasn't home. She was a sweet girl, as if taken out of a book of manners and crafted into a little girl from the paper.

Aloysius was eleven. Agnes nearly had to lock him in the closet to keep him from going up to the apartment. Agnes could still feel the brute force of his shoulder against her sternum as he tried to break free, run up the stairs to help. He was always a strong boy, always trying to do good, always too large for his own good, with too large a heart for his own good, always trying to be the hero he thought his father had been and Agnes never had the heart to tell him otherwise—that the man's body did not lay buried in the same graveyards as those nameless heroes, the ones who gave their lives for France. Aloysius's father couldn't even give his life for his family; instead, he gave his life for a card game, for pride after being called a cheat, for a knife to the belly that should have bled out all the liquor inside him, that revealed the cards he had hidden up his sleeve covered with blood from when he grabbed his stomach and fell to the floor. But that was a story Agnes never shared with Aloysius, instead letting the boy think his father one of the great heroes of a war no one understood, that turned the vibrant streets of Paris into a city of old men, young boys, and the women in between, the ones who shed all the tears when their husbands, brothers, and sons didn't come home.

Agnes calmed Aloysius down by saying she would check on Odette and her mother but only if Aloysius stayed in the apartment. He stood at the door and watched his mother ascend the stairs. She took her time, as if counting the seconds before each step. Aloysius huffed from the doorway. Agnes sped up, not wanting to risk her son running up into the fray. Then the vase, then the thump, then the sobs, then the calls for *maman*, then the understanding. Agnes stood in the doorway. If she had hurried, stepped quicker, followed her son up the stairs, perhaps the grocer would have stopped. Perhaps Agnes could have saved a life, even two. Instead, she walked in on Death and found him in the form of a big man collapsed over a petite woman with a tiny child silent beside them kneeling on broken glass like the penitent. Agnes could imagine her son below waiting to hear the news, waiting to know that Odette was safe. What would happen if he found out what Odette had done? He wouldn't let her get rid of the body on her own. He would want to help. He would try to help to make sure

Odette wouldn't get in trouble. What would he know to do at eleven years old? But Agnes had to know what to do, Agnes had to save Odette so she could save Aloysius.

What can we do? she asked herself. *What can we do*, she wanted to scream. She nearly grabbed Odette and screamed the question into the girl's face, less concerned with what the girl had lost and more concerned with what she had lost—and could lose.

"You need to get rid of the body," Agnes whispered. She bit her fingernails to keep her hands busy, to keep herself from lunging at the girl, at the body, at the person who could have been alive and warm and blushing if Agnes hadn't hidden away.

A soft knock echoed against the door.

"Madame Moreau?" The butcher's voice slid beneath the door with the bang of his hand. He didn't try to peer inside the apartment and instead knocked, content to stay in the hall. Agnes quickly opened the door.

"Mr. Devereux," Agnes said. "Why are you—" she paused and noticed his clean shave, clean clothes. The absence of blood, of an apron, of a bloody apron. Her posture softened. "It is good to see you. May I offer you a coffee?"

"Chicory and bark?" he smiled. "Normally, I would be delighted, but I don't have much time today."

"How may I help?" Agnes said.

"I promised you an extra chop, but you did not come by the shop today." The butcher passed Agnes a bag. She tried not to take it.

"Not now," she said. "I thought we had—"

"You make your own decisions," the butcher said. "But so do I."

The butcher turned to leave but stopped. "How is your boy?"

"I don't think you've ever asked about him," Agnes said.

"Normally, you tell me."

"I always thought it courtesy," she said.

"It was. It is. And so is the bag." The butcher winked. "You look yellow today. It suits you."

Agnes blushed. Her cheeks felt warm. He was the only man who could make her feel warm, to turn her cheeks red with charm instead of anger.

"Please don't forget to open the bag and take out all the items."

"All of the—"

"Please," he said. "Just between those of us who are invisible."

Agnes closed the door and placed the bag on the table. She had known the butcher's favors would require a turn eventually but had hoped he would have been preoccupied to call the favor in.

She held the bag and crinkled the paper. She hesitated to open it. Her mouth watered at the thought of the bag. She opened it. The chop was at the bottom wrapped in butcher paper. A canister stuck to the side. Agnes opened it to find real coffee. The scent of caramel caressed her cheek. A note sat on top of the beans. It said:

Mr. Tureshko

As if he knew, Mr. Tureshko started playing his violin and bathed the streets in music.

Twenty-one

The dining room of Café de Flore was warm, known to have a coal-fired heater that could warm the room and the upper floor. The heater sat in the center of the café, easily distinguishable between the tables, chairs, and the lounging Dr. Eugéne who sat at a table with a half-drunk cup of coffee—actual coffee—in a room filled with the smell of crisp, burnt tobacco. He held a newspaper, and Odette smiled to herself, thinking of the stories Aloysius read as a child about spies sitting on park benches pretending to read the paper. He had a red carnation in a black suit, just as Mr. Tureshko had said. Odette moved through the room and sat at the table. The man didn't move. Odette closed her eyes and inhaled what was left of the coffee aroma. She noticed another familiar odor—slightly sweet, partly musty—but she couldn't place it.

Dr. Eugéne rustled his paper but did not put it down.

"Where is Mr.—"

Odette straightened her position. She hadn't expected to speak so openly about Mr. Tureshko, about the documents. When she found Dr. Eugéne reading a newspaper, she had imagined, for the moment, she was a spy, and they would speak in code passing the money and the documents between them.

"He sent me."

"Is he so old he couldn't come himself?" Dr. Eugéne said. "If he can't come to a simple meeting, how would he ever stand the trip south?" Dr. Eugéne put his paper on the table and looked at Odette. His eyes moved from her face to her torso and back to her face. It was a progression Odette knew well but most often the men's eyes lingered much longer on her breasts, the ones she had kept hidden under wraps for so long. Except Dr. Eugéne's eyes didn't linger. They moved absently over her; for all Odette knew, she could have been a hippopotamus for all Dr. Eugéne cared.

"If you have what he asked for, I have what you need," Odette said, easily sinking into the role of a spy. She pretended to be someone else each time she followed a man home, each time she lured them back to her cellar; how was this any different?

"I'm afraid there's much more to it than a simple transaction," Dr. Eugéne said. "It's a matter of defense and protection."

"Are you worried you cannot trust me?"

"I know I cannot trust you," Dr. Eugéne said. "That is beside the point. My network doesn't work if the person doesn't show up." Dr. Eugéne lit a cigarette. Beneath the smell of sulfur and charring nicotine, the familiar smell surfaced again. Dr. Eugéne inhaled. "There are plenty of people who take trips. They all need to be healthy. I'm a doctor, madam. I need to make sure they are healthy by giving them an inoculation. Your…friend, was meant to meet me here and return to my home to receive the injection. It's just safer that way for everyone. If he isn't here—"

Odette leaned closer to the doctor. His suit was clean and pressed but the odor came from the sleeves—no, the cuffs. She lowered her voice and leaned in closer.

"I have the money."

"If only it were about that," he said. "It comes back to trust." He took the cigarette from his mouth and pointed it at Odette. The smell came back, pushing through the smell of tar. Odette grabbed Dr. Eugéne's hand, pulled the cigarette from his fingers, closed her eyes once more, and inhaled the scent of death.

The man didn't try to pull his hand away. He smiled. Odette smiled back, seeing a reflection of herself in the doctor sitting before her.

"You smell familiar," she said.

"It takes a certain person to know that smell," Dr. Eugéne said.

"I'm a nurse," she said.

"And I'm a doctor."

"Where are the documents?" Odette said.

"At my home," Dr. Eugéne said.

Odette squeezed the doctor's wrist. He twitched but remained quiet. With every lie he told, her grip tightened, and her smile grew. If she could, she would have removed his wrist altogether.

"Where are the documents?" Odette asked.

Dr. Eugéne shrugged, his smile returning.

"And the inoculation?"

The doctor shrugged again. "Perhaps not everyone who gets inoculated goes on the same journey," Dr. Eugéne said.

Odette let go of his hand.

"What if I promised to do the same to you?"

"You wouldn't be the first," Dr. Eugéne said. "You won't be the last."

Odette grabbed the doctor's cup and drank the dregs of his coffee. The bitter soil hit her tongue. Her mouth watered. She wanted to lick the bottom of the cup and let the grinds cling to her teeth, let the flavor last one more day, one more hour, one more second.

"What is your real name?" Odette said. "For if we ever cross paths again."

"We won't," Dr. Eugéne said. He nodded his head.

Odette walked through the smoke unsure what to tell Mr. Tureshko, unsure what she had seen in the café, unsure she had liked the person she saw staring back at her.

Twenty-two

The room was dark with sporadic shadows crawling down the wall cast by the random light poking through the curtains. Odette should have been asleep. Her mother was in the kitchen scrubbing the pots clean. No matter how much her mother scrubbed, the pots were never clean enough, her mother had said. She could stand over the sink for hours, brush in hand, or metal wool clasped tight between her fingers. The scrape and scratch filled the room, skulked beneath the crack in the door separating the bedroom from the kitchen, and joined the shadows, twittering like monsters eager to jump out from beneath Odette's bed.

The apartment door pounded with a knock. It resembled the sound Aloysius made when they played cops and robbers in the street. He would pound on wooden gates and walls, imitating the American cinema when the officers slammed their fists against the door of a club or some gangster's house, ready to raid the inside. Odette pulled the covers up to her chin. The knock came again. Her mother stopped scrubbing in the other room. Her feet dragged against the tile. The soles of her shoes scraped the floor between sink and doorway. Hushed voices replaced her mother's movements; the scratching metal disappeared; her feet against the floor stopped; her mother spoke with intense whispers. A deeper voice responded. When Odette went to the market with her mother, she often heard the same heavy whisper. Odette wasn't naughty, but when they went to the market, the rainbow colors of the candy shops would entice her. She would wander down the halls between the produce stalls. While her mother knocked on watermelon or squeezed potatoes, smelled artichoke or sampled a blueberry, Odette sampled a lemon tart or a gumdrop without telling the vendor until her stomach began to ache or the vendor caught her shoving a chocolate croissant into her pocket; he would then grab her wrist and shout for Odette's mother, demanding payment as her wrist turned red from the pressure, and sometimes black and blue. Her mother would then take the same wrist, squeezing harder than the vendor. She would shove her finger in Odette's face and scream through her whispers, not wanting to draw attention to them in the heart of the arcade. Tears would hover around her chin stalling before they fell. Her mother would let go of her hand, the tears would fade, and Odette would shove her hands into her pockets to rub her fingers against the spoils she had taken from the candy store or bakery without anyone else knowing. Her wrist would ache for days, but the bruise didn't hurt. She had learned to look sad and regretful by watching other children in trouble. They would look to the floor, avert their eyes from their parent, cry, pout, apologize, promise they learned their lesson and that it would never happen again. Odette did the same when she got caught, but she never felt the same.

The monsters once beneath her bed had escaped, slithered beneath the doorframe and entered the other room. Her mother whispered to them to get back home, Odette thought. Someone must have found them on the street and brought them back; that was why she had that tone.

The man's voice grew louder. His words became more comprehensible. Odette knew his voice. He was the local grocer. Odette passed him almost every day on the way home from school. He would call out to her, ask about her mother, and offer an orange or lemon or whatever was fresh to take home. "Remember to tell your mother who it's from," he would say. For the first three weeks Odette had given the gift to her mother. Each time her mother took the orange or lemon or even once a kiwi and threw them in the garbage.

"We do not accept gifts like these," she said.

"We don't accept fruit?" Odette asked.

"Not from men like him."

For another two weeks, Odette hoarded the gifts, eating the fruit on the way home or hiding it in her room. Then her mother found an orange beside Odette's bed. She demanded to know where Odette had gotten it. Odette lied. Her mother slapped her cheek. Odette lied again. Her mother slapped Odette again. Odette tasted copper on the inside of her cheek. Blood spread across her teeth. She smiled to show her mother how the thin crimson spread over her mouth. Her mother slapped Odette a third time before asking. Odette admitted she had taken it from the grocer.

"From now on, you go a different way home," her mother said.

"But that will take more time," Odette said.

"Let it," her mother said.

The voices on the opposite side of the door grew louder. They growled and groaned. Odette brushed away the sheets and cracked open the door. The grocer stood above Odette's mother. He loomed over her the way a tree hovers above its shadow. His chubby fingers swallowed her wrists. Her fingers crunched and turned pink and red.

"You took my fruit," he said. "You took my fruit and never came to say hello."

"Please," she said. Her voice no longer carried a harsh whisper and instead whimpered. His neck fat poured over his shirt collar. The neighbor turned on their radio. A fast-paced violin bounced off the walls, drowning out Odette's mother.

"My husband—"

"Is dead," the grocer said. "I have been kind to you!" His skin leaked. The room smelled of rotten eggplant. The single lamp in the kitchen turned her mother and the grocer into half-shadows. One side of her face turned to agony; her mouth twisted in an attempt to scream. The grocer's fat stomach backed her against the wall. Her arms wrestled to be free but lost.

Odette's father died before she was born, one of the last casualties of the Great War, her mother had said. He went off to fight and survived the battle, recuperating in a hospital after the Battle of the Marne. The Germans had regained ground, and hundreds of thousands of lives had disintegrated for both countries to reach the trenches from which they had started. Odette's father had taken a bullet to the leg and was rushed off the battlefield. While he was at the field hospital, a wave of Spanish flu spread from bed to bed like a pack of wolves tearing through a field of unguarded sheep, finishing what the Germans had started. The military burned the bodies. Odette's mother, pregnant and working at a laundry, didn't receive her husband's medals or his duffel that might still have smelled of him. She received a letter from the military months after the war had ended explaining extenuating circumstances about the field hospital, how nothing could have been done, and that he rested in the fields with his men—except his men had been buried at the cemetery in Dormans; he had turned to ash and been released to the sky. It made Odette wonder what it would be like to let the wind take her.

"Stop, please," her mother said once more. The grocer stuck out his wet pink tongue and leaned closer. He pushed Odette's mother to the floor. He stepped towards Odette. She stepped back. It was a perverse dance that smelled of rot and vinegar. Odette ran at the grocer. He grabbed her, held her tight, smelled her hair, licked her cheek. "You," he said. "You took my fruit, too. Your mother is ungrateful. I wanted to help. Your father has been gone for a long time." The raw slime of his tongue lingered as Odette screamed and tried to kick him.

"You have grown. She can keep the ghost of her husband. I'll give you all the fruit you could ever want." Her breasts hadn't formed yet. His breasts pressed against her neck. The putrid sweat splashed against her cheeks. He pressed his chapped, crusty lips to hers and forced his swollen, drenched tongue into her mouth. She kicked but couldn't loosen his grip. His erection pressed against her thigh, indenting her nightgown, turning each rub of the warm, soft cloth. The grocer breathed heavy like the rhinoceros at the zoo Odette had seen years ago. In the winter, its breath puffed like a factory. Her knuckles turned white.

Odette clamped down on the grocer's tongue. The fleshy muscle clenched between her teeth. He screamed and tried to pull away. The more he pulled, the harder she clamped down. The familiar taste of blood filled her mouth, tinted with the vinegar flavor of the grocer's skin. He tried to push Odette away.

Her mother crawled to the grocer's leg and bit his ankle. Odette released the grocer's tongue. He screamed. He threw Odette down.

"You bite like a bitch," the grocer said. He reached down and pulled Odette's mother from the floor. "If you want to act like a bitch, I'll treat you like a bitch." He dripped his tongue into her ear. She elbowed him, slapped him, but he wouldn't let go. The floor was cold on Odette's skin. The grocer grunted like a hog, too heavy for his own body. He swarmed over Odette's mother; a sewer pipe ready to burst.

Odette found a vase her mother had put on the windowsill. In winter, purple buds decorated the windowsill filling the room with lavender. In summer, sunflowers glowed against the glass. The sunflowers had died the same day Odette's mother had found the orange. Odette grabbed the cold glass. Swampy water swished around the inside. She pressed her cold toes to the tile, trying to sneak across the room. She raised the vase over her head. The grocer turned, loosening his grip on Odette's mother. Odette slammed the vase into the grocer's neck. He bent forward and groaned. The water splashed against his brown blazer, sopping the edges and dripping to the floor. Odette's mother kneed the grocer in the groin. He doubled over. Her mother folded like a box beneath him. His teeth were the color of lemons. His breath smelled of rancid meat.

The shattered glass crunched beneath the grocer's feet. Odette's hobbled over loose shards. Her skin broke. Bloody footprints left traces of her backward steps. She had never met her father but swore he would never have hurt her, her mother; he would never have made her step on glass or choose between her mother or him.

Her feet continued to bleed onto the tile. The room began to smell like moldy copper. The shadows had enveloped her mother, the grocer, Odette, with the single light flickering across the room. Odette's mother raised the knife. Her mother slammed the blade into the grocer's skull. The crack of the bone sounded the same as the shattering vase. The grocer blinked. He turned towards Odette's mother, took three steps, and fell to the floor covering Odette's bloody footprints.

Odette breathed heavily. Sweat, some Odette's, some the grocer's, drenched her nightgown. But it wasn't sweat. Blood flooded into the thin strands of Odette's hair and leaked down onto the tile. It flowed out of the grocer. It stepped across the floor with her bloody footprints.

"I need you to help me now," Odette's mother said.

It was the first dead body Odette had ever seen. She expected his eyes to close or for him to stand up and attack them all over again. His eyes stayed open and stared at the floor. His legs and arms twitched. Her mother grabbed Odette's shoulder. But it wasn't her mother. It was Agnes. Her mother lay crumpled and lifeless beneath the grocer.

"Odette," Agnes said. "I need your help now."

Odette nodded. The pool of blood began to lick at the fringe of her nightgown, seeping into the fabric.

"We're going to do this together," Agnes said. She brought out blankets to place beneath the bodies. They took turns lifting the grocer. The blankets soaked up the blood. They stripped his clothes away, leaving bare the folds of his back, the way his flaccid penis contracted like a scared turtle into its foreskin. Odette couldn't remember the whole night, or what happened after they cleaned the blood, but she remembered the kiln, the heat, the licking flames, the smell of burnt hair as it caught fire and disintegrated. Mostly, she remembered her mother, how one second, she was cleaning dishes and then wasn't. How one second, she was in the room and then wasn't. How one second Agnes held Odette's mother, then a man at door with large forearms and his hands stretched out and the sound of coins jingling and then silence; no questions—a strangled woman's limp body as typical in the city as a passing bird before being carried to *Cimetière du Montparnasse*. Odette remembered Agnes, as if the woman stepped from out of a mist and into the fire. And the grocer's dead eyes—fearful gaze with an eternal smirk. But also, she remembered his head, detached from his body—a lifeless peach with its juice spilling onto the floor.

The sun peeked over the city's edge. Odette kneeled over the streaks of blood the blanket hadn't sopped up, the footprints she had left behind, and the twittering monsters returned as she scrubbed away the night.

Twenty-three

The girl was meant to get better, Ilse thought. She had shown all the signs of getting better. The girl had gone from pale to colorful, her lips dour and chapped to full, filled with moisture. She smiled. She laughed when Ilse made faces. She held tight to a teddy bear Ilse had given her. She smelled of roses instead of rot. Her hair had grown back, first in patches but then thick, dark brown, like chestnuts. Ilse once found herself hugging the girl, digging her nose into the girl's scalp, and finding the scent of pine, of hazelnut, absent of lice, flees, and pestilence Ilse had found on the other patients.

Instead, Ilse kept finding reasons to connect with the girl, who she had chosen never to name, as if she were a stray dog, one to whom she couldn't get attached, who needed to stay feral and dirty. But even without a name, even with a number or by pointing her finger, or referring to the girl as *the one with the hair*, the lips, the scent of the forest in autumn; they only made her want to name the girl, to call her a sweet Austrian name, to name the girl after Ilse's mother, Emma. And Ilse did name the girl, not out loud. Ilse whispered the girl's secret name in her head whenever she pointed to the girl, whenever she needed to give her another dose.

145

Ilse documented Emma's progress. The more time Ilse spent with Emma; the more Emma progressed. Ilse couldn't see the veins in Emma's arms or the ones in her neck in which they first injected her. Ilse remembered the way Emma didn't cry, didn't call out or squirm. Emma sat there and made eye contact with a single tear running down her cheek. Ilse convinced herself the tear had sprung from defiance as opposed to pain. That was the first treatment, but she had been injected before, not by Ilse, but by the others working in the hospital. They had given her the sickness in the first place, waiting and watching what would happen. Those who lasted longer than forty-eight hours entered the hospital. Those who hadn't made it the full forty-eight hours hadn't made it at all, had fallen long before they ever had a chance at help, too weak, too bland for this life. Too meaningless in a city filled with meaning, too powerless in a battle for power. And in the end, Ilse would take it all on the backs of those powerless fools who lasted long enough for her to climb over. Except Emma.

When the rest of her kind cried and pleaded, she sat silent in the room and grew stronger. Ilse's father always said, "Pleading only makes you look like a fool when you already know you're dead." Ilse never understood what he meant until the day she took a knife to his back, when he kneeled with his fists pressed to the floor apologizing for the mistakes he made, begging for his life, for forgiveness, knowing it was too late yet still trying. Then Ilse twisted the knife and told him to ask her mother. Even if Ilse had believed in an afterlife, a biblical version of heaven and hell, her father would never have asked her mother; they would have been on opposite ends of the heavenly spectrum, one accompanied by angels, the other leading demons.

Emma never cried or pleaded. She took her medicine. While others coughed up blood, sneezed out bloody mucus, shriveled from collapsing veins, Emma sat up in her bed and asked for milk. She spoke to Ilse. She laughed with Ilse, played cards with Ilse.

"Why do you shoot me?" Emma asked.

"I would never shoot you," Ilse said. She played her cards hoping for another heart to shoot the moon.

"Why do you give me the shots?" Emma said.

"They make you feel better, yes?" Ilse pulled another heart from the deck. She needed to get rid of her remaining spades.

Emma nodded and picked up a spade. "They are like black hearts," she said and turned the card upside down.

"You are a child," Ilse said. "What do you know about black hearts?"

"I had a black heart."

"Who told you that?"

"The nurse," Emma said. "My momma had one, and so did my papa. That is why they are gone. The nurse said I'll be gone too." She put the card back in her hand.

"You could never have a black heart, no? That is too much. How could someone say such a thing, I will never understand."

Heavy silence hung between them interspersed with the swish the cards made as they brushed against one another.

"Let's play a game," Ilse said.

"We are playing a game," Emma said.

"I meant another game."

"But we aren't finished with this game."

Ilse smiled and touched Emma's nose with a single finger, the way her mother did to her before bed. "I meant, what if we continue to play our game but we also try a memory game, as well."

"How do we play?" Emma picked up a club before realizing it wasn't a spade. She tried to hide her pout behind her hand.

"I'm going to ask you questions about the nurse who said you had a black heart, and you can answer them as best as you can remember, yes?" Ilse discarded a diamond. They were always useless anyway.

Emma nodded again and avoided the diamond. See, Ilse told herself, useless.

"Did she have hair like gold?" Emma shook her head. "She had brown hair, like yours? Like dark oak?" Emma nodded. "Was she thin, like a lamp post?" Emma shook her head. "She was bigger, yes? She looked like a bear maybe." Emma nodded again. "Was she fuzzy like a bear too? Especially with a mustache and a beard?" Emma laughed like wind chimes adding a sense of levity to the heavy air of the hospital. "I think I know who this nurse is. We can't have our nurses saying such terrible things to our patients."

"A hospital makes sick people better," Emma said.

"Of course," Ilse said.

"Then why are so many people getting sicker?" Emma asked.

Ilse paused, took the final heart from the deck, placed down her cards and said, "I win. It looks like our time is up for the day."

"But—"

"But you need rest if you want to get better," Ilse said. She took the cards and placed them in her jacket pocket. "We'll play again tomorrow when I check on you. I am a busy doctor you know. I can't spend all day playing cards with you." She smiled and touched her finger to Emma's nose once more. Ilse stopped a thin nurse walking past and asked her to find the bear Emma had described. "Tell her Dr. Kohler wants to see her." The thin nurse clicked her heels and walked away, trying to escape whatever storm followed Ilse using her formal title, she thought.

In her office, Ilse pretended to read memos, shifted papers around, stared at the inner spine of her medical terminology book until the bear entered the room.

"You asked to see me, doctor?" the bear spoke. She filled the doorway. Ilse's heart skipped a beat at the size of the woman. She realized now she had never stood close to nurse Gerhardt. Her shoulders reminded others of a bear, creating the frame that held a powerful neck, one that could withstand the gallows and break through the rope. "Am I interrupting?"

Ilse pushed away the book of papers. "No," she said. "Of course, not. Have a seat."

Ilse stood the moment nurse Gerhardt sat. The shift in size mattered little. Ilse felt as tall as the bear when she sat. She could only imagine how small she'd feel if Gerhardt remained standing. The thought of someone towering over Ilse made her palms sweat. She walked to the door and shut it behind the back of the sturdy bear. The cards still filled her pocket with all the hearts facing inward against her chest.

"I've heard rumors you are talking to the patients," Ilse said.

"Nothing more than what we're permitted to say, Ilse—"

"Doctor," Ilse said.

"Yes, doctor."

"What are you permitted to say to them?"

"Very little," Gerhardt said.

"That is an odd thing to say to patients."

"I meant—"

"I know what you meant," Ilse said. "But that is not what I asked you. I did not ask *how much* you are permitted to say to the patients, I asked *what* you are permitted to say to them."

"We can tell them mealtimes," Gerhardt said.

"Is that it?"

"We can tell them to keep quiet or to try and pacify them if we feel they are getting better."

"Are you allowed to tell them they have black hearts?"

"Pardon me, doctor but what does—"

"Are you permitted to tell these patients they're dying because of their black hearts? Did you say it was because they are vermin, dirty Jews, and deserve what your god has in store for them, or perhaps their god will not greet them on the other side of this life?"

Ilse placed her hand on Gerhardt's shoulder and pressed down. Her palm couldn't indent the thick muscle of Gerhardt's trapezius.

"I said what I was permitted to say."

"I didn't know you were that creative. Perhaps you should have worked with Minister Goebbels. You could find new ways to present the news, the stories, the propaganda. Perhaps you could even model a new character after yourself, 'Gerhardt the Bear, Nurse Extraordinaire.'"

"My name is not bear," Gerhardt said. "It is—"

"At this moment, you are whatever I choose to call you. If I wanted to call you shit-stain, that is what your name would be. Understand, Bear?"

"No, Ilse," Gerhardt said and stood up. "The girl should be dead like the others. She is—"

"A child," Ilse said.

"A pest," Gerhardt said. "A stain on the world."

"I've read the books too," Ilse said.

"Then maybe her black heart is rubbing off on you," Gerhardt said and gave a slick half-smile.

"Yes," Ilse said. "I keep her black heart and mine here." She patted her pocket where she had placed the cards. She took a scalpel from the same pocket and jammed it into Gerhardt's inner thigh. She took the cards and shoved them into Gerhard's mouth, pressing the paper as far down the bear's throat as she could. She took the scalpel from the leg. The artery opened and sprayed across the office covering Ilse's white coat. The doctor scraped the scalpel across the bear's neck. The cards fell from Gerhardt's mouth. Her neck splattered blood across the room before her body fell to the floor. Ilse wiped the scalpel on her stained coat. She took the cards, all of which now looked like hearts after soaking in blood. She placed her jacket over the body and reached for a new white coat from the closet. The bear's legs twitched. Ilse needed to find Odette.

The problem with living so long, Agnes thought, was that she couldn't help but remember everything, the good, the bad, and the bloody. After the Great War, she had tried to give up meat. She had seen too many legs butchered, gangrenous fingers, torn flesh, the smell of rotten flesh, the blood on the floor, that she could have never seen another cut of veal or a slice of pork again and been fine.

Pork was the worst. It not only looked like skin but if felt like human muscle too. When she trained at the field hospital, long before they ran low on provisions, her instructor would bring out a pig and have the nurses practice on the body. The pig would dangle from a hook upside down, the blood already drained, and Agnes would pierce the skin with her knife and look for the kidneys, the liver, the heart, the bone.

She remembered the smell of the pig, and how on the hot days, it imitated the smell of war, the putrid aroma of dead bodies littering the fields, when the sun baked down on the ground, and instead of the perfume of flowers or the herbaceous scent of grass, the children who played soldier decayed and their bones turned back to dust, but not before the flies swarmed over the fields—black clouds that buzzed and bit.

Agnes remembered all of their faces, the scared boys, the disillusioned men, and the stone-face girls who, like her, filled the tents and sterilized needles, mopped up shit, and held those *strong* soldiers down as they sawed off limbs while never flaring more than a nostril inside the tent, while her insides roiled or they finished bandaging the stump before they stepped away from the wounded and vomited chunks of potato stew.

She remembered Paris after the war and how the smell of the apartment carried asparagus and flowers. She tried to keep the scent of meat far from her flat, but when her husband came home drunk and threw a steak on the burner, Agnes wouldn't look at the meat as it sizzled in the pan. After the second time, her husband didn't expect less than a charred brick. But after the third time, Agnes refused to cook any more. It wasn't long after that she kicked him out for good.

She remembered Paris filled with the aromas of celebration, simple scents the war could not offer, like the buttery fragrance of croissants or jasmine perfume. The city swelled with little details she hadn't known she missed until they returned, the taste of thick wine on her tongue, the sound of butter frying in the pan, and warmth of a fire on a cold day.

But most of all, she remembered Aloysius as a child, sick with polio, when the doctor told Agnes there was nothing more he could do.

Odette opened her door to find Ilse standing in the hall.

"Hello, Ilse. I was not expecting—"

"Of course not," Ilse said. "Is that a cat?" Ilse moved past Odette and entered the apartment. She reached for Martine who hissed and scattered under the chair.

"May I get you some coffee?"

"Acorns and tree bark?" Ilse asked. "I'd rather drink toilet water."

"Would you like—"

"Please," Ilse said. "Stop with the pleasantries. I came here for a reason."

Odette stepped deeper into her apartment. Martine remained hidden and stiff beneath the chair.

"Why is that?" Odette said."

"Do you believe we are friends?" Ilse said.

They had spoken little at work but nothing to make Odette feel they were friends. But Odette didn't have many friends to begin with. Perhaps that *was* a friend.

"I suppose," Odette said.

"I am not of the belief that friendship is a supposition." Ilse sat on the chair and peered out the window. "You have a charming flat. It feels nothing like the home my husband and I have tried to make here. We keep a different kind of home, but I believe that is why I like yours. Ours is too…cold. Too old. Yours looks like what I imagined Paris to be like."

"Small and cramped?" Odette said.

"Bohemian, no? It is a city of intrigue and artistic ingenuity. But it is not just those things. Ingenuity can take on many forms even when shaped by a single inspiration, yes?"

Odette nodded unsure of what to say or what Ilse meant. The air felt still in the flat, and Martine had not yet emerged from beneath the chair.

"Again, I ask you if we are friends."

Odette hesitated but then said yes. She sat down on a chair opposite Ilse and looked into the doctor's eyes. She did not see fear but concern as if her calculations had gone awry. Odette knew that feeling, like the time she had followed a cobbler to his mistress's home only to find the man had drunkenly knocked on the wrong door, waking half the floor with his incessant demands and the screams of the woman who answered.

"Good," Ilse said. "I don't have many friends. The curse of a professional life and moving often."

"But you have a husband?" Odette said. She had thought for so long that her life, her death mask, the fire raging inside her meant she could never have a family. These things kept her from Aloysius, from drowning in his sheets each day for good. Ilse ignored Odette's question.

"I need your help and discretion. I know you are good for the latter, but can I count on the former?"

"As your friend, I will do what I can." The word felt foreign on Odette's tongue. But she found it felt good. She wanted it to linger.

The doctor told Agnes to pray, but she left her prayers at the field hospital with the sawed-off limbs and decayed bodies. She hadn't thought about what happened to them, but if she took a minute, she would have believed that they, like the soldiers, sunk back into the soil. She kept her prayers far in the past and silently nodded to the doctor. Aloysius lay in bed sick and feverish. *He had always wanted to follow in his father's footsteps,* Agnes thought. But instead of praying, Agnes drew a bath. She boiled water until it seared her skin pink. The steam wafted through the room like smoke, a screen making it difficult to differentiate between the flat and the field, a soldier and her son. For days, he had only shaken with fever.

She remembered how he didn't cry when she dunked him into the tub. He whimpered but kept his eyes closed like a sick lamb waiting to die. Like all the other lost boys she had watched before him. But this time it felt different. She couldn't look away. She couldn't call over another nurse when she needed a cigarette or fresh air away from the tinny stink of blood. This time, she let the hot water envelope Aloysius, her son, her child, her baby, and as he whimpered, she sobbed. The sound of the droplets splashing down from the rag into the water imitated her tears. Odette's mother, Lorelai, would run to the kitchen when the kettle boiled and return to the tub. She held Agnes's hand. It always felt soft and warm, unlike Agnes's which felt leathery, cold, lifeless. She wished she had Lorelai's hands. As if these hands could bring Ali back, could pull the sickness from his spine. She wanted to beg Lorelai. After all the boys at war, after all the boys sunken into the soil.

"Let me use your hands," she wanted to say. "Give me your hands. He needs them."

But instead, selfishly, she kept them for herself. She held them sweet and soft.

She poured the hot water into the tub for him and clung to those hands for her. The water stayed hot and singed her son's skin, and in doing so, could burn out whatever sickness remained inside him—possibly. And she remembered how he stopped whimpering. She remembered her sigh after the sobbing stopped. She remembered the sweat that dripped down her chin and into the tub. She remembered watching and waiting for her son's chest to rise, fall, and rise again. She remembered how her heart stopped each second she couldn't tell whether Aloysius breathed. She remembered how she fell into Lorelai's arms. And she remembered when he breathed again, and how she fell to the floor, dug her arm into the water, and rubbed his chest until the pink of his skin turned back to white. The tears left a salty taste in her mouth. Her flat smelled like lavender and black licorice. She took Aloysius out of the tub, wrapped him in blankets, and set him in the bed for the night. By morning, his strength had returned. Agnes remembered how she stayed in bed with her son and let the water pool on the floor. She wondered if she left it there long enough, would it evaporate on its own, like steam, like sweat, like a sickness, like her prayers.

They stood in Ilse's office with the door locked behind them. A lake of blood swarmed around the bear. It reminded Odette of the water at Lac de Minimes, glossy and reflective, as if she and Aloysius could have strolled along the surrounding footpaths and snack on a gateau as the grey herons search for food. If the cuts hadn't killed her, it looked like she could have drowned in her own blood, Odette thought.

"I can't help with this."

Her voice didn't waver. A part of her was not surprised that Ilse had killed someone and was only concerned with Ilse asking her for help. Most surprising to Odette was the white coat covered in blood splatter as if a child tried to dry a wet paint brush and got Ilse by accident. It looked nearly as chaotic as the day Odette first met Ilse, with the stains on the coat already turning a rusty brown.

"I don't believe you," Ilse said. "You have done things like this before."

Odette stepped away from Ilse and into the lake swallowing the bear.

"Excuse me?" Odette said.

"With the former head of the hospital, yes?"

Odette sighed. Relief swelled in her chest.

"That was different. Everyone knew he was dead. I just took him to the morgue."

"We cannot take her to the morgue."

"Then throw her in the Seine," Odette said. "It doesn't matter how you get rid of her, but she can't stay here."

"Obviously." The calm veneer of Ilse's voice had cracked. "I face death every day. It's always for the common good. What good is this?"

"I'm sure you had a reason," Odette said.

"Are you?" Ilse said. "What reason would you have?"

"Pardon me?"

"If you killed someone, what reason would you have? What could someone possibly do that would make you kill them?"

"I would have rules," Odette said. "Just like you. For the common good." She reached toward the door eager to leave. The room grew hot and humid. The hotter the room, the quicker the blood would spoil.

Ilse moved to the door and blocked it.

"I cannot let you leave now. I need you."

"You cannot panic," Odette said.

"I've broken so many rules, but none like this. Please. How can I go on?"

"We can get through this," Odette said. "I have never done—what I mean is…no women or children."

"She was always more of a bear," Ilse said and cracked a fake, forced smile.

"Can you get her to my apartment?"

"It is across town," Ilse said. Odette's stare did not waver. She forced an answer from Ilse in her silence. Ilse nodded. "I can use an ambulance."

"Give me one hour," Odette said. "Until then, get some bleach and rags. Wipe the room down. Get her naked and bring it all with you." Ilse gave the slight nod of a person not used to taking orders.

When she arrived, Odette helped bring the body into the cellar. The body had lost nearly all of its blood already. Odette handed Ilse the saw. Without question, Ilse cut away the body parts with the eagerness of a medical student. Odette wrapped each piece of the nurse into cloth and found space in the kiln. The cloth quickly burned; the fat dripped and sizzled as it melted away.

The fire sung. The body was slowly disappearing along with the bloody clothing and rags. The adrenaline seeped away.

"This isn't the first time," Ilse said. "I always know when people are holding secrets."

Against the smell of melting fat and charred skin, Odette found the aroma of lilies. It had become settling, soothing, especially amongst the constant smell of garbage enduring along the city streets.

"Everyone has secrets," Odette said. She had already given too much away, too much to someone too dangerous. At least this was a secret she felt could save her, rather than condemn her. "Even you."

Ilse nodded. "Unlike others, I don't hide that I have secrets."

"I broke a rule," Odette said. Agnes's voice cracked in Odette's head, roaring over the fire; *I hope you know what you're doing*, it said. "For a friend."

Ilse smiled. The scent of lilies grew powerful.

For the first time in years, Odette didn't know what she was doing. And if felt exciting.

Twenty-four

Agnes stood at the doorway to the butcher's shop. The rain poured over the windows acting like a veil between her and him. His apron held less blood than the days before the war. The counters and meat hooks held less pig, less cow, less sheep, more emptiness. In summer the putrid scent of innards, gizzards, and entrails swept through the alleyway after the butcher tossed the remains of the animals or those elements that hadn't turned and needed refuge in the refuse onto the streets for the cats. Anything he couldn't sell, couldn't put in a soup, couldn't turn into something better, got tossed away. Agnes felt similar in the way their romance had ended, treated the same way he treated the parts of the animal that carried the shit. And now he sat cleaning the counters, checking his shelves repeatedly as if something new might magically appear, or worse, something old disappeared. He kept the pencil behind his ear stuffed between the protruding cartilage and his bald pate. He wore his spectacles with pride, even after the war, as if daring someone to laugh at him. He had grown up slim in need of milk for strong bones, in need of meat for strong muscles, in need of attention for a strong soul.

He hadn't had any of those until he stumbled into the butcher's shop with his thick forearms but little else and attempted to steal a full pig from off the hook. This was before the war, before he grew into his forearms and bald head, when the boys in the neighborhood picked on him for his broken lenses he couldn't afford to change, when he saw the world cracked and bloated from each eye. Agnes didn't know him then. She imagined his eyes cut into threes through the frames, saw the way he fingered his glasses to his nose until he tried to grab the meat from the hook, when the smell of the offal in the summer heat grabbed him by the brain and dragged him into the shop. He hugged the meat, cried into the ribs of the pig as its snout dangled down to his chest. He held it close like his mother, ready to suckle for health, strength, comfort, knowledge. The old butcher screamed at him, but his words bounced off the young miscreant whose skin had become leather through years of heartache, of bullying, of his mother beating him with a wooden spoon, of the boys in the neighborhood kicking him with the toes of their boots until his elbow shattered, until his toes bent inward, until the lens of his glasses broke. But the old butcher saw through the tears, saw past the leathery skin, when the young butcher's sleeves lifted up to reveal his forearm, their thick and bulbous shape like unripe furry pears.

They clung to the pig ready to lift it off the hooks but instead of lifting, they released the pig and fell into the old butcher. The old man's beard rubbed against the head of the young butcher, whose hair was already thinning by the age of twelve. The old man had blood on his shirt—on his apron, on his cheeks, in his beard, but kept the faded pink away from the boy as if the violence of the butcher shop was more than he could bear, more than the violence of the streets, of his home. The boy wanted the violence of the butcher shop, wanted the violence to have meaning beyond him, beyond his feelings he had done something wrong, wanted his broken glasses to show him more than the shattered world he stared at every day. The old man took an extra pair of spectacles from his shelf, the shelf the boy would one day check and re-check. He handed the spectacles to the boy, who took off his tired and broken lenses and replaced them with the used but healthy glasses. The world turned focused with a slight tint. The gypsy on the outskirts of their neighborhood would talk about auras in the night after she finished her third glass of absinthe, crying about the outline of colors emanating from those passing her shop. The boy could now see those outlines too but unlike the gypsy, he didn't know what the colors meant. He gave them attributes based upon the way the people had treated him in the past. The blood covering the old butcher spread to his aura outlined with a pink hue. The boy believed pink was a good sign. His mother glowed red, which leaked from her angry face to her silhouette. Red meant bad. She screamed at the boy for his new glasses, took the spoon from the drawer and swatted it down over the boy's back. He turned, held up his arms, and the wood cracked, splintered, and split over his forearms leaving his bones untouched. The boys in the neighborhood had a similar red, one streak that connected them all. They ran after the young butcher in an attempt to break his glasses once more, tear away the colorful fuzzy outlines of those around him, and return the world to the fractured way he once viewed it. But the episode with the wooden spoon had given the young butcher confidence— hope. The young butcher faced the lead boy and threw his forearm into the boy's nose. The pop had a similar ring to the sound the young butcher's glasses made when the boys had broken them. The head boy's nose cracked and caved with blood dripping down to the floor, the blood the young butcher thought of pouring from animals, from pigs, from cows, from sheep, from goats, but those animals bled for a reason. Why did these children blead? Why did they make others? The young butcher returned to the old man the next day with a white apron.

"I want mine to look like yours," he had said.

"It'll take time," the old butcher said.

"I have time," the young butcher said. "I need blood."

"I have plenty of blood." The old butcher smiled and welcomed in his apprentice who had found saving in the dangling pig. His master gave him meat to use for stews in the winter, offered lesser cuts or pieces about to turn in the summer to poach in butter, garnish with fried sage, pair with eggplant, puree, and stuff into an artichoke. His master didn't give him an education; he showed him food was more than satiation, it was worth living for instead of needed for living. The young butcher grew into his arms—plump—and his cheeks turned rosy, and he filled out into the same glasses that showed the customers' auras. The old butcher would ask his apprentice about the different colors their customers emitted each day.

"What did Madam Lucerne wear today?" He always referred to the customers by name, making sure his apprentice remembered each of them like a house guest. He would then respond with their clothing, the way they held their face in the cold or hot air outside the store before entering versus how they acted once inside the store. The boy would end with the color wrapping around their body like a cold front, a wet blanket, or soothing hot water bottle. On that morning, Madam Lucerne glowed orange. The boy had only seen one other woman glow orange since receiving his glasses. It was the gypsy after she stumbled out of her shop to the street corner. She wrapped herself in a shawl and lifted her dress to reveal a naked ankle. She lit a cigarette and took a swig of brandy. The orange shined brighter than the fruit, than the juice, than sherbet. A man stumbled out of the door and repositioned his tie. He turned to the gypsy woman and kissed her, stealing the brandy from her hands. She looked at the boy and laughed.

"Orange is for lovers," she said and laughed again as if reading the boy's mind before stumbling back into her shop.

During the Great War, the boy used his forearms at the front, his knowledge of complimentary flavors, but nothing complimented dirt and mud. He returned home with more blood on his cuffs than he had ever gotten on his apron and once again wondered the reason the boys around him bled and caused bleeding, finding solace once more in the blood he took from the cows, from the pigs, from the goats, from the sheep to give life to the neighborhood and flavor to life.

It was at the tail end of the Great War when Agnes met the young butcher. He had lost the plumpness and grown into his arms. Her husband had returned with her but kept late mornings and later nights. The young butcher had known her husband in the war but never said more than, "I knew him." Agnes visited the butcher shop daily, watched the young butcher pull the meat from the hooks, smile at the men and women, wave to the children, provide recipes to everyone, and nod at Agnes. Then one night, when her husband remained lost amidst the mist of smoke and haze of champagne at one of his "card games," Agnes found herself standing at the doorway of the butcher shop as the apprentice cleaned the counters and the floors. He pulled blinds down over the windows but saw Agnes waiting across the street—staring. He welcomed her in with the same nod he offered her during the day. His white apron had taken on tints of pink, of blood stains. He washed the apron to take care of the smell but never wanted the color to fade. It always faded. Yet the blood from the front never did, even though he had burned those clothes nearly a year before. Agnes kept her hands in front of her with her purse clasped between her fingers. The butcher wore the same glasses his master had given him before the war. They had kept his mind healthy during the war, filled his heart with stories about home and about the boys with whom he shared the trenches.

"You glow," he said in the quiet of the Parisian night, a rarity since the war ended.

She blushed, heightening her colorful aura. She opened her mouth to speak but put her finger to her lips as if she had only thought a word he must now guess.

"You have an outline of orange," he said. "It's as if the sun follows you wherever you go."

"Is that what your glasses tell you?" she said.

"It is what you are telling me," he said.

Agnes dropped the purse and pulled the butcher to her. They spent the hours leading into the late night forgetting about the blood of the war, of the neighborhood, of the butcher shop, and basking in their shared orange glow.

After Agnes kicked out her husband, she broke off the affair between her and the butcher. Her aura had turned from orange to blue. He imagined his wasn't much different. She continued to come into the shop, and he would greet her with the same nod as always. She would blush for a brief second before turning away. His master retired, Agnes grew large with child, and the thought crossed his mind whether the boy belonged to them, instead of the man he once knew who had gone—good riddance. But he never asked. Their romance heated up once more for a brief period of time before this new war, after Agnes begged for his help, even though she knew she never had to beg him for anything. She said she had wanted to beg, wanted to show how desperately she needed him at that moment. She needed his bloody hands and quiet mouth for the night. And he said yes because he would always say yes to her. And he said when the time came to return the favor she would say yes, too. And he asked her, and she said no, but here she stood outside his shop once more, now in the rain, knowing she must say yes. The butcher pulled down the blinds and welcomed Agnes in with little more than a nod.

"You glow," he said.

"I haven't even seen the sun in what feels like forever," she said.

"You turned blue long ago," he said.

"Like water," she said.

"Like sadness," he said.

"Is that what color sadness is?"

He nodded.

"I guess I couldn't expect it to be lilac," she said.

He touched her arm with his strong hands, his soft hands stained pink at the tips of his fingers.

"How much blood have you seen in your lifetime?" she asked.

"Too much," he said.

"Was it—" she pulled her finger to her mouth and sighed. "Was it ever worth it?" The rain outside smacked against the window and splashed against the dents in the cobblestones.

"Outside of this place," he said, "never." He pushed his glasses back up his nose, the same glasses from before the Great War, that survived the trench, their romance, her absence, their heartache. She dropped a letter onto the counter. Her coat left droplets of water behind. He took the note. She walked into the rain without saying goodbye, the same way she had ended their affair. Over the sounds of the rain, the storm of Mr. Tureshko's violin echoed in the night. The butcher didn't need to check his watch. He knew the time by the song Tureshko played. He opened the note where she had written a single word: yes. He locked the door and took off the apron stained with the day's blood.

Twenty-five

Odette stepped down the stairs from her apartment to a morning steeped in radiant sunlight and an odd quiet as if the city held its breath like a predator waiting to pounce. A bus stood empty at the end of the road with a series of gendarmes breaking the silence, their boots stomping on the cobblestones with a snap, crack, and thud, the same sound Odette had heard the day the Germans arrived. Monsieur La Page sat behind the wheel of the bus marked with green and yellow colors, the sign of public transport. He hid his eyes behind his slumped shoulders. A police officer exited a building closer to the bus pushing a family into the streets. The woman shed tears in the quiet, the street filled with the new grumble of the bus, the sporadic clack of boots, and the clamor of a dropped suitcase thrown open with a shirt, a blanket, and hidden packets of food spraying across the pavement. The officer stepped on the food, pushed the woman forward, and the man dropped to his knees to grab the clothing, the blanket, the crumbs. The officer took out his baton and smacked the man across his back replacing the thud of police boots with the smash of the man's body on the ground, limp. Odette knew the type, not dead but not awake. And when the man woke, Odette wondered what he would see, a hospital bed, a jail cell?

A police officer with tufts of dark hair protruding from beneath the side of his hat squeezed past Odette. He rushed through the door trailing the smell of sweat and stale wine. His thin mustache blended him into the collective faces of French police, but his smooth cheeks gave away his youth, his need to obey, to be accepted. He made Odette think of Aloysius.

"Favre," the inspector down the street called. A short, chunky man appeared from a doorway. "Favre, this one fainted."

"Fainted?" Favre called with a voice thick with smoke. "Why? Was the Jew too afraid to take public transportation?" Favre laughed with a gravel in his lungs until a coughing fit erupted. The inspector waved Favre over, and they lifted the man into the bus leaving his open suitcase in the street.

A scream tore open Odette's building. The young officer pushed through the door carrying a girl.

"You can't. You can't. She's just a girl." The mother's voice boiled with blood, but not anger, fear. Odette had spent enough time with people at the edge of their sanity to know the difference, when all the rage they had turned to mush after realizing they had no escape. The officer said nothing as he carried the girl out. She screamed. She kicked. She flailed her small legs. But the officer held her tight. The mother cried harder.

"Please, I will go with you. Leave her alone." She fell to her knees to beg, Odette thought, but instead, the woman wrapped her arms around the officer's leg. "I will go. You do not need to take her."

The officer dropped the girl, who ran down the hall and out the door. He turned to the mother and took out his baton ready and eager to clout the woman across the jaw. She turned her head and winced in anticipation.

"Don't be stupid, boy." Agnes had poked her head through her door but didn't show her face. Odette could discern her voice through a crowd of chanting football fans. The officer looked to the headless voice, turned down to the woman, looked back at his cudgel, and hammered down dragging the lifeless body of the woman out of the building. A waiting officer collected the woman and carried her to the bus where the seats had begun filling.

"Why didn't you stop him," Odette asked Agnes.

"Why didn't you?" she spat back.

The young officer returned. Droplets of sweat dripped down his cheek. His eyes squinted in the new light peaking over the buildings causing a slight golden tint to spread across the city. Odette thought about running to her apartment, locking the door, finding a new place to hide the candlesticks. All it took was one wrong step, one knock against the hollow floor, and she'd join the woman.

"Keep your head down," Agnes whispered.

But Odette had spent too much time keeping her head down, keeping her breasts wrapped, keeping the mask on, sticking to the shadows and darkness. But Odette wanted to lift her head up in the daylight. She stepped into the officer's way. Agnes huffed.

"Pardon me," she said.

"You should stay inside, mademoiselle."

"I should say so," Odette said. "Or I might end up like that poor girl? Or perhaps her mother. Where, may I ask, are you taking them? I should say, where is that bus taking them because we both know where you dragged that poor woman."

The swagger in the officer had melted away into a puddle wet at his shoes. He stuttered in response, making Odette look into his eyes to make sure he wasn't Aloysius. But this officer had black, wavy hair and green eyes without any hint of happiness or hope left. Perhaps it had abandoned him the day the Germans arrived in Paris or maybe on the day he returned from the front, or maybe he had never been allowed at the front to begin with, so he used this moment as his war, his time on the force to prove himself a man.

"Official police business," the officer said.

"I'm sure official police business requires the cudgeling of women and children. Lord knows we need protection from the meek, mirthless, and starved. How could we ever have survived without your help, officer?"

He scoffed and entered the complex once again stepping over the trail of blood left in the hall. His feet pounded against the stone stairs with every step.

"You're going to get yourself killed," Agnes said through the cracked door.

"Where's Aloysius?" Odette said.

"At work."

"I'm sure he is. But where? You don't think—"

"I won't ask him of his business any more than I'd expect him to ask me of mine."

"That didn't answer the question," Odette said.

Agnes opened the door and poked her head out. Her gray hair had frizzled turning the air around her frantic as if it contained a life of its own pulling at each strand.

"Don't you get it, girl," Agnes seethed. "I don't want to know. Go bother some other poor old woman."

The swarm had only grown in the city. A rush of wind brushed Odette's arm. Agnes's door stood open a crack, but Agnes had disappeared. Odette still expected to find the scent of rose and sandalwood or coffee and dough from the open door, but it had felt like a lifetime ago since Agnes had any type of comfort left.

The young officer searched the halls for the girl. An older officer called for him.

"Don't bother," the older officer said. "One girl won't matter." The young officer shuffled down the steps and huffed, angered that a child had bested him, that a girl had bested him?

"Pardon me, officer," Odette said.

The young officer turned and looked up at Odette with the same youthful, eager expression he had held when first entering the complex. Except a touch of fear had crept onto his face turning the corner of his lip into a sneer showing his true youth through the wispiness of his mustache.

"Perhaps you and I will meet again, monsieur."

The young man's sneer turned into a smile. "I would like that," he said.

"I am sure you would."

And the officer blended into the river of people and faded beneath the current of screams moving toward the bus where monsieur La Page kept his face hidden behind his shoulder.

"Get in here," Agnes said, her door finally opening all the way. She grabbed Odette and pulled her inside softening the morning cries the city would not be able to pretend were the sounds of roosters. Beneath the flood of screams and stomping feet outside, Odette swore someone hid in the room sobbing.

"Take this," Agnes said and handed Odette a cup of coffee.

"Is someone else here?" Odette said.

"Of course," Agnes said. "Don't you know I make it a habit hiding people in my apartment?"

Odette shook her head. Of course, Agnes wouldn't risk her life for these people.

"It could have been any of us," Odette said.

"With what you have hidden—" Agnes said.

Agnes barely wanted to help Odette, why would she help strangers? The aroma from the cup hit Odette. It smelled rich and chocolatey, without the overwhelming smell of dandelion and endives from the chicory they've been drinking.

"Where did you get real coffee?" she asked.

"You don't need to know," Agnes said. "Just drink it."

"I don't understand," Odette said.

Agnes sighed. "Girl, it's better if you don't know."

Odette waved away Agnes's response. "I mean about the people, about the officers, in broad daylight. I won't even—" Odette's hands trembled. The coffee cup tinkered and tinned against the saucer.

"No, you wouldn't, would you," Agnes said. "Do you think yourself a monster?"

Odette didn't respond.

"it's ok, girl. I'm asking."

Odette inspected her feet, the scuffs on her shoes she hadn't shined away, the way her skirt needed hemming. Before the Germans arrived, these little details would have made her stand out, would have shown her differences from the rest of the Parisian women who always looked well kept, fashionable, the object of European affection, but now these small details helped her blend in with most of the women in the city. They walked with wooden soles and clacked down the alleyways with a pathetic percussion that contrasted the German tourists and soldiers. It embodied the differences. The Germans, oiled, clean, and modern, walking through the city of Paris, a relic of Old-World charm with colorful storefronts filled with people who resembled wooden dolls. It started with their soles but worked its way up until the best they could do was stare when a German entered the café or pin a yellow star to their dog in solidarity with people they never cared for in the first place, people they once called neighbors, or maybe even friends, people Odette had become a part of without ever knowing what that meant.

"You, the people in this city, all want to believe—hell, we hope to believe—monsters only attack at night," Agnes said. "We want to know our monsters so we can avoid them. But take a look at them. You saw them— boys, men, fat, old, tall, thin, even good looking. You saw them, girl. These monsters want to be seen in the daylight. They want you to know."

Agnes encouraged Odette to drink one last sip of the coffee and took the cup away.

"Know what?" Odette asked.

"That they can kill you just as easily in the daylight," Agnes said.

Twenty-six

Since Odette had helped Ilse, the hospital had the same type of light as a cloudy day when the sun hid behind the gray sky letting faded bits of yellow through, enough for daylight, but otherwise no different than the slate of the night sky. At first the days seemed harmless enough with Odette helping Ilse with patients and never speaking about the bear.

Rumors crept through the halls about the disappearance, but most of the staff settled on the information Ilse provided. She had transferred back to Germany. "She couldn't stand the taste of French beer," Ilse had said. The staff laughed. But not Odette.

Odette continued issuing gauze to patients, assessing their wounds, and helping doctors diagnose illnesses. The patients all seemed so timid, scared, reprehensible in Odette's mind. She had watched men in the face of death, as she posed as the face of death, and seen their moral texture, their dignity, their attachment to pride, dissolve into something less than watery shit as if they had turned into shit themselves, a watery, malleable figure stinking of acid and rotten butter. They would plead for Odette to stop. The men always devolved into clichés, offering her unlimited monies, unlimited food, endless supplies of clothing, and even, in the case of the low-level bureaucrat, an amount of favors disappearing those Odette had placed on her list so she didn't have to work so hard. They never believed that once they wound up in front of her bound and gagged, it was already too late, that she looked at them as the face of unwavering Death, with hands stiff as rigor mortis and resolve much more concrete than theirs, because they, like her, had been flawed. Only she had discovered it; they couldn't go unpunished.

Had the bear held the same look on her face? Was it different for a woman? Her mother hadn't begged for her own life but for that of Odette's, for Odette's purity, future, sanity, but with the grocer went the spoils. And with it brought only the face of death Odette wore. She had wondered about the day Death would take a new face, a new disguise, and how she would stare at Death: with dignity, with disgrace, with welcoming arms, or with the same fear that gripped these *proud* men, these *aristocratic* men. She dreamed, partially, that in those moments she would look into death's gunmetal gray eyes and smile with grace and die, *like a woman*.

But the patients in the hospital didn't even fight. They entered the hospital like timid dogs shaking in the cold without a sense of will. If they couldn't carry a sense of pride, of reason—maybe they could survive, maybe their empty eyes wouldn't stick to Odette as she walked through the room—of course the patients would wind up on the gurneys bound for the morgue. Of course they would die in the same forgettable quiver in which they arrived. Odette couldn't forget them—Odette couldn't forgive them.

Each patient burned their memories inside her mind and filled her with hate and resentment. She would dress their wounds, and they would stare at the floor. She would take their temperatures, and they'd stare at the wall. She would reach to console them, touch them, and they would cower away. She would smile, and they would cringe. She would say hello, and they would scream, to the point they sounded like rats, the same rats that scurried through the trash and the sewers.

Their screams turned to screeches. Their fingers turned to claws. They moved with a scurry and scraped their nails against the metal bedframes and tiles. Because they acted like rats, they turned into rats, and Odette treated them like rats, unable to see them for anything more than vermin, until the smell became unbearable to her; their matted fur reeked of wet garbage, whether they had just arrived in the hospital or had been in the ward for weeks. The smell probably killed them in the end, an infection Ilse never found, or one that didn't show in the wounds Odette carefully tended to daily like some sort of rot only Odette knew, resulting in her always wearing a mask, adding another screen between her and the patients—not patients, vermin.

Then Odette asked Ilse to enter the room, a gallery beyond the hospital beds. It was a hall past the nurses who dressed patients with bandages, beyond the private stations where the staff attended to German tourists with scraped noses after a drunken fall, or SS officers with venereal diseases, or SS officers who had a proclivity for nurses' outfits. Ilse carried the key around her neck, like a piece of jewelry of which she was proud, one that should have glinted in the light, but not beneath the hospital light because the hospital light was too dim, flickered too much—the hospital light made Odette squint endlessly, never supposed to be used for long periods of time, hoping people would get in and out quick, a color reminiscent of faded candles just before they burnt down to the nub, with one dying gasp of wick and wax remaining.

The stench of the room hit Odette through the mask like a mallet. She fumbled backward and reached for the wall. Ilse watched with intent, with the focus of study, wondering how Odette would react to the room, but Odette had only smelled it, finding the scent of decay, akin to the back of the butcher shops when they would throw the innards out onto the stone. The blood would seep into the cracks until the dogs and cats tore at the soft, graying viscera and lapped at the dried crusting carnage.

It was always worse in summer, when the heat turned the intestines that much faster; the rot attracted the flies, the flies laid the maggots to the point no one could walk down the street or open their window without inhaling a mouthful of flies. Odette expected, even with the mask over her mouth, to crunch a fistful of flies between her teeth with every breath. Patients lay in bed on sheets smothered with dried brown, acid yellow, layered with sweat that had dried, moistened, and dried again. Odette wandered along the rows of beds, trying to count the patients in the bed, in the room, but lost count near fifty with more to go. The women's hair had been shaved or fallen out in clumps leaving patches. Their cheeks sallow, their noses the only appendage keeping their faces from looking like skeletons buried deep in the ground for years. Their arms resembled tree branches in the winter, when the lack of leaves showed true frailty, an unnoticed feebleness shaped by the elements, reaching out from the proud trunk. If Odette touched their desiccated skin, they would surely flake and float away, disappearing before her eyes like mounds of ash in the wind. The rows seemed to stretch forever, far longer than the building could accommodate, farther than the possible, as if mirrors had been placed at opposite ends reflecting infinite beds soiled with those Odette couldn't stand and, before entering the room, thought deserved to die.

"Is it what you expected?" Ilse said from behind, shattering the fugue Odette had stepped into.

"I'm sorry?" Odette said. The smell of lilies brough Odette back to the room, back to Ilse, the doctor's blonde hair a light in the dark room, the aroma a guide out and way from the stench of decay.

"I had seen you walk by the room before. There was always a…curiosity?"

"It was the only room in the hospital that was locked," Odette said.

"That isn't true," Ilse said.

Odette shook her head. "I meant, it was the only room not everyone was allowed into. A door with only one key—"

A groan grew from the bed beside Odette. A man whose nose had caved in; his two front teeth had cracked. The groan turned to a gurgle. Odette turned to the man, noticed the way his eyes kept shut, his eyelids too heavy to open in his weakened state.

"Hides something, yes?" Ilse said. Odette nodded. "You did not care for these people."

Odette turned to Ilse. Her eyes grew wide with terror, confronted by the truth she had ignored, not that she didn't care for those that walked in the door, but the fact that she had forgotten they were people, refused to believe they were people, and had seen them for too long as less than animals, as insects meant for the bottom of her shoe. She gasped at the realization. The thick, putrid air caught in her throat. She coughed and took off the mask, expecting to find masticated flies drowning in the spittle. She found neither. She took another deep breath. Ilse patted her on the back.

"You were the first to wear a mask in this hospital. The other nurses, the orderlies, they followed you. They must have thought you knew something they didn't. Do you know why I brought you in here?"

Odette welled with tears, lingering on the brink, ready to drop, as she tried desperately to keep them inside. *They are, from the smell*, she told herself, but knew better deep down as she looked away from the man on the bed.

"You had started with such…shall we say, empathy?" Ilse said. "But there was always something different about the way you worked, I noticed. From the beginning you had a methodical approach. You focused on the task at hand. When you touched a patient out of kindness, it didn't look like you wanted to but had to. If you had the choice, you wouldn't have touched them at all. You had a tone too, a flatness hidden beneath your words. I heard it. I don't think many others did.

"Then you changed. You stopped touching them all together. You stopped trying. You didn't see them as sick anymore. You saw them as lost. Why reach out to a dead man?"

Odette drifted back to the times in the basement with the men strung on their backs, a rag placed in their mouths, their screams muffled by the fabric, forcing them to swallow their past until, Odette always hoped, they choked on it. But they never did. Her favorite moment would be the first cut along their wrists, along the artery, upwards, with the skin splitting, as simple as slicing the seams of a dress, rewarded by the effortless flow of blood, a millisecond of silence, the tap of liquid in the metal bucket, and then the men would cry, the tears trailing up their eyelids, over their foreheads, and onto the floor. At the last moment their eyelids would flutter. Their screams would gurgle. Their breaths labored. Their gaze would turn opaque. Odette would lean down, brush the final tears away, and whisper into their ear, "Maybe one day someone will forgive you," reaching out with one final hope to the dying men.

"I knew it was time," Ilse said. "I knew you could handle this place now. And then you asked to come in. And I could use your help."

A nurse brought Ilse a tray with a syringe. Ilse grabbed the syringe. The nurse placed the tray on a side-table and helped lift the man. He leaned against the bedframe with his chin slumped into his chest, his eyes still closed. He breathed slow, shallow, labored breaths. He would be dead soon, Odette knew, by the sound of the gush and murmur in his lungs when his chest heaved, similar to the last gasp of dying men. Ilse rubbed the man's arm with alcohol and readied to plunge the needle. She leaned over.

"Stop," Odette said.

Ilse turned to Odette with a simple, twisted smirk. Odette held out her hand, ready to take the syringe. Ilse backed away from the *patient*.

"Show me I wasn't wrong. Show me you are ready for this room."

"What is it?" Odette asked.

"It will help," Ilse said.

"Help who?"

Ilse took a breath, made a deep sigh. She scratched her nose. Odette realized the smell didn't bother her anymore. *With time,* she thought, *I can get used to anything.* "The world has cracks and fissures in it," Ilse said. Odette nodded. "It has mountains and valleys. Then you find canyons, gorges, or even cracks in the street. The world isn't smooth. But we figure out ways to use the world to our advantage no matter how big those cracks grow. This is the same. Medicine is not smooth. But we use what we can, when we can, to smooth cracks, build along the canyons, conquering the mountains. Do you understand?"

Odette nodded. Ilse urged Odette to take the syringe. The man continued his laborious breaths. Odette took it. She looked back at Ilse for a brief second, finding whatever chasm had separated them before, narrowed. She plunged the syringe into the man's arm. The resistance between her thumb and the plunger grew, like trying to shove a fork into solid stone. She pressed harder. The syringe budged and slowly the liquid dove into the man's body. The man didn't react. He kept breathing. Odette leaned in close to listen. The nurse took notes, jotting down the time of day, the man's reaction, the amount of medicine they had used. His breath slowed. His eyelids never opened but fluttered. Tears formed on his cheeks. Had he been crying the whole time? Had he been aware, listening, knowing he was a small part of a big machine, one that paved over the hills and valleys to create a uniform world free of the fear of undignified death, the way they—she—Odette—had made him die? She leaned in closer to his ear and whispered, "Maybe one day someone will forgive me."

The man stopped breathing. His arms splayed over the sheets. The light in the room flickered with white rather than yellow.

"The dosage might need to be upped," Ilse said with a dry, pedagogical tone. "There are no mistakes when studying medicine, only teachable moments." Odette kept the tears at bay, stood, and nodded. The nurse walked away.

Ilse rubbed her fingers on Odette's shoulder. It made Odette feel fragile. It made Odette feel like a child. It made Odette want to lean in close and rest her head into the woman's neck, to find the scent of lilies drifting off her skin.

"You can take the remainder of the day off," Ilse said. "I am sure this room came as quit the surprise." Ilse walked away along the infinite rows leaving Odette beside the bed, beside the man whose name she didn't even know, whose life she had taken without knowing if he deserved it, whether he had children, a wife, a brother, a sister, a father who waited for him, a mother who doted on him, a cat who wanted milk in the evening, a girlfriend wanting flowers before dinner. The orderlies appeared out of the ether, took the man onto a gurney, and left, leaving Odette beside the bed stripped of sheets, with the stained mattress, absent of any sign of the man she hadn't healed.

Twenty-seven

The morning gray had faded, but the cold lingered in the air. It bit at Odette's skin, flushed her cheeks, and made her nose run. She wiped it away on her sleeve, the same as the boys who fought over the ball. They kicked at one another's shins, threw elbows at their chests, headbutted with everyone watching. The game took place in the street. One good thing about the lack of cars, Odette thought, they rarely had to stop to let someone pass. Instead, people watched from their windows, cheered for boy they knew best, or perhaps jeered the boy they knew best.

Odette had played with these same boys since childhood. And since the arrival of German soldiers and tourists, it seemed the only thing that made them all feel like children again, for Odette, almost the only thing. From the street, she could keep track of the steam rising out of the cellar, hear the puffs and groan of the kiln as it heated, dried, and cooled the ceramics of what would soon become past tense. A man who *was*, not *is*. A man who people could refer to only as a memory rather than a nightmare.

"Your left," Aloysius said. He passed the ball to Odette. She trapped it with her right foot, touched the ball to the outside, and quickly took her shot. The keeper trapped the ball and held it tight. He rolled the ball to his teammate, winced, and rubbed the point on his chest where the ball had hit him. Odette smirked before chasing after the ball. She preferred the brutal and rough nature of street soccer instead of the regulated soccer that took place on the fields around Paris. Just like in life, Odette knew, the rules only worked if both teams followed them, but usually one team followed the rules, the other defied the rules, and the cheaters always won. She thought of the Germans.

In the street, they were all on equal footing. Both teams could elbow, both could kick their shins, cup their ears, or even grab their balls and twist, which only happened once. But whatever one team could do, the other could respond in kind. On the field, Odette had too often felt subjugated by the rules, a slave to her inability to throw a punch at one of the men who rubbed their hands on her chest during a corner kick or another man who tried to stick his finger in her crotch during a throw-in. She stood on their field, kicked their ball, scored on their goal, and yet they thought they owned her. During a penalty kick, she paid the man back—no, not a man, a boy—who had tried to stick his fingers in her crotch. He stood behind her, his breath hot and rotten with egg. He inched closer to her rubbing himself against her back. She reached behind her, grabbed his balls, and squeezed. He screamed. Then she pulled down until his scream turned to silent gasps. He fell to the ground. The teammate kicked the ball. She found it. Took it. And was then removed from the game. But not before the boy was taken off the field, unable to walk on his own. But Odette knew he had gotten lucky. She could have met him off the field instead.

She passed the ball to Louis, who had grown into a great handler after he healed from Odette's elbow to his nose nearly a decade ago. His brother Francois never did get over it. He would flinch whenever Odette walked past until he moved to Lyon. Louis dribbled around the defender, shoved his way past the goalkeeper, and tapped the ball into the makeshift goal. They cheered with their feet tapping against the cobblestones. The crowd booed or clapped with nothing more to do on the Tuesday afternoon. Then the crowd hushed. A troupe of German SS walked down the sidewalk. The leader carried the look of an arrogant lost tourist who refused to admit he had taken a wrong turn.

"Ah, yes," he said. "I knew there was a game around here somewhere."

He turned to the other soldiers. They nodded and gestured around the street. The crowd remained silent with the hiss and groan of the kiln suddenly chaotic in Odette's ears.

"May we join?" the leader said. "We may not live up to *French* standards, but we have competed well in Germany." Aloysius held the ball and walked up to the man, a contrast in a mirror of air; the German chiseled from marble with honey hair, Aloysius made of glass with curls of mud dangling from his head.

"I'm sorry Truppführer," he said. "We already have full teams."

"Come, now. I'm sure we could make something work."

Aloysius looked back to the team, to the players, to the onlookers from the apartments. He gave a slight shrug, as if asking the crowd, *what can I do?*

"I know you, yes?" the soldier said.

"I don't' believe so," Aloysius said, his cheeks reddening as if splattered with blood, the blush of embarrassment, not the cold. Odette knew his faces, how he hid from people when the center of attention, and the last thing anyone wanted in front of the Germans was to be the center of attention.

"It'll come to me," the Truppführer said. "I'm very good with faces." He took off his hat, placed it in his jacket, took off his jacket, folded it, and placed it away from the street. He rolled up his sleeves revealing chiseled forearms. His hair slicked back. A smirk plastered his face. "Shall we play then?"

He stepped onto the street with his team. Louis and Aloysius avoided him like a raincloud on a summer's day. Odette gravitated to him.

"Wait, wait," Truppführer said. "You are a woman."

"And you are not," Odette said.

"She doesn't play like a woman," Louis said.

"And you don't need to play like a gentleman if that's what you are worried about," Odette said.

"Fine, fine," Truppführer said.

The air had a faint scent of cedar and tobacco that drifted from the German. Odette stayed in that aroma for a moment, too eager to think of the times in the country before the Germans arrived, before the grocer pounded on her door. At first, no one on Truppführer's team wanted to pass him the ball. By not passing him the ball, Odette had no one to defend. Truppführer took his fate in his own hands. His teammate had double coverage and still wouldn't pass the ball. Truppführer ran behind him, stole the ball from his own player, and dribbled around the defenders. Odette ran after Truppführer. She caught him quickly, tried to put her foot in front of the ball and got an elbow in the nose. She fell to the ground. Blood trickled onto her lips. Truppführer kicked, scored, and celebrated with his team.

Louis helped Odette up from the floor.

"It's ok," she said. "The irony isn't lost on me."

Louis smiled kindly. The dimples made his cheeks look chubby, the last baby fat left on his entire body.

"You elbowing me in the nose was the best thing that ever happened to me," he said. "For Francois, not so much." They both laughed. Odette dabbed the blood away with her sleeve, letting it join the dried mucus around the cuff.

"He learns quickly," Odette said. "Perhaps he needs a different lesson."

"Keep your head," Aloysius said.

"Or what?" Odette said. "He'll ship me away because I beat him at football?"

"Do we really know?"

"Maybe he's right," Louis said.

"Is that all?" Truppführer yelled. "This is a competition, is it not?"

Louis, Aloysius, and Odette took their positions. Their goalkeeper rolled the ball to Aloysius. It always amazed Odette how his limp almost vanished when he played soccer. He shuffled and hopped, ran and side-stepped but never limped, almost as if he was meant for motion. Too often his fear kept him stiff and still. When the ball reached his feet, he couldn't stop moving.

He passed to Louis, who tapped the ball and touched it to Odette. Truppführer waited for her. He kept his eyes on the ball and not her, a constant error with the boys she played with, who easily fell to the wrong side anticipating a different move. The ball felt heavy. The cobblestones pounded against the pads of her feet harder than usual. Truppführer stuck his foot between her feet, avoided the ball, and let her spill onto the stone. Her skin scaped at the palms. Her knee thudded against the ground. She ignored the pain, stood up, and ran back to Truppführer. The cedar aroma created a mist around him. She broke through and dug her elbow into his ribs shoving him down. The crowd fell away in a hush. Odette stole the ball, rounded the fallen Truppführer, and broke down the street kicking the ball into upper left-hand corner of the goal.

Louis cheered. Aloysius shook his head. The crowd stayed silent. Truppführer stood up and dusted his hands together. He walked over to Odette and stared down at her.

"You may be more aggressive than I anticipated."

"We're sorry Truppführer—" Aloysius said.

Truppführer raised his hand. "No, no. I enjoy the challenge. You remind me of a wild boar. Have you ever hunted a wild boar? They are quite exhilarating. Stubborn and violent. They'll circle their adversary and attack from behind. I've hunted my share of wild boar."

"I have hunted my share, as well Truppführer," Odette said.

"Of feral boar?"

"Of feral men." She smiled.

Truppführer laughed. He placed his hand on his belly but nothing jiggled. "You remind me very much of my sister. But she never would have let me get back up. "

"The thought crossed my mind," she said. Aloysius nudged her.

Truppführer held out his hand to Odette. "Good game."

She shook it. And with that, the thought of following him into the night evaporated with the steam from the kiln. She would no more punish Truppführer for winning the game than she could imagine him punishing her for the same.

Twenty-eight

The sweat collected beneath Agnes's armpits as she walked causing an audible squish with every step. She was too old to mind the noise, but it felt the same as wearing wet socks as if she had taken them and shoved them under her arms the way she had for Aloysius when he had a fever, but the fever stemmed from the city and not her body, as if it rejected her, those around her, or perhaps tried to purge itself of the soldiers dressed in black laughing in the cafes as it absorbed the heat. Except those men, those in black, and shimmering silver, and polished boots, could refresh their bodies with cool cream, with honey tea. Agnes's mouth salivated from the thought of the tea, the idea of mint and honey brought back from North Africa, the way her father drank it. The simple combination kept them refreshed as a breeze swept through the open door and into the courtyard; as others thought they needed an escape to the mountains; Agnes and her father would sip the tea and felt their bodies relax from the inside out.

She strolled through the garden at Parc Monceau hoping the shade beneath the canopy would shield her from the weather. Instead, it made the day's warmth more oppressive, turning the moisture heavy and making it feel as though she carried a boulder on her back. A group of boys stood at the edge of the pond watching the water lilies. Except they licked their lips as if thirsty, as if wanting to lap up the pond near the stone bridge. And they did, Agnes thought, except not with their mouths but with their skin, as they sat like sponges in the water and soaked up the cool, refreshing feeling all over their bodies rather than stay stifled in their clothing, the garments their mothers most likely made them wear, especially on a hot day, when their shorts would only itch more and their collars would constrict around their necks as if the very garments they wore attacked them, killing them slowly.

The smell of nearly rotten fruit wafted up from her grocery bag. Food had become the endless focus of Agnes's day. She didn't know if it was the heat or simply the bad crop from the grocer, but all she could grab had already started turning. She had visited four grocers to find a half bag of fruit and a few vegetables ripe enough to eat, ready to cook, even if the last thing she wanted was turn on the stove and let the fire roast her kitchen more than the day already had. The turnips and Jerusalem artichokes she tried growing in the apartment had died in the winter frost, too cold and bitter for even the roots nobody wanted. The rabbits she had tried to keep fed. Agnes ate them shortly after. The nights only made the intensity of the temperature worse because she expected the darkness to bring a different climate, a touch of softness, but unending heat only built anger, only grew tension, and made her blood boil.

The boys stood longingly at the pond, their eyes growing even more intense at the possibility of plunging into the water. A year ago, they would have thrown sticks at the ducks who dipped their feathers beneath the surface bathing or dunked their beaks into ripples in search of food. No one had seen the ducks; no one spoke about where they had gone. Same with the pigeons, as if one day they just disappeared from the city or knew better than to bathe in the fountains anymore. One boy broke the delirium. He slipped off his shoes, sat on the ground, and pulled off his socks. The other boy watched in amazement and horror, his mouth a veritable fish unable to close and breathe. The sockless boy did not jump or plunge into the water but slowly touched his toes to the pond as if worried it would swallow him up. He smiled and laughed. He flicked water at the second boy. Once it looked like the first boy was safe, the second boy followed, taking his shoes off, then socks, and joining the first boy in the water with the simple act of compliance making them much more comfortable, much more capable to endure.

Two officers, one a *Polizeiführer*, stood in the shade near the bridge and watched the boys. The boys' mother called to them. The fear in the boys' eyes showed like a rabbit before the hunter. They scrambled out of the water only making their clothes wetter, splashed and soaked in random places. They huddled to get their socks on but stumbled to the floor with dirt caking their legs, their socks, their shorts, clinging to their skin. If they had only taken their time, Agnes thought, panic won't get them anywhere.

Their mother turned the corner on the footpath and found the boys. She started screaming, slapping the back of their heads. The Polizeiführer laughed with a soft, jovial smile with a touch of chalk in his lungs from smoking a pipe like a new grandfather watching his first grandchild stumble and fall after attempting to walk. The boys put on their shoes, and their mother pulled them away from the edge of the pond by their ears, one pinched between the fingers of each hand, the boys bent at an awkward angle leaning down to their matriarch even as she yelled, "Wait until your father hears about this," but Agnes knew their punishment was their mother's alone, and while their father may have been a screen of control, their mother held the power, and at that moment she used it to cuff and clasp their ears and guide them all the way home while the Polizeiführer stood laughing; a Frenchwoman's worst nightmare, a reason for a German to laugh at them.

The man had a gentle smile and soft-looking skin like milk. For a moment, Agnes thought the man could have been a secretary back in Germany or a librarian who always misplaced his glasses on top of a book to which he had grown attached. But his uniform betrayed a hardness even if not visible on his skin. Sometimes Agnes had to remind herself that ugliness or evil didn't get a mark, she knew firsthand; she thought of Odette and the ugliness surrounding her but never touching her, marking her like Quasimodo, except he was never evil or bad—rather he acted as the opposite, as the embodiment of Agnes's point.

A warm breeze rustled through the park. Agnes caught the scent of stale and near rotting fruit. Her stomach rumbled. The cries of the mother and her boys had faded by now, but their looks of contentment remained drawn over the stoic surface of the pond broken by a reflection of the Polizeiführer. Agnes sighed and took it as a sign.

It took Agnes three tries before getting the Polizeiführer's attention.

"Good afternoon, madam," the Polizeiführer said as Agnes approached.

"I have—" Agnes said. She stopped and looked at her shoes, the point of which she felt with her toe about ready to poke through. It was about time to take out a new pair stuffed in the closet behind the base of papers.

"What was that?" the Polizeiführer said.

"Good afternoon," Agnes said. She nodded her head and hesitated to take a step. The hot breeze returned and with it, the scent of rotten peaches. She stopped and looked at the Polizeiführer noticing how dry he was. It only made her sweat more. "I know of…the rumors."

The Polizeiführer didn't respond and instead raised his eyebrows and looked down at Agnes. The feeling of wet socks stuffed under her arms returned. She wished she had joined the boys by dipping her feet in the pond.

"I thought—" she said. "I had wanted—good afternoon, Polizeiführer." She turned to walk away.

"That fruit does not look fresh," the Polizeiführer said. "Perhaps two or three days too old, I would think. Perhaps you should get a new grocer." Agnes nodded. "If you would like, I know a great grocer. A French grocer.

If you do not mind my saying," the Polizeiführer lowered his voice as if in a conspiratorial whisper, "all the best grocers are French." Agnes nodded again. She forced a small smile not knowing if the tone made her want to vomit, scream, or make friends. The Polizeiführer took a pen and scribbled an address on a piece of paper. "Go to this address, and you should never have rotten berries again." He winked.

Agnes knew the address and knew she couldn't be seen walking through those doors.

"Thank you Polizeiführer."

"I'm sure I will see you around at the grocer's," the Polizeiführer said. And Agnes nodded once more knowing she would go, knowing she would sit at his desk and tell the Polizeiführer exactly what she had planned to tell him now but couldn't. And in return, he would give her ripe fruit, fresh vegetables, and the chance for her stomach to stop growling, a chance for her to look as contented as those boys in the pond. And all she had to do was tell the Polizeiführer what she had already planned on. And she would tell him, giving him names and apartment numbers. All of them gone the moment she had felt their names on her lips even before they slipped into sound.

Twenty-nine

On the night the music stopped completely, Odette had returned home late from the hospital. Odette had expected mutants with rat noses and half-scalped heads to hobble through the streets attempting to grab each passerby with claws, not hands, stuffed with garbage and blood between skin and nail. The night had filled with people Odette swore she knew, without the rat noses, without pockets stuffed with gold, without warts and shriveled skin, and hunchbacks. They were fragile men, proud women, families with fur coats and gold rings, husbands and wives with patched coats and holes in their socks, each as scared as the next, unsure of what would come.

Instead, Odette returned from the hospital after having helped Ilse inject six subjects, not patients, because they didn't have the same status as a patient. They didn't deserve the same courtesy as a patient, who would have needed a savior. These subjects didn't need protection from life; life needed protection from them. If one broke free, then so would Death, brought by disease, pestilence, the plague of those lesser than them—than Odette, than Ilse, than Aloysius, those too weak to carry on living. Odette

192

brought mercy, the angel of mercy, which was more than any angel gave to her…or her mother.

Before she left, Ilse pressed cheek to Odette's, once, twice, three times, and on the fourth, Ilse brushed her lips against the corner of Odette's lips. And for a brief moment, Odette felt the mercy.

Aloysius stood on the stoop with his hair gnarled in his fingers. His eyes bulged red. Officers of the SS stood outside the door. Odette paused at the corner of her apartment waiting to catch his eye for a sign that they had come for her. The city lights no longer twinkled around the streets at night. They had faded to something more sinister, more generic, akin to the bland yellow of the hospital. They polluted the night sky and cast a piss-colored glow against the once beautiful buildings of the city. Instead of palaces, they looked stained by urine in the night and ashen gray in the morning, sick with the rest of the city by the occupation, with no German doing good except for Ilse—with the help of Odette. The officers stood beside Agnes and spoke louder than necessary. Their respectful French pummeled the walls and the cobblestones. Odette expected to see dents around the street where their words had landed. They thanked Agnes for her help, except they called it "Patriotism." They wanted to help scourge France of undesirables the way they wanted to save Germany from the same blight, but they called them fleas or lice, less than human, less than dogs, less than the fish in the Seine.

Mr. Tureshko exited the building, followed by two soldiers. He seemed so small with his small hunch, his tweed coat, his hands pressed to the violin case tucked into his chest. The soldiers didn't look at him but stared ahead, worried they might take pity on someone so feeble, but not if he wasn't human, Odette thought. He looked human enough. That, said the propaganda, was what made them so dangerous.

Monsieur Tureshko shuffled down the stairs clutching a small case. The liver spots on this his forehead looked more prominent in the morning light like fresh scabs brutally opened instead of the natural decomposition of old men in a decaying world. Odette had told him the man at the café had never showed up, sparing the old man the details of the visit, of what could have been his future—buried in a pit and dusted with quicklime to cover the smell, to increase the rate of decomposition. Odette had spared Mr. Tureshko that fate, for what? For this? His soft feet once soared across the stages of Europe, "like swans," he had said. But now he shambled and slouched down the hall keeping tempo with the thump and thud of the gendarme's boots stomping down the stairs. Monsieur Tureshko stopped in front of Odette and nodded his head.

"You don't have to," Odette said. She tapped the soft fabric of his tweed coat. She glared at the soldier. Aloysius tried to pull her aside. The soldier turned his eyes away attending to an interesting crack in the doorway.

"It has been a blessed life," Monsieur Tureshko said. He leaned in to give Odette a kiss on her cheek, then the other but lingered leaving the scent of sautéed onions in her nose and whispered gently, knowingly, "Sadly, you won't find any more books in my flat."

"Maybe I can still find music," she said.

He opened his mouth to speak but the soldiers pushed him along.

She grabbed his arm with more resolve hoping to leave a trace of her fingertips in his clothing, as if those could keep him rooted to the floor and allow her to pull him back from the bus the way a fishing line would. He gave a light, nearly imperceptible shake of his head. Odette let go and Monsieur Tureshko joined the street beneath the flood of people watching from their windows, where the afternoon quiet had shattered into a collage of silent screams, a collection of imperceptible noises to which Odette couldn't connect, too often comfortable in the familiar cry of a single person—man, whose voice rasped with tension after straining his vocal cords for so long before all the hope died leaving only resolve.

They took him into the wagon and stole him away. Time didn't slow. No one popped out of the windows to save him. The snow didn't fall early offering a surprise for the Bosch and a quick escape for the man. He stepped out of the doorway, walked to the car, stepped inside, and by the time the doors closed on him, the rest of the world had already forgotten.

The officers thanked Agnes. She stood stoic, faceless, a white wall against the endless black buildings. The car drove away. Aloysius didn't look up. Odette walked closer to the door, to home, which in the absence of music felt empty, in the absence of the scent of sautéed onions felt soulless. She walked slowly so her footsteps wouldn't clack against the stone.

"Pull your head up, child," Agnes said. The venom in her voice poisoned the air. "You are not so valiant."

Aloysius pulled at the threads of his dark hair, the black deeper than night, black enough to find streaks of blue in the right light, in the golden daylight, which Paris hadn't seen since the occupation began.

"I am better than—"

"Are you?" Agnes said. "I saw no fight in you. I never see any fight in you. Not unless you count that crazy girl in front of you. You spend more time trying to impress her than trying to stand up for yourself."

"Good evening, Agnes," Odette said.

Agnes's voice shrank but the spite held the words firm. "Good evening."

"What happened to Mr. Tureshko?"

"It is none of your concern."

"Aloysius?"

"He had nothing to do with it either," Agnes said.

"I wanted to know if he was ok," Odette said. "He looks distraught."

"He is as fine as ever; no thanks to you."

Aloysius leaned his back against the complex, his feet planted on the floor as he crouched. He hadn't looked up from the cracks on the sidewalk, the cracks that led to the ghost of where the car had been parked, the path Mr. Tureshko had walked.

"I don't understand," Odette said.

"Of course, you don't," Agnes said. "You never do, and you will bring death to us all because of it."

Aloysius stood, wiped the wet away from his cheeks, and grabbed Odette's hand. He paused in front of his mother and pulled himself to his full, wiry height. For a moment, he looked like a man, not a boy, with a broad chest, full arms, thick neck, and the muddy hair falling around his strong cheeks. He peered down at his mother until her body shrank back. Aloysius pulled Odette into the complex bound for her flat. Agnes's body remained tired and small and overcompensated with her voice—loud, shrill, and carrying. "That is the only courage you ever had, boy. She won't always be around to stoke that fire…" Aloysius slammed the door to Odette's apartment. He ran to the sink and vomited. Odette poured a glass of water and left it on the counter for when Aloysius recovered. It wasn't the first time he had wound himself up so much. Aloysius washed the vomit from the sink and gulped down the glass of water. Odette waited until he caught his breath. She sat on her chair facing the window. Martine rubbed his raggedy fur against Aloysius's leg. The cat hated bathing in autumn and waited until Odette tried to bathe him before he groomed himself again.

Aloysius sat on the floor and rested his head against Odette's knees.

"He's Jewish," Aloysius said.

Odette said nothing. She knew Mr. Tureshko was Jewish. He had fled from Russia to Poland after the Pogroms and found refuge in Paris after that. He didn't talk much, worried about his accent, his grasp of French, even though it was always better than most native speakers. He spent more time playing music, music he wrote, music he copied, music he found somewhere in the depths of the forgotten caverns of Parisian history when composers, writers, artists settled in the city to grow. Some grew too large and floated away. Others shrank too small and disappeared. Mr. Turehsko didn't grow one way or the other. He fit perfectly into his quiet, musical life on the fifth floor.

"What's the difference between a Jew, a Christian, and a Muslim?" Odette's mother once asked. Odette shrugged. She tried to imagine the different skin tones, the way they prayed, the gods they believed in, the way they smelled but knew her mother wasn't asking about these. They ate differently, prayed differently, spoke differently.

"Nothing," her mother said. She pointed to the differences between French people that weren't any of those religions, then those that were, and showed how they all acted the same at the end of the day; the lesson became much clearer after Agnes showed Odette the candleholders. But the longer the Germans occupied France the more her mother seemed wrong. The more the French turned on their own, Odette wondered if there was a difference in how they viewed Jews and themselves. Those who turned on one another called the SS because a neighbor had fur, had pearls, had furniture to trade in exchange for cheese, wine, and coffee. They wanted to be good citizens—they claimed—to turn in those who never fit the model French citizen. But greed was often as powerful and venomous as jealousy, Odette knew. How long until someone turned on her, without ever knowing the truth?

"My mother turned him in," Aloysius said.

Odette stirred. The pressure of his head dug into her knees, but she wouldn't dare move him. "She turned him in? But she—"

"Would do anything to protect herself," Aloysius said.

"Or you," she mumbled.

"You heard her. It isn't me she's protecting."

"It isn't always what it looks like." Odette hoped she was right, hoped there was more beneath the action, but Agnes had always said, *you are what you do*. Odette could only judge Agnes's actions, and not her intentions.

"It always has been what it looks like," Aloysius said. He shook his head and sighed. "Why would it be different now? For Bananas."

"What?"

"She told me; she gave up Mr. Tureshko for a bunch of bananas."

Odette looked back on the previous months and wondered where she had been. She had been spending more time at the hospital, more time with Ilse, and never once questioned where the subjects came from, but the endless supply became clear. Maybe by tomorrow Mr. Tureshko would show up in the room and Odette could quietly slip him out the back of the hospital, shoo him away like a stray pet needing freedom.

"Do you feel safe?"

Aloysius shrugged. "They know her now. They know she'll help. They trust her, so she said."

"So she thinks," Odette said.

"I wanted to—"

"You couldn't," Odette said. "They would have killed both of you. What good would that do?"

"She is right," Aloysius said. "I'm a coward."

"No. She doesn't know you."

"She's my mother."

"That just makes it worse."

Aloysius turned to Odette's knees. He kissed her skin lightly. It tingled up her thigh. Martine closed his eyes and purred. Odette combed her fingers through Aloysius's hair. It felt like a mixture of silk and cotton. He lifted his face to hers and kissed her lips, softly, gently, quietly. The clock read 9.05. The music wouldn't crescendo tonight. The chilled autumn breeze carried emptiness. Odette guided Aloysius from the floor. She dropped her coat down. She pulled his coat away.

"I am sure," she said before he had a chance to ask. He nodded and rubbed his hands against her shoulders, inching towards the buttons on her uniform. She had never spent much time imagining how it would feel, how it would happen, or where, or when. It seemed right now, in the forced silence of the night, without Paganini, without the racket of pots and pans.

"We can do important work here. We can make a difference. You can make a difference."

"How?" Aloysius said. "I've heard the rumors. Is this what Mr. Tureshko deserves? What any of them deserve?"

"It isn't true. It can't be." But Odette looked at her hands and saw the ghosts tainting her fingers. But it was for prosperity, for humanity. A broken egg for an omelet that would save tens of thousands.

"It's not just—" Aloysius said.

"It must be," Odette said.

"It—I…" Aloysius turned away with the words anchored him in place heavy and hard. "I did it. The Val d'Hive. There were so many of them. I should have—but I didn't."

"But you still can," she said. But with every chord lost, it felt less true, brittle even.

"Like Mr. Tureshko?"

"Like me," she said.

"We could leave this place," Aloysius said.

"And go where?" Odette said.

"I know someone. We could get papers."

"To where, Ali?" To Spain? To England?"

"To America, maybe."

"Why? Soon the whole world will look like this."

"Don't say that! I won't believe it." He pushed away from her, but she tried to hold him back. The warmth, the comfort of him always seemed too short lived, gone in an instant and back to the cold absence she felt always.

"I want to show you," she said.

She pulled the carpet back, took away the floor, and brought out the candlesticks.

He said nothing and she couldn't stand the silence. She couldn't stand not being able to read him, not see him flinch or turn to steel. He didn't react, and that scared her most of all.

"I wanted you to know," Odette said. "I needed you to know."

"Since when," he said. "How had I never—"

"I didn't either," she said. "But now I do. Now, you do."

She pulled him back. Another chill ran down her spine, but she brought Aloysius in. He blanketed her with his arms, clothed her with his bare chest. Their bodies no longer silky but callused and rubbed together as she felt him hard against her, felt her hands move towards his pants as if she had done this hundreds of times before. The clock turned 9.06, the night felt empty, but Odette and Aloysius didn't notice for the moment.

Thirty

The bodies lay in a pile at the center of the room as if they were presented on stage, a sight for passersby, anyone with two sou could peep in and witness the dead bodies, a sideshow in the heart of the city, nothing more. The flab of the grocer slipping, sliding, oozing over Lorelai's body, his skin no longer able to contain his fat. Odette sat near the pool of blood leaking from the grocer's skull protected by a broken levy made with the shards of glass from the vase she had broken over his head. She looked like a broken doll, chin tucked into her chest, her hair hiding her eyes.

For the best, Agnes thought. She didn't know what kind of eyes the child would have now, now she had killed someone—no, not exactly an innocent; not an innocent at all but a death, a spirit, and ghost stained into Odette's fingers. *That kind of debt takes everything*, money, any promise of a future, any memories from the past, the light from someone's eyes. It was better if Agnes didn't have to look at the child who could have turned into a monster beneath the strands of hair covering her face, a raggedy boudoir doll who had fallen from the bed. The room smelled like iron, iron and wine, iron and wine and piss. Perhaps the girl had drenched herself in the process; Agnes couldn't blame her. But the only puddle near her was the

201

creeping blood. *It must have been the grocer*, Agnes thought. It made sense, the slob. He probably pissed himself before he barged through the door. The girl stirred, wiping sweat away from her forehead—parting the curtain of hair from her face until Agnes could see her eyes, but the woman turned away, not yet ready to know. She turned back to the bodies, the undignified way the grocer seeped out of his clothes over Lorelai, the way she hid beneath him as if it were a game, one where Odette would search the apartment for her friend unaware Lorelei could hide beneath the massive boulder until she poked her head out and smiled, her teeth beaming with sincere revelry, the red lipstick punctuating the colorless room. But the smile never surfaced, her face never emerged, and Odette only imagined the bruises forming even now around the woman's neck, each indentation of the grocer's fingers may have made, the swirl of his thumbs, the waves of his—Odette stirred again, sniffling, a sign of awareness, Agnes thought.

"Girl," Agnes said, the disdain dripping from her lips like thick vinegar. She couldn't help it, but she didn't understand from where the bitterness in her voice came. She tried again, put her hand on Odette's shoulder, "Girl," but the same acrid sound came out, accompanied by a rough shake of Odette's shoulder forcing Odette to look, forcing Agnes to look, until their eyes met and the playful glint in Odette's eyes, the one that always reminded her of two coins in a pond, that had reminded her son of flecks of gold in a river he had said—having never seen gold outside a store window—had disappeared. Agnes swallowed her gasp and instead clenched her fingers tighter into Odette's shoulder. The girl didn't flinch. Words caught in Agnes's throat—thick with confusion, uncertainty, unknowing—wanting desperately to ask Odette what they should do next. Odette stared at Agnes absent of joy, absent of life, barely prescient, barely present—and the time in the field hospital returned, when they had to remove the bodies from the tent, not to keep the place sterilized like the administration had said, but because they had to make room for the new bodies. Agnes croaked the words, "We need to get rid of him." Her voice broke. She couldn't catch her breath. She managed to find enough force in her lungs to push out the words, "We need to get rid of them both."

Odette's face remained blank, impassive, as if she sat beside a pair of dolls like her, a broken doll, empty of the promise of a playmate, a decorative dress, more like the doll Agnes's mother had once made out of hair and potato sacks. Her mother had placed it on her bed where the crooked button eyes flashed whenever the candlelight flickered in the draft, and the stitched mouth made Agnes think of a witch whose last words were stolen from her when an inquisitor sewed her lips shut.

"Girl," the venom in her voice returned. Agnes shook Odette harder. A glimmer of life returned to Odette's eyes without the color, without light. "The bodies. They need to go."

"How?" Odette asked. Agnes didn't see her lips move. Instead, the voice echoed in Agnes's head and rattled around. A single word made the whole apartment turn upside down. How could they get rid of the bodies? They couldn't exactly drag them to the Seine. And even if they could get the bodies to the riverbank without being seen, how could they possibly carry the lard-ass through the streets of Paris? If he hadn't been so large. If he hadn't been so heavy. If they could take him in shifts, like medieval stoneworkers who carried one at a time to the castle keep. If they could carry one arm at a time, one leg, his torso last.

"I have an idea," Agnes said. Odette didn't acknowledge a word. She stared at the bodies on the floor nearly registering the blood, Agnes thought, almost ready to remember the woman hidden beneath the mass of grocer. Agnes snapped her fingers. "Girl!"

Odette cracked her head to the woman.

"You need to stay here. Get this floor cleaned up. I'll be back in a minute. Do not leave this flat."

Odette turned back to the blood, the bodies, the shards of glass.

Agnes nudged Odette's shoulder once more. "Do you understand me?" silence. "Nod at least, girl."

Odette nodded. Agnes left the room, shut the door behind her, and locked it. She turned and startled when Aloysius stood at the base of the stairs. The lines on his forehead made him look decades older, like his father, concerned, if his father ever could show concern for anyone other than himself.

"Is Mrs. LaFebvre ok?" Aloysius asked.

"Get back inside," Agnes said.

"Is Odette—"

"The girl is—" Agnes hesitated. The creases on Aloysius's face sharpened, deepened. Could Agnes say Odette was fine? She lived. She breathed. For Aloysius, for now, that was enough. "She's fine."

"But her mother?"

"She—" this time the words stuck in her throat, heavy and thick like the blood pooled on the floor. When Lorelai hid beneath the grocer, it almost seemed fake, a nightmare, the same one Agnes had now and again about the Great War, the operating rooms, the soldiers burned at the front, the young men gasping for air with holes in their chests or lungs poisoned with mustard gas. She couldn't. She didn't. She shook her head and looked at the floor to hide the tears from her son, the least she felt she could do in the moment—like her mother who cried only when hanging laundry on the line thinking her children couldn't see her through the sheets or realize their clothing always smelled faintly of tears. Mothers are strong, Agnes always thought growing up; and children should never see their mothers' cry. So now she hid the tears from her son.

"You need to get back inside and make sure no one goes into that flat."

"I want to help," Aloysius said.

"Then make sure no one goes—"

"I can help, Maman!"

Agnes slapped Aloysius across the face before she realized she had even raised her hand. Spittle dripped from his lips, but he did not bleed. He held back the well of tears the same way Agnes had seconds before. She gripped her fingers around Aloysius's face. He flinched but did not turn away.

"Boy. Son. Ali. I need you to understand." She swallowed hard. It felt like a jagged pebble butted down her throat. "You need to go inside and make sure no one goes into that flat. Yes?" She stared into his brown eyes, pools of uncertainty, of cowardice like his father hoping for a moment to prove himself, a moment like this in which he would back down, pulling his head back into the shell he had made of his life. *Where would my boy be if not for that girl*, Agnes thought, long enough to fill the pause until he finally consented.

"Wait," she said. He stood with his back to her, almost to the door, almost out of sight, almost gone from her reach. "Instead, go to the butcher. You know the one I mean." Aloysius did not turn around. He nodded. He ran. He disappeared.

Agnes ran down to the cellar where she kept the cleaning supplies and junk she hadn't looked at in years, decades even, including an old French kiln she had taken from a tenant who had long left Paris and didn't have the space or concern to take with them. For three months, she took pottery lessons instead of rent thinking it could be an extra income for her and the boy until the sweat she put into keeping the kiln fired was much more work, more sweat than she wanted, as if she steamed clothes in a laundry. She moved aside all the miscellaneous rubbish she should have thrown out years ago. She located the extra wood, pressed her fingers into the splinters and found it dry, perfect, even after years untouched, possibly protected by all the other garbage scattered around the room. She placed the wood on the third shelf over the fire bars feeding the flame. The wood took to the heat and burst as she stoked and stoked watching the ash fall over coals below and eventually collapse to the floor. She spread around the burning rocks to feed more oxygen to the fire. She had a few minutes as the kiln warmed, knowing after all the modifications it would still take a few hours of constant attention before it reached peak temperature. The fire grew. The heat in the basement became more intense turning the perspiration on Agnes's face to a river of sweat dripping, dropping, and sizzling on the stone floor. The kiln wouldn't wait, and the bodies two floors above her head couldn't wait. A feeling lingered, one of forgetfulness, not like the opposite of remembering but the absence of an object. But what could she have forgotten in the basement beside a disremembered kiln? She noticed the rusty hatchet beside the old wood. She took it with her. She ran up the stairs taking two at a time with the crack and creak in her knees echoing in the stairwell. She stood in front of the door, wiped the sweat from her face, and patted down her hair, smoothed her dress. She unlocked the door. Odette had covered the bodies with a sheet with the blood from the grocer sinking into the fabric until stained, a moist stain like spilling red wine on a summer dress.

Agnes exhaled hard and fast. "This won't do. This won't do. This won't do. This won't—"

"Why do you have that hatchet?" Odette asked. Her voice remained a small wisp in a room empty of sound but barely audible over Agnes's heart.

"We need more linens," Agnes said shouting louder than she had anticipated. Odette winced.

"Go to my flat and grab all the linens you can, the dour ones. Ali will know the ones. Make sure he gives them to you. Do not bring him up here." Odette nodded and walked out the door.

Agnes stepped to the bodies. She tore away the sheet and pushed, nudged, and shouldered the grocer attempting to free Lorelai from beneath him, but the man barely budged, except Agnes could see Lorelai's face, the fear impressed on her lips and stuck in her cheeks forever-more, no longer an echo of her smile. Agnes fell to the floor with the tears damming up harder behind her eyes stinging as she attempted to push them back down. She ran her fingers over Lorelai's forehead tracing the forced, eternal lines. Her skin felt soft, still warm as if her body didn't yet know she had gone. A groan settled in the air. Agnes pushed back from the pile. The groan slipped through the flat again. Agnes's heart thudded against her chest thinking for a moment Lorelai may still have life in her after all. She lunged back to the body waiting for another groan. She pressed her ears to Lorelai's lips feeling for breath, any air at all, or perhaps another gentle moan. And then it came. It drifted from the bodies and filled the open space in the flat but not from Lorelai, from the grocer. *From the goddamned grocer!* Agnes thought.

The man moaned once more and turned his face to Agnes, his eyes glassy, the fortified wine still putrid in his pores. Agnes waited for a sign of recognition, for the moment his eyes turned from glazed to focused, a spark of detection, lucidity. And then it came, and he opened his mouth to speak. But instead of words, Agnes clenched her finger around his nostrils until she couldn't feel any air. She grabbed the sheet and stuffed it as far down his throat as she could manage. His body limply flailed, *like a beached whale. How fitting.* And he moaned, grunted, until the light once again broke in his eyes, until he had nothing left to recognize but death. And when he stopped moving, she pulled the sheet out of his mouth. And the tears finally poured out of Agnes mixing with the sweat. Agnes turned away from the grocer and back to Lorelai because her tears weren't meant for him; he wasn't good enough for her tears. They slid from her cheeks like a hand running over silk and faded into the strands of Lorelai's hair. Agnes dipped her lips down and pressed them on the creases of Lorelai's forehead, where her lips, she thought, would now make an eternal impression.

Odette returned with the linens, a combination of sheets, towels, and clothes they no longer wore.

"What will we do with these?" Odette asked.

"I told you we needed to get rid of him?" Odette nodded. "These will help. There is a kiln in the basement. Do you know what a kiln is?" Odette nodded again.

"But how will we get them to the basement?"

Agnes glanced to the hatchet.

"No," Odette said. She stepped away from Agnes shaking her head with the fear Agnes had always expected to see dripping onto the girl's cheeks. "No, I can't. No. No. No. No There must be another way. No—"

Agnes grabbed Odette's wrist and clamped her fingers around the skin. "We have to."

"But—please."

Agnes looked back to the bodies, to Lorelai's aged face, to the grocer, to the crumpled sheet, and she turned away. "I will help you."

They laid sheets across the floor, one over the other until thick with layers. They worked together rolling the grocer off Lorelai and onto the sheets. A gentle knock at the door; Agnes answered. She tried to give the butcher money, a small token for his help, a fee for a taxicab coming to the apartment late in the night, coins to help Lorelai cross the river Styx. When the butcher held out his hand to try and hug Agnes, to try and bring her close to him, she filled his palm with coins. She looked away from his face, too broken from seeing Lorelai to see another person she cared for shattered by her action—her inaction. The butcher refused the coins. He took Lorelai away in silence.

The door closed. Agnes raised the hatchet ready to strike. Odette watched transfixed, unable to turn. *She's had enough for one day*, Agnes thought. She lowered the blade to the floor.

"I will take care of this," she said. "You know how to stoke a fire?"

"Of course."

"Go to the basement, feed the kiln, make sure the fire doesn't weaken."

"But you said—"

"Damn it, girl, I know what I said, and now, I'm saying different."

"Yes, madam." Odette took off out of the room.

Agnes lifted the hatchet once more and started with the grocer's hands, the ones he had used to strangle Lorelai, cutting through the bone at the wrist. The blood spurted out on the linens darkening and yet disappearing into the fabric. Then she went for the shoulder. By the time she had finished with the bodies, she wrapped them in the soiled cloths and took trips carrying them down into the basement, placing them in the kiln as best she could as Odette continued stoking the fire, ensuring the coals had room in which the oxygen could move, dance, and burn.

"What happens next?" Odette said.

"We wait," Agnes said.

"For how long?"

"Tomorrow should work."

"What then?"

"We fix what's left," Agnes said. She bent down and pointed her finger in Odette's face. "We always have to make sure we fix what's left." Agnes stood and stretched her back adding cracks and creaks to the sound of the roaring fire. "Go upstairs. Your mother keeps bleach under the sink. You make sure you scrub the floors hard. And when you think you're done, do it again. It's my turn to stoke the fire." Agnes stood in the room on her own ready to stoke the fire knowing that without her, the flames would fizzle to nothing or engulf the entire building.

Thirty-one

Odette relished the moments she could cycle along the open streets of Paris instead of suffocating in the crowded buses where she had to guard her breasts from the grabby men or the curious boys. On the days she couldn't take Aloysius's bike, she had to settle for the misanthropic groping of married men longing for some escape from their solitary existence in the bedroom, even if the last time she rode the bus she nearly stabbed an old man with a fraying mustache who for once had accidentally squished her breast while trying to steady his stance after an inadvertent jerky stop. But on the bicycle, Odette had the rare feeling of freedom with her blood pulsing fast enough for her to hear the thump in her ears tuning in to the movements around her as if she knew what would happen before anyone else. The only other time she felt this way was before a kill, when she knew exactly how the man would react, cry, flail, muted screams, sweat through his bindings, or on the rare occasion, accept his fate, close his eyes, and give in.

She cycled near Champs Elysées on her usual route to work. Since the Germans arrived, only certain cars were allowed on the road, and those who drove either embodied some sort of self-importance or were deemed important by the Gestapo. The absence of cars on the road made riding a bike through the city much easier and allowed Odette to speed through stop lights without worrying about another car running through the intersection and swiping her. In summer, it also meant the scent of jasmine in the streets in addition to the subtle acrid smoke from burnt rubber and the sweetness of the smog emitted from the petrol.

A car slowed close to Odette. She ignored it thinking of the day ahead at work and the vases cooling in the kiln she hoped would be ready by the time she returned home from the hospital. The car pulled beside Odette on the left with the passenger nearly able to touch her.

"Excuse me Fraulein," the passenger said. Odette didn't know the ranks of the German soldiers, but she presumed this man was part of a higher level, with a shoulder strap resembling a zeppelin with silver lines and two gold stars. Strands of black hair poked from beneath his hat showing bits of premature gray. His stone chin told Odette all she felt she needed to know about the man. Small Nazi flags clinging to the front of the car rippled in wind with a loud, obnoxious flap. "Hello, miss. Excuse us." The driver kept his eyes on the road and Odette for a second wanted to commend him on not crashing into her. "Can you please tell us where the Grands Boulevards is?"

Odette did not make a habit of consorting with Germans but never wanted to draw attention to herself unnecessarily. *If they don't see you, they won't remember you. If they don't remember you, they can't point you out in a crowd.*

"You are going in the wrong direction," she said. And pointed them down a different street. "When you get to Rue du Louvre, you're close."

She tried to peddle faster in the hopes of leaving the car behind, but the driver kept pace with her. A slight smirk formed, crinkling around his eye. Odette quietly huffed. *Maybe I should have taken the bus today*, she thought.

"You should come with us," the officer said. "It's too hot for a bike. We will help you cool off with a nice, cold German beer." The soldiers laughed. The light at the intersection turned red. The soldiers stopped. Odette kept riding through the light and waved farewell to the soldiers. She wiped away the sweat forming on her forehead happy to have moved beyond the soldiers for the day. She returned to her steady pace passing the remaining boutique shops and elegant cafes along the road with a variety of Germans enjoying the sun at outdoor tables, smoking cigarettes, and sipping coffee, coffee Odette had run out of ages ago. She spat and noticed the polished black car pulling closer to her on the left once again. She rolled her eyes and bit her lip.

"Fraulein," the passenger said again. "You are too fast for our car. Slow down and we can show you a different side of Paris." Odette's thoughts wandered to the type of Paris they could show her, one filled with soldiers in a beerhall, soldiers in a brothel, soldiers standing beneath the Arche de Triomphe, soldiers visiting a German bookstore. Perhaps she should invite them see her side of Paris and the breadlines, the starving children, the boarded-up restaurants, the closed-down shops, and the freezing apartments in winter. She shook her head.

"I am sorry. It sounds like a delight, but I'm on my way to work."

The soldier reached out for her hand, but she swerved the bike. The driver stopped the car at a red light and Odette sped through the intersection. She sucked in all the air she could, letting her chest inflate as large as possible before blowing out in one hard complete breath.

Agnes had always pushed the importance of diplomacy, the act of letting her pursued think they had the upper hand and never giving into the urge to yell, throw a tantrum, or cry…unless absolutely necessary. She wasn't afraid of these two idiots but worried more about what would happen tomorrow, what would happen when the soldiers didn't show up for duty, for their roll call? No one would ever find the bodies. No one would ever consider searching for bones inside a working kiln, finding hints of a person turned to ash, turned to clay, turned to a vase.

"That's enough, Fraulein," the passenger said as the car sped up to meet Odette. It turned and stopped in front of her forcing her to stop or smash into the door and perhaps fall into the lap of the passenger. She skidded and twisted the handlebars narrowly avoiding a collision. "How dare you disrespect officers of the Reich with your…your…bicycle."

"I apologize if I offended you, sir," Odette said. "But—"

"There are no excuses for your haughty attitude." The passenger stepped from the car and loomed tall over Odette in his polished boots. He looked back at the driver and sneered. "What is it with French women? They think so highly of themselves, of this country. It took us longer to defeat Poland than to march through *your* country."

"I'm sorry you feel that way," Odette said holding back the contempt in her throat as it grew thicker; she almost choked on it.

"The whores at that brothel on *Rue de la Lune* understand their place. They welcome us with open arms."

"Then you might not be getting your money's worth," Odette said.

"What's that supposed to mean?"

"They're supposed to welcome you with open legs."

The driver snickered. The passenger raised his fist and Odette flinched waiting for the blow to sting. Instead, the passenger pulled off his hat and slicked his hair back. He pointed to Odette with a smile that made his eyes look sick, that broadened his chin turning it from stone to a boulder.

"You should learn a lesson, you and all the other French *girls*."

Odette clenched her fingers around the handlebars. She knew, if she had to, she could lure the passenger into one of the nearby arcades but how would she get the driver? And then what would she do with the car?

"Yes, you need a lesson in humility," he said. "Empty the air from your tires."

"Excuse me, sir?" Odette said.

"We were nothing but nice to you. We spared your godforsaken city. But you and your *ill-tempered* neighbors don't give us the time of day. I'm going to stand here and watch you empty the air from your tires. To show you what a good sport I am, I'll steady your bicycle as you let the air out." The soldier reached for the handlebars with his stubby, callused fingers almost grating against the back of Odette's hand as she pulled away.

"Go on then."

"Sir, I—"

"You think you can disrespect me by passing my car on a bicycle? When you disrespect me, you disrespect the army. You disrespect Germany. You disrespect the Fuhrer. This cannot stand."

He was posturing for his driver, she knew. She embarrassed him, and now he needed to reassert his masculinity. She would love to show him how masculine a dead man could be, if he gave her the chance, if she didn't need to fear the repercussions. She knelt down and twisted the cap from the back wheel first. The passenger pressed down on the handlebars trying to force the air out faster.

"And the front," the officer said.

"Of course," Odette said and smiled. She repeated the process with the front tire.

"Thank you," he said. "I'm sorry we had to learn such a harsh lesson today. Perhaps you'll be more careful—humbler—in the future." The man returned to the passenger seat and drove off with the screech of the wheel leaving a small scar on the road.

Odette replaced the caps on the tires. She had barely enough air to make it to the hospital, but she would have to peddle much harder than she had planned. She mounted the bike. The heat sat on the city with nowhere to go but push down harder on her shoulders. The sweat turned from beads to droplets falling from her forehead. As she peddled, she thought about how lucky the passenger was for having a driver, for having a car, for not having met her in the back alleys near the Rue de la Lune at midnight where his uniform made him a target instead of an authority figure. She sped through the intersections, the red lights, and past the small collection of cafés hosting German soldiers with French women being more than hospitable. She pushed and trudged along as she wondered if it would be easier to walk or join the crowds of the bus at this point. A second wind pushed her after four blocks when she noticed a black car stopped at the side of the road. The driver bent over the car hood, his face hidden behind a veil of steam. The passenger stood with one hand on the car and one hand on his back kneeling over the engine like a supervisor without a clue. The Nazi flags that had rippled in the wind as the car drove beside Odette stood still, invisible without motion. The passenger looked up at Odette as she passed. But she looked forward with a hint of a smile forming at the corners and the flat tires feeling as though they had filled themselves with new air.

Thirty-two

Aloysius watched as Odette strolled down the street arm in arm with another man. He watched as she laughed and patted the man on his arm. He watched as the man caressed her shoulder and gazed into her eyes. The night was inelegant and sticky. The streetlights seemed dimmer than normal.

Aloysius had always avoided Odette's life outside of their bubble, pushed thoughts of her with other men away and believed in a world where he would one day be brave enough to take her hand in his, leave this city with her, build a life with her. In that part of his imagination, she went to work, worked on her pottery, and walked through the park with Aloysius—never with other men.

Odette's shoes grazed softly against the cobblestone street while the man's shoes clacked and clanked awkwardly. The smell of shit lingered in the air, a putrid scent Aloysius had noticed more and more often since the night of the roundup. It clung to the city now. It seeped into the crevices between the cobblestones, the mortar between the stone buildings, and the winding waters of the Seine. Or perhaps, he hated to admit, it just clung to him. And now, that same smell came from the couple wandering down the street near Aloysius's flat.

Odette's finger ran up and down the man's arm, a motion Aloysius had rarely felt. One he had imagined repeatedly, them intertwined in bed laying naked beneath the sheets, the smell of jasmine drifting from her skin—jasmine and sweat—jasmine, sweat and sex—and the smooth tip of her finger would run up and down his arm as if tracing his history through the freckles on his skin. As a child, he once wondered if his freckles were like the rings of a tree but instead of telling his age, they told him how many past lives he had. He had one hundred and forty past lives. Then he and Odette spent the rest of the afternoon trying to think of the lives he had lived, one as a baker, one as an imperial warrior, and one as a Spanish explorer. None of the past lives were of a child with a lame leg. All of those lives found glory in some way. And all of them eventually led to the same image of Aloysius and Odette embracing. But now, Aloysius watched as Odette trailed her finger down the coat of another man, and the heat grew in his cheeks, and it roiled in his stomach, and it drew him deeper into the shadow.

Could the man have been German? A high-ranking Nazi? Odette could not have needed food badly enough for her to collude with a Nazi. She could have come to him instead. But what could Aloysius have given her? Affection, a bed? He received the same rations she did, even as a gendarme. But A Nazi could give her cream, could remind her of the taste of cake, could keep the lights on later into the night. But it didn't look like they would need the lights on at all. Aloysius tried to glimpse the man, but they were too far, the man wore too many layers, the night was too dim— the man's face never left the darkness.

Aloysius blew out a hard breath and recoiled back from the street. He watched as the man leaned in for a kiss and Odette turned away. The man brushed his lips against her cheek. She smiled, giggled, and tapped the man's shoulder. Aloysius had never seen this side of Odette before, the giddy side, the side that resembled a schoolgirl. Even when Odette was a schoolgirl, she did not act like one. What other reasons could she be acting this way, with this man, with a man other than Aloysius? He spent so long thinking arm's reach was the closest anyone would ever get to her, he was convinced that was affection. But this man broke through the perimeter of arm's reach; a sharp pain ran up Aloysius's heart and into his eyes as if the pain of seeing Odette with another man would blind him.

Odette leaned against the cellar door. The man leaned in and once again tried for a kiss. Odette turned her face again, this time pouting. Aloysius watched as she opened the door, as the man entered the cellar, as she followed behind and closed the door. Then the street once again turned silent, as the smell of shit returned after the brief respite inside his memory of jasmine. And Aloysius's idea of Odette disappeared behind the same cellar door leaving emptiness in its wake.

Thirty-three

Odette crept beneath the gentle stream of umbrellas and awnings. If she stood still, maybe the water wouldn't even reach her shoulders, only splash up from the puddles between the stones and flick her ankles. She clasped her overcoat wondering if the beige of the fabric would blend her into the surrounding facades. The raindrops splashed against the streetlights, tapped atop the umbrellas, thudded down onto the awnings. Mostly, people ignored the water as a part of life in the city, in France. Odette didn't mind the rain as much as the cold. She clasped her hands so tight she felt her knuckles whiten, strained from the pressure and the indentation the seams made on her skin.

SS officers stood in slickers with the water collecting into the fabric of their hats. The droplets bounced off the brims or dribbled down onto their coats without the notice of passersby because to them, and Odette, the droplets resembled more raindrops, infinite raindrops, that sooner or later would cause the Seine to rise, the streets to flood, and the need for an ark to return, once again leaving behind the people two-by-two.

The shops on Rue de CauMartine were closed. The blue door of the neighboring boutique framed a naked female mannequin surrounded by

219

velvet drapes Odette knew wouldn't last much longer. If the owner couldn't afford to clothe the mannequin, she would soon use the drapes for a blanket, a coat, as a trade for food. The drapes shouldn't have lasted as long as they had, but it was just as hard to find planks of wood to board up the windows as it was to find extra money for fabric. Odette had already patched the same tear in her jacket at her elbow three times. She fingered the scar on the jacket as if drawn by the memory. The window glowed in the darkness above the city's noticeable absence. Odette stood across the walkways hiding in the semi-dry comfort underneath the stone head of the doorway.

The perfect husband and wife sat at a table. The husband with rouge cheeks and parted hair sat with rigid posture. He smiled at his wife before biting into a piece of beef, a juicy, tender piece of beef, the likes of which Odette hadn't tasted in far too long. He wore a black coat and had light brunette tints. His teeth glinted in the light of the room. He sipped a glass of red wine, wine not thinned with water to make it last longer. The woman, the doctor, Mrs. Ilse Köhler, with each blonde hair kept in place, a curl draping over her temple, her white blouse always tucked into her brown skirt, smiled back at her husband, as if earlier that day she hadn't had her hands bathed in blood, she hadn't shot needles into the hopeless and innocent, hadn't stood in the gallery of the hospital surrounded by the pleads and screams of children, women, old men—as if the day stopped at the door and she shed her skin like a snake to reappear in a new life inside her home.

She had a husband. Köhler had a life outside of work in which her lips curled past the ever-present smirk smothered in red lipstick. Odette had learned to hate that smirk; it haunted her like the ghosts of those she had killed who should have haunted her, a simple smile, an uncaring smile, absent of malice or desire, pleasure or pain, like a painting devoid of the spirit, a still life without the life, just still. Ilse smirked throughout the day, welcoming new patients, laying them down on the bed, stroking their hair, pricking their arms with the needles, watching as their faces turned from stoic yearning, eager to be understood, to twisted in pain, wretched pain, as they held their stomachs, turned to their sides, vomited into a bucket, missed Ilse's shoes, and vomited again, filling the room with acid and the faint scent of bad fish. Only then, after weeks of vomit, after weeks of emaciation, when their skin wrapped around their muscles as tight and as brittle as twine, just before their pupils turned from black to white, did Ilse's smirk turn to a smile just as twisted as the patients' insides, as if the smile pained her as much as the poison she had put in their systems.

Ilse's smile with her husband was different in its absence of pain, in its ability to show any joy, an emotion Odette had thought the doctor incapable of knowing, which would have connected them, a way Odette would have been able to understand the doctor's actions, her ways of wrecking life, of taking life, of twisting life from a series of bearable hardships and unforgettable moments of passion and love, to remaining garbage alit with unbridled gasoline. Odette was happy for a moment, for a brief second even, just to see that her and Ilse were not the same, that they didn't share all the same characteristics as the doctor had said—had thought. Then the happiness faded, overcome by a sense of dread, of jealousy, of anger, that this woman—more vile than Odette could have ever been—could smile a joyful smile, could feel a moment of pleasure away from her destructive hands, her terrorizing thoughts, the way she measured the fluids into the vial, the way she swabbed the patient's arms with alcohol, the way it looked as if she wanted to cure them, to help, but instead watched the microbes enter their system and tear at their cells from the inside out, patiently writing down how they felt, how they looked, and how the world would soon forget them.

This was a woman who could have a family, have a smile, have a husband who looked at her lovingly from a window overlooking the crowds of the city Paris once was. Then there was Odette, who had spent her life pushing people away to not reveal to them the monster underneath, when she could have hidden it from them the way Ilse hid it from her family. The doctor didn't deserve happiness. She didn't deserve dinner. Her husband didn't deserve a life apart from the turmoil of the war. The heavy rain turned to a shroud of mist, coiling through the streets, around the streetlamps before curfew tormented the night. Ilse laughed with her entire body. Her shoulders shuttered. Her husband covered his mouth as he chewed to not spit out the food. Odette wanted revenge for the joy she couldn't feel, the love Ilse could, to prove they were different in the end.

Thirty-four

Aloysius never dreamed he would find a dead body in the basement of his mother's apartment building. The room sweltered with cancerous heat. Odette must have finished a batch in the kiln recently, Aloysius thought.

Had this been the man Odette was talking with? Had he crossed a line? Could Aloysius have saved him; could he have saved her? Now, Aloysius stood eye to eye with a dead man in a room that stank of vinegar. Slice marks decorated the body around the neck, along the forearms, and around the upper leg. Each cut had been made precisely along an artery. The room stank of embalming fluid. The body almost glowed white in the dim light filtering through the window. The body had been washed, absent of blood streaks or any marks that would signify the blood had touched the skin. Aloysius took a pen from his pocket, the pen he used for writing notes when patrolling the city. He dug the tip of the pen into the open slit on the forearm checking for signs of seepage. He peeled back the tiny flap of skin, then pushed the other side open hoping for a better view. His mother had once said sunshine was the best disinfectant, but no amount of sunshine could disinfect his pen after it touched a dead body. But the body was beyond dead; a dead body still had some essence of its past life, a lingering glance of its final moments, a grotesque expression emoting the ability that at any minute the body would spring back to life. A thought struck Aloysius like shock: could this be the man for whom he searched? Aloysius took his pen and crept it between the man's lips.

The teeth hadn't shaken Aloysius; he had seen teeth busted from outside someone's head. He had seen Odette knock a tooth from the mouth of a bully one afternoon when the boy had dropped his pants and chased after a group of girls in the alley. The girls had wanted to look at the new kittens drinking the milk Odette had left out. The boy, who was closer to a man at that point, elbowed his friends, telling them to watch what he would do. He dropped his pants and waddled down the alley with his arms reaching out to grab the girls. The gaggle screamed and ran. The murder of boys laughed their stupid laughs, their unquestionable laughs, as if they laughed only because they hadn't known any better. Odette poked her head outside of Aloysius's apartment after hearing the screams. They saw the running girls, the boy picking up his trousers, the last glimpse of his pale hairless ass. Odette rounded the corner on him, threw him to the ground and kicked him in the teeth. Blood splattered onto the cobblestones with a cacophonous splat. The boy spat his tooth onto the floor. He didn't bother picking it up. He left it there like a sacrifice to Odette, to the city, to the cats, like a totem in an apology to the girls he had scared away. Except, Aloysius hadn't watched the boy. He had heard the spit, listened to the rattle of the tooth hit the stone, the clutter of footsteps when the boys ran away, but for the first time, Aloysius noticed a change in Odette. She had always been reserved, respectful, but quick to temper after her mother's death. It wasn't the temper that surprised him, it was the hints of joy he found at the corners of her lips, the slight glint in her eye from the blood, the tooth, the throbbing in her knuckle after she hit the boy in the stomach. When her chest heaved, Aloysius no longer thought it was from exertion but pleasure, the type of pleasure a woman gained from stimulation.

Aloysius thought back on all the times Odette ran into a fight, even the fights that hadn't drawn her in. Fighting, it seemed, was a magnet, and she was the metal.

Then one day, it stopped. Her fighting, her thirst for blood, one day Aloysius and Odette walked past a hidden garden they enjoyed using as an escape from school, then from work. A teenager and his date picnicked under a secluded tree. They kissed quietly under the scent of orange blossoms. Aloysius realized it wasn't a teenager at all, but a man, but the girl still looked like a girl, rosy cheeks, innocent smile covered by her hands. She giggled when he whispered in her ear. It wasn't an uncommon sight. They ignored Aloysius and Odette who chose instead to stare at the birds and discuss the latest poetry from Zelda Fitzgerald, a favorite of Odette's. Aloysius preferred the paintings of Salvador Dali. They could never see eye to eye on art or on most things. Aloysius was passionate about stories of knights, French history, the idea of chivalry. Odette loved cats and always participated in conversation, but other than an interest in moving pictures and a new-found interest in ceramics, she didn't thirst for much more than what she had. She had taken up studying anatomy to become a nurse, spending time with Agnes to learn more about the Great War. Aloysius had never known his mother participated in the French efforts.

"The amount you don't know about your mother," Odette told Aloysius, "could fill the Palaise de Louvre."

Odette began spending more and more time with Agnes, to the point Aloysius grew jealous, angered by the time his mother soaked up and stole from him. But in the park that day, the man became forceful, turning from the façade of a gentleman to a hurried beast unable to stand reason. His hands grabbed, gripped, and tore at the girl. The girl's giggles turned to pleas, at first whispered so no one could hear her, so no one would judge her because she must have gotten herself into the deplorable situation as a girl of loose morals or questionable character. The invisible mark would stain her for the remainder of her life like an inkblot on her forehead.

Aloysius looked to Odette, but she stared at the ducks wading in the pond, who ignored the sounds of struggling from the girl as if familiar with the cries. The girl whimpered, the man argued, urging her, blaming her. Aloysius stood from the banks of the pond and stared, hoping his presence would deter the man, but his presence went unnoticed. Anger turned Aloysius's cheeks flush, anger at the man, and fury at himself for not doing more, for not being more.

"Excuse me," Aloysius sniveled like a child just waking from a nap. The man did not turn. The girl cried again. "Sir," Aloysius said with more force, but it still sounded like a question rather than a command. The man finally stopped. He looked to Aloysius with half-sunken eyes and a mustache disheveled from forcing his lips onto the girl's skin. "I was…I think you—"

"Go away, friend," the man said. His breath heaved. "I am busy."

Aloysius didn't want to turn. The girl glanced with imploring eyes before her gaze fell from view.

"You should—"

"I should what?" the man said.

"I am lost," Aloysius said. "We need directions back to the Palaise de Louvre."

"Foreigners," the man said. "As good as trash." The girl sat up from the ground, dusted herself off, and sulked away. The man looked at Aloysius and huffed, following at a half step behind the girl. Aloysius didn't know if the man caught up to her.

"How could you do nothing?" Aloysius said.

Odette threw a piece of bread to the ducks. They fought over the stale piece turning soggy in the water.

"You always fight for—"

"For what?" Odette asked. "What am I always fighting for? I can't hit every bastard in this city. All I'd get is bruised knuckles and a line of people waiting to stab me in the dark."

"No one is going to stab you," Aloysius said, which was the exact wrong thing to say.

"And who is going to protect me? You? Who had to ask the man for directions, so he'd stop trying to rape that girl. Did you need those directions to find your prick?" Odette tossed the remainder of the bread into the pond. The mound sunk into the water like a stone before the ducks swarmed. She skulked away kicking up dirt along the unpaved trail leading out of the park.

"You always fought for something," Aloysius said to himself. And he always wanted to fight for whatever she believed in because she always believed in what felt right. Now she didn't fight at all.

Aloysius exhaled with relief. This man had all his teeth. This wasn't the dead body; it was a corpse. He took his pen, wiped it with a handkerchief and put the pen back in his shirt pocket. No one ever used this room but Odette.

"It couldn't be," he said to himself. He traced all the times Odette disappeared, the times she returned with sweat pooling around her body. She never let anyone look inside the cellar, not that anyone ever bothered. Then the truth came crashing down, the time he asked her what she hid. She hadn't been joking. What seemed funny at the time, heartwarming even, turned sinister.

The sounds of scraping etched against the window. Odette's heels clacked against the sidewalk. The door to the complex squeaked when it opened. Her shoes tapped on the stone stairs leading to the cellar. Aloysius tried to find his voice. He tried to speak her name, but it caught in his throat. He tried again and pushed the words out attempting to sound stern.

"Odette!"

She was startled. "Aloysius, what are you doing here? And in the dark?" She looked around the room in search of objects that could incriminate her, beyond the dead body at the center of the room. Her eyes never rested on the pulled away sheet, the ghostly white of the man's skin, his closed, lifeless eyes, his naked body, or the precise slits made into his arms, legs, and neck.

"I can't imagine—" he stuttered. "I know losing your mother was a shock. But how could you—you did this? You did this. How could you do something like this?"

Odette tried to hide a thin smile behind her hand. She spoke through her fingers.

"You are right," she said. "I cut him." She walked closer to the dead body. An innocent person would have flinched. An innocent person might have fled or vomited. Why did Aloysius try to prove her innocence even after she admitted to it? Her finger hovered over his left leg. "First I cut him here." She traced the slices she made over the body. "Then here, on the arms. I made the incision on his neck last."

Incision, he thought. She kept a methodical tone as if it was just practice or a book of study and had nothing to do with human life.

"You killed this man," he said and took a step back from the body. He backed against the cupboard holding a variety of tools. Had Odette used one of them to kill the man? He should have hidden before she came down the stairs, then he could have continued his investigation unimpeded.

"I did not," she gasped. "This was a good man. He had a family he cared for. He had grandchildren who wept when he died. He did not deserve to die."

"What do you mean deserved?"

"He had a heart attack," she said. "He was to be cremated."

"Why is he here? Why does he have these incisions? What have you done to him? I don't want to have to arrest you but I—"

"I did not realize it was an offense worthy of arrest. I thought perhaps a fine or a stern warning."

"You cut this man. You murdered—"

"I have told you I did not murder him. Don't you know what that smell is?" Aloysius had noticed the strong scent of vinegar. "You see dead bodies more often than a regular person. You should know when a body is freshly dead versus preserved. You didn't think it strange there was no blood left?"

"Why would you embalm a body if it was going to be cremated."

"The crematorium has been struggling to get resupplied. We have plenty of embalming fluid. We keep them at the morgue until the crematorium is ready. Sometimes…"

Aloysius took a deep breath. The acidic scent of formaldehyde remained prevalent and almost caused him to cough. He realized he hadn't been breathing. "This doesn't make sense. Why is this body here?"

"So I can practice," Odette said.

"Practice? Murdering people?"

Odette blushed and turned away. Aloysius regretted the words the moment he said them. He had known Odette since they were children, pined after her for as long, how could he accuse her of something so vulgar?

"It is important to understand the human body," Odette said with a whisper. "You should know. I take my work seriously. The more I know, the more work they give me and the more they teach me. It's not my fault I was born a woman. I don't have to be happy about it."

"You don't like being a woman?"

She turned and slammed her hand on the cadaver. A puff of gas emitted from the man's mouth. The formaldehyde grew thick, mixed with the faint scent of rotten flesh.

"I can do the same work—better work!—than those, those—"

"Pigheaded?" Aloysius said.

"Yes," Odette said "Better work than those pigheaded doctors who think god gave them insight. If god gave them anything, it was the ability to see while their head is so far up their own asses."

"Then where did you get this…body?"

"Ilse, the German doctor, Dr. Köhler. She said this is how she learned."

"But how is it here?"

"Are you always awake? Always staring out the window keeping track of the comings and goings on the street?"

"You make me sound like my mother," Aloysius said.

"A German—a German doctor—a high ranking German doctor can get a lot of things done in this city without anyone asking questions. Most of the time—" Odette swallowed hard. She rubbed her hand to her chest. She cleared her throat and it sounded like sandpaper rubbing against wood. "Most of the time, people don't want to ask questions." She looked Aloysius in the eyes. It felt like the first time in his life he did not turn away from her, did not blush. He stared back. He couldn't say why; he didn't know if it was because the story she told nagged at him or because he wanted to believe her story so desperately he could quickly push the doubt aside. Perhaps Odette sensed his apprehension—she probably tell based on his stare, his sudden boldness.

"Taxis, bikes, ambulances, you never would have blinked twice if one of those passed down the street," Odette said. Aloysius nodded. It wasn't so unbelievable.

"This person was once alive," Aloysius said.

"And now he isn't," Odette said. "You of all people should know when they are dead, they are not coming back."

"The body—"

"Is going to be reduced to ash. No one will even know it was gone."

"Is this what you hide in here all the time?" He moved to brush his fingers over the cadaver but recoiled. Odette nodded. "Even before this Dr. Köhler?"

"She caught me the last time," Odette said.

"She caught you?"

"No one is usually in the hospital at midnight. I always check. The last time, I forgot."

"How long have you been doing this?"

"Long enough." She glared at Aloysius. He was asking too many questions. He realized his tone nestled somewhere between accusatory and frightened. When he looked at her, at the raw fear on her face, those feelings melted away. She wanted knowledge, she wanted to be a doctor, she didn't want to skulk through the city hiding dead bodies. He moved around the table.

"Do you want help taking the body back?"

"His name was Mr. Bertrand."

"He had a name?"

"Of course, he had a name. He wasn't raised by wolves."

"How could you look at him knowing he had a name?"

"How do you look at victims knowing they had a name? You want to find their murderers, so do I. They just come in different forms."

Aloysius sighed. "I'll help you take Mr. Bertrand back."

"I don't need your help," she said. He touched her hand, and the heat from her pulsing blood contrasted the lifeless skin of Mr. Bertrand.

"You never have," he said. "But it doesn't mean I won't stop offering."

Thirty-five

The cobbled lanes of the city narrowed around the neighborhood of St. Germaine. Paris had emptied of cars seemingly overnight; since the Germans arrived the motor cars appeared as lifeless obstructions, boulders growing out of the streets. A milkman tipped his hat to Odette as he passed. Two large dogs pulled the cart; horses were as hard to find in the city as working cars, with petrol rationed to nearly empty by the Germans who needed the gas for their tanks and jeeps at the front. The fragrant, roasted aroma of coffee that once prevailed over the smell of sewer had disappeared with the cars, replaced by the scattered char of chicory that resembled burning bark. Taxi drivers on bikes rolled down the lane, pedaling with ease when no passengers sat in the back cab. They waved to Odette, a sign they could take her the rest of the way, but she didn't want to pay the high tariff the drivers placed on their exercise. A Bosch officer drove past in a slick, shimmering black Citroen. He must have been SS, Odette thought. Unlike soldiers or members of the Wehrmacht, the SS liked to flaunt their status as occupiers, as the new aristocracy in the city—in their eyes. They were better than the Parisians, than the French. Their shiny cars, polished boots, and dinners of beef bourguignon confit only proved it. The opposite of the regal depiction of a German, a soldier. Instead of blond hair and a chin chiseled from granite, the grease practically seeped through his pores and the fat rolls of his neck nearly spilled over his collar.

A thin layer of fog covered the sky, but the light managed to glint against the car. The wheels rolled over the cobblestones, unaffected by the cracks and uneven surface the way the horse cart—no, dogcart—had rumbled over the street. The engine roared louder than Odette remembered. She thought of the gentle purr that said both power and luxury. The officer honked at the taxis. The dogcart had moved to the side of the road with the milkman gone, disappeared inside a store with his remaining crates. The dogs barked at the engine, fearful of the passing beast, trying to sink behind the cart and hide but stuck in place by their harnesses. The milkman returned from the shop and stroked the dogs. They trembled in the man's hands. He fed them torn, muddled, and gray scraps from his pocket.

Odette salivated at the sight of the scraps. The man had hidden them in his hand, glancing from side to side in search of someone who might notice. He hadn't counted on Odette seeing him from across the boulevard. He had kept his palms closed until they reached the snouts of the dogs. The dogs yipped with excitement. He shushed them. Odette wanted to run across the street, Citroen be damned, and tear at the milkman, rip open his pockets, murder him for the scraps of meat he withheld, for the slivers of putrid, rancid scraps he had given up to his dogs. The dogs licked the milkman's fingers, his knuckles, the man's face, leaving a smile of broken teeth squeezed between his unshaven cheeks.

Is this how far Odette had come in the city starved of information and literally starving? At least in the country they had chickens or cows or horses or wheat or even scorpions. Paris had rats and even those seemed to have dwindled. Whether because of the cats or the people, she wasn't sure. The government had put out a statement about cat meat making people sick, which protected the strays in the street. She couldn't imagine someone trying to eat Martine, nor did she want to. And worse, she also wanted to tell people hoarding rabbits on their balconies that sooner or later it would starve them. Rabbit meat was too lean, not enough fat to satiate them. In fact, their body would work harder to process the rabbit meat than the nutrients provided. But like the pigeons, people just missed meat after a while and didn't care about the repercussions. The dogs rubbed their snouts into the man's hands. The man glanced at Odette and nodded with a slight wink; it could have been a lazy blink—one that said, "We're in this together."

Her ire turned to the Citroen whose black glimmer streamed down the road. The taxis hadn't gotten out of the way. The loud, high-pitched horn hadn't driven the drivers to the sides of the road. Odette imagined the men with wry smiles, silently agreeing to keep a steady pace side-by-side so the officer couldn't pass. The German horn gave way to German yells. The officer's voice sounded similar to the horn, long-winded, loud, and surprisingly high for a burly man. He waved his hand out of the window to shoo the taxis aside as if they noticed, as if he had the power to throw them from the road with a wave of his fingers. He revved the engine; the taxis kept their pace. He honked again; the taxis didn't stray. The officer pushed forward. The wheels screeched against the stone. The car lurched forward. Odette cried out to the taxis. The milkman had taken his dogcart back the way he had come, the sound of the creaking wooden wheels a memory beneath the crying rubber of the Citroen. The slick, black bumper crashed into the cab. The back axle bent; the wheels turned in. The driver swerved into his neighbor. The other taxi driver screamed. The bicycle careened from the road. The officer kept honking. The taxis wrapped together, swerved together, and ran into the tables of the café. Chairs scattered. The tables toppled. An elderly couple, too afraid to move, grabbed their watery chicory coffee before it fell away beneath them. The taxi drivers flew from their bicycles. The officer waved goodbye, the couple sat amongst the pile of tables and chairs that once resemble a quiet place to watch the city pass until the city rolled into them, but still left them unharmed. One of the drivers had hit his head on the stone after flying from his bike. The other driver carried his arm as if in a sling. He checked on the fallen driver. The man looked pale, a mask of himself seconds before. Odette should have run to him, checked his pulse, steadied his head, diagnosed the situation, but just like when she saw the milkman feed the dogs bits of meat, rage boiled in her stomach, where she found anger resided most often. It sat there, heated there, bubbled there, until it erupted into the other parts of her, filling her heart, her head, even tingling in her toes as they carried her forward, not toward the cab driver but following the officer. He could have killed the drivers, that couple, or anyone that had happened to have walked by the café at the time. A man like that must have done worse things when he actually thought about it. A man like that was dangerous. A man like that would hurt others on a whim. A man like that shouldn't go on; imagine all the lives Odette would save just by killing this one man.

Odette passed the taxi driver and stopped. She knelt down near his head. The old couple and the maître d' added to the crowd around the fallen driver, who still hadn't moved or blinked. His breath had shallowed to imperceptible movement. The stones were dry, showing no signs of a head wound, which was a good sign. Odette told the couple to stay with the driver and slowly grabbed a knife close to the edge of the driver's head, sliding it into her bag. Odette followed the car, picking up her pace, listening to the sound of her footsteps on the stone, her breath in the muggy air, the way the fabric of her blouse rubbed against her shoulders as they swayed leaving a slight itch. It was the hyper-awareness of a hunt, before a kill; a primitive feeling, she told herself, which allowed her ancestors to focus on their prey while staying aware of their surroundings.

The car had turned onto a side street. She followed the trace of the shiny stream, like a spiritual residue that stayed behind for a heartbeat. Like the butcher, she thought. The colors he always claimed to see. She was a lion, hiding her true self in the concrete jungle from the men who hunted for sport. She, in turn, would hunt them for sport. The Citroen stopped in front of the SS headquarters on Avenue Foch. The officer walked into the main building and disappeared. The black of his uniform couldn't slim him. His leather boots swelled around his feet and calves. His shirt nearly burst, and his hat barely hid his greasy hair. A slob. The slob, who left a trail of slime wherever he went. A barbarian dressed as a man. But hadn't that been what Odette had expected of the German's all along?

Odette could wait for his return or go in the building after him. Her ears tingled with hot fury, the same as her toes that had carried her so far from where she started the day, past the flailing cabby and near the Arc de Triomphe, where people left flowers atop the tomb of the unknown soldier in acts of quiet protest. Odette was tired of silent protests; exhausted with the thought of all the times in her life she had stood by and watched a child take a beating from their father; or a wife take a fist in her jaw to protect her daughter; or a daughter take the belt from her father to protect her brother; or a soldier pick a fight with a drunk; or a soldier rape an unsuspecting woman; or a soldier ridicule, demean, belittle, shame, puncture any sense of morality and dignity a woman may have left after the rape.

Odette had watched the aftermath, women empty shells of their former selves, eyes open with no brightness inside, going through the motions of their day like a machine rather than a person, with no joy, no time to smell the fresh macarons, the roasting chickens, the foie gras, the robust wine. And then, like those women, Paris emptied of light, a city once known for its radiance, then turned into a hallow shell where brightness once attracted creativity and curiosity from around the world. She hadn't bothered or cared before, hadn't wanted to deal with the aftermath putting on her death mask to meet with a German soldier, no matter how deserving. Especially after the mistake she had already made. She had practically begged for Agnes's help, her protection. She couldn't make a mistake like that against. But she couldn't put it off any longer. She couldn't watch any longer. But she couldn't start with this man. But she could start with his Citroen.

She took the knife she had taken from the café out of her bag. The metal had been smooth once, now rusted a touch around the handle, unpolished for weeks and washed too often without replacement. It felt flaccid and weak. She gripped the handle as tight as possible and pretended to drop something from her bag. She leaned down to grab the imagined object and thrust the knife into the tires, first the back, then the front. She picked up the fake object, placed it in her purse, and walked away, eager to find the focus of her new objective, no longer relying on the sad men intent on building themselves up with their boot on their wife's throat. She would do this for herself, she would do this for her mother. Perhaps she could convince herself, she could do it for France.

Thirty-six

The restaurant stunk of fat. Butter, duck fat, German fat, and the grease melting down the chins of the whores inside who smiled, laughed, sipped wine, and rubbed their fingers over the bloated cocks of German officers. Odette sat at a table alone and sipped at her wine, a red glass. The scent of tobacco and blackberries swirled upward from the table. How long had it been since she had taken in the scent of a wine not muddled by water? Of hints of tobacco instead of sunflower leaves? How long had it been since she could taste the wine before she even had a drop? How long had it been since she sat down in a restaurant and ordered wine without thinking about the cost? And for a brief moment, Odette forgot about her reason for being there. She wanted to stay at the table, order a chicken, and nibble on potatoes roasted in the fat. But then the SS officer laughed. Spittle flew from his mouth. The napkin tucked into his collar looked greasy and stained.

Odette took one last sip of her wine and dreaded leaving the remainder of the glass. She wore red; her dress, her lips, the fire that roared in her chest where her heart should have been. The dresses had lined the walls of Lévitan when she returned with Ilse, and while Ilse once again fingered the furs or tapped the porcelain, Odette coveted the red dress. She practically tasted the blood. Her mouth watered at its promise. Ilse had muttered about someone special in Odette's life. Odette nodded; Ilse hadn't been wrong.

Odette had stayed clear of the German soldiers for so long only to watch them grow and spread through the city like leeches sucking at the very soul of Paris, of France, of her. And rather than take care of the infestations, they—her—let them multiply. She swayed her hips as she strutted past the officer's table. Her best imitation of a Hollywood femme fatale. She dropped a piece of paper. The officer bent down to retrieve it.

"Madame," he said, his voice high but brutal as if his cheeks slapped every time he spoke. "I believe this is yours." He held up the paper.

"You must be mistaken," Odette said. "That's yours." She winked. The officer blushed. She walked away toward the WC where stairs led to the cellar, where the cellar led to the catacombs, where the tunnels led to Death—to her. And this time, she wouldn't bother leading him to her kiln. And this time she would let the man rot beneath the city, give the German what he wants, to become part of the city, and fade into the nauseating mold with bits of detritus. And her heart pounded with anticipation beyond the hunt. And her thighs quivered from the excitement of shirking routine, unable to bring an SS officer to her street, to her building, to the cellar. And she knew he opened the paper. And she knew he would follow her. And she knew she would wait in the soft glow of the lantern in red. With her death mask staring into the future.

And he knew with that whisper he wouldn't make it out alive. The funny thing about drowning in your blood, you can feel it bubble with every breath. You know it shouldn't be there. You think maybe you can cough if out. Maybe you can vomit it away, like a hole in a dyke. You feel it creep in and settle like a bog. Perhaps mosquitos will lay eggs in it, and they'll bite at your tissue, or better yet, drink the blood until they are fat and lazy and drowned in it too. Even with his hand to the wound, with the blood spilling from his chest, through his fingers, dripping down his skin, the whole of him would fade until soaking wet, dried up, and evaporated. Ashes to ashes, dust to dust, face to dirt, blood to mud. These quiet nights, as in the endless absence of sound that took up more space than silence, made the drum of his slowing heart echo in his ears, pound against his temples. The dead had a way of rising up when committed, when convicted, when even their desiccated veins moved enough blood around to keep their muscles active for a last second, a vengeful second, to leap out and grab the knife, the hand holding the knife, the throat of the woman who wielded the knife. He had grabbed her, a woman, a soft hand in washed gloves, a glove he could have eaten from, with fingers he could have licked once, sucked the sweet saccharine juice of tart strawberries from, with a hint of chocolate tucked into the corner of his lips for a slightly bitter ending. He always loved a bitter ending.

How could he not have seen a woman, this woman from the start, the way she leaned into him, the way she walked and spoke, poised, elegant, a woman of schooling, not from a proper boarding school but lessons from the street. He knew, he had seen them with his own eyes during the war, not this sham of a fight, good for Germany but bad for pride, for morale, for honor with the way the planes flew hard and fast at night. The men no longer saw the face of their enemy, the whites in their eyes, the bloodshot cracks from lack of sleep, on the brink of insanity due to nonstop artillery shells and gunfire, hints of mustard gas and blood-soaked bayonets. Honor had fallen into the mud. And here he slouched, a man of honor, one humbled by the hand of a woman in the catacombs of a city they should have flattened. But no, the Fuhrer wanted it—needed it as a trophy. He took hold of it like a boy stealing his brother's favorite toy, only to find it wasn't as shiny as he had thought. Now that he had it, he didn't know what to do with it. And he, like the other officers, was left to hold it in place, keep it looking shiny to the outside world, to the folks back home, to the people inside the shiny toy. He spat blood on the dusty floor. It soaked the dirt and turned into a glob. A trickle of water dripped, dripped, dripped away from the blood on the floor, except it wasn't water, it was blood seeping from his wound. The gurgle grew worse. He had given his life to Germany and now for Germany only to have his life fade from the world unbeknownst to it by a common whore. If he believed his own hype, she must not have been common because she bested him. He wheezed, spit, and wheezed again. The blood rushed in his lungs. A gendarme spilled out of the darkness. He caught the ghostly white of the man's face, his blood-soaked uniform, the knife in his hand. The gendarme studied it, the blade, the handle as if he had never seen death before. Without comment but with a slight hesitation, he limped to the officer, and shoved the knife back into his chest. He pulled it out, plunged it back in, out once more, and shoved it back down deep into his ribs. The officer smiled. With one last breath filled with the gurgling of his bloody lungs, he laughed, coughing blood onto the gendarme's face thinking the entire time, it was never the woman. Thinking, this is honor.

Thirty-seven

"What the hell have you done?" Odette screamed.

She gripped Aloysius's lapels. She felt the roughness of his hands on her skin as he tried to pull her away. Tears, hot and salty, fell to the floor. But when was the last time she had cried? When was the last time she had a reason, let alone felt enough anger to cry. Because for Odette, crying was not about sadness. She never felt the need to cry when sad but when angry; the fire boiled in her heart, as if it were a pot, and when the water gushed over, it spilled from her eyes promising both tears and aggression. And that was how she felt now. She couldn't tell if the pounding she heard was her heart or the footsteps of soldiers chasing after them.

"Why—" she stuttered. The word caught in her throat and wouldn't fall out. She finally understood when people asked if there was a frog in her throat because, out of all the times she needed to speak, it felt like a frog had leapt into her mouth and lodged itself in her esophagus. She might choke. She might vomit. Then would the frog come out and leap away unharmed? "Why would you—? He was—"

"Odette, Odette!" Aloysius moved his hands from hers and pressed his fingers to her cheeks. His skin was cold and covered in smeared blood already drying when the red turned form crimson to brown. "He was going to hurt you."

"No," she said. "You don't understand." She pressed her face into his shoulder. She grabbed his coat. She pounded her fists against him. "You don't know. You think you know but you don't know."

"Odette, please." He pulled her face from his shoulder. He tried to kiss her. She wanted his lips. She was desperate for his touch. Because unlike him, she knew it would be their last. She pulled herself away from him.

"Damn it, Ali," she said. She pulled out a knife from her coat, unused, glinting in the dark. It wasn't supposed to look innocent.

"But, why?" Aloysius said.

"You never wanted to look past the book cover did you?"

"What are you talking about?"

"I always told you I was the beast. Even when you thought it was you. You never wanted to listen."

He dropped his hands from her face. She didn't think the air could have felt colder than it had a second ago. But when Aloysius pulled away, a windstorm struck her skin. It was cold, icy, and lonely.

"What have you done?" Aloysius said. "What have I done?"

"You did what you thought was right," Odette said. "You always wanted to do what you thought was right."

Aloysius shook his head. He brought his palms to his face but stopped before his hands reached his eyes. He stared at his skin, the bloodstains on his fingers, the way it crept up his sleeves, dug underneath his fingernails. With each passing second it seemed like the blood caked to his skin became a part of him. Odette understood that feeling; it had happened to her with the grocer when the blood spilled across the floor and she sat in it, let it pool around her and she sank into it. She wanted her skin to absorb the blood at the time, as if that would have made it ok, as if it would have made her capable of turning into the grocer and therefore capable of turning back time, repenting for his actions but repenting was always for the sinner and never for those sinned against, which only meant even if Odette could have taken the grocer's blood into her body, she never could have turned back time, and her penance never would have brought her mother back. Instead, the grocer's penance would have made him feel better and still would have left Odette with nothing. So instead, she took the blood. And now, Aloysius took the blood.

"Lord, forgive me," Aloysius said.

"No," Odette said. This time she grabbed his face. His cheeks were cold and not from the damp air of the catacombs but from fear, his fear that shone through his pale skin, that beamed from his eyes. "You do not need forgiveness." Her voice seethed; each word poured through her teeth. "He was a terrible man. Less than a man. A demon. And the world is better without him."

"And what about me?" Aloysius said. His breath erupted from his mouth in visible puffs. The catacombs grew colder. Odette still couldn't tell if the pounding was her heart or the soldiers, or perhaps it was the sound of Aloysius's heart. Maybe he would see her not as a beast, and not as a beauty but as someone like him, trying to do good in the world. "Will the world be better without me? Without a murderer?"

"Would it have been better if you had done nothing? If all good men did nothing?" She tried to kiss him, to implore him with her lips the way he had tried with her. She tried to tell him all the things she could not say, how she hid her life from him, how she wished to show him her true self, how she wished to tell him what brought her to this, how she wished to have killed the officer herself, how she wished to have that man's blood on her hands, how she wished to take away the pain from his eyes, how she wished—but then Aloysius pulled away from her kiss, and she knew that was all they would ever be, wishes.

"Good men don't kill," Aloysius said. He hung his head down and sank slowly to the floor. Odette tried to fight it, tried to keep him lifted. If the pounding she heard were footsteps, they'd have to run.

"Ali," Odette said. "We need to go. You need to go."

He sat on his heels shaking his head mumbling the word "no" over and over. The blood was barely visible on him in the dark.

"What have I become?"

"Damn it, Ali." Odette smacked Aloysius on the cheek, hard enough for him to snap to attention. "Are all soldiers bad men? You wanted to be a soldier. You wanted to protect France. You wanted—" the words once again caught in her mouth. "You wanted to protect me." Her chest heaved. She couldn't catch her breath. "You have. After all this time, okay? You have always protected me—from myself. Please. Let me protect you now."

"But you always fought for me. You never needed my protection."

"You stupid man," Odette almost laughed. "You think you can only protect someone when fighting. When will you realize that you protected me from the world, you showed me beauty." Her voice dropped knowing she was too much beast to ever have a happy ending; now more than ever, she knew. "You showed me love. You showed me there was more to the world than that night, than demons, more than myself. Ali, please." Aloysius stood up. Odette breathed a deep sigh. She took his coat and put it on. She tore her coat and left it crumpled in the corner.

"You remember Mr. Debusier?"

"The butcher?" Aloysius asked. Odette nodded.

"Go there. If his shop is closed, knock four times in equal measure."

"Are you saying—"

"I'm saying he is going to protect you. He is going to protect us." This time Aloysius nodded. He leaned in to kiss Odette. She turned and he kissed her cheek. For all the times she had wanted his kisses, felt she deserved his kisses, now she only felt shame. She had dragged him into the one mess she had promised Agnes she would never do. But promises rarely last.

"Odette, I—"

She pressed her finger to his lips.

"Not now. Tell me later."

"Later," he said.

"Give us something to look forward to." She tried to smile but the weight felt too much.

They walked to the edge of the catacombs where the tunnels led back out into the Parisian night. Aloysius left first. Odette watched him turn from body to shadow to emptiness. He never looked back. Odette walked in the opposite direction. She took the emptiness with her.

Thirty-eight

Odette kept her journal in the drawer beneath the counter where she stored the knives. The sharp edges pointing down to the counter felt protective as if they'd strike someone reaching for the drawer in her absence to protect her secrets. Except she didn't keep many secrets in the journal, or any that would harm her life beyond the emotional layers she shouldn't have. She opened the journal and ran her fingers along the yellow, dry pages. The moisture in the apartment had caused the pages to dampen, dry, dampen, and dry over again, making them crisp and brittle to the touch. One time she touched the corner of the page too vigorously and the paper tore from between her fingers.

"All little girls keep a diary," her mother had said. "I kept one when I was your age, and now you are old enough to keep one too."

"What's the point?" Odette said.

"Sometimes we have thoughts or feelings we aren't allowed to share," her mother said. Odette swore she had seen the narrows at the edge of her mother's eyes turn down as if her eyes had frowned for her.

"But what about—" Odette said.

"There are some things in this world you cannot share." Her mother's tone held heat; she spoke quick and quiet. "That journal is yours and only yours. No one sees it but you. No one reads it but you. Write stories, draw, I don't care, but a little girl cannot go around making others bleed or breaking their bones with rocks."

Odette understood her mother referred to the fight with Francois and Louis. She couldn't have known Odette's reasoning; otherwise, she wouldn't be defending them over her daughter.

"Those boys were—"

"I don't care if they said I work at the Moulin Rouge!" her mother shouted. "You keep your hands clean; do you hear me? Someone won't always be around to wash the blood away before the dust settles."

"What dust?" Odette asked.

"It's an expression," her mother said. "It means if other people notice, you can get in big trouble. What if Francois had hurt you?"

"He's a big oaf."

"Bigger in his bulk maybe but obviously not as oafish as you in his thoughts."

Odette couldn't understand from where her mother's anger rose. It seethed through her clenched jaw and pulsed in the veins on her neck. Odette wondered if she looked like her mother when she was angry. She clenched her fists, not her jaw, and breathed through her nose like a bull, or what she imagined a bull to breathe like when angry through the cartoons she read. Odette looked to the floor, averting her eyes and keeping her hands behind her back.

"I will always be worried about you," her mother said.

"Even when I am grown?" Odette said.

"Always," her mother said.

Odette had never opened the journal until the night her mother died. After Odette and Agnes had disposed of the body, after they had cleaned the floor, after she had walked past the lower apartment and seen Aloysius waving to her from the doorway, she opened the journal to the second page, the one after her mother had written "thoughts, hopes, dreams."

The blank page hadn't yet yellowed. Her mind had emptied with the first sign of her mother's blood. She had scrubbed any sign of the grocer away from the floor and swept away the glass. She had picked out the small pieces embedded in her knees and palms and threw them into the linens where the grocer had lain. With any luck, even after death, he could still feel the glass dig into his skin, she thought. Odette took a pencil and wrote, "I no longer need groceries." Tonight, in the clean, quiet of Paris, Odette took her time flipping through the pages. She sat on her chair and sunk into the soft cushion. Martine gave a short *meep* and stared at her, telling her she sat in his seat. He jumped onto her lap, which meant it was okay, *for now*. The passages in her journal were not what her mom had hoped. She hadn't drawn pictures or written stories, at least a story another person could read. The sentences were terse and reflected that of her first entry, of all the things she no longer needed. But each object said more than what she didn't need, and instead told her of what she had gotten rid of, a world unburdened by the reddening of a sliver of darkness. Three pages in the book said, "I no longer need shoes," or "I no longer need to put money in the bank." The cobbler she had killed beat his wife and his children because he thought they judged him too harshly on his days off. The banker cheated his clients out of money and left them rotten poor. To the unknowing reader the journal meant what it said, a checklist of sorts to remind Odette of what she might have bought. To Odette, each sentence was a moving picture of the men who deserved to die, the banker who she bled quickly from his wrists and the cobbler who she beat with a bag of oranges across the face and left an open wound on his belly to account for the child he killed when he beat his pregnant wife before Odette bled him from the wrists. There were plenty of empty brittle pages in the book, but Odette couldn't turn away from what remained absent. Martine purred on her lap. She turned the pages again, this time with eagerness, tipping her fingers against the edge of the paper, not finding what she wanted. She kept such fastidious notes in her life of intimate details to always stay ahead of anyone or anything. But she hadn't given space on the page to the hospital—and to those in it. She turned another page. The paper cracked, tore, and crumbled beneath the frantic flip of her fingers. The remaining crisp edge tore through her skin. Odette flinched at the paper cut. She stuck her finger in her mouth and sucked away the blood. She hadn't given space to any of the patients. How would she remember them? Something told her she wouldn't need the journal. Her tears felt cold as they carried the image of each patient she had seen in the hospital. Each tear a projection of their death—of her as Death—as they sunk away from life with a whimper.

She glided down the hall tracing her fingers down the cold stone, the cracks that told her the age of the structure, that started at the base along the shattered rocks and crept up the wall breaking with every step she took. The building looked ready to collapse from the weight of Odette's memories, absent of the strong foundations once by her mother, Agnes, Aloysius, Mr. Tureshko. She descended the stairs into the cellar where she could count on the fire; she could always count on the fire with the wood Agnes had harvested, with the lives Odette had harvested.

I'm not Death, she realized. *Agnes was right. I am the devil.* Death takes and ferries souls, but the devil keeps them. And the plates, the cups, the bowls scattered around the cellar revealed the hell she had created, another layer of the Inferno, but whose? The men she had killed or the unending cycle she had created? The fire in the kiln roared. She threw the journal into the pit. The fire flipped and ate the pages. It spoke out of turn. She couldn't remember lighting the fire. But she rarely remembered starting the fire, only that the fire existed, after the first, the first that Agnes had sparked, that Odette had kept alive. Until it took over. And the cellar steeped with heat, the wood crouched beneath the table. How many cold nights could she have stayed warm in her flat? How many old women she could have helped in the winter? How many children could she have saved from the frost?

"I did save the children," she said.

"No, you didn't," the fire roared. "You saved yourself. Every life you took was never for them. It was for you. Always for you. Including Agnes."

"That isn't true."

The fire cackled.

"Stop it."

"Prove it. But you better do it soon. I'm getting hungry."

"You're always hungry," she said.

"No," the fire said. "You are always hungry." It raged, and the door flew open ready to take the food it wanted. Odette flung the door shut and burned her fingertips, the rot of charred skin replacing the smell of ash and wood.

The hatchet glowed in the firelight. Odette gripped the handle and let her waxy fingers melt into the polished wood. It felt heavier with the weight of the building resting on the blade.

She swung the hatchet. Shards of porcelain flew across the room. Cups shattered. Plates cracked then crushed, pulverized. The blade cut into the table. The table split. The table broke open. The remaining pottery avalanched to floor.

"What does that prove," the fire spit.

Odette turned to bricks. Her fingers fused to the hatchet handle. The sweat dripped, then dropped, and then sizzled on her skin. She swung and the kiln fractured. She swung again. The kiln splintered. Once more and the kiln ruptured falling in on itself, a model of the building around them ready to collapse at any second and fall into the pit Odette had created. The fire sputtered beneath the brick. Odette spit on the flame. It fizzled to a whisper beneath the hot brick, the suffocating brick, the broken brick where the dust mingled with the shards of lifeless pottery. Odette's chest heaved, unable to catch a breath in the storm she had created. On top of the mound of bricks, over the broken pottery, sat the first bowl Odette had ever made, where she would put peaches, where the peaches would rot, where the scent would remind her of a time before ash-coated fingers. Her mother, split down the middle—again—Odette had caused it—again— and Odette couldn't protect her—again—and the dust blended with the smoke—still— and she abandoned the cellar, bound for her apartment—voices called from outside—she pulled back the rug and fell to the floor—and footsteps fell hard up the stairs—and she pulled back the floorboards—and rough hands pounded the door—the space in the floor dark and open—and rough hands grabbed her—and rough hands pounded her—and rough mouths spat in her face—but the candlesticks she had expected to find were gone—and her building came down around her.

Thirty-nine

The room spun with darkness, turning Odette upside down, twirling to the right and left until she couldn't tell from where she had come. The scent of damp, putrid water filtered through the catacombs until the flicker of light brought her back to the hall. She had been down here before. The light brushed against the wall and fell on the indentations of the forgotten limestone. The pockmarks reminded her of the ways the statues in the Louvre once took on the elements of their surroundings, absorbing the outside world into their pores. What a difference the environment makes, Odette thought, as she touched her fingers to the crags in the wall imagining what the Venus de Milo would look like if it was stuffed inside the catacombs hidden from the view of the outside world, instead remaining fodder for rats, bats, and passing piss from the dripping sewers. What tainted color would the marble hold? What feral scent would lift from the beauty's porous skin? Who would want to embrace her as a treasure then? Odette moved to sniff her fingers, finding the aroma of petrol blending in with the subtle stench of rat and human shit.

Odette had experience with human shit, after all the bodies she had wiped down over the years, in the hospital and in the cellar of the apartment complex. In those years she learned the layers of shit, the way it carried particular aromas different than other animals. Rats shat human refuse, absorbing the necessary nutrients from whatever they could find as food. Their pellets carried small whiffs of wood shavings and trash, but trash was never the hardest smell to which she needed to acclimate. Human shit, depending on the texture, had different smells all on their own. Thick and firm shit held a unique stench to the sick, slick diarrhea of fear when the bowels loosened without control. The smear left an incredible odor on par with pure stomach acid and rotten tomatoes with fungus. The stench clawed its way into the nostrils, into any available fabric like a virus. It was why Odette always burned incense in the cellar while she worked, because the fear of death, then death itself, always led to shit.

"This is where he died," Ilse said. Her lantern glowed against the wall. "Yes?"

Odette turned, having forgotten Ilse led her back down into the catacombs, back to the scene of the crime she had said she didn't commit. "You were here, you said. But you did not kill him."

Odette nodded and sniffed her fingers again. The petrol must have leaked from the restaurant above. Ilse shouldn't hold the candle so close to the wall or the entire catacombs could go up in flames. For a brief second, Odette wanted to push Ilse's lantern closer to the fumes, break the glass and let the underground chamber erupt. It would take care of both of them. She had never had a problem killing before. But now her fingers trembled. She felt faint. Aloysius had given up his life for her to survive. She couldn't repay him now, especially not with *her* own life.

Ilse leaned closer to Odette's ear. "He's dead you know," she whispered.

"I know. I was here. I have told you."

"No," Ilse said. "Your police friend." The light cast a narrow beam through the catacombs and died quietly in the darkness, useless after three feet. "Did he save you? Paris can be such a frightening city." Ilse pulled her free fingers to her teeth and chattered before breaking into a smile. "Please, child. Men like your policeman are not becoming to us. We need excitement, danger. We want to be tested, yes? You have known him since childhood, I'm sure. Has he ever suspected?"

"What about your husband?"

Ilse slapped Odette. The smack echoed through the empty chamber. The lantern swung and twirled. Odette almost lost her footing. She bit her cheek. Her mouth filled with blood. She sucked on her teeth and let the thick taste of iron coat her tongue. It kept her from smiling.

"You can't change the subject," Ilse said. "You are still so young. So naïve. You don't understand the difference between a challenge and an understanding." Ilse rubbed her fingers down Odette's face, this time tapping against her chin with the soft tissue of her gloves. She leaned in close, her lily perfume prominent, her nicotine breath alluring, her plump limps draped in red. "Your policeman didn't challenge you. He couldn't even challenge those idiots at his precinct. He spent so much time wallowing behind his puppy eyes worried they'd torment him again. He always saw his lame leg as a weakness." The heat from her breath made Odette's upper lip prickle with sweat.

"It kept him out of the war," Odette said.

"And so did being a woman," Ilse said. "Is that a weakness?" They walked down the catacomb until Ilse stopped and smeared her foot over the slick mess of dark liquid. "How about your...weakness? Do you know what happened here?"

"This is where you found the captain," Odette said.

"He had a curious wound," Ilse said.

"In his neck," Odette said.

"It looked methodical. Why would someone make a precise cut and then stab him repeatedly?"

"You should have asked my policeman," Odette said.

Ilse put the lantern on the ground. They stood in a drying puddle of blood, still shiny from pockets of wetness. "I did. What do you think you are standing in?"

Odette jumped away from the puddle. She stomped her boots on the floor. She screamed and tried to take the boots from her feet if the blood wouldn't wipe off. Aloysius's blood had tainted her, an innocent man now stuck to her soles.

"Stop it, you weakling!" Ilse laughed and pushed Odette to the wall at the edge of the light where the shadows crept in. She spat in Odette's face. The sludge dripped down her chin. "Where is the strength I once saw in you? When did you become this sniveling—thing?"

"His blood," Odette said. "It's his blood. He didn't deserve—"

"But the men you've killed did?"

"Yes," Odette screamed into the void. She flailed her legs to kick the boots away but they clung fast to her body.

"No," Ilse said. "They didn't. Your policeman didn't. And certainly, those poor fools in the hospital didn't." Odette felt weak, absent of bone and muscle, made of gelatin and ready to melt. "But you did it anyway. You did because you believed in something. You believed they earned death. They needed to see your death mask. Your policeman earned it too, for his cowardice."

"He wasn't—"

"You are going to tell me he wasn't a coward? He was made of mice and in the end ran like a mouse." Ilse made a squeaking sound, bucking her teeth in a brief impression. She let go of Odette, picked up the lantern, and traced a trail of half-bloody footprints deeper into the catacombs, down to a place that smelled more of mold and emptiness.

"This isn't his?" Odette asked.

"No, dear. This is the captain's. This is the mess I have to clean up for you."

"He earned it," Odette said staring into the darkness. Ilse stepped in front of Odette and once again pressed her hand to Odette's face. Her soft touch had a motherly affection, almost calming Odette, consoling her, reassuring her.

"Yes," Ilse said. The light shined against half her face, leaving the rest of her body in the blackness of the underground. "He did deserve it. We all do." The candle flickered in a soft breeze that blew through the catacombs. "Someone must have opened a door. We should find our way out." She moved to walk away. Odette reached out and grabbed Ilse's hand. Odette thought back to walking with her mother in the park, feeding the ducks, and returning home to cook a peach cobbler or roast a chicken.

"Am I safe?" Odette asked, for herself, for Aloysius.

"Are any of us?" Ilse said, turning back to the door and pulling Odette along as a guide back from the blood hidden in the underworld.

Forty

The butcher shop's lights were off, and the windows blended into the surrounding street as if it could have been any butcher shop on any street in Paris. But Odette knew better. She had been coming to this shop after hours since she was twelve, since Agnes first gave her a knife, since the first time she needed help dissecting a body without remorse. After the grocer died, she didn't touch the body. When she killed her first prey, Agnes had helped her break it down and dispose of it. That was how Odette considered her work, disposal. But the butcher had helped Odette understand that a person, a body, was just another animal. While she may not want to eat one, they can be slashed, dashed, and diced like any other cut of meat.

She knocked the glass, one-two-three-four times. The windows remained dark. The painted letters had begun peeling. Business owners would rather spend their money on the black market than on repairing their shops, Odette thought. And it was true. Why should they starve just to keep their shop open when barely anyone could purchase goods legally, let alone afford something illegal? The butcher, she had thought, would be careful.

But—she had learned—the more someone tried to look innocent, the more suspicious they became.

The butcher shuffled out from the back and opened the door. He waved Odette in. His glasses sat askew on his face, barely touching the bridge of his nose.

"You shouldn't have come," he said.

"I wanted to make sure—"

"I know. Of course, but you shouldn't have."

Odette nodded. She knew but she couldn't help it. She needed to at least know Aloysius had made it to the shop.

"Is he—"

"He's long gone."

Odette kept glancing at the back door not wanting to draw too much attention. The butcher blocked her glance and made it look as though she stared at him, his movement, his tired eyes. His shoulders had slumped since the last time she saw him, not with age but with exhaustion, too tired to hold up his world much longer.

"We couldn't keep him here, you know that."

"Where—"

The butcher shook his head. "I *won't* tell you that."

"*Can* you tell me?" She was pulled to the echo of her night naked with Aloysius when she touched him like she knew how, with soft, juicy lips, with welcoming open hands, with an excited wet body, and he slipped into her the way she fell into sporadic dreams: peacefully and focused, hard but not forceful, until they both burst from excitement, falling onto the bed in exhaustion. When she entered her apartment alone, the ghost of the memory overwhelmed her, making her stir more than the wrathful recollection of her mother's death. She would lie in bed before falling asleep with her body reacting to the absent silhouette of Aloysius above her, the imagined weight of him on top of her, the tingle of him inside her until she broke out in a sweat and needed to break away from the memory, from the world around her, from the beast inside of her.

"I won't tell you," the butcher said. "You took a stupid risk coming here tonight." He looked at her hands. "You didn't even wash the blood." He disappeared into the back and returned with a rag soaked in ammonia. He scrubbed at her fingernails. "It's been days. The longer you wait—"

"The tougher the stain. I know."

"If anyone would know, it's you," he said with a lazy smile. The blood started to disappear. Odette savored the Butcher's touch, not like with Aloysius whose hands always felt unsure and a bit rough with calluses, but she basked in the surety of the butcher, how he knew what his hands were for, how the muscles always remained tense as if he always carried a knife, how his fingers always felt soft, even after all the years gripping, chopping, cutting, and slicing.

"You were always my best student," he said.

"That's because I was your smartest student."

"I didn't say that." He offered Odette a different smile, one of tiredness and warmth. It made the wrinkles around his eyes crinkle unlike the smile he had shown her previously. "You would have made a great butcher."

Odette shrugged. What could she say? That she was, in some way, a butcher? That she took what he had taught her into a different area of expertise? She tried to conjure some words, any words, that might show her gratitude but also not give away too much of where she had taken what he had taught her.

"But I think you already are," he interrupted her thoughts. He winked.

"Excuse me?"

The butcher looked up from scrubbing her hands with the rag resting its coarse hairs against the edge of her fingers ready to slowly scrape each fleck of dried blood and from beneath the nail and perhaps away from the memory.

"At the hospital, of course," the butcher said. "Your skills come in handy there, I'm sure. Lord knows doctors are little more than butchers anyway."

Odette tried to hide her sigh thinking of what the butcher would think if he saw the relief in her face, felt it relax in her body. Instead of telling him the truth, she said, "I'm just a nurse."

He patted her hand. "Good. I've always liked nurses better." He frowned giving away his true thoughts, those that turned to Agnes, their lost love, their time together, or perhaps the child they could have had if not for the stupid choices he made, the choices Odette now felt the weight of—not because of him but because of how her choices mirrored his, how her life pushed away the one she loved rather than brought him closer. But if she was honest with herself, she would have known that she had been pushing Aloysius away ever since the night with the grocer, ever since Agnes told Odette who she really was. And by keeping Aloysius at arm's length, she could continue to be that girl, that woman, that monster, that thing. But she didn't want to be that anymore. At what point could she stop, turn back, and take the path of the person she had wished to become?

"You can't—-" the butcher said, reading her thoughts.

"Pardon me?" Odette said.

"You can't ever know where he is. It's too—"

"I understand."

"This is going to break her," the butcher said.

"Who?" But after she said it, Odette knew. It was just another thing she wished she could take back but couldn't. "I'll check on her when I get back."

The butcher held up his finger and went to the back room. Odette had never noticed how the shop smelled like lavender at night as if the butcher cleansed the shop from the stench of blood or spoiling meat to create a new, earthen space each night, somewhere that felt pastoral, absent of death, absent of blood, and reminiscent of the countryside. The smell of blood reminded everyone of the war, even those who had never been to the front, never bothered with politics, and ignored the German soldiers, but lavender brought Odette into the parks before the war, when flowers bloomed, ducklings swam in the ponds, and children ate ice cream as it dripped down from the cone onto their sticky fingers. The butcher returned with a small photo.

"Please," he said. "Give this to Agnes."

The photograph pictured two bicycles leaning against the butcher shop window. He didn't write a message.

"Can I ask—"

"No," he said. "It's a joke between old friends." He patted Odette's shoulder. "I wish so many things had been different for you. You are a good girl."

"If only—"

"Stop. You are." He turned and opened the door for Odette. "Please give that to Agnes the moment you get home."

Odette nodded and stepped out. She turned back one last time to thank the butcher, but he had already closed the door. The keys jangled together as he turned the lock. He stared down and never looked up at her before returning behind the back door leaving the shop empty. It wasn't cold, but Odette felt the cold creep down her spine.

Forty-one

The sun hung low over Paris, almost hidden by the palaces and villas of a past grandeur, the same palaces and villas that now fluttered with swastikas on rippling fabric. For weeks after the German arrival in the city, the flags hung to the light posts along the Champs Elysée, over the facades of German offices, homes, the palaces of the French capital hidden behind the dark lines of a dark empire, with anywhere that hid behind the flag reeking of the same smell the flag represented, or worse, emanated the vitriol through the flag or because of it.

Odette sat in Agnes's kitchen. She hadn't slept. It felt like days but had been only hours since she returned from the butcher. She sipped a cup of tepid tea. She had stared too long at the steam rising from the water. Sporadic leaves drifted around the surface, having escaped from the steeper. Agnes only made coffee if she could source actual beans. "If you can't make it right," she had said, "better to not make it at all." That didn't account for the fact that Agnes made terrible blueberry tarts but always made them for Aloysius because they were his favorite. The tea smelled faintly of flower petals more than herbs or spices Odette's mother would drink before bed. It had a sweetness coffee lacked, but when steeped long enough, it ended up just as bitter without the same punch. When was the last time she had had any dessert? Aloysius had shared a custard he had found months ago. He had taken it from the kitchen after a German officer had finished less than half. Aloysius had scooped away the part of the custard the German had touched, then threw out the spoon too—considered *tainted*—worried that sharing what the officer had eaten would turn Aloysius more like *them*. Odette wanted to argue that "German" wasn't contagious—that by talking like that Aloysius sounded like *them*. Instead, she took a bite of the custard, closed her eyes, and let the thick, malleable cream coat her tongue. Agnes didn't have any custard. Stacks of papers, mail she had intercepted over the years, mail residents had never picked up, mail Agnes found reason to never throw away, lined the shelves beneath the nearly empty canisters for flour, sugar, coffee, and rosemary.

Years ago, Odette had modeled what she had in her kitchen based on what Agnes had in hers. Odette always had butter out on the counter and sugar near the stove for coffee. She had placed plates in the cupboard closest to the sink where they were easier to put away. The glasses were the easiest to reach. She had olive oil at the front of her pantry alongside the items she used most often. If Odette modeled her kitchen after Agnes's now, it would have nothing more than empty space where life once was.

"Why did you get him involved?" Agnes asked. Her voice cracked. Her eyes glowed red with sleeplessness, anger, and tears.

"I did no such thing, and you know it."

"His father was a damn drunk, and his son was a goddamn martyr."

"Don't talk like that," Odette said.

"Like what?" Agnes said.

"In the past tense."

"You don't know anything," Agnes said.

"And you didn't know him."

"He was my son!" Agnes slapped her hand onto the wooden table. Odette's teacup clanked. Water spilled onto the table. Forgotten mail soaked up the hemorrhaging, thinning the envelopes to reveal post no one had ever read, words no one cared about, stories no one knew.

"And you cared more about saving yourself than saving him."

"I cared about protecting us!"

"But not your souls," Odette said, knowing that was how Aloysius felt.

"You are not one to talk to *me* about a soul." Agnes's voice turned to a low gravelly whisper. "Of all the devils here, you by far are the worst."

When Odette and Aloysius were young, he had led her to a hidden park behind the Sacre Coeur Cathedral on Montmartre. They walked beneath the verdant arches in the scent of jasmine. They kissed in the quiet until an old man with his dog wandered into the park. He waddled with a cane. He took a look at the young couple, the way Aloysius blushed, but not Odette. The man tipped his hat, smiled, and put his finger to his lip before walking in the opposite direction, leaving Aloysius and Odette on their own once more.

"You remember *Beauty and the Beast*?" Aloysius asked.

Odette nodded her head. She hadn't heard many stories growing up, beyond the tales her mom would tell of the fabulous places they would travel to in their life together. They would visit London, New York, Tahiti; they would even spend time in the jungles of the Congo and on the sands of the Sahara in Morocco. The closest they ever got was when they saw a moving picture that took place in the palaces of Rajasthan.

"You told me about the story," Odette said. "You don't remember."

"I told you it's a great story about a prince who gets turned into a beast, naturally. Then Belle, the beauty, finds him, and he realizes his humanity. She sees the beauty in him. That's the point."

"Oh," Odette said. "I don't think I caught that." Her stomach rumbled. Her hands shook. She fought back a desire to run. She wouldn't cry; she couldn't cry; she had never cared how anyone thought of her before. She had never wondered how anyone thought of her before. But on the park bench, in the shade of the blossoming arches, Odette grew hot, knowing her cheeks flushed with anger, with shame because she learned, without Aloysius saying so, that he thought of her as the beast. And worse, she considered herself the same. It had been a month since she last killed someone. She relished it, took her time, listened to the blood, basked in the way her heart pounded as she stood at the precipice ready to jump. Even beasts didn't kill for fun. Lions hunted for food. Gorillas fought for dominance and territory. Martine gave warning when he didn't want to be touched. But Odette killed because it made her feel better, made her feel human, because it made her feel. Now, in Agnes's kitchen, Odette realized she was never the beast; she was never more than Death.

"The devil you know—" Agnes said.

"Wrong," Odette said. "Every devil is just a devil in the end."

"You're no better than them," Agnes said. "With all those bodies you've hidden."

"At least those bodies deserved it. What did the man upstairs do to you? Play his music too loud?"

"That is not the same," Agnes said.

"Better to learn to live with what you've done than not live at all. Your son knows better."

Agnes bit her lip, looked at the table, and grumbled.

"What was that?" Odette said.

"Knew," Agnes spat. "My son *knew* better."

"We don't know he still doesn't," Odette said.

Agnes put a knife on the table between them. She slid it to Odette.

"You won't need the kiln," she said.

"What do you mean?"

"I'm old. He's gone. Don't make me beg."

Odette stood. She nudged the table, tipping the tea.

"What makes you think I would—after all this time, you really think I'm a monster? I thought, I truly believed these things you said were for him, to protect him. I thought you actually—"

"Sit girl," Agnes said. Her voice wasn't harsh the way she often spat the word, and instead it floated out like a balloon. Odette stayed standing.

"Odette," Agnes said. "Please." Odette took her seat. Agnes stood and went to a container on the counter.

"I have been saving this for a special occasion," she said. "I don't think it will get more special than this." They sat in silence as Agnes brewed fresh coffee. Odette inhaled deeply taking in the scent of the chocolate, caramel, and char only found in coffee grounds. The machine dripped and echoed through the kitchen. Agnes poured the coffee, no sugar, no cream but real coffee, and placed it in front of Odette, pushing away the cold, dirty tea water.

Agnes waited for Odette to take a sip. For half a second, the terrors of the world melted away as the familiar, comforting, warm flavor of the coffee coated Odette's tongue. Then Agnes reached across the table and placed her hand on Odette's. Her voice turned nurturing, a tone Odette hadn't heard in ages, too often laced with acid or anger.

"I never thought you a monster, and I don't now," Agnes said. "I never wanted you to get hurt. You or Ali. But this is what the world's become. A place of hurt."

"But all those things you've done, you've said—" Odette said.

"I had to protect us. You should know, not all things are so black and white." Agnes looked back at the knife resting between them. The silence clung heavy to the air but linked them like a spider's web, strong and buoyant.

Odette took out the postcard from the butcher. She slid it across the table into Agnes's hand. Her leathery fingers traced the bicycles, the shop window.

"Old and rusty," she whispered.

Odette said nothing.

"This," Agnes said. "I meant something to someone."

"To more than someone," Odette said.

Agnes looked up from the postcard with a look that said she hadn't heard Odette.

"I—" Odette said. She took a sip of coffee to try and compose herself. Her heart pounded like thunder, so loud she swore Agnes could hear. The coffee, so fresh and sweet as a treat, had quickly turned bitter. "Why me?" Why not—" Odette looked at her hands unable to finish the thought.

"After so long," Agnes said, "I always hoped I would meet Death as a friend."

Agnes swept her fingers through Odette's hair and pulled through the strings with softness, absent of their usual leathery texture, comforting instead of scolding.

There was a hard knock at the door. The Gestapo had finally arrived.

"It's too late for waiting," Agnes said.

Odette grabbed the knife.

"You don't have to watch," Agnes said. "You've seen so much…too much."

Odette took Agnes by the hand. She stroked her skin from wrist to elbow. She stood behind Agnes, kissed the old woman's cheeks and slid the knife up. Agnes made no sound. The room absent of the cries, the screams, the pleas Odette had known, had taken comfort in, replaced by a resigned acceptance.

Odette turned away from the blood flowing from Agnes's arm like a waterfall. But Agnes grabbed onto her, pulled Odette's hand back.

"I forgive you," she said.

The door flew open. The soldiers flooded the room and knocked over the stacks of mail around the lounge, the kitchen, and the bedroom. They tapped the butts of their rifles against the walls and floor. The soldiers grabbed Odette, wrapping her up. She kicked at them. Her voice grew hoarse. They didn't listen. She grew limp and made them drag her through the doorway. She cried that she had done nothing. She yelled asking to know why they had taken her. And Agnes sat at the table, the cup of coffee thick with steam. Alone but no longer lonely.

Agnes ran directly to Mr. Tureshko's apartment and banged on the door, her heart matching the frantic thud of her fist against the wood. The old man with liver spots on his forehead opened. He took off his glasses and held them in his hand, like a knife, Agnes thought. *And he should stab me and get it over with.* She didn't wait for an invitation and instead barged past him into the apartment where the sounds of Lutoslawski's "Symphony No. 3" bounced off the walls of books, the torn chair, the table covered in notes beneath a single butterflied book.

"Mr. Tureshko," Agnes said. "You—" she stopped, stepped to the door. "This should be closed." She stepped back into the center of the apartment nearly knocking over a stack of books. It wavered and jittered with every step she took pacing back and forth until the tower leaned ready to fall.

"Madame Moreau," Mr. Tureshko said, "please sit." He handed Agnes a cup of cold tea. She waved it away unable to hold the saucer or the cup.

"I did it," she said. "I did it and I can't go through with it." She hid her face in her hands, the skin felt dry, absent of moisture when only an hour earlier she couldn't escape the heat, the sweat, but now her body had turned into a desert.

"Madame Moreau," Mr. Tureshko said. He looked at his book and back at Agnes, as if the pages were more important.

"No," Agnes said. She stared desperately at her hands wondering when they had become so wrinkled, so old, so detached from the rest of her. Mr. Tureshko turned up the music and took a sip of the cold tea. Agnes noticed how the book looked against the table and thought about the surface of the page, the sentence, the word she must have interrupted.

"It's about a man whose family turned into butterflies," he said.

"This has nothing to do with butterflies," she said.

He nodded his head to the book. "They fly away, and he spends the remainder of the book looking for them, trying to trace their existence along the migration route. It gave the character a sense of purpose."

She stood up and put her hands on Mr. Tureshko's shoulders gazing into his eyes at the same height. Bursts of green hid behind a lush brown matching his mahogany chair, the bookshelves.

"He finds them," Mr. Tureshko said. "In the end."

"You must leave," Agnes said. "They know your name. They know where you live. They know everything about you. And it's—you must leave."

"I tried to tell you," Mr. Tureshko said with a gentle voice that reminded Agnes of when she would try to calm Aloysius down. The faint scent of chamomile drifted from Mr. Tureshko's lips. "It could not have been easy."

Agnes shook her head. "I didn't think it would be so hard. I thought by now, after all this time…" her voice trailed into silence as she dipped her head and spoke the last words into her chest.

"You told them about me," he said. She nodded. "Good." He shook her shoulders gently and creased his lips into a sad but contented smile.

"You could go now. You, Mr. Tullis, Madame Seline."

"Where would we go," he said. "Where could we go? We have no family left."

"Then why this?" Agnes said. "Why have me name you?"

"It isn't about what they knew or didn't know. It's about what they thought they could get from you." Mr. Tureshko sniffed the air, "or perhaps what we hoped you could get from them, instead of just fresh fruit."

"I would never have done this for fresh fruit," Agnes said.

"Of course not. But now you'll have more access because of the fresh fruit you have given them."

"And what about you?" Agnes said. "What about all of you?"

"I have no one left. I never should have left Poland. My family stayed there, rounded up and frozen out of the community they had been part of. It was only a matter of time. It will be ok."

"You can't believe that," Agnes said, the cold bitterness of her voice pushing Mr. Tureshko a step back. He grabbed her hand, and with quiet warmth, patted her, caressed her skin, calming her.

"It is all I can ever believe. You did the right thing. You did what he had asked of you. You'll be able to protect far more than we ever could. When it's time for us—" he shrugged. She patted his hand this time reassuring him with a single touch she would do all she could, cling to their agreement, protect those she could. She sighed.

"If you'll excuse me," Mr. Tureshko said. "I have some reading I must finish." This time a genuine smile radiated from the center of the room.

"I can let myself out," Agnes said. Mr. Tureshko took his seat and picked up his book.

"Madame Moreau," Mr. Tureshko said. Agnes turned. "And what of the girl?" Agnes cracked a smile.

"Safe."

"And the boy before her?"

"Safe."

"And the others before them?"

Agnes said nothing.

"And now many others will also be safe. It isn't selfless. I'm old.

As Agnes closed the door, she wondered about the last time she had seen a butterfly, another disappearance in the city since the German's arrived.

Forty-two

The cell crowded Odette. Not from the concrete walls and the iron bars. Not from the cot and the bucket that hadn't been washed out, with black, bobbing pieces of shit inside the brown sludge that once was solid waste and urine. It made Odette think of the dusty banks of the Seine when the cobblestones got pulled up revealing the sand and the rain poured over the city turning the walkways to mud and muck. At first, the smell made Odette gag. It carried the same scent of a man she once left in the basement for too long in the summer heat. She had been called to work and was unable to get rid of the body for another two days. The blood spoiled before the sinew and skin. Odette hadn't known blood could spoil. The color had turned from crimson to rust, the same color of wet metal. The iron and medicinal smell of the blood turned putrid, sulfuric, emphasized by the desiccated skin, the caved chest cavity. The stink filled the streets until everyone checked their homes, their pipes, the water closets, the garbage, wondering what produced the stench. The blood looked clumpy in the buckets.

His skin had turned the gray of rotten meat. The man had been a banker. He had cheated clients out of money. He had gambled away his money and replaced it with other peoples', stealing what little they had to help himself, but in the end, he used what should have paid his debts and gambled it all away again, perpetuating the cycle, and those left with nothing could say nothing because those with something never believed those with nothing. The night Odette took the man back to the basement, she first cut off the fingers on the hand he used to hold cards. Then she cut off the fingers on the hand he used to tap his chips, narrating her reasons as she sliced near his knuckles. The rag in his mouth ate his screams. Men bled faster the more they screamed and jerked. Odette tried to calm those men she admonished, the ones she hated the most, who had done their worst, who Odette felt needed one more lesson in life before dying. She'd soothe their beastly cries before slicing into them again, making the pain last, making the blood take its time to drip from the body. She didn't care for the banker, but she didn't need him to linger longer than necessary. She cut his fingers, slit his wrists, and let him die. Then let his body linger. Then let the street fill with his stench. It was hard to move his body that night without the alley cats pawing at the window trying to get a peek or a taste of the meat inside. After a while Odette had gone nose-blind to the smell until she returned from using the toilet and it all hit her in one quick breath. That was the smell that hit her now inside the cell. But it wasn't the putrid perfume that narrowed the walls.

It was the writing etched into the cold concrete, meant to empower the imprisoned from past prisoners, strong words, phrases of resistance, "Never confess," "France above all," "Julien. 20 years old. Headed for the post." The words didn't embolden Odette; they closed her in, told her of all the people who had been in the cell before her, of those who Paris had already forgotten. Did their families survive, continue, remember? Was Julien another name erased from existence: past, present, and future? Odette traced her fingers over the letters in an attempt to find solace among the only headstones these people would ever have with their resignations, their obituaries engraved in concrete. That was the third day of her incarceration. On the first day she had ignored the writing on the walls, too busy pressing her face to the cold iron bars and screaming at the guard there must have been a mistake, a plea they must all have heard. On the second day, she sat with her back to the bars, her throat scratched raw from the screams. Then the words found her, and she felt the gritty letters with the tips of her fingers. The longer she rubbed, the smoother the words became, the more tender her fingers grew, until she had rubbed the skin pink, on the brink of bleeding, and some of the letters looked faded, making her as culpable as the Germans in erasing those like Julien from the world. Except worse. Then the words and the walls—the words on the walls—inched closer around her.

Odette screamed again, finding her voice in the silence of the cell. She pulled at her hair. The walls kept inching closer. She pounded her fists against the concrete. The walls closed in. She kicked and pushed and shoved until she missed the wall, knocked over the cot, and spilled the bucket of shit over the floor. The mist of urine and shitty water splashed under her heels. Then the guards came. They looked young like students, clean shaven, doe-eyed, one with green, one with blue. One had brown hair; one had blonde hair. Their black uniforms were pressed, ironed, with rigid creases. Their buttons gleamed in the dim light—lights like the hospital, not meant for healing.

"There was a mistake," Odette said. She stood at the center of the pool of feces and piss. The soldiers hesitated to grab her. They stood at the open cell and grimaced at the odor leftover. With one look Odette had turned from a woman, a French woman, into a slob, a pig, an animal that rolled in its own filth. The guards didn't see her as a woman. They saw her as the reason they had to wade through a puddle of refuse, the reason they had to dirty their uniform, the reason they couldn't be out in the brothels of Paris with a real woman, not a shit-loving animal. The scowls stuck to their faces, one with a pug nose, the other with a pointed nose and flaring nostrils. The walls swelled behind her and pushed her to the guards. They grabbed her arms and dragged her through the hall. The cell had constricted, but the hall extended endlessly, infinite doors, infinite lights, one stretch of hall. The guards' jackboots pounded on the tile. They huffed through their scowls. They didn't alter course. They marched with Odette between them, hungry, tired, with shit rubbed in her shoes and splattered over her stockings up to her ankles. A door at the end of the hall opened. She couldn't remember if she walked in, or the guards pushed her through. A woman told her take a seat, a woman whose voice sounded familiar, but Odette couldn't see. The light from the ceiling glared behind the woman, turning her into a silhouette, lifeless in the shadows—her voice as soulless as the shade.

"Take a seat," the woman's voice said. Odette hesitated, wanting once more to tell someone—anyone who might listen—it was a mistake. She mumbled. Dribble slipped from her mouth. She tried to hide it, wipe away any remnants on her sleeve. The woman repeated her demand. Odette stumbled while looking for a chair. A tub of water sat at the heart of the room. There wasn't a chair. The tub rippled and dripped onto the floor. The serene sound of crackling ice filled the room. If it was an empty bucket beneath a table Odette might have laughed, tickled by the turn her life had taken. Was this the mask Death wore for Odette? How cowardly Death must be, to wear a cloak on his face after how often Odette showed herself as the angel of death, unafraid to give those waiting to die the satisfaction of knowing who had come for them. Odette spat on the floor as an attempt to insult Death. But her attempt failed when the glob of goo turned to spittle and dribbled down her chin. The shadow nodded in the dim light. Then Odette couldn't move. She kicked her legs and shuddered but went nowhere. The familiar voice, the cold calm told her to relax. "It's worse if you struggle." If she struggled, maybe it would take her faster. They had strapped her legs to a bar across the tub. The shadow shushed Odette, a soothing sound, the way her mother calmed her when she cried as a child.

The shadow pulled at the chain. Odette crashed into the tub. She froze with the ice. She gasped, swallowed, choked, coughed in an air pocket, swallowed, choked, drowned—she was drowning. She emerged from the tub. Her body was blue; she knew it. She shook and shuddered. The stale air felt as cold on her skin, felt like knives on her skin, like a shot to the stomach; all the air in her lungs had been sucked out. She gasped but couldn't get the air past her throat. The shadow spoke, her voice as calm as before.

"That is what happens if you don't listen," she said. "Or if I think you are lying. If you are telling the truth, you can stay dry. Do you understand?"

Odette nodded. She hoped she nodded. She tried to nod. She blinked away the water from her eyes. The room was dark now, the way the shadow must have preferred it.

"Who was Agnes Moreau working with?"

"No, no, no," Odette said. The cold fogged her mind. The water clogged her throat and kept her from making sense. She stuttered and mumbled. "I do not know where Aloysius is." She must have heard them wrong. They must have said Ali. Agnes was old and had given up long ago. They must be looking for Ali. And she must stay silent.

Odette fell back into the water. Her heart shot into her mouth. Her teeth chomped together. She barely missed her tongue. The taste of frozen lung flooded her mouth. They dragged her from the water. She gasped.

"We will try again," the shadow said. "Who was Agnes Moreau working with?"

Odette had heard right; they wanted Agnes. But she lay dead and empty at her kitchen table surrounded by mountains of paper.

"Come now. We found piles of forged documents in her apartment. Papers of transit, adoption papers, even false identities. She is lucky she took her own life. We would have been much less pleasant." The shadow's voice dropped. It prickled into Odette's ear, a harsh, low, chilling whisper.

"Perhaps you are too soft on the woman. You didn't know her. She put you here. So, tell me, who was Agnes Moreau working with?"

"I don't—"

Odette fell into the water once more and was quickly yanked free.

"Let us try something different," the Shadow said. "Where is Aloysius Moreau?"

Odette shook her head. The water flew away from her skin. A modicum of warmth touched her. She plunged back into the tub. She swallowed the water, choked, surrounded by the freeze. The shock hadn't worn away. The shadow pulled her back up.

"You were picked up at his home. You were there when his mother died. And you expect us to believe you know nothing of her activity, nothing of his whereabouts?" The shadow made a sound with her mouth, a tsk that splashed in the concrete room over the sound of settling water. "This is not a trusting start to our friendship."

Odette stammered. "You don't have any friends," she told Death. The shadow submerged her into the tub and drew her quickly out.

"We have plenty of water and ice, mademoiselle. How long do you want this to continue?"

"How long do you?" Odette managed. She swore the shadow smiled before dropping Odette back into the tub. The plunge was quick but effective. Odette couldn't get warm. She couldn't breathe. Her entire body shook and ached. The straps dug into her ankles and wrists. Her shoulders strained each time they pulled her up. The straps cut into her skin when they yanked her into the tub.

"We have simple questions," the shadow said. Her voice hadn't wavered. "He has already betrayed you by betraying us. He dragged you into this. You don't have to be a part of it anymore. Answer our simple questions and you go home." Odette's eyes burned. She tried to blink away the tears, but they swelled and bubbled over, dripping into the freezing water.

"You are safe," the shadow said. "You are safe."

Forty-three

The breeze had carried the pear blossoms over the pebbles in the garden. An old couple sat on a park bench. On a normal spring day, after the thaw of an unpredictable winter, the woman would throw breadcrumbs to the ducks. The man would read a book of poetry or the pages of Le monde. But this spring, the ducks had long vanished from the park. Even the pigeons had disappeared. Aloysius had said the people of Paris had eaten them. Odette hadn't seen or heard one since that day. She and Aloysius had spent time in Tuileries Gardens, amongst the German tourists sipping cappuccinos and eating pastries with real cream. These days the only ones who could afford real coffee, fresh pastries, and thick cream were Germans and those who spoke to Germans. On the historic streets of Paris, those listed on the German tourist maps, shops glowed with shimmering clean glass windows. The shopkeepers swept the aisles each day. The cafés swelled with music. On the hidden alleys away from the SS headquarters, off from the Champs Elysées, the windows held grime instead of displays if the glass hadn't already shattered altogether. Blockades closed the lanes to cars and pedestrians unless a person could prove on their papers they lived on the street. The German tourists paraded

279

around the city as if a war had never happened, wasn't happening still. They cooed and awed over the city; they sat in the cafés, held their cigarettes like Parisians, used French words, and pretended to be from Paris, at least for a day, a week, while those who had grown in Paris, breathed Paris, knew the sounds of the Seine in summer and winter, the calls of the pigeons in fall and the way the bells of Sacre Coeur sounded duller after the rains in spring, hadn't eaten a proper meal, hadn't bathed in hot water, hadn't had a sip of true coffee in year—spring once pronounced a rebirth but Paris looked as dead as it felt, taken over by a German parasite eaten from the inside out with all the scars still visible.

Odette hadn't eaten in days. She hadn't had a sip of water in a week, other than the frigid water she swallowed each time the shadow dropped her into the tub and pulled her out without pause, without a moment for Odette to catch her breath, to shake off the endless cold. The shadow would ask more questions Odette had no answer to until she would spill a lie, a fib, an outright fabrication so not to be dropped into the tub again. By the last night in her cell, the guard had opened the gate to find Odette on her hands and knees trying to slurp up the puddled water washed over from the earlier mopping of the floor. Odette looked into the guard's green eyes. He slapped her across the face. Her cheek split. The blood trickled down. She wiped at her cheek and smeared the blood on her fingers. She sucked her skin to suck at the liquid. She sobbed uncontrollably. This is where her life had led her. Death didn't have the decency to even show his face, not as the shadow, but as thirst, as hunger, as emptiness, as the constricting words on the wall, but no face, not tangible, eyes to stare into, bones to break, teeth to shatter, smirk to tear away at. Odette understood why the soldier hit her; she found it in his eyes when she bore into him. The pity for a brief second that he found in her pitiful action, her need for libation. If she couldn't drink something soon, she'd die, so she resorted to the mop water. The soldier was disgusted by her, by his own pity for her, and took it out on Odette. The only way he knew how, with force.

Odette began to look forward to her time strung above the tub, at least then she'd have a chance to drink and hopefully, drown in the process.

Today, the soldier, the one who found her lapping up the dirty puddle on the floor, dragged her down the hall. It no longer took two men. Odette no longer resisted. The men in the room strung Odette up above the tub. The shadow walked into the room in silence; even her shoes didn't squeak.

"Who did this?" The shadow said. She grabbed Odette by the chin and turned her cheek to the light. The cut had stopped bleeding but hadn't healed. Odette had tried to draw more blood from the open wound in desperation, an attempt to soak her fingers in the liquid once more, then suck the blood from the tips of her fingers as if her body were a fountain. It hadn't worked. The less water she drank the less blood coursed through her. She remembered the desiccated, sallow banker on her table in the basement; was that what her future looked like?

The room remained silent. The shadow turned to the guards in the room. They didn't answer. They didn't move. She leaned in close to Odette. Her voice was soft, a whisper. It made Odette shake harder than the promise of pain and freezing water.

"We can be honest with each other, yes?" she said. Odette nodded. She closed her eyes tight. The shadow's breath smelled of mint and black licorice. "Who did this to you? Who marked you like this?"

Odette didn't know how to answer. Should she blame herself? How would the guard react if she pointed him out? Would the shadow believe her? Odette kept quiet but looked to the door where the guard stood waiting to take her back to her cell.

"You don't have anything to fear in this room," the shadow said. Odette didn't respond. The shadow tightened her grip on Odette's face— her fingers dug into Odette's cheeks. The scabby flesh wound opened again. Thin droplets of blood dropped down her face into the tub. The water splashed and trickled. "You have nothing to fear girl. Nothing to fear in this room—except me." A dark tone swirled in the air, turned the spiced scent acrid. Odette looked to the guard by the door once more.

"I see," the shadow said. She let go of Odette's face, smoothed her clothes, and said, "Henrich, come here."

The guard took four steps into the room and stood to the side of the shadow. Her eyes, hollowed in the darkness, still stared at Odette. Odette felt a familiar iciness crawl down her skin.

"Did you strike our guest?"

"I beg your pardon madame?"

"I am your superior, yes?"

"Of course, madame."

"I said no one is to touch this guest of ours, correct?"

"Yes, madame."

"Now I am asking, did you lay a single finger on her in a manner unbecoming to a German soldier, a German man, and a member of the Nazi Party?"

"But madam," the office trembled. "She was drinking water from the floor, leftover from the mop. She looked at me—"

"She looked at you?" The shadow stepped back to Odette. She gripped Odette's cheeks once more, harder, and pulled Odette's face towards the guard. "Look at him," she told Odette. "Look in his eyes." She slapped Odette on the cut. "Not his shoes, his eyes. This is the man who hit you, yes? This is the man who couldn't stand to look at you." Odette couldn't swallow. Her tongue swelled, and the shadow's nails dug deep into her cut. Her cheek.

"Look at her, Untersherfurher. How does she look to you? Weak? Did she make you feel weak? Did she scare you?" The calm had disappeared, replaced with scorn, anger. "Is this the face of fear to you? Hers or your own?"

The shadow kept her hand on Odette's chin. "Are you looking?" She pulled a pistol from a hidden holster, pointed it at Henrich, and shot.

Odette screamed. The sound was involuntary, a gasp of exasperation, fear, relief, on a day she hadn't expected to wear her death mask, a time she hadn't believed she would ever wear that mask again.

The guard dropped to the floor. The look of confusion stuck like shit on a shoe.

"He disobeyed a direct order," the shadow said. "Get her back to her cell, then get this disrespectful person out of my building."

The Shadow stepped to the body, and he looked at Odette. She couldn't look away. She needed to memorize his face, the way she did for all the others she had killed in the past, this one was no less deserving. The shadow took her toe and turned the guard's face away.

"I hate it when they stare," she said.

The guards took Odette back to her cell. By morning, the same guards led her to the lobby of the SS headquarters. She could barely stand on her own. The guards had walked with her, not dragged or pushed. Odette waited for the shot, a pain, and bullet to the back. But the guards said, "We apologize for the inconvenience," and walked away. Bureaucrats and secretaries passed unnoticing. Odette looked around the lobby, took a short step, then another until she reached the door. A German soldier opened the door for her; she cringed, took control, and walked out combing her hair down, suddenly self-conscious of her clothes, the cheek. A car pulled to the front of the building.

"It looks like you could use a ride?" Ilse said. "It is a hot day. Let me help you home, yes?"

Forty-four

In the morning, the clouds hung high above Paris but held a grayness Odette found familiar and longed for the day the clouds would lose their tint of foreboding, lying in wait endlessly for the summer rain to come and wash away the nightmares. She hadn't seen Aloysius in months. But it felt like years. The days swirled together into a puddle, and the nights seemed to disappear before she realized they had even come.

Martine sat in the sliver of sunlight filtering through the window. He blinked his eyes shut. If Odette could sleep so soundly, effortlessly, but when she closed her eyes, Agnes's face appeared, like a moving picture, a silent picture, gray and black like the clouds over Paris now. She said nothing but her mouth continued to move in agony. After a night in the cellar, Odette would fall into a blissful sleep without dreams and often wake to Martine, to his gentle purr as he nestled beside her head on the pillow. She would wake up refreshed and excited for the new day. Agnes had haunted her every night since Aloysius's disappearance, since Odette's abduction. She tried to fall back into her routine, thinking it would ease her mind, but she found it hard to walk at first after her time in the cell. She tried not to question why they had released her but imagined it had something to do with Ilse; it was the only way to explain how she had known where to find Odette. Odette's knee had heeled fine since being back home, but the slight limp had remained, more out of habit now as opposed to necessity. When she didn't think about walking straight, her leg would return back to the shuffle she had become accustomed to. How could she outrun a ghost? Agnes could be difficult, but she didn't deserve to die, she didn't deserve to see Odette's death mask. Would she ever be able to separate herself from the mask even when her time came?

It had gotten worse. Whenever she blinked, she saw Agnes's face. Her sallow cheeks and pale hair framed her thin lips, her dry lips, dour lips. Odette kept her eyes shut, tried to look deeper into Agnes's mouth to understand what she wanted. What could a ghost want? She had asked Odette to do it. A small voice echoed in Odette's head. A light drizzle fell outside. Paris used to bustle in the rain and sun, day and night. Since the German's arrived, familiar sounds of the city continued filling certain pockets while the emptiness of the countryside filled the remainder of the streets, or worse, the sounds of sirens and the absence of birds, reminding Odette once again of what Aloysius had told her about the pigeons and the desperation of Parisians.

The complex felt empty. Agnes was gone, Aloysius was gone, Mr. Tureshko was gone. How many had left while Odette was gone? If any had stayed, they stayed clear of Odette. She couldn't blame them. A loud shriek poured through the window. Martine woke with his hair on edge. The cats in the alley fought over their boxes and the dumpsters filled with what little scraps remained, which wasn't much to begin with. Then the familiar voice emerged once more. Odette let the gray light stuff her apartment, not wanting to waste gas or candles. When night fell, sometimes she used the faded and rationed streetlights or remaining lights in the abandoned City of Light to read by, live by. It sounded like Agnes, but with the strain of something deeper without the ever-present contempt she had for the world. It sounded like more of a motherly tone, a supportive note in a soft, low moan distant from the sirens.

"Dead," she said.

"Who's dead?" Odette asked. But the voice repeated "death" once more. Martine growled at the window, and the shrieking cats overtook the ghostly hum. Odette took her coat and stepped outside. The drizzle had turned the cobblestones nearly black. Before the occupation, the cafés had businessmen enjoying an afternoon glass of wine or couples purring to one another while listening to the rain, or friends chatting over lattés while watching their city pass by. The cafes that remained open remained empty. Their tables and chairs as ghost-like as the voice Odette heard. She stood on the Pont Marie where she used to stand with her mother to watch the boats float below. The drizzle felt like mist shrouding over the city, wetting the streets, the trees. The people, for reasons beyond Odette, kept their pace in the gardens or lingered inside small, cozy stores in the accompaniment of German tourists. A piece of paper floated on the water below carried by the current. It looked like a letter, maybe a love letter, one that carried the names of a couple torn apart by the occupation or their love of France or distance, one now in the country while the other resigned herself to the confines of the city too afraid to leave her family behind. The last letter Odette's mother had received was accompanied by a medal; one her father had earned during the Great War. The medal had a rainbow ribbon representing the international coalition, connected to a coin engraved with a winged angel. Odette learned later that many soldiers or their families received the medal after the servicemen died of disease or injury. It had been a gray day, with looming clouds, with a letter written in black ink on aged paper, with words Odette didn't understand. Her mother stared at the words but did not move or sigh, cry or scream. When her mother read letters from her cousin in New York, she would regale Odette with stories from across the Atlantic Ocean or place her hand over her chest, cluck her tongue, and exclaim, "Oh la la la la." Her mother took the letter, tore it in half, then tore it again. She took the medal and grabbed Odette's coat. They walked out over the Pont Marie and into the Par Monceau in the eighth arrondissement. It drizzled like now, and her mother squeezed Odette's hand, unlike now, when she had no one to hold onto. Her mother pulled her forward until Odette could barely keep up, almost tripping, regaining her balance, only to trip again. Her coat didn't fit right, pulled on too quickly, making her sleeves bunch around the shoulders. The drizzle formed large droplets on her mother's forehead. They walked past the Egyptian pyramid and Venetian bridge. On a sunny day, children of affluent families would fill the park. Artists would set up easels and paint the budding roses. Storytellers would try to make new legends about the stones on the pyramid. Her mother dragged Odette to the edges of the lily pond and threw the medal into the water. Then the rain started. They stayed looking at where the ripples had long disappeared, replaced by the waves caused by the fat raindrops. Odette huddled into herself to keep the hard rain from hitting her neck. Her mother continued to look at the pond and the way the rain pounded the water lilies, breaking the weak blossoms away from the thick pads.

"Miss," a man said. He had been walking past but stopped upon seeing Odette and her mother. "Please, take my umbrella. Your daughter looks ready to drown."

Her mother continued to stare at the water. "We shall drown from the bottom up and not the top down." She turned away from the man, pulling Odette once again, and leaving the medal at the bottom of the pond.

The drizzle made Odette blink away the memory as the letter on the Seine continued to drift below, wading beneath the Pont Marie. Odette made her way to Parc Monceau. The drizzle had scared away lovers or families from the pathways. Water dripped down onto the lily pad where her father's medal still lay for all she knew. The word death whispered in the wind again. Odette had nothing of Aloysius's to throw into the water. She found a patch of damp sand on the shores of the lily pond. She dug her finger into the gritty dirt and wrote Aloysius's name deep into the earth. The small letters spoke silently of the person of whom she could now speak to no one. The drizzle turned into hard rain. The drops fell, fat and ugly, over the park. The rain turned the pond into an undulating pool. The water rose and fell like an ocean in a storm. Odette took a step away from the shore. It took only seconds, or possibly an hour, the mix of rain and pond water washed over Aloysius's name and brushed it away from the world, leaving only a shallow imprint where the last "S" had stood, the same way Odette held the last of Aloysius in her because he, like his name, was gone.

Forty-five

The hospital had taken on the same black as the city. Paris no longer held color and light but the absence of light, which permeated the streets, the trees, the architecture, even pierced the buildings. The food tasted of absence. In the breeze, Odette often took pain at noticing what wasn't there as opposed to what was. The new aromas didn't smell familiar and instead only brought more awareness to the smells she missed, the scent of almond croissants, dark chocolate, baguettes, peppermint. A few arrondissements held fast to their aromas. Those were more or less on the main streets and connected to the German tourist trade, catering more to officers, well-to-do visitors, and the collaborators eager to bask in their good fortunes with real cream, real apples, and an overabundance of bacon grease and coffee. The hospital had once smelled of antiseptic and gardenias, a mixture of what kept patients healthy and what kept workers and visitors calm. Odette didn't know if the blandness, the absence had poured into the hospital from the outside or the hospital had poured out to the city.

She wore her hospital mask and walked through the aisles of the beds without looking at the people. She had stopped seeing people in those beds long ago. The moment they stepped into the hospital they became objects, like the scalpel, like paper, like bed sheets or the posts. They no longer looked or sounded like people. They had once resembled rats to Odette, or worse, lice. They were less than human but more than nothing. Odette couldn't pinpoint when they had devolved into less than rodents, into something once easy enough to kill but hard to dispose of, into objects easily torn up, ripped up, thrown out—garbage in need of collecting, far past their usefulness. Her limp had subsided, giving way to a walk of absence, an airy stride, not one of tranquility but passivity, like a ghost where all signs of existence had drained when they didn't know they were dead. She walked to the subject and drew the injection. The chart listed sections in which Odette should have checked the physical and mental state of the subject, in which Odette should have listed temperature, skin tone, pupil dilation, motor functions, but Odette didn't look at the chart, and didn't look to see how any of the conditions today contrasted with the conditions of yesterday. She flicked the needle, grabbed the subject's arm, and searched for a vein. Needle marks pocketed the subject's elbow like bloody mosquito bites no one had taken the time to clean. Last week, Odette couldn't find a vein in the subject's arm and had to search for a vein in their neck. The week before, the subject hadn't had any veins left in the neck or in their arm. Odette and an assistant had to find a vein between their toes. They shoved the needle into the webbing. The subject wiggled their big toe but otherwise remained unmoved. Odette couldn't look at them as anything other than objects now, subjects and instruments. She had once been able to see them as animals, rats or lice, vermin to be terminated beneath her feet. Now they took on no more importance in her life than a piece of paper, a scalpel, or a shoe, an inanimate object ready for disposal, a piece of garbage. Odette readied the syringe.

"Did you check the chart?" Ilse asked. Odette startled.

"I didn't realize you were—-I was about to."

Ilse tapped her pen to her teeth. She looked the subject up and down before turning back to Odette.

"And?" Ilse said.

Odette took the chart and looked over the subject for the first time. Their hair had fallen out. Their teeth had cracked. Their lips were swollen and dry. Even their eyebrows had gone. Their cheeks sallow and nose ready to cave into the crevices of their own face. The fact Odette and others were having trouble finding veins meant the subjects were living longer, but it was hard to tell by looking at them. As Ilse liked to say, "If there was a one percent chance the vaccine could save a German life, then there is a one hundred percent chance they would keep trying."

"Her fever has dropped," Odette said.

"You can tell that by looking at her?" Ilse said.

Odette had once struggled with every person she injected in the hospital. She would stroke their hair, touch her hands to their cheeks, and whisper hopeful words; that was when she saw them as people, when she could tell whether they were men or women, girls or boys, before they all resembled fleas. This was a woman or a girl in front of her, but how could Odette have known? The girl's chart had an "F" under gender but otherwise didn't even have a name, just a number. Odette hadn't noticed how long the numbers had grown since starting at the hospital.

"No, Ilse," Odette said. "I have taken her temperature." She lied. Ilse must have known she lied.

"You did not write her new temperature on the chart. You must always write changes on the chart. You have worked here long enough to know this."

"Yes, doctor." When Ilse gave criticism or had to assume authority, she needed reassurance by being called her professional name, so she knew whomever she spoke to understood they were being chided without Ilse needing to raise her voice.

"Your documentation has not been efficient as of late. Are you well? If there is anything I can help with, please Odette, you must let me know. This is far too important, and we are much too far along for any mistakes."

"I understand," Odette said. She felt queasy. The room rocked back and forth. She had spent her life meticulously following every rule and capturing every detail. Since when had she not followed instructions?

"Have you read the updated guidelines to injections?"

"No, doctor."

"Please," Ilse said. "You know I prefer to be called Ilse," which meant Odette's punishment was over. They were back to being friends.

"No, Ilse. I have been having. . . home trouble." She spoke as if they weren't in a hospital, surrounded by sick subjects, surrounded by garbage, atop a freshly cleaned floor to keep the doctors and nurses from slipping or tripping in dried shit and puddles of urine. The room reeked in layers with a top layer of ammonia and a bottom layer stinking of death, blood mixed with the acidity of vomit.

"Then you should come to dinner at my home tonight," Ilse said. "After all, we are friends."

Odette nodded. She still held the syringe and reached down for the subject's arm.

"You have not read the new guidelines," Ilse said. "Let me." She reached for the syringe with one hand and held the girl's hand with her other. "We noticed subjects have a better reaction to the serum when feeling comforted. They did not live as long at the beginning because we had the dose wrong. With the proper dosage and the right encouragement, we are getting closer. It is what you used to do when you first started. Remember?"

Odette nodded and looked back to the chart, ashamed of her diminished work ethic but not about the way she saw the subjects. Ilse rubbed her manicured hand over the girl's. The girl had a faint smirk that looked too full against her hollowed features.

"You are safe," Ilse said. "You do not have to worry. You are safe."

The words struck a familiar note, pulling Odette back into a dark room surrounded by stone with a tub full of ice at the center. Odette hung above the tub and plunged up and down with that voice calling to her, repeating, *you are safe; you are safe.*

The lights flickered in the room bringing the familiar faded look to the hospital. The bland gray had washed away. Odette looked back at the subject and found traces of a girl, around sixteen, who should have been meeting a boy at the cinema or smoking a cigarette while at a café near the Tuileries Gardens. The faces of the subjects came back, returned to Odette from out of the absent gray, showing the true features of each person, boy and girl, woman and man, not garbage, not lice, and not rats. Ilse continued in her soft voice, "You are safe." Odette stepped away and hit the bed behind her. A groan escaped from the subject—no—from the boy, maybe eighteen. The girl and boy could have been together, could have snuck kisses under the arches at Parc Monceau. It could have been Aloysius and Odette. Sweat erupted from Odette's skin, her hands, puddled at her feet but left her face dry.

Ilse stood from the bed, handed Odette the syringe, and said, "I will see you tonight." She caressed Odette's cheek. "You are safe." She smiled, her lips red like blood, and she kissed Odette's head and walked away. Her small heels clacked against the tile on the way out of the room.

Odette turned to the returned faces and began to search each bed, each face, the lips she had memorized, the slick hair she had known since childhood, no longer floating but stomping in a panic up to each bed in search of Aloysius. She had clung to the chart the entire time, not finding Aloysius, and returning to the bed of the subject, the patient, the girl, whose breath turned shallow. Odette placed the chart back on the bed and the girl stopped breathing. And Odette wanted to follow her.

"Forgive me," Odette whispered.

Forty-six

Ilse answered the door in a white dress. She always wore white, Odette thought, except when she wore shadows. Her blonde hair fell effortlessly to her shoulders. How often had Odette wished she had hair like Ilse's when younger, blonde, silky, with a bounce whenever she turned her head? She felt as though she had tufts of hair, dark, curly, and unruly, perhaps just another physical manifestation of the beast inside especially after her time in the cell. Had her hair been the same before her mother's death? She could barely remember a time before then, a time when her mother was alive. Even in her memories, her mother felt absent.

The aroma of butter slapped Odette, made her mouth water. Music drifted through the flat on the back of the butter, familiar, intense, like the start of a fire that never made it. Ilse grabbed Odette by the shoulder; the doctor's fingers firm but reassuring, and she pulled Odette into the doorway, into the apartment, and into her lips—full and red and burning. Ilse pressed her mouth hard against Odette's where Odette found the stench of tobacco and the taste of wine joining the ever-present aroma of lilies. They pulled apart and the world felt hazy.

"Oh, hurry inside," Ilse said. "No need to let the entire building know what we're having for dinner." Ilse shuffled Odette into the flat. Her husband stood with an apron on over his suit, his pudgy stomach pressed against the tight apron, fit for the shape of a woman. He held a glass of red wine in his hand. Ilse took the glass and passed it to Odette. Then the scent of tobacco of blackberries from the wine. The familiar aroma of duck fat mixed with the butter. And Odette saw the restaurant, saw the catacombs, Aloysius's bloody hands, his pale face, his back, his ghost. Then the music, Mr. Tureshko's music. Like a cat playing with its dinner but Martine had never played with his food. He tore into it with pleasure. And when he caught a mouse, he would pounce on the meat and lap up the blood, worried it wouldn't last.

Ilse wasn't Martine.

Odette wasn't a mouse.

"Please," Ilse said, "sit. You are right on time and dinner will be ready in just a moment."

Odette took her seat and sipped her wine. She nearly choked on the smell, on its thick body, and the jam-like texture. It had turned sanguine in her mouth.

"Tell me," Ilse said, "However did you survive your time—"

"Liebling," her husband said. He raised his eyebrows. Ilse shrugged. "That is not a polite thing to talk about."

"But we are friends," she said. She grabbed Odette's hand and squeezed. "Friends can talk about all sorts of uncomfortable subjects. Yes? Is that not what friendship is, safety?"

The questions—again. The assurance of safety—again. The voice of the silhouette with a light now fully shone on their form. Odette was desperate to pull her hand away but froze. Perhaps she was more like a mouse after all. And here was the moment Ilse would bite down. Odette would see it coming and still not move, her body frozen with fear. After so many years of wearing Death as a mask, Death never made her fearless. She was fear disguised as judgement, and now Death showed his true form ready to take payment for all those she had forced into acceptance. Then Ilse cut her again with a memory, a scent deeper than the butter and the wine, but she couldn't place it underneath the stench of pooling fat.

"We also have peach tarte tatin for dessert."

Ilse played the music, simmered the butter, poured the wine, offered peaches, and Odette bathed in it. Perhaps she had been the mouse after all, but instead of pouring blood, she spilled memories from her veins. And Ilse left Odette face down to drown in them with Odette unsure which would kill her first, the cut or the lack of oxygen, the past or the present.

"Odette," Ilse said shaking her hand. "You look ghastly. Are you alright?"

Her husband sat at the table with a glass of champagne for himself. "A ghost of yourself," he said.

"I haven't slept much since…" her voice trailed off. It sounded like she was underwater, garbled by blood making it bubble with every work, every sound. Where had her voice come from? It couldn't have been her. She hadn't breathed in minutes, in weeks, in years. When was the last time she had taken a breath? The last time her lungs expanded? She had died. Yes, she had died a decade ago at the hands of the grocer, and her life since that moment was only a memory of the future. She was probably still dying, lying still in the flat with her mom beside her, the grocer's gaseous body between them, as they all bled out waiting for Aloysius to find them the next day.

"How could you have?" Ise's husband said. His voice drew Odette back into the present, breathed life back into her. "Those savages at the, what have Parisians been calling it, 'the Street of Horrors?' It will certainly make your skin crawl."

"Philistines," Ilse said. "The lot of them. Can't see a millimeter past their own dicks."

"Liebling."

"I won't apologize for talking truth in this house."

"Which truth?" Odette said. She took her hand away from Ilse's and grabbed the wine. She drank the glass quick and soundlessly. She ignored the smell of blood on the body.

"There is only one truth," Isle said.

"Now that is an interesting proposition," Ilse's husband said. "Perhaps we should think about this for a longer moment." He sipped his champagne. The bubbles fizzed and popped against his lip.

"Yes, Hans, ever the philosopher. Always looking for a way to justify either side of an argument. There is no justification for what they think. There is no truth there. Isn't that right, Odette?"

Odette wiped her mouth. The thickness of the wine stuck to her lips, clung to her teeth, coated her throat. "I think—"

"Not about their truth," Hans said. "The truth of the French, your truth, my truth. Who's to say which truth is correct?"

"There is only one truth!" Ilse raised her voice. It made the crystal glasses sing. Odette dropped her glass. It shattered.

"It's fine," Ilse said. "I'll just get another set from Lévitan."

And with it went the veneer of the night. And with it the illusion of the restaurant, the catacombs, Odette's mother, Aloysius finding them on the floor of the flat with the grocer half naked and fully flabby. The music played low. The duck burned. Ilse sprung from her chair and directed Hans to grab rags and peroxide, a doctor who spat orders to the very end. And none of them understood a single truth, the ultimate truth, the only truth they all must face.

And Odette put on her mask.

And Odette grabbed a knife.

"The shadow," she whispered. She spat blood into the crystal shards on the floor.

And Ilse stared, blank eyes, blank face, blonde hair, her entire body turned to fresh snow that hid the story beneath. And the room disappeared.

And Hans disappeared. And they floated in darkness, the cat and the mouse. But now the mouse had a knife. But a cat could see in the dark.

"The mouse," Ilse said.

"You tortured me," Odette said.

"You said nothing," Ilse said.

"You killed that man."

"I have killed many men."

"You—"

"I have killed many women, and boys, and girls. There was always a reason, wasn't there? You killed. How many have you killed. How many have you judged? What about the first man—when you entered the room and smelled death?"

"I didn't touch him," Odette said.

"You didn't have to. You saw him. You left him there. You said nothing."

"I kill for a purpose," Odette said.

"So do I," Ilse said.

Odette dropped the knife. The room returned. Hans stood in the doorway with a rag. Ilse pointed to the floor, the glass. And Odette knew Hans would rake his knees over the shards before he disobeyed Ilse. Ilse knew it too. And before Hans dropped to the floor, the light hit the shards and flickered into color, a rainbow against the crimson. And each shard turned into a face. And each face looked familiar. Each face looked absent. Each face looked haunting. The patients, the vermin, the lives she had taken without question and without any sense of contentment, believing in her non-commitment to their deaths, that they did not matter. What made her matter more? She was still here.

Hans blotted up the wine and swept up the shards. Odette ran to the door.

"Remember mouse," Ilse said. "It was never for nothing." Her voice carried a smile. Odette shed the scent of fat as she ran from the flat. On the street, she swore cats followed her as she ran home. But no, she couldn't go home. And somewhere in the night—long past curfew and for the first night in years—Paris was still awake.

Forty-seven

And the morning tasted like dirt; with the air dry and thick, it filled Odette's mouth like broken glass, ready to cut her tongue and bleed her dry. She had spent the night out in the city, with the city, too scared to go home, scared Ilse would be waiting for her the way Odette wanted to wait for Ilse in the darkness, in the corner, once more the face of death. For the night, Paris glowed by candlelight, absent of the electric hum, but filled with an angelic glow. Black clung to the first night of the city like what Odette imagined the sea to look like under a sky absent of the moon, but she had never seen the sea. But the city must have been like the sea, must have ebbed and flowed like the water with a storm knowingly on its way to churn the air with life. Last night, the city stirred, slow at first with a current belying the sweltering heat everyone felt, the heat the city could no longer take. It started with rumors, with an inclination the Allies approached, with inclement curfews, with less light, with less food, with less wine, with less of the fake air the German army had given the city as if the people, the cafés, the theaters were meant to be gawked at; they had been puppets for years, and when the Germans were done with it, they tore their puppets apart like petulant children bored of their toys. But now the toys would fight back. General Dietrich von Choltitz would retreat, they all knew, they had all heard, they had all bitten their nails back to the cuticles until they could only tear at the skin in anticipation. Then the rumors flew like fireballs: when the Germans retreat, they would take the city with them, leaving salt pillars in their wake.

Odette had stood in the corner of Ilse's house after work, in the dark, breathing the air of coming death. She closed her eyes to relish the quickening pace of her heart, one of the few times she felt alive in a city known to celebrate life—the reason she always felt closer to death, because if you don't celebrate with others, how can you know life? She felt this way with Aloysius—when he was alive—in those moments they spent walking in the park, listening to the music blaring from Mr. Tureshko's apartment, enjoying the soft coo of the pigeons in the crevices of the building before Martine attempted to snatch them from their perches. Then, when those moments ended, Odette sunk back into the muddled life of the undead, when even the brightest colors turned gray, the tastiest fruit turned bitter, and every smell turned to shit. When she gripped tight to her knife, she could see in the dark, leap over buildings, hear her victim's heartbeat through the door before they even entered their home. And now she listened to her heart quicken, the blood rushed through her veins, tingling in her toes, in her fingertips, pulsing in her neck. The key entered the lock. The tumble clicked and clacked. A sliver of light opened and closed with the door. Ilse was at the hospital. She wouldn't be home for at least two hours, more than enough time.

Ilse's husband placed a bottle of wine on the counter. He went into the bedroom and grabbed a suitcase from underneath his bed. It was full. They planned to leave soon. He didn't bother with the lights. Odette clung to the darkness. Then death took on the distinctive aroma of chloroform. Hans leaned over his suitcase making room for the bottle. He sniffed and wiggled his nose. Odette pressed the handkerchief to his face, wrapped her arm around his neck, and waited for him to stop flailing.

Hans woke up naked and strapped to the bed. Odette thought it the most fitting example in the best attempt to imitate the hospital beds in which Ilse had killed so many—in which Odette had allowed so many to die. Odette poured ice water over Han's flabby, pasty stomach, over his bony shoulders. She shoved a wet rag in his mouth. She didn't want the cold water to feel good in the hot summer's day, but the water reminded her too much of the time she spent in the cell, the tub dangling from the ceiling. She poured the water over Han's head, letting the rag soak with the water unable to go anywhere but down. Tears splashed his face as much as the water. He tried to spit but the rag held tight. His grogginess waned; Odette watched the lucidity return to his eyes, the pupils dilate and focus, the harsh blue light return, framed by white, always white, so much Nazi white. Odette had taken the time to fold Hans's clothes and placed them neatly atop the closed suitcase. Odette had placed the wine by the door, so she wouldn't forget it on her way out.

"Nous allons jouer à un jeu," Odette said. She chose her words carefully, claiming they would play a game he didn't have a choice in. He nodded his head.

"It is called, 'How much do you want to live?' It starts when I take the rag out of your mouth. If you want to live, you don't scream. If you want to die, you scream." Odette grabbed the knife from the bedside table. She ran the blade down Hans's chest, cutting a small piece of him open near his pale nipple. Hans screamed in pain. He was not a soldier; he worked in an office, pushed papers around, sipped Champagne, ate strudel. He did not know torture, Odette thought, look at his belly. He does not know pain. But he will.

"Now you know I am serious," Odette said. Hans nodded again. He winced and writhed but remained silent. Odette took the rag from his mouth. He moved his jaw around, rolled his fat tongue over his white teeth. He raised his head from the bead.

"Why?" he said without pleading. Maybe he was stronger than Odette thought.

"Ilse—" Odette said.

"She brought you into our home," Hans whispered, his throat scratchy, the cold water on his face from sweat, not the ice. "She treated you like a daughter, like a sister, like a…".

"Like a German?" Odette said.

"You were family," he said.

"Why would my family leave me behind?" Odette said. She tapped her toe to the suitcase, giving an audible thud. Hans turned his eyes away.

"You look so strong with your clothes on," she said. "Does Germany know about your little…issue?" Odette pointed the knife to Hans's penis. It lay flaccid and shriveled drooping between his legs.

"There is no problem," he said. His voice quaked, his body quivered. Odette ran the smooth edge of the knife down Hans's stomach until the tip reached his forest of pubic hair. It resembled the bushes in the hidden corners of Tuileries Gardens, which once had been the pride of the city but hadn't been tended in far too long. She dug the metal into the top of his groin to make a point. He flinched. "The Germans are retreating!"

"The whole world knows," Odette said.

"Tomorrow," Hans said. "We're all leaving tomorrow. I handled the paperwork myself. The chancellor wants to tear the city down when we go. If we can't have it, no one will."

"You're going to kill everyone?"

"I've never killed anyone," Hans said.

"What about Mr. Tureshko? What about Aloysius? What about those who will die when you level the city?"

Hans cried, his penis hardened the harder he cried, which made him cry harder. "I have never killed anyone," he said. "I never had the courage. I thought we could just send them all away." His body shuddered. Snot poured from his nose. Odette used the wet rag to wipe away the thick paste of mucus and tears, then shoved the rag back in his mouth. Odette felt the death mask wear away. She went over the list in her head, the collection she had amassed over the years, the ways in which they all pleaded, they all wanted to live. Except Hans didn't plead for his life, he pleaded for his name, for Odette to know he hadn't killed anyone, but he never asked to live, he never asked to be spared. For that reason alone, Odette believed him.

He was a man. He had done bad things. He hadn't killed anyone. How many had Odette killed with her bare hands, with the *vaccine*, by thinking of others as less than she? Between she and Hans, she should be an inch from death, not him. Hans continued to cry. Odette took the knife, leaned into Hans's ear, and said, "Tell your wife I'll be waiting for her."

That night the city knew what Hans had said as if he had broadcast it over the BBC radio programs no one should have been listening too. Maybe it was the heat. Maybe it was the story about the man who had slapped a German soldier on the metro just for being in the city. Maybe the fire had sat for too long and had its first taste of oxygen, making it ready to erupt. Odette took the bottle from the apartment and stepped onto the street. German soldiers paraded around the city in groups, not causing trouble but not backing down from trouble either. The city smelled of smoke. Candles turned to fires. Kids threw rocks and bottles at passing soldiers and anyone who looked like a German tourist. Odette took the knife and cut the bottle open. She took a gulp. The wine streamed down her chin and plopped on the floor. A boy who resembled Aloysius passed. Odette caught his arm.

"What's happening?"

"We're fighting for France," he said. Odette handed him the bottle. He took a swig and attempted to give it back.

"Take it," Odette said. "For Paris." But she meant, *for Aloysius*. She and the boy went in opposite directions; he to where the fires had started, she to where the fires would end.

Forty-eight

Within hours, the Germans were gone. The streets continued to scream, but not with anger or fear, now with joy. Tanks roared in the distance from the incoming Free French army. Planes glided overhead with bombs pounding the outer reaches of Paris, where the roads turned to gravel, but the sounds still made barely an impact over the jovial cries of the city. Barriers people had made along the narrow alleys and streets to keep the Germans on the main roads turned into hills of celebration. People drank wine and found champagne in the hidden cellars once cut off from Parisians, meant for the drunken SS officers and German tourists. The city had returned to its rightful owners, those who wanted to rejoice in life, those who wanted to celebrate with every breath, to watch people pass them along the streets, to indulge in the scent of fresh espresso, to walk along the banks of the Seine, to bask in the boundless shake of a body in orgasmic ecstasy before lighting a new cigarette.

Then there was Odette, who didn't feel like joining the city, who would have rather fell into the shadows or worse, the pale gray of the cobblestones left behind by the retreating Nazis. Women did their hair, paid special attention to their makeup. The dance halls around Montmartre reopened without delay with signs assuring French men and the newly arriving allies the women will be happy to welcome them home.

Odette hadn't yet been home. It had been days since she had stepped into her apartment. She had given Martine extra food and trusted him to graze whenever he needed. She couldn't return yet, not until she was sure Ilse had gotten the message. She couldn't let Ilse escape. Odette hadn't planned on letting Hans live, but despite all the proposals she ever made, the grand design she tried to follow, sometimes life had other plans. She passed a storefront empty of a display with a sign that read, "Went south for the winter. Be back when the birds return." In the empty glass Odette noticed the redness of her eyes. The welling water burned inside the dry cracks, trying to return the moisture. She spent so much time trying to fit in, blend in, that she couldn't help noticing the ways in which she now stood out, how her shoulders drooped forward, the tears in her stockings, the tiny holes in her gloves, the way one heel had nearly torn away. Whenever she walked, the heel would flop away from the sole of the shoe. For the first time since deciding to kill Hans, Odette looked at the people in the city, not just the joy, but the details of Paris, and realized they too looked like her. They too had holes in their coats, wore hair out of place, but they all wore displaced smiles, irregular smiles as if they had forgotten how, like walking after sitting on your ankles for too long; they started clumsily, until they remembered what a smile felt like.

Odette stumbled half aware through the streets. The bombing on the outskirts of town gave way to sporadic rattles of gunfire. A burst, silence, a scream, another burst, then an explosion. The city didn't shake as it once had. The rumble of tanks had gone. The cobblestones felt erratic, unstable; at any minute, they'd crumble into the catacombs below. The boy who had looked like Aloysius stood atop a barrier made of chairs and broken tables. He drank from the wine bottle Odette had given him. White wine spilled down his shirt. He used the bottle like a chalice, refilling it with whatever he could find, king of his mound, chief of a Parisian tribe with a mask made of dirt and soot. Odette turned to the hospital and pushed open the doors. She didn't walk but floated, with her heals no longer needing to clack against the tile. The scent of death lingered, even though all the patients, the prisoners, had been cleared. Papers rustled in Ilse's office. Glass broke. Odette opened the door. Ilse shoved files into an otherwise empty suitcase. The drawers of the cabinet remained open with the shell of the cabinet pushed over. The room smelled of fumes. Ilse's hair looked frail and strained, frayed from frantic electricity. Her lipstick had smeared at the edges of her lips. Her usual controlled demeanor lost beneath this other woman—this scared animal. Odette remembered the other animals in the hospital and found it fitting Ilse should be another trapped among them even if only the memory of them.

"It was you," Odette whispered.

"You came into my home!" Ilse screamed. She slammed her hand on the desk. The clap echoed in the room. She shoved the mound of papers from the desktop and created a blizzard of files, some soaked in gasoline, others with trace drops of the bitter fragrance. "How dare you! You have ruined all of this."

"No," Odette said. "You did." She hid a scalpel in the waistband at her back. She wanted to grab it but didn't want to give Ilse a reason to charge any more than any reason Ilse had already formed.

"If we could keep going—you and me. All of this..." Ilse said. The cracks in her voice softened. Her lips were no longer red; they had paled—pink, lifeless, stillborn. She turned her words into whispers, the way she would talk to Odette in the quiet of the city after dark, as if sharing deep, dark secrets. And her secrets were dark, but unlike Odette, Ilse never hid her true self. She wore it proudly like one of her pristine white coats.

"You were so strong," Ilse said. "We could have done so much together. Think of how many we could have saved," the words sounded like a plea, as if Odette could change the coming army, as if Odette could change the fate that awaited Ilse, as if Odette wanted to. Ilse looked at the empty table. The fumes lingered, controlled in the canister at the corner of the room near the fallen cabinet. The scent of lilies—the aroma of Ilse, long gone, replaced by the stench of gasoline, charred paper, and the memories of the Bear whose blood had practically spread through the office, from wall to wall.

"How about all the ones you already killed," Odette said.

"Kill one to save one hundred," Ilse said.

"What about killing one hundred, or one thousand—"

"Lose the melodrama, child. I am not the only murderer in this room. You think you will be spared judgment?"

"I've already been judged," Odette said.

"You don't know how much you have until you lose everything."

"Then you have nothing."

"No," Ilse said. "Then you have nothing to lose." Ilse took a lighter from her pocket and dropped it on the stack of papers. She jumped over the desk and lunged at Odette. The air erupted from Odette's lungs. Their bodies tumbled against the back wall. Odette lost her footing and fell to the floor, taking Ilse with her. Her hair smelled like a bird's nest. Her coat felt like burlap stuffed with moldy potatoes. Ilse punched Odette in the ribs. Then again. Odette held her elbows close to her body to lessen the blows, to cover her face with her hands. Ilse yanked Odette's hair. She slammed Odette's head against the floor. Odette threw her head up and hit Ilse in the nose, crunching the soft cartilage. She didn't wait for the blood to gush. Flames licked at the doorway to the office already engulfing the room where Ilse's crimes had been documented, now lost to the heat, to history, to the memory.

Odette scrambled through the double doors, falling into the room that once held the patients. The metal beds had remained, the stained mattresses empty but present. The scent of sterilizer overtook the putrid aroma of smoke. Ilse burst into the room. Blood streamed from her nose. The crimson color matched her lipstick. She held the door open, framed by the dim light, the growing smoke.

"I am the one who will judge you," Ilse said. She licked the blood from her lips. Her shoes had fallen off in the scuffle. Odette crawled between the beds, trying to hide for long enough to catch her breath. "I knew who you really were from the beginning. I have known all along. You weren't happy before the war. You won't be happy after. You had freedom these last few years. You could kill at will. We had rooms full of cretins ready to die. They had given up their will to live! That wasn't good enough for you, was it? You didn't just want the kill; you wanted the hunt. You and I are alike, you know. You remember. It is not just the kill we savor. I gave you endless chances, but you couldn't be happy killing vermin. You needed a person, someone who didn't want to die, the same reason you couldn't kill Hans. Did he plead to live?"

Odette lay beneath a bed at the far end of the room. Once the gallery seemed infinite, filled with rows of beds and decrepit bodies. Now, when Odette craved infinity, she found the room's true nature small and frail, easily navigable. Her lungs ached and burned. Her heart pounded like a wet drum, the room grew, Ilse's voice slowed. *This is what fear feels like,* Odette thought, giving her the same emotion as when she hunted, when she killed, the same adrenaline coursing through her body. Her breath slowed. She closed her eyes. Smoke drifted over the ceiling like coming fog.

"Of course, he did not plead," Ilse said. "He is pathetic. He has been too afraid to live for a long time, ever since he saw the Russian front. We were lucky to transfer here. I was lucky to meet you. You were what I was missing. I needed someone like me to help my research. You made others in this hospital like you. They turned their backs on the rodents in these beds because you did. You gave injections with such abandon; the nurses wanted to be like you. Don't you see that? Don't you see what we could have done, what we could still do? Come out. I forgive you." Ilse walked barefoot across the room. Her stockings were singed from the fire and blackened from the smoke. Odette scrambled beneath another bed, took the scalpel from her waistband, and waited for Ilse to walk past, slashing at her Achilles. Ilse folded but caught herself on the bed. She pulled herself onto the mattress. Odette pulled herself out from beneath the bed. Ilse grabbed for Odette. Odette pushed Ilse's arms away. She sat atop Ilse.

Ilse reached for Odette's neck and squeezed. Odette didn't fight or struggle. She gasped only once.

"I don't want to hunt anymore," Odette said. She took the scalpel to Ilse's exposed wrist, slicing down the vein. At first the blood seeped out, then squirted onto Odette's face, her mask, and Ilse's eyes grew wide in terror. She dropped her hands and tried to stop the bleeding, clenching her wrist.

"I don't want your forgiveness," Odette said. She stepped from the bed and walked away.

"Wait," Ilse said, her voice losing strength. "Help. Please." She tried to stand but dropped to the floor, too weak to hobble, with blood gushing from her nose, her heel, her wrist. The fire had grown, tearing from the office and down the hall, pushing open the doors. Odette coughed in the forest of smoke, using the tiles she knew so well to guide her out, hoping those she had wronged while in the hospital could forgive her as she pushed through the doors and into the fresh air.

Forty-nine

Odette woke up and brushed the sheets away as if they hadn't been washed in years, more like cobwebs molding to her skin, rather than sheets at all. Her kitchen remained dark. Paris hadn't stopped celebrating, hadn't stopped erupting with laughter from cafes, from bars, from apartments swimming in champagne, from cats rejoicing in their nightly howls. Except in her apartment, the faint scent of peaches remained but little else covered the musty scent of accumulated dirt. Months had passed. The city felt like life once again, but Odette barely noticed, stuck in a routine that woke her up, took her to the hospital where she bandaged, she soothed, she found soldiers emaciated and raw—found Parisians emaciated and raw—found her fingers emaciated and raw. She would return home, fall asleep, wake up, go to the hospital, where she found the hospital emaciated and raw. The city felt different, but behind the feeling, not much had changed.

Martine purred when Odette woke up. He greeted her by rubbing against her feet, by jumping on the counter expecting his breakfast, by looking to the door expecting someone who would not arrive. The apartment looked the same, the complex felt the same, but that was why she'd rather be like a building, not necessarily a building but an inanimate object. They kept going whether noticed or not, full or not. They kept going as if she had never been there. *And when you are gone, the world won't remember you anyway*, Agnes had once said.

But what about those who remember Agnes the way Odette did? What about those who remember Aloysius the way Odette did, the way Martine did? When the memory of them hurt too much to hold on to, could she let them go like a balloon and watch their faces float gently through the sky until disappeared? Is that how memories work? *What then*, she thought. What of them after their faces drift beyond the skyline? Will Odette no longer remember them, and would that be worth it? Is she willing to let all her memories go, to stop the pain of it all from roiling in her stomach, making every moment feel like she was about to vomit?

She and Paris had awoken from the same nightmare, where she was smothered in dirt and cobwebs made of blood, made of brick, made of all her ghosts. *You made your bed*, Agnes always said, *now you lie in it*. How much of this bed had she made versus how much of this bed had she inherited?

Martine rubbed against the door. He didn't touch his breakfast. Odette couldn't blame him. He could smell the sausages cooking in the other buildings. Other tenants poured the grease from their windows as if it were gold, flooding the streets with the fat Paris had missed, the fat Odette would have stolen once, and Martine wanted to roll around in it. Odette did as well. She wanted to dip her head beneath an espresso machine and let the actual taste of coffee fill her mouth. Enough of this carob shit, Odette thought. She grabbed Martine, ready to amble through the door, but realized she hadn't changed her clothes. She still felt the cobwebs clinging to her arms, to her feet like a nail in a cross. She was stuck in this apartment more now than ever before. Martine purred against her chest and Odette realized for the first time in days, the city was quiet, absent of the celebrations.

The light from the window wasn't pouring in from the sun but from the lamp Odette had forgotten to turn off earlier in the night. The silence hit her like a slap on her tender skin, when she didn't know she could feel tender anymore. She had grown accustomed to the sounds of grease splattering on the cobblestones, the popping corks of the champagne, the off-key renditions of Les Marseillaise. It reminded her of the way Hollywood had imagined the Great War with soldiers dangling out of train cars and kissing their partners on train platforms. It was romance, a romance that was never present at the front or during the celebrations at home, she thinks—she wasn't there. She only heard stories, and now those stories had become dogma, reinforced by the levity that had filled Paris days ago when the streets emptied of fleeing Germans but filled with dying soldiers, crumbling buildings, and blood, not Odette's blood—Ilse's blood. Odette had never thought about those she had killed before, those whose lives she had taken for a better city, a better world, believing if she could take one life to save countless others, how much of the world could she save in the end? How many dominoes could she keep from falling by taking out one? But Ilse drove Odette to bed, drove Odette beneath the sheets listening to a world beyond her grasp once again knowing she wasn't meant for it. Ilse tried to tell Odette, gave Odette a way out, a way into a world Odette could join. It wasn't worth the price of admission, Odette thought, another phrase Agnes had once said, on the night Odette spoke openly about sex.

Odette wanted to know why men fell absurdly for women, what a woman could do, and if women felt the same. They stood in Agnes's kitchen. Agnes stared, surrounded by the leaning unopened envelopes, and spoke frankly about where, why, and how sex should be, but then pointed her spatula at Odette before she flipped a crepe and said, "but at your age, it isn't worth the price of admission." Odette laughed then, a real laugh, not the fake kind she had perfected over the years to try and fit in with the other kids. Agnes knew because she laughed too, then sighed, then added cheese to the crepe and pretended like the conversation never happened. In the silence, Odette recalled these memories in the silence—and in the silence she ate these memories like charcoal—and in the silence they made her gag.

Martine nuzzled into her neck. She pet him twice. Then he swatted at her hand. She dropped him and sucked the blood from her finger. She used to love the look of blood, its elegant color, the way it could flow like a stream or drip like a leaky faucet. She felt a kinship with blood, the way farmers felt connected to the land. But now, she couldn't even look at the gash Martine made in her finger. She stuck it in her mouth to suck out the blood but also to avoid seeing the blood. It didn't taste the same either: heavy on the iron, on oxidized metal instead of the subtle sweetness she once found lurking beneath the surface thick like honey.

Martine scratched at the door.

"There is no one there," Odette said.

Martine looked at her but then ignored her, scratching at the door once again. Odette ran to the door, unable to stop herself. The morning silence had drilled into her head, shaken her, reminded her of the silence in the cell; moreover, it reminded her of the loneliness of it, her last conversation with Agnes, the last time she saw Aloysius as he ran from the stumbling body of the German officer, the last time she saw Ilse as Odette took the scalpel from Ilse's wrist, the last time Odette heard the violin play from the apartment upstairs, the first taste of cream she had after leaving the prison, the first life she took, her mother, the peaches, and she wanted to throw the door open and tear down the building along with the rest of Paris if she could find the strength. She picked up the cat and pulled the door open but instead of emptiness, a man stood ready to knock. Martine purred.

"I couldn't stand it in the other apartment," Aloysius said. He wore a torn blue trench coat. He had a patchy beard, a renegade's beard, a beard that said he had run all night to see Odette.

"You are dead," Odette said. "You are a ghost." She shook her head in disbelief. Martine wiggled from her arms and brushed against the ghost at the door.

"I worried it was too late to knock."

"The German officer," Odette said. "They found you and—"

"It took me weeks to get back here. I needed to bathe before I saw you. This place feels empty. I was—"

The silence swung between them like a pendulum, and she wanted to speak but couldn't get the timing right. Ali looked different, his cheeks thin but his mustache full, no longer the wispy strands of a boy.

"I was brave," Ali said.

"I know," she said and turned away.

"No," he said. "You don't." He looked to the floor—away from Odette. He couldn't look her in the eye, she thought. She wouldn't be able to either. He pulled two candleholders from his pockets. They glinted in the light. They looked more precious in his hands, priceless when held between his strong fingers. "I always wanted to be brave because I thought that's what I had to do. But I was brave because I finally found something to be brave for."

"I missed you," Odette said. The words tumbled out of her mouth before she could help it.

"They didn't want me to come back. I needed to."

"The butcher?"

Aloysius nodded. "I hear he's starting over by the sea. Eze, I think."

"He wouldn't let me—"

"I know. He took me out of the city, but I never wanted to leave."

"Your mother," she said.

"I know," he said. "The butcher told me."

"What did he tell you?" Odette asked, worried what he might think.

"You did the right thing," he said.

"Mercy?"

"Because she asked you to," he said. He limped inside the door. Martine followed him. Odette went to the floor and pulled back the rug. Except, she didn't need to open the floorboards. She didn't need to hide her mother's past—her past. She replaced the rug, took the candleholders from Aloysius, and placed them on the table. For the first time, she thought they looked good on display. For the first time, she thought they belonged.

Aloysius nodded, walked to the window, and looked at a display of fireworks popping over the rooftops. He pointed to the bright lights as if reading Odette's thoughts, the lamps, the time of day, the silence. "I didn't want to miss the celebration."

Odette moved to the window and sat on the sill beside him. He pressed his hand to her leg and hesitated. She held his hand to her skin, letting his body warm beside her. The fireworks flittered, cracked, popped, and faded. She pointed to the sky as well, moving her eyes away from the light and to the building across the street. Two pigeons perched on the lip of the roof. She imagined them cooing beneath the light, against the sound, taking away the night's silence. She wasn't even sure about the time anymore, nor did she care.

"They've come back," she said.

"They must," he said. "It's home."

Odette looked around the apartment. Martine jumped onto her lap. The cobwebs had swept away in the soft cool breeze rushing through the open window. Aloysius looked to the birds. She brushed her fingers across his beard and kissed his cheek. *This is home*, she thought.

"I'm thinking of learning the violin," Odette said.

"What about your pottery?" Aloysius said.

"I would rather take up painting," Odette said. "Or perhaps, sculpting. I'm very good with sharp objects."

Aloysius cringed but said nothing. He stroked Martine across her lap. "What happens now?" he said. She hadn't thought about now or next. She'd been too wrapped up in then.

"We mend," she said.

"I am glad you're a nurse," he said.

"Perhaps one day I'll be a doctor," she said.

The sun began to rise over the city taking away the anxiety of silence. Odette had made it to a new day, she thought. The cafés along the street set out chairs, tables, and opened their doors to give passersby the scent of something new, something rare, something still a treat, but somehow familiar and comforting. Odette had emerged from the darkness to find solace and contentment in the sun. What was it Agnes had said, *Light is the best disinfectant*? And Odette wanted so badly to be disinfected.

"Aloysius," she said. He turned from the window. Martine jumped to the floor. "Let's go to bed." She guided him to her sheets but kept open the curtains to let the light shine through.

Acknowledgements

This book could to have been written or completed without the help of Lisa Weissman, Martin Pousson, Charlene de Leon-Urbanski, Lowell Rottenberg, Kimberleh Weissman, Deb Alix, and Abby Brookshire.

Douglas Weissman is the author of eight novels including The Deep Freeze series and Life Between Seconds. He is a travel writer, graduated with an MFA from the University of San Francisco, and lives in the Los Angeles area with his wife, daughter, dog, and cat.

* 9 7 8 1 9 5 8 9 0 1 7 6 2 *